Spies, Lies, and Allies

ALSO BY LISA BROWN ROBERTS

THE REPLACEMENT CRUSH

LISA BROWN ROBERTS

Entangled Publishing, LLC
2614 South Timberline Road
Suite 105, PMB 159
Fort Collins, CO 80525

Entangled Teen is an imprint of Entangled Publishing, LLC.

Visit our website at www.entangledpublishing.com.

Edited by Liz Pelletier
Cover design by Anna Crosswell, Cover Couture
Cover art from Depositphotos: Stockasso
Depositphotos: Valuavitaly Depositphotos: Aletia
Interior design by Toni Kerr
Wikimedia Commons #2265761

ISBN 978-1-63375-698-4
Ebook ISBN 978-1-63375-699-1

Manufactured in the United States of America

First Edition May 2018

10 9 8 7 6 5 4 3 2 1

entangled teen
an imprint of Entangled Publishing LLC

For my father, who I miss every day.

Chapter One

I t's the second Saturday in May, and I'm counting the days until I'm free of Clarkson K-12 Academy. Tonight—awards night—my school sparkles like a scaled-down version of the Dolby Theatre on Oscar night, fancied up in twinkling lights, ruby-red velvet stage curtains, and glittering decorations. Our private school is jokingly called Harvard High; everything is overfunded and insanely competitive.

Like all the Oscar almost-winners say, it's an honor just to be nominated. And in my case, that's true. All I want is to stand on stage and see my parents in the crowd—well, see my dad. Mom will be there; she always is. But Dad? Odds are low that Dad Vader will tear himself away from Emergent Enterprises, AKA his evil empire.

Is he here yet? I text my mom. I'm in violation of the no-cells-on-stage rule, but I don't care.

Her reply is quick: **Not yet.** Which in our family is code for *he's not coming.* My heart, which had been fluttering around hopefully, folds in on itself and sinks back into my chest. Despite my low odds, the fantasy of actually winning the photography award and standing at the mic to thank my dad for buying all my equipment, watching his face light up with pride…that fantasy has played in my head for days.

"And now for the photography award." Our principal's voice jolts me to attention. I squint my eyes against the lights, searching hopefully for my dad's dark hair, but I can't distinguish faces in the crowd. Where's my zoom lens when I needed it?

"As most of you know, Clarkson Academy prides itself on its award-winning photojournalism classes," Dr. Farnham says, her spikey silver hair glinting under the spotlight. "Our top photographers often continue their studies in college, and at last count we had five Clarkson graduates working in major media outlets across the globe."

The crowd applauds politely as I rattle off those graduates' names in my mind. I stalk them in the news and social media because one day I hope to follow in their footsteps.

"This year we have an outstanding slate of nominees," continues Dr. Farnham. "Without further ado, I'd like each student to stand as I call their name."

I zone out as she rattles off the names. I already know that Blake is going to win. Awards always go to seniors, which he is, and his photos are as jaw-dropping as his attitude is annoying. If he had a halfway decent personality, I'd be madly in love with him, but unfortunately, he's as pretentious as he is gifted.

We each stand as Dr. Farnham calls our names. As I rise from my chair, I'm keenly aware of how wrongly I pegged the event's attire, wearing one of my mom's one-of-a-kind yarn and fabric creations instead of something sleek and sophisticated like all the other girls on the stage. I feel like a hippie flower girl trailing in the glamorous bride's wake.

My phone buzzes in my hand again and I sneak a glance at the text.

You look amazing! Followed by a thumbs-up emoji and a heart from my best friend Lexi.

That means I *don't* look amazing, and Lexi feels the need to give me a bad-outfit-choice-pre-award-loss boost. I chew on my lip to hide my bittersweet smile; Lexi knows me better than anyone.

"A selection of our nominees' best photographs is displayed in the hall outside the auditorium. Please take time to view them later, if you haven't already." Dr. Farnham clears her throat and glances at us, then proceeds to open the envelope. I can hear the Oscar drumroll in my imagination as her finger slides under the tab and she removes the ivory card.

"And our winner is Blake Hamilton! Please give him a round of applause!"

Even though I knew my odds of winning were miniscule, a tidal wave of disappointment floods through me. I try to keep a "Yay, Blake" smile plastered on my face as Blake pushes past me in his rush toward the mic, stepping on my toes. Dr. Farnham presents him with a certificate and a crystal disc engraved with his name, the year, and an etching of a classic Brownie camera, circa 1940.

I've been picturing that award engraved with my name on it for weeks. My shoulders slump as I sit down, since standing is for winners.

It's just as well Dad's not here to witness my failure.

Two hours later, Mom and I sit on our patio under the stars sharing a pint of Bonnie Brae ice cream—the best in Denver, according to me. It's a warm spring evening and we don't want to waste it, even in the face of my crushing defeat.

Dad's text, sent minutes after I left the auditorium, had

seared my heart and hastened my exit from the parking lot. **Sorry to miss the awards, kiddo. At least you didn't win.**

"He didn't mean it as an insult," Mom insists, dipping her spoon into the red-and-white striped tub. "He's proud of you for finaling. He just meant he would've felt bad if you'd won and he'd missed it."

"Because he only shows up for winners." The words bite at my throat. Deep down I don't believe them, but right now I'm wallowing in self-pity. Not only did I lose, my finalist certificate has my name spelled wrong: Laura Kristoff instead of Laurel. I've been battling that mistake since kindergarten; you'd think my K-12 academy would have it right by now.

"Now, Laurel, you know that's not true." Mom's green eyes glint in the flickering light from the candles on our patio table. "Your dad loves you and he's so proud of you and your sister." She shoves a huge bite of ice cream into her mouth. I can tell by her wince when the throat freeze hits.

"So you say. I wouldn't know, since I only see him about ten minutes a day." An exaggeration, yes, but not by much.

Mom sighs. "Your father runs a demanding business. And he does it all for us."

As if on cue, the hum of the garage door sounds, followed by the crunch of tires on our gravel driveway. Mom checks the ice cream tub to make sure we've left some for Dad. Mom doesn't keep much sugar in the house, but Dad always consumes an unfair share.

A few minutes later, his tall silhouette appears in the French doors that open onto the patio. It's easy to imagine the Vader cape flowing off his broad shoulders.

My dad emerges like a king onto a palace balcony, striding toward us like a true victor, unlike me. His movie-star good looks are ridiculous, especially when paired with his name:

Rhett, just like Rhett Butler in *Gone with the Wind,* my grandma's favorite movie.

"How are my girls?" He sinks into a wicker chair. Mom hands him a spoon and his eyes light up. "Chocolate brownie? My favorite!"

It's my favorite, too—probably because it's his.

He takes a big bite, but unlike Mom, he doesn't wince from throat freeze. Ice cream doesn't dare mess with Dad Vader. He leans back in his chair and smiles at his subjects. Without warning, I flash back to my sixth birthday party.

I'd dressed as Princess Leia, of course, and Darth Vader made a surprise guest appearance. When he'd stormed the party, brandishing his lightsaber, I'd shrieked in fear until my mom scooped me up and whispered in my ear, "It's just Daddy in disguise." Relieved, I attacked him with my own lightsaber. He fought valiantly but suffered a well-deserved demise, flattened on the grass by me and ten of my saber-wielding friends.

That party was the beginning of my love affair with Denver's famous Bonnie Brae ice cream, and cemented my childhood hero worship of my dad. When I was young, Dad was around a lot more for my sister Kendra and me. I remembered burnt pancake mornings and piggyback rides, tickle fights, and cozy story times when I fell asleep against his chest.

But that was a long time ago, before his business succeeded and took over our lives. Now I count myself lucky if I see him more than twice a week for dinner. When my friends complain about their overbearing parents, I nod as if I empathize, but the truth is I miss my dad.

"Sorry you didn't take home the trophy, kiddo." Dad scrapes the bottom of the ice cream tub with his spoon. He glances up. "Next year you'll win."

On the one hand, it's a rare moment, the three of us sitting outside together, my dad relaxed and smiling instead of stressed and scowling. On the other hand...

"I wish you'd been there." The words tumble out of my mouth, surprising me.

"Laurel, honey. I'm sorry I wasn't there, but I had to wrap up a client proposal, and we've got the interns starting in two weeks and—" Dad's smile fades, along with his excuses.

"I wish *I* was an intern." Then maybe I'd see him for more than ten minutes a day.

"What?" Dad blinks in surprise. "Don't be ridiculous, Laurel. The intern program is for students who can't afford college tuition, who need the scholarship we provide." He cocks an eyebrow. "Unlike you or your sister. Sometimes I wonder if you realize how fortunate you are."

His words hit me like a punch. Dad's new scholarship program is a big deal; it was in the local news a few weeks ago, a feature story with photos of him and his top executives. One lucky intern will win 100K, enough to cover an in-state tuition full ride. The runners-up will each receive five thousand, but the full-ride is the holy grail everyone will vie for.

"I'm calling it a night," Dad says abruptly, rising from his chair.

Guilt tugs at me as he ruffles my hair before turning toward the house. For someone who wants to spend time with her dad, I did a great job chasing him off.

I started badgering my dad the next day, hoping to turn my offhand comment into reality. Why *not* be an intern? Without competing for the money, obviously. If nothing else, I'd get two long car rides each day with my dad in which he wasn't distracted—unless he spent them yammering on his Bluetooth.

Thirteen days ago, he gave me a curt one-word "No" answer.

Ten days ago, he sighed and stared at the ceiling. "I said no already."

Seven days ago, he crossed his arms over his chest and pinned me with an intense stare. "And what exactly would you do at the office?"

I wasn't prepared for that, so I stalled.

Five days ago, I suggested working as the assistant to the interns. Or I could help out Miss Emmaline at the reception desk. Miss Emmaline is an eighty-year-old, ninety-pound holy terror, but I was getting desperate.

"I can give you feedback on the interns," I told Dad. "Honest feedback, to help you decide who wins the scholarship." His only response was a disapproving frown. "A peer review," I pressed. "One college-bound student assessing the others."

Four days ago, I pulled out my best card—emotional manipulation. "You're going to be an empty nester in a year. Then you'll wish we'd bonded, Vader, but instead I'll be on the other side of the galaxy, joining the Resistance."

My sister Kendra just finished her freshman year of college at UC San Diego, but she'd stayed out there this summer to do her own internship with some start-up tech company full of hot nerds, according to our most recent text convo. A year from now I'll be off to college, too, mostly likely somewhere out of state—hopefully somewhere with my own batch of hot nerds to crush on.

Now it's D-Day, the Sunday before the internship program starts. I've given up on convincing Dad. Tomorrow I'll start my search for a summer job, which I've procrastinated on due to 1) laziness and 2) my intent to spend my summer taking photos for the Faces of Denver contest. I probably don't have a chance of winning that contest, either, but I'd love it if one of my photos made the final portfolio voted on by the public.

My dad studies me from across the kitchen table. We're in the process of devouring an extra-large Hawaiian pizza, a Sunday night tradition that he still makes an appearance for. Tonight, it's just the two of us; Mom is at a church meeting. Dad takes a long sip from his microbrew, then stretches out his legs and narrows his steely gray eyes.

"All right, princess, you win. Tomorrow morning be ready to leave the house by seven thirty."

Stunned, I gape at him.

"You'll earn minimum wage. Interns earn fifteen bucks an hour." He takes another bite of pizza, his eyes still on me. If the pay disparity is supposed to dissuade me, it doesn't. Instead, I'm giddy with victory.

I raise my glass in a toast. "You're on, Vader."

Dad narrows his eyes, but his lips quirk. I hope I made a chink in his business armor. My fun dad is still under there somewhere.

Maybe by the end of summer I'll rip off the Vader mask and find that guy again.

Chapter Two

"So, what am I doing for the Empire this summer? Plotting the destruction of peaceful planets like Alderaan?" I thought a *Star Wars* joke might be a fun way to start our first morning as coworkers, but Dad Vader doesn't look amused.

"I'm not the enemy, Laurel," Dad snaps. "Also, I'm your boss, so watch it."

Mom slides us both plates of scrambled eggs, toast, and bacon as we sit at the kitchen counter. Well, I sit. Dad stands, glancing at his watch anxiously.

"Have some breakfast, Rhett," Mom insists.

"No time to eat." Dad slaps together the eggs and bacon inside the toast and gestures for me to do the same. He's in conquer-the-universe mode, so I decide to knock off the jokes, for now.

"You're okay with me eating in your car? What if I spill?" Dad's car is immaculate, unlike Mom's and mine.

He scowls as he yanks a paper towel from the roll, handing me one and wrapping his makeshift sandwich with the other. "We need to go, Laurel. Kristoffs are never late.

And they don't spill."

Mom and I share a smirk, but fortunately he doesn't bust us.

"Try not to kill each other today," Mom says cheerfully. She takes a sip of coffee from her "I'm a knotty hooker" mug patterned with colorful skeins of yarn.

"For my part, I promise a homicide-free day."

"No one's going to die," Dad grumbles, grabbing his briefcase.

"In case he's wrong, tell Kendra I love her," I stage-whisper to Mom, who snort-laughs.

Dad's dark eyebrows bunch together, but when Mom stands on tiptoe to kiss him goodbye, he reciprocates way too enthusiastically for this early in the morning.

"Kristoffs don't have time for PDA," I call over my shoulder, grabbing the messenger bag Mom made for me from vintage *Star Wars* fabric.

Five minutes later I'm a captive in my dad's spaceship (AKA Mercedes SUV) as we begin the stressful rush-hour drive from our faux ranch outside of Castle Rock into downtown Denver.

Dad passes a slow-moving minivan, then side-eyes me. "I'm not a villain like Vader, you know. I prefer to think of myself as Yoda."

"Really? You see yourself as a—"

"Wise warrior? Yes, I do."

Dad returns his focus to the road as I stifle a laugh. He's the most un-Yoda person I know. As he passes another slow-moving car, I wonder if he's pretending to levitate all the other cars with the Force and fly us straight to his LoDo office.

"I'm excited about the job, Dad. Thanks for giving me a chance." I clear my throat. "What exactly am I going to do?"

"Help out the interns." Dad's frowny face returns. "Isn't

that what you wanted?"

Even though I pushed him hard for this opportunity, I'm getting that Han Solo feeling, as in, *I have a bad feeling about this.* I'm worried he's a corporate dictator, an unyielding Scrooge to a cowering army of Bob Cratchits.

What if my dad really is like Darth Vader and the interns end up hating me by association? Then again, with a huge scholarship on the line they'll probably put up with a lot. That thought makes me even more uncomfortable.

Dad sighs like he just read my mind. "You won't have to foil any secret plots to destroy innocent planets, Princess Laurel. Contrary to your overactive imagination, I don't run an evil empire. Ewok's honor." Dad raises three fingers in the air. "No enemies to take down, either."

Ewok's honor was something he made up when I was eight years old and scared to play soccer with girls more experienced than me. Dad swore on my stuffed Ewok I'd have a great season. I hadn't, but then he'd created a new family motto: *Kristoffs Never Quit.* Almost ten years later, I've proven his point by earning a spot on the varsity soccer team.

"Let's hope you're right," I say. "My saber skills are rusty from lack of practice."

Dad sighs. "I'm one of the good guys. My company is full of them."

"We shall see," I say dramatically.

We don't argue for the rest of the drive. By the time he pulls into the underground parking garage, I dare to hope this summer will be what I wish for—the chance to reconnect with my dad.

"*A New Hope,*" I whisper, cracking myself up with a nerdy joke.

"Ready, princess?" Dad's eyes meet mine.

"Take me to your Death Star, Vader."

His gaze narrows but I spot a flicker of amusement in his gray eyes. "I hope your opinion of my business changes by the end of the summer, Laurel."

I hope so, too, but I'd bet my Carrie Fisher autograph that it won't.

The reception lobby of Emergent Enterprises is urban and trendy, with exposed brick walls covered with canvas prints and metal wall sculptures from local artists. Steel beams crisscross overhead, wrapped in plastic tube lights. The building used to be a paint factory back in the horse-and-buggy days, but now it's one of the trendier buildings on Market Street, close to the baseball stadium and hipster bars and restaurants.

"Laurel Kristoff!" A voice booms across the lobby as a determined figure bears down on us. His shiny bald head glows under the lights and his body practically bursts out of his clothes, like the Pillsbury Doughboy stuffed into a too-small suit.

It's Mr. Mantoni, one of Dad Vader's lieutenants. I remember him vividly from last summer. He pumps my hand. I'm embarrassed by his enthusiastic welcome.

"Hi Mr. Manic—um, Mr. Mantoni." My dad's eyebrows shoot toward his hairline. I'd nicknamed Mr. Mantoni the Manly Manicotti last summer and made the mistake of sharing the joke at dinner one night. Mom had laughed, but Dad wasn't amused.

Mr. Mantoni's sweaty hand releases mine. "So glad you're back with us!" His voice is stabbing my eardrums. "We're looking forward to you helping out the interns this summer." He lowers his voice. "Great idea, having you vote on the scholarship winner."

What's he talking about? Apprehension skitters up my spine.

"Get Laurel settled, Tom," Dad says. "I'll stop in later to meet the interns and lay down the law." Dad squeezes my shoulder, then strides away, abandoning me to the Manicotti.

"Vote?" My voice squeaks when I finally speak. "What do you mean?"

Mr. Manicotti puts a finger to his lips, then glances suspiciously at a couple of employees heading our way. Once they pass, he claps his hand on my back and steers me past Miss Emmaline, ferociously guarding the front desk.

In an office like this, you'd expect a multi-pierced hipster at the front desk, but Dad has Miss Emmaline, who looks one hundred and two years old but doesn't miss a thing. I learned that last summer when she busted me Snapchatting in the bathroom, taking an extra-long break with a pile of free snacks from the kitchen.

Miss Emmaline squints as I pass her desk. I wave, trying to look sweet and innocent, but her scowl doesn't waver. Mission number one: make her laugh before the summer is over.

"You know how this scholarship contest works, right?" The Manicotti steers me down a narrow hallway of more exposed brick walls lined with framed magazine covers featuring Dad's company. "Four contestants. No mercy! Only one can be victorious!"

I've always wondered why my dad hired the Manicotti. If my dad had served in a war, I'd assume the Manicotti saved his life and Dad owed him, but that's not the case.

We pause outside a conference room with a closed door. "I'm keeping them waiting," he says, rubbing his hands together gleefully. "Made 'em show up at seven. Round one: the elimination. One of them still isn't here, so he's off the island even if he does show up."

"Wow. That's, um…intense." It seems unfair, too, since all of the interns need the salary from the summer job, not to mention a shot at the scholarship. Maybe I need to worry more about the Manicotti than Dad Vader.

"That's how I like things. Intense." His beady eyes gleam behind his rimless glasses. He grins in a way that makes me wish I had pepper spray. "We're counting on you for inside information, Laurel."

"You are?" Imaginary warning bells clang in my mind.

He nods, sweat gleaming on his forehead. "Yep." He glances around the hallway like we're hiding behind enemy lines, then drops his voice to a whisper. "Your dad says your vote counts twice."

"Vote?"

He blinks rapidly, like a cartoon. "On who wins the scholarship, of course!"

Stunned, I open my mouth to protest, but before I can, he throws open the door and pushes me inside. I stumble, then compose myself to take in the sea of faces around the conference table.

I'm not sure what I was expecting, but it's not this. Somehow "underprivileged" had converged in my mind with… unpresentable. And that couldn't be further than the truth. I feel myself blushing at my awkward entrance and my unfair assumptions.

As I take another hesitant step into the room, I catch the eye of one of the guys. His shaggy dark hair could stand a haircut, but he's wearing the right suck-up clothes, including a tie that looks like a casual afterthought. His deep chocolate brown eyes lock onto mine, his wide mouth briefly curving in a smile that could easily slide into smirk territory. My heart does a little kick start as I take in his angular good looks and self-assured demeanor, but then I remember last year's winter dance debacle, in which a guy like this humiliated me in front of the entire school.

I turn away, my gaze landing on a pretty blond girl, who may as well be a supermodel compared to me. I can't help but wonder if there's a brain hiding under all the pretty. Sitting next to her is a guy with close-cropped curls and smooth brown skin wearing a suit. He's even more beautiful than the supermodel. He flashes me a quick grin that may or may not be genuine. I hope it is.

A disgusted snort startles me, and I turn around. Snorting girl leans against the doorjamb, chewing gum like it's her mortal enemy. She has vampire skin—pale and translucent—spiky neon blue hair, and a glittering nose stud. She's definitely not dressed for success, wearing ripped jeans and a black T-shirt with the anarchy symbol. She's riveting, in a scary way.

"Well, look who's here. Daddy's girl." Her slit-eyed glare makes me wish for a disappearing cloak.

My cheeks heat as I sink into the nearest chair. I didn't want to reveal who my dad is, but she's just blown my cover.

"Patricia, that's enough," Mr. Mantoni snaps, and the puzzle pieces rearrange themselves in my sputtering brain.

Mr. Mantoni has a daughter who just finished her first year of college. Trish—that's what Mom calls her when she and Dad talk about work people. She used to attend the company holiday parties at our house, but I haven't seen her in a few years. Last time I saw her she didn't have blue hair, though she did have the attitude.

"Whatevs." Trish flings a hand dismissively, then saunters around the table and plops into a chair next to Suit Guy. She arches an eyebrow and runs the tip of her tongue around her lips, eyeing him like he's a delicious snack and she's ravenous. Even though I suspect she's going to make my life miserable,

I'm in awe of her brazen technique—especially in front of her dad.

"Interns of Emergent Enterprises!" booms Mr. Mantoni. "Welcome to your own version of *Survivor*." Tiny drops of spittle fly from his mouth, making me flinch. "May the best intern win!"

A cough sounds behind us and everyone turns to stare.

Especially me, because framed in the doorway like a dream come to life is Jason Riggs, a guy for whom I've long harbored a secret, pointless crush. Me and half the girls I know. It's cliché, crushing on the quarterback, but I think it's a high school requirement, like taking U.S. History.

"Sorry I'm late." Jason's gaze darts around the room, then lands back on Mr. Mantoni. "My car broke down and I had to run for the—"

"Off the island!" Mr. Mantoni points a finger in the air. "Tardiness will not be tolerated."

Jason takes a step back, his green eyes wide. "B-but I—"

"Do you know what the world needs less of, young man? Excuses, that's what. Your car breaks down, you have a plan B. Your flight gets canceled on the way to close a deal, you have a plan B."

Mr. Mantoni wipes a hand across his sweaty brow. I study the other interns, all of whom look as shocked as Jason—except Trish, who's aimed her tongue skills at the fresh meat hovering nervously in the doorway.

I can't believe this is how the interns are being welcomed. I feel awful for Jason. He's one of the few scholarship students at my school; rumor is he got a full ride because of his stunning athletic abilities. I have no doubt his ancient clunker broke down.

"Aw, come on, *Mr. Mantoni*," Trish says, smacking her lips. "Cut the guy a break. It's the first day."

Crud. I wish I'd said that, especially when Jason gives her a dimpling, grateful smile. Instead, I covertly ogle Jason from under lowered lashes. That's *my* technique, honed with years of practice.

"Interns!" Mr. Mantoni booms, jarring me out of my Jason trance. "I will put this to a vote. Who believes we should give this young man a second chance and allow him to stay?"

The interns stare at each other as I sneak another glance at Jason, who looks like he wants to bolt. His wavy blond hair needs combing and his blue dress shirt is half-untucked from his khakis. His tie looks like he borrowed it from his grandpa. In spite of, or maybe because of all this, he's adorable.

"Show of hands!" Manicotti's voice thunders. "If you think he should stay, raise your hand."

Supermodel raises her hand tentatively. Surprised, I revise my snarky first impression of her. It was brave of her to do that. Suit Guy narrows his eyes suspiciously at Jason, while Chocolate Eyes shrugs and leans back in his chair like he doesn't care one way or the other, but he doesn't raise his hand. Guys are such competitive jerks, never giving each other a break.

I stare hard at Trish. *Come on,* I will her with my Jedi mind control, *raise your hand. You're the one who practically licked him by osmosis.* Her gaze locks onto mine and her eyes narrow, but I don't look away. Slowly, like it's killing her to do it, her hand creeps into the air.

Mr. Mantoni huffs. "Two against two. A split decision can make or break a man." He whirls on me. "It's up to you, Laurel. Let him stay or cast him back into the ocean without a lifeboat?"

I don't have to think twice. I raise my hand without hesitation and smile at Jason, who blinks and swallows, then graces me with a gorgeous grin, his gaze fully connecting with mine, sending my heart rate into the stratosphere.

Supermodel smiles at me, Trish rolls her eyes, Suit Guy frowns…and Chocolate Eyes? He studies me with an unnerving intensity that jolts me right out of my fuzzy Jason daydream. I blink and turn away from him.

A girl's gotta take what she can get, and so I do, focusing on Jason's sweet face because I'm afraid it's only a matter of time before this summer job blows up just like Alderaan.

Chapter Three

"Mr. Kristoff will be here shortly," says the Manicotti as Jason settles himself at the table. "You'll introduce yourselves and tell us what you hope to do at Emergent. You each get two minutes." He points at me. "Laurel, you'll time everyone."

"I will?"

He glowers at me, and Chocolate Eyes smirks. I'll be glad when we do the introductions because I need to stop with the nicknames.

"Laurel is your personal assistant for the summer," Mr. Mantoni says. "Which is much more than a secretary. Not that there's anything wrong with secretaries. It's a noble profession for women. Ah, men, too, if that's all they want. I mean…" He breaks off, clearing his throat.

This guy desperately needs help digging out of the hole, but I'm not going to hand him a shovel. I'm appalled by his bumbling sexism and his attitude with the interns. Dad and I are going to have a serious chat on the drive home about the way the interns are treated, and this crazy idea of me being the final vote on the scholarship winner. What the heck is my dad thinking?

I glance at Trish, feeling a twinge of sympathy for her. I'd be a fan of anarchy, too, if the Manicotti were my dad. She looks like she wants to throttle him, but she keeps her mouth shut. I bet she's planning an after-work dad chat, too.

We sneak peeks at each other, look away, then sneak more peeks. Jason eyeballs Supermodel, which sort of breaks my heart but isn't surprising. He's got a type, and she's it. Trish sits with her arms crossed over her chest like a shield, giving everyone the slit-eye. Suit Guy eyes Mr. Mantoni warily, like he's half-expecting a racist comment. Chocolate Eyes's steady gaze sweeps around the table, making me flush when it pauses on me, then returns to Mr. Mantoni. The door swings open, saving us all from more painful, awkward silence. Everyone sits up straight, even Trish, because my dad has that effect on people.

"Welcome to Emergent Enterprises," he says. Even though he's my dad, I know he's exceptionally handsome in his dark gray suit. He's even rocking cufflinks today, which I didn't notice earlier. I try not to roll my eyes at the affectation. His thick dark hair, shot through with a few distinguished strands of silver, won't dare move between now and the end of the day.

Dad takes a seat and graces us with his practiced public relations smile. "I'm Rhett Kristoff. Please call me Mr. Kristoff, or Mr. K."

Mr. K? Seriously? I wince with embarrassment.

"You've met Mr. Mantoni, of course, when he interviewed you for the intern positions. Mr. Mantoni and I go back many years and he has my full trust." Dad's penetrating gaze takes in each of the interns, but he avoids eye contact with me. "I'd like to go around the table. Each of you tell us a little about yourselves and why you want to intern here." He flashes a smile. "Besides the financial reason, of course."

The Manicotti raises his eyebrows and taps his watch. *Great*. I open the timer app. Dad frowns at me.

"I'm timing them. Two minutes each."

Dad turns to Mr. Mantoni. "I think we can allow more than that. This is a chance for everyone to get to know each other." He shakes his head at me ever so slightly, so I dim my phone's screen. "Does anyone want water? Coffee? Soda? We have a big selection in the kitchen. Laurel can get us drinks."

Though Dad's calm demeanor is a relief from Mr. Mantoni's intensity, I'm not thrilled he's treating me like a waitress. I catch Trish smirking from the corner of my eye. I sneak a peek at Jason, whose eyes are fixed on my dad. He looks almost…worshipful.

"I'll take an iced tea," Trish says. "Two sugar packets and a straw."

It takes all of my self-control not to fry her with my death glare.

"Me too," chimes in Supermodel, beaming at my dad. "But Splenda for me."

"Coke for me, please," says Suit Guy.

"Coke would be great," Jason says eagerly, like my dad invented the red can.

Hiding my annoyance, I turn to Chocolate Eyes. "How about you?"

"I'm good. Besides, that'd be too much for you to carry." He shrugs and gives me a smile that does something unexpectedly swirly to my insides.

"Be right back."

As I head into the hallway, Dad calls out, "I'll take an espresso, Laurel."

So much for *Dad* worrying about how I'll carry all the drinks. I close the door more forcefully than I should and head toward the kitchen.

"Laurel. How nice to see you, sweetheart."

It's Ms. Romero, Dad's personal assistant. As usual, she looks terrific, dressed like a female version of my dad, except her suit is red, and she wears awesome shoes with clear Lucite heels. I wonder if I'd look good in those shoes or like a kid wearing a Cinderella costume.

Mom and Dad talk about Ms. Romero a lot at home; she's been with Emergent since a few years after Dad started the company. They think she's amazing. Brilliant. Loyal. Hardworking. All the ideal qualities my dad talks about ad nauseam.

"Hi, Ms. Romero." I tug at my hair. I inherited my mom's curls, though the color is boring brown unlike Mom's strawberry blond, thanks to Dad's DNA. Like Mom, I usually let my hair do whatever it's going to do. Today I should've put it in a hairnet since I'm apparently in charge of food service.

Ms. Romero takes a granola bar from one of the snack baskets and tears it open. "There are homemade brownies in that basket." She points to the end of the counter. "I thought you and the interns might want them." She winks like she knows exactly how Mr. Mantoni is behaving.

"That's great, but I can't carry those plus drinks." I open the fridge and retrieve two Cokes and two iced teas.

"Here." She opens a cupboard and removes a lacquered serving tray. "Ta da."

She's a genius. I stack the drinks on the tray, count out brownies, then grab napkins and the required sweetener packets. I'd better earn bonus points for this.

"You let me know if you need anything, Laurel. You can come to me with any questions or concerns. Okay?" Her warm brown eyes are full of sincerity.

"Thanks. I will."

"Let me know if you want to grab lunch one day. We're surrounded by great restaurants." She grins. "My treat."

Maybe I should be her assistant for the summer. I hesitate, then grab a Coke for Chocolate Eyes and head back to the room of doom. Balancing the tray in one hand, I open the door with the other.

"...then in 2008, I bought this building," Dad says. "You're all too young to remember, but it was a rough downturn for the economy. Real estate was hit especially hard, so I got a great deal on this place, and a few other buildings in the area."

Dad pauses his Emergent history lesson as I set the tray on the table...and that's when I realize I forgot his espresso. My cheeks burn, and I straighten, ready to return to the kitchen, but he stops me with a raised hand.

"Never mind, Laurel. I'll take a brownie, though."

Is that shimmer in his eyes frustration or silent laughter? Dad Vader is so hard to read. I slide a brownie down the table, and he grabs it, tearing open the plastic enthusiastically. Maybe this is the reason Mom keeps us mostly sugar-free at home.

"Help yourselves," he says to the interns. I push the tray across the table and watch everyone dig in. Chocolate Eyes points at the extra Coke, then himself, brow furrowed in a question. I nod, and he reaches for it, his dark eyes fixed on me. Must. Not. Blush.

"All right." Dad swallows the last bite of his brownie. "Let's start with you." He points to Jason, who tries not to choke on the soda he just swigged.

"I, um, I'm Jason Riggs. I, um, wanted to intern here because it's a cool company. And I think I have a lot to offer. I mean, I hope I do."

Oh, you do, I want to say. *So very much to offer me, in particular.* My cheeks heat at my naughty thoughts, so I duck my head, but not before Chocolate Eyes narrows his orbs at me like he's calculating something in his head. I glance up, and his lips curve slowly, deliberately. My cheeks burn even hotter under his scrutiny. I turn back to my dad, hoping my blush will fade.

"What do you want to study in college?" Dad asks Jason.

"International business." Jason sits up straighter and I swear his chest puffs out. It's easy to picture him jetting around the world, making deals. Being adorable. Meeting gorgeous French girls. Okay, scratch that last one.

"And what skills do you have to offer us?" Dad asks. "I understand you're quite the athlete."

Jason's ears turn red. "Um, yeah. I'm good at teamwork. Been doing it all my life. I'll be captain of the football team next year." He chews his lip. I hate seeing him so nervous. He's different here than how he is at school, swaggering through the hallways with his posse of jocks. Today he reminds me of a giant teddy bear stuffed into the wrong clothes.

Dad nods, looking thoughtful. "Teamwork is critical to any business. I'm sure you'll excel."

He turns to Supermodel. She blinks her lovely eyes and every guy at the table stops chewing to stare at her, except my dad, who's doing serious damage to a second brownie. Trish shoots me a look and I think it might be one of solidarity, but she turns away before I can be sure.

"I'm Ashley Goodson. I want to study art history. Maybe work in a gallery someday." She gives everyone a beauty queen smile and I try not to resent her, reminding myself she was the first one to champion Jason when the Manicotti wanted to toss him overboard.

"I can bring a sense of the aesthetic." She blushes prettily, unlike me, who blotches. "You have so much wonderful artwork here already, Mr. Kristoff. My skills might also be helpful for advertising. Some of your campaigns have used iconic art in such clever ways."

Somebody did their homework. I dart another look at Trish, who rolls her eyes, and for one brief moment I know we're in agreement. I don't bother looking at Chocolate Eyes and Suit Guy because I know they're salivating like dogs. Jason probably is, too, and I don't need to see that.

"What period of art interests you most?" Dad asks, surprising me because he sounds genuinely curious.

"The Renaissance and Baroque periods. I'd love to attend Colorado College; they have a fantastic program." She tosses her hair over her shoulders and I can feel the testosterone levels in the room spike. I'm impressed with how at ease she seems. Another assumption popped like a balloon.

Dad turns his attention to Suit Guy. "Your turn."

Suit Guy flashes a gorgeous smile that must get him free stuff from smitten clerks everywhere he goes. "Elijah Sampson. I'm hoping to get into Fisk." He keeps his focus on my dad as he talks. "I applied here because you've done a lot of work with minority-owned businesses." He glances at Jason. "I'm planning to study business, too. Finance."

A bean counter? He's going to be the sexiest accountant ever. But then I scold myself because that's just as bad as me discounting Ashley's intelligence just because she's pretty.

"Excellent," Dad says. "You speak my language." He even cracks a smile, which is more than he's done for anyone else. He nods at Trish. "Patricia."

She lifts her chin like she's ready for a fight. "I'm Patricia Mantoni but everyone calls me Trish. I'm here because I have to be." She shoots her dad the stink-eye. I smash my lips together to hold in laughter, then glance at the Manicotti, whose face is rapidly turning purple.

"Also," she adds quickly, "I know this is a good company.

My dad has worked here forever, and he likes it." She tugs at her choppy Smurf hair. "I'll be a sophomore at CU Boulder next year. My major is Women and Gender Studies."

Of course it is. I'm both impressed and terrified.

"I see," Dad says. "And how can that benefit us, Trish?"

Careful, Dad. She's armed and dangerous. I dart a glance at Elijah, who shoots me a wink, I think. Maybe it was just a nervous tic.

"I can spot sexism a mile away." She glares at the Manicotti and I cringe. "Also, generational stereotyping."

Dad clears his throat. "Can you elaborate?"

She rolls her eyes again and I try not to laugh. Dad hates eye-rolling almost as much as he hates texting.

"Like if you put together an ad you think is hip and cool, but it's really not. No offense."

This time I'm certain Dad's jaw is twitching with suppressed laughter. "We do our best," he says. "We have millennials working here for that very reason."

"But what about Gen Z?"

Dad glances at me. Uh-oh. I do *not* want to speak for my generation.

"We don't have clients who advertise to consumers that young," Dad says, "though we will soon, I'm sure." He smiles at her. That's two people now who've earned them. "And what are you hoping to accomplish this summer, Patricia?"

Trish sits up straight. "I want to work with a nonprofit. I had another internship lined up but it, um, fell through, so I'm working here instead." She glances at her dad, who nods. Trish squares her shoulders and looks at everyone but me. "You should all know that I'm not competing for the scholarship."

I'm relieved to hear she's not in the running for the money. Dad always refers to Mr. Mantoni as his right-hand man, so I assume he makes decent bank. I study Trish, wondering why her other internship fell through, but she's scowling at her purple fingernails.

"Thank you, Patricia," Dad says. "All right, next?"

I finally get a chance to check out Chocolate Eyes without being obvious. He doesn't exude the awkward jock adorableness Jason does; instead there's an energy about him that makes it impossible to look away.

"I'm Carlos Rubio. I hope I can get into CU." He pauses and shoots a significant look at Trish. "Probably CU Denver, not Boulder, unless I…" He clears his throat and I know what he almost said: if he doesn't win the full scholarship he can't afford to live on the Boulder campus, so he'll attend the downtown commuter school instead.

He takes a swig of Coke, then continues. "I haven't decided on a major, but I'm interested in political science. Maybe pre law."

I check to see if Dad's smiling, but he's not. Instead, he steeples his fingers as he returns Carlos's intense gaze.

"I see. And what interests you about Emergent?"

Carlos leans forward, and I can feel the intensity pouring out of him like he's channeling his own version of the Force.

"You started with nothing and now you're a huge success. I'm starting with nothing, too. I want to know how you did it." He hesitates, then plunges ahead. "Your employees are loyal, like Mr. Mantoni, who's been here since the beginning. Your assistant, Ms. Romero, she's been here for what, thirteen years? You're always rated one of the best local companies to work for. Even though you could cherry-pick clients at this point, you still take on new start-ups who don't have much money. Your business is diversified: corporate and residential real estate, branding and marketing, even an art gallery. You win awards every year. You do a lot of pro bono work for the causes you support. You work people hard but they're loyal.

So are your clients."

Carlos takes a deep breath and I feel like all of us are holding *our* breath because holy crapoli, how does he know all this? He just made Ashley look like a ten-second Googler, whereas he's clearly dug deep on Emergent, and my dad.

Also, since when does Dad own an art gallery? No wonder he was interested in Ashley's major. I bet she's thrilled to learn that tasty morsel of data.

"I think you've just proven what you can bring to the table, Carlos." Dad leans back in his chair and his lips curve into a full smile.

A quick flash of what looks like relief lights up Carlos's eyes right before he ducks his head. My stomach dips, transmitting a traitorous oohh-he's-intriguing-keep-ogling-him message. Rattled, I turn to Jason, who looks awestruck and a bit envious.

"Well, then." Dad places his hands on the table, signaling he's ready to leave, but Mr. Mantoni clears his throat and inclines his head toward me. "Oh," Dad says. "I almost forgot. Laurel, please introduce yourself."

Way to make me feel like chopped liver, Dad Vader. I'll remember this when the Rebels storm the Death Star. Although, based on all that data Carlos just spewed, maybe the Empire isn't *quite* as evil as I've always assumed.

"I'm Laurel. Laurel Kristoff." I tilt my head. "He's my dad, so that's why I'm here." I smile tentatively at Trish, hoping she'll appreciate my echo of her introduction. She doesn't smile back, but Carlos is watching me as intently as he watched my dad. I take a breath and continue. "I haven't decided which college I'll go to yet. I want to study photojournalism, but…"

I dart a glance at Dad and decide it's best to keep our family feud private. Dad thinks it's an impractical major, but Mom is on my side. I'm hoping I can wear him down eventually, like I did with this job.

"Anyway, I, uh…I'm here to support all of you." I twirl a strand of hair around my finger, a nervous habit I can't seem to kick. "I know a lot of software programs so maybe I can help with, uh, proposals and graphics or whatever, so…" My voice trails away. Compared to everyone else's introductions, I feel like I just showed up at a kegger with juice pouches.

"You get props for snack delivery skills." Elijah grins and I'm ridiculously grateful for the acknowledgment.

"Agreed," Carlos says, lifting his soda can in a mock salute.

Dad stands up. "All right, I need to get back to work. Mr. Mantoni will fill you in on the details. I expect to see each of you here every day, other than excused absences cleared with Mr. Mantoni or my assistant, Ms. Romero." He narrows his eyes at Trish. "Patricia, we do have a dress code. It's reasonable, but it doesn't include shirts with inflammatory slogans or torn jeans. Save those for your free time, please."

Trish's pale skin turns the color of a ripe tomato and I feel bad for her. I wonder if she and her dad argued about her outfit this morning.

After Dad leaves, the Manicotti stands up. "How about you all take a ten-minute break before we dive into things? Laurel can show you where the kitchen is. Bathrooms. Whatever you need." He exits quickly, probably to run after my dad.

"Take me to your snack bar," Elijah jokes, making me laugh.

Trish jumps up. "I know where everything is, too." She sounds defensive.

A stab of guilt slices through me. She has the better dad/daughter summer gig, an intern instead of a personal assistant, but my dad embarrassed her. I hope she doesn't try to poison me with arsenic or whatever poison anarchists use on their enemies.

Elijah and Ashley leave with Trish. Jason digs through his messy backpack, then heads for the door. I want a few minutes to myself, but Carlos hasn't moved. I send him silent Jedi vibes to follow the others, but he's immune to my powers.

Jason stops at the door and turns to me. "You go to Clarkson Academy, right?"

"Yeah." This is where he confesses his secret crush on me, right? And how grateful he is that I voted for him to stay.

Jason scratches the back of his head, looking slightly baffled. "I sort of knew that, I guess." He studies me like he's never seen me before and my body tingles. I wish we didn't have an audience, but apparently Carlos isn't going anywhere.

"Your sister is Kendra, right?"

Of course he remembers her; everyone does. She's the brilliant social butterfly and I'm the awkward nerd. He gives me a lopsided grin. "Wish I'd known who your dad was in advance, right? I could've pumped you for info."

"That's what he said," Carlos mutters under his breath.

Seriously? It's bad enough he's witnessing my humiliation, but he has to make a rude joke, too? I refuse to be the butt of a smug guy's mocking humor; I've had enough of that to last a lifetime, thank you very much. I shoot him a warning glare but his long eyelashes flutter with fake innocence.

"Do you, uh, do sports and stuff at CA?" Jason asks me, apparently deaf to Carlos's stupid joke. "Clubs?"

His question stuns me. I was in the Harry Potter parody skit with him in seventh grade. How can he not remember I was Dobby to his Draco?

"You gave me your stinky sock to set me free." The words blurt out of me, desperate and pathetic. Next to me, Carlos choke-laughs on his soda. I ignore him.

"What?" Jason tilts his head like a confused puppy.

"The Potter Parody. When you were Draco and I was

Dobby?" This is beyond humiliating. I want to crawl under the table, but instead I grip the chair arms like they're lifesavers.

"Maybe you don't recognize her without the ears," Carlos suggests. We turn to him and he shrugs. "I assume you wore house-elf ears in the play. And maybe a burlap sack?"

Is he mocking me again? Or is he trying to help? Those melty eyes of his are distracting, as is the permanently smirking mouth. Still, I know better than to trust this type of guy. I shoot him another death glare and refocus on Jason.

"That must be it." Jason nods. "The costume and makeup crew did a great job, so good I didn't know it was you." He grins affably, and I don't know what to say.

I side-eye Carlos, who cocks a dark eyebrow. "I wouldn't cast you as a house-elf." He rubs a thumb across his chin like a casting director considering my role. "You've got more of a Hermione vibe going on." He flicks his hand like he's holding a wand, then he and Jason laugh.

I know just how Hermione must've felt when she wanted to bash Ron's and Harry's heads together. Heaving an exaggerated sigh, I roll my eyes to the ceiling.

"I'm gonna grab another drink," Jason says. "You guys want anything?" We both shake our heads. As soon as he leaves, I scoot my chair away from the table, anxious to escape, but Carlos's voice stops me.

"I'm sorry. About my dumb joke."

His apology surprises me, but I'm not letting him off the hook easily. "Which one?"

"The, uh, first one." He blinks those eyelashes again, then grins, which throws me off-balance. It's a showstopper of a smile, with a dimple and everything.

"You're fine with mocking my house-elf self?"

He shrugs. "Actually, I was mocking him for not remembering you. I bet you were a great Dobby." He glances at the empty doorway. "He was Draco? But Lucius gave Dobby his sock, not Draco. Unwillingly, of course."

His Potter knowledge makes my heart skip a beat.

"It was a parody. We changed stuff up."

Carlos's eyes stay on mine. "Is he a good actor?"

The question surprises me. The truth is, Jason's not a great actor. He's…workmanlike. He memorizes his lines and understands stage direction, but he doesn't have much stage presence. I assume he performs so he'll have something artsy on his college apps. Still, it feels disloyal to reveal this to a guy I've just met, so I lie.

"He's great."

Carlos studies me intently and I'm convinced he knows I'm lying. He inhales deeply, nostrils flaring.

"You've gone to school with him for how long?" He drums his fingers on the conference table. He should definitely become a lawyer; he could stare the truth out of criminals.

"Are you cross-examining me, counselor?"

"I'm just curious." His cocky grin reappears, and I can't decide which is more discombobulating—his smile or his stare-glare.

"You and the monkey."

His nose wrinkles, then he laughs. "Curious George? That's me."

The last time a guy this good-looking talked to me for more than five seconds it ended with mortification. For me, not the guy.

He takes another long swig of his soda and I decide to tell him the truth. He'll probably just find it on Google, anyway, since he's great at research.

"I've known Jason since the third grade, when he transferred to Clarkson. I mean, I've known who he is." My cheeks start to burn. "Obviously he doesn't know who I am."

Carlos nods slowly as he scans my face. My hair. Every part of me that's visible over the table. My skin burns under the heat of his perusal.

"Well," he finally says, "it's too bad you girls voted him back on the island."

My hackles rise. "Why?"

"Because he's obviously an idiot."

"He's not," I protest. "He's smart." At least I hope he is, though in real life he's never at the honor roll assemblies with me. Still, some people struggle with classwork even though they're geniuses, like Einstein. I'm sure Jason's brilliant at something; I just don't know what it is. Yet.

Carlos's eyes narrow, never leaving my face. "Not the type of smart that matters. Like remembering someone he's gone to school with for eight years."

I feel like I've just spiked a fever. I glance at the wall clock; our break is over soon. Carlos leans back in his chair, clasping his hands behind his head like we're old friends just hanging out.

"You want to study photojournalism but…"

"Huh?"

His wide mouth curves and I hate how my body responds, like he's fresh spring water and I'm parched. *Shields up*.

He flashes the dimple again, like a missile aimed straight at my protective shield. "You started to say you want to major in photojournalism, but then you stopped yourself. Why?"

"Maybe *you* should major in journalism," I say. "You definitely know how to research." I take a deep breath. "No offense, Carlos, but you're, uh, sort of freaking me out."

"How so?" He unclasps his hands from behind his head and grips his chair arms, a frown knotting his forehead.

"You knew all that stuff about my dad and his company and now you're, um, sort of putting me on the spot."

"I don't mean to freak you out. I'm just curious." His eyebrows meet in a dark slash over troubled eyes.

I swallow and glance out the window, but all I see is the wall of another brick building. I'm starting to feel trapped, like Leia and the gang in the trash compactor.

Carlos tugs at his tie and suddenly stands up. "Sorry. Didn't mean to weird you out. I'm going outside to get some air." He shoves his hands in his pockets and exits the room before I can think of a response.

Squeezing my eyes shut, I blow out a long breath. Surviving a summer on the Death Star is going to be trickier than I thought.

*E*veryone gathers in the conference room after the break. The Manicotti opens a cabinet mounted on the wall to reveal a whiteboard. He grabs a marker and slashes out "***THE RULES***" in black letters, then underlines it three times.

"Number one," he says, writing quickly. "No cheating." He glances over his shoulder. "That means no stealing other people's ideas, no copying ideas that are already out there. Got it?"

Everyone nods. Ashley opens a grown-up portfolio and takes notes. I figure I should do the same, so I grab my Hello Kitty notebook from my messenger bag and start scribbling.

Note to self: buy a fancy leather notebook so I don't look like a dork.

Mr. Mantoni resumes his hyperactive scribbling.

2. BE ON TIME! 8:30-5:00, MONDAY – FRIDAY. ONE HOUR FOR LUNCH.

3. PROFESSIONAL ATTIRE. JEANS OKAY ON FRIDAY, NO TORN ONES.

He glances over his shoulder at Trish, who folds her arms.

She isn't taking notes. Neither is Jason—or at least he isn't until he leans over to Ashley and asks to borrow a piece of paper. And a pen. I scribble in my notebook. *Note: Jason, while adorable, is not very prepared. Get him supplies from the supply room.* That's something I should do as the assistant, right?

Across the table from me, Elijah and Carlos have unearthed laptops from backpacks and are typing quickly. I study Carlos's laptop, which is covered in stickers for local bands, breweries, and a few cryptic acronyms I don't recognize. He must feel me staring because he glances up. Embarrassed, I refocus on the Manicotti, who's finished numbers four and five.

4. DEADLINES MUST BE MET. NO EXCUSES!

5. CONFIDENTIALITY: YOU MAY LEARN OF NEW BUSINESS VENTURES OR POTENTIAL CLIENTS. THESE ARE NOT TO BE SHARED OUTSIDE THESE DOORS!!

Mr. Mantoni is quite the fan of the exclamation point. My English teachers don't allow them, so I'm surprised to see them sprouting like rabbits all over the whiteboard.

Trish lets out a long, bored sigh, and Mr. Mantoni's shoulders bunch. Elijah slants her an amused look and she squirms in her chair. *Note: Does Trish like Elijah?*

Hello Kitty is going to fill up fast at this rate.

The Manicotti spins around and points at me. "You getting all this, Laurel?"

"Y-yes." I try to look responsible, like I'm taking important notes, not gossipy ones.

"Good. You'll be the first line of defense." He studies everyone from behind his invisible glasses. "Laurel will report any rule violations directly to me."

Omigod. Everyone side-eyes me suspiciously, even Jason. This can't be happening. I'm supposed to be an assistant, not a mole. The Manicotti has just destroyed any chance I had at making friends. Or anything more than friends.

I sneak another glance at Jason, who's watching Ashley. They share a look that isn't hard to decipher: basically, I'm the devil. I drop my gaze and draw a spiral design in my notebook, or maybe it's a whirlpool, since I can see my myself being pulled under, hands flailing for help.

Carlos clears his throat and raises a hand. Mr. Mantoni nods his permission to speak.

"What if one of us notices, uh, violations? Do we let Laurel know? Or you?"

Holy crapoli. No no *no*!! I want to yell, with all of the Manicotti's exclamation points.

"Hmm, good question, Mr. Rubio. How about you start by letting Laurel know."

"Will do," Carlos says, shooting me a sly grin. I pick up my pen. *Note: Carlos is trouble.* Hot trouble, yes, but trouble nonetheless. I raise my hand.

"Yes, Laurel?"

"Mr. Mantoni, I…well, I don't think this is a good idea. I thought I was supposed to help everyone. Not, um, spy on them." I hate how wobbly my voice is, but I have to do damage control and stop this tattletale nonsense.

Also, I *really* need to talk to my dad about all of this because it's too harsh, even for Dad Vader.

Mr. Mantoni glowers, looking a lot like his daughter. "Laurel, we will discuss this later. For now, everyone do as I say."

I duck my head and draw a face with Princess Leia hair rolls and *X*s for eyes because that's me: sentenced to death and it's not even lunchtime yet.

7. WINNER TAKES ALL.

"At the end of your internship," Mr. Mantoni says, pointing at the whiteboard, "you'll each do a presentation on your project. Key staff will vote and the winner, as you know, earns one hundred thousand dollars. It's an incredibly generous opportunity that will change the course of one intern's life."

My Spidey senses tingle. Is it wise to pit them against each other? I glance at Trish and she's staring right at me like she's read my mind. She shakes her head slowly, like she's answering my unspoken question. Either that or she's sending me a "don't screw with me" message.

I sneak a peek at Carlos. If I had to vote today, I'd vote for him. He was so passionate when he spoke, and he did so much research and he—he— My brain shuts off as he raises his head and meets my gaze, one corner of his delicious mouth quirking up.

Delicious? What is wrong with me?

I cannot fall headfirst into another stupid crush. Dad will kill me if I waste my summer swooning instead of working, especially after the pressure I put on him to hire me. Plus, this scholarship is hugely important. I need to focus on that.

Ashley raises her hand. "Can you please explain how the voting will work? And how we can best position ourselves to win?"

I study her closely. She wouldn't be here if she didn't need the scholarship, even though she dresses and acts like the some of the richest girls at my school. I doodle a prom queen sash and a crown in my notebook, wondering what her story is.

"Are you sure you're getting all this, Laurel?" Mr. Mantoni prods. He's scribbled a matrix on the whiteboard, with columns labeled Effort, Creativity, and Leadership. "This is what you'll be judged on." He frowns pointedly at my hand, which isn't taking notes.

"Got it." I grab my phone and snap a picture of the whiteboard.

He sighs, probably at the laziness of my generation

taking photos instead of notes. "All right," he says, "I assume you're all wondering who will cast the deciding votes for the scholarship."

I stop breathing. Please God, don't let him mention me.

He clears his throat and continues. "Just like in real life, we're going to shake it up. You'll be observed all summer, by myself, Mr. Kristoff, and other staff members." He shoots me a knowing glance, but I quickly look away, hoping no one notices.

The interns all exhibit varying degrees of anxiety—even Trish, which surprises me.

"This is going to be a great summer." Mr. Mantoni's lips spread into what might be a smile. "I know I just scared you with all the tough stuff, but it's important we set the tone for success. Everyone walks away with experience for your résumé, even if you don't win the grand prize."

Too little, too late, Manicotti, I scribble in my notebook. Then I add an exclamation point, since they're encouraged here in the Empire.

"All right, interns, time to move to your work space. Grab your stuff and follow me." Mr. Mantoni brushes his hands like he's been using chalk instead of a dry erase marker.

We traipse out of the conference room and follow him to the reception area. There's a lot more activity in the office now. A few people nod and smile at me as we pass them like dancers in a conga line. We take the curving steel staircase from the lobby up to the second floor, then Mr. Mantoni leads us down another long hallway to a doorway opening to a narrow, steep flight of steps. This part of the building feels original, not retrofitted like the rest.

"The third floor is where we have room for expansion," he calls over his shoulder as our footfalls echo in the stairwell. "Don't think you'll be unsupervised. We've got a few of our finance department employees up here, too, and they'll be keeping an eye on you."

That probably makes Elijah happy. I glance over my shoulder to smile at him but instead it's Jason who's right behind me. Distracted, I stumble on the steps and he reaches out to grab my arm, sending a few tingles from my elbow to my chest.

"Watch your step, Laura."

The tingles evaporate. "Laurel. My name is Laurel." Looming behind Jason, Carlos rolls his Hershey's Kiss eyes.

"Right. Sorry." Jason brushes past me to catch up to Mr. Mantoni.

Mr. Mantoni opens the door and we emerge into a huge open space full of exposed ductwork, glass, and metal everywhere I turn.

"Sweet." Carlos whistles next to me, clearly captivated by the setting. I can see why; we have a great view, with floor-to-ceiling windows facing the Rocky Mountains, a dusting of snow visible on the highest peaks from a late spring snowstorm.

Ashley pushes past us, tossing me a blinding smile. Her perfume fills my nose. "Can we take any empty desk?" she asks, heading toward the windows.

"Winner takes all," Carlos says softly, amusement threading his voice. "Gotta give her props for staking her claim."

"I guess." I tighten my grip on my messenger bag. Snagging the best spot isn't my style. I steal another peek at Carlos, whose eyes are trained on the supermodel. Guys are so predictable.

"What are you waiting for?" Mr. Mantoni's voice echoes in the room. "Stake your claim."

"Ha." I smirk at Carlos. "He stole your line."

"Or maybe I'm a mind reader."

"That's a mind I wouldn't want to read."

His laughter curls around me, sending a not-unpleasant shiver up my spine.

"Don't you want to grab a desk by the window?" I need him out of my personal space. Now.

"I'll let everyone else choose first." His eyes meet mine and I swallow. He's…intense is the only word that fits.

"Why?"

He shakes his head. "Sorry, little spy. Can't tell you my secrets."

Embarrassed, I turn away, but not fast enough.

"Hey"—his voice softens—"I'm kidding."

"Yeah, right," I mutter. "You're just the only one willing to say what everyone else is thinking."

I step away from him, heading to a far corner of the room, selecting a desk off by itself. My sliver of a view includes part of Coors Field, so I can't complain too much.

Everyone else chatters and laughs as they settle in at their desks, while the finance employees watch, bemused. I'm glad I've chosen an isolated desk so I don't have to listen to the bantering and flirting, because I know that's what this is going to turn into, once everyone gets past the rules freak-out.

Carlos chooses a desk halfway between the other interns and me. This must be part of his secret strategy. Weird.

"All right." Mr. Mantoni claps his hands together and everyone goes quiet. "Go ahead and get settled, then it's time for lunch. I expect you all back in the office at thirteen hundred hours."

Military time? *Great.* I scowl out the window. I'm going to find Dad, so we can have lunch together. We need to discuss my role and the Manicotti's rules. I wait until everyone else has fled before I leave the room. No one wants a spy trailing their every move.

...

*M*s. Romero's desk is located in Dad's outer office like a protective sentry, but she's not there. I knock on Dad's closed door. Muffled voices rise, giving me pause, but this is urgent. The door swings open and Dad activates Vader mode when he sees me.

"Laurel? What is it?"

I almost lose my nerve.

"I, uh, well…I thought maybe we could have lunch together?" I whisper because now I'm embarrassed, like a little kid clinging to her parent's leg on the first day of kindergarten.

Dad's mouth tightens and annoyance flickers in his eyes. Crud.

"I have a meeting for the next couple of hours. Maybe another day this week."

I swallow and nod, officially rebuffed. I turn away, but his voice stops me.

"Is everything okay, honey?"

Honey? What happened to Vader? I shrug and force a smile. "Everything is fine. I'll see you later." He closes the door, still frowning.

"Laurel?"

Ms. Romero has returned, carrying a large bag from Smiling Moose Deli.

"Hi. I was just…I thought maybe Dad and I could have lunch, but he has a meeting."

She sets the bag on the credenza next to a multi-colored vase full of fresh flowers. It's the only spot of color in the office.

"He's got a working lunch meeting. Want to eat with me? There's plenty here; I always order extra."

I hesitate, then figure why not? It's not like the interns asked me to join them, and I don't feel like eating alone.

"Sure. Can I help you set up?"

"That'd be great. Grab some drinks from the kitchen and a serving tray."

We prepare lunch quickly. "You can take it in," Ms. Romero says when the tray is ready.

"Are you sure? I already interrupted him once." I don't want to rattle Dad Vader's cage.

"It's not an interruption when you have food." She smiles encouragingly.

This time when Dad opens the door, his eyes light up, especially when he spots the cookies. "Just put it on the conference table, Laurel."

Everyone thanks me as they reach for food. I wave at my dad as I leave and right before I close the door, I spot the hint of a Vader smile.

"Sit down, honey." Ms. Romero has prepared two plates for us at a small corner table.

Two "honeys" in fifteen minutes. Trish would be appalled, but honestly it feels good right now. I'm reeling from the crazy morning, and my feelings are sort of hurt that none of the interns asked me to join them for lunch. But who wants to hang out with the boss's daughter who's supposed to report rule violations?

"So, how was the morning?" Ms. Romero pauses between bites of sandwich.

I release a defeated sigh; I can't help it. Last summer when I worked here, she was nicer to me than anyone else, and I know my mom thinks she's awesome, so I decide to confide in her.

"Weird," I say. "Really weird."

Her forehead wrinkles with concern. "What happened?"

"It's…a lot of stuff. Mr. Mantoni is…super intense. And he has all these crazy rules for the interns. He wants me to report back to him whenever they break a rule or do something wrong." I take a huge bite of ham and cheese to shut myself up.

Ms. Romero taps her manicured fingers on the table. "I know Mr. Mantoni can be intense, as you said," she says carefully. "He's very devoted to your father and this is the first time we've sponsored this program. The scholarship is a big deal; it's gotten a lot of press. I'm sure he doesn't want anything to go wrong."

Maybe so, but Mr. Mantoni sure isn't giving us the warm-and-fuzzy, go-team-go vibe.

"Do you want me to talk to your dad about it?"

I shake my head. "No, I will." I need to tell him firsthand about the bizarre morning.

We finish eating, changing the subject to talk about my mom's new clothing line, why my sister chose to stay in San Diego for the summer, and what colleges I'm thinking of attending.

I glance at my phone and realize it's 12:55. "I've gotta go." I jump up. "Mr. Mantoni will kill me if I'm late coming back from lunch."

"You go on; I'll clean up." She waves me away and I practically sprint down the hallway, wondering if it's faster to take the elevator or the two flights of stairs. I decide on the elevator.

"Come on, come on," I mutter as I press the button. I glance toward Miss Emmaline, who watches me suspiciously. I wave and smile, but she doesn't even blink.

The elevator opens, and I rush in, coming face-to-face with Carlos. I try to act nonchalant. "Where'd you come from?"

"Garage level." He takes a drink from a large soda cup, eyeing me over the straw as the doors close. The elevator is suddenly very small. And very warm.

"Where's everyone else? I thought you all went to lunch together."

"Nope." He doesn't say anything else. I'm grateful it's a short ride to the third floor.

The elevator stops with a lurching thud, then spits us out like human hairballs. We head into the giant room I've decided to call the sky box. Everyone else is already there, including Mr. Mantoni, who glances at his watch, then pins Carlos and me with a suspicious squint.

"Cutting it close." He crosses the room and hands us each a glossy booklet. "Last year's annual report." He motions for everyone to gather around him, so we do.

"All right, interns." The Manicotti crosses his beefy arms over his barrel chest. "Study this report, thinking about your areas of interest. We'll reconvene at three o'clock in the room where we met this morning." He glances at me. "Laurel, put another snack tray together for the meeting."

My gaze slides to Trish. I expect to see her gloating, but she looks as annoyed as I feel. Working women solidarity, maybe? I can't figure her out.

No one moves until Mr. Mantoni claps his hands together. "What are you waiting for?" Everyone scatters to their desks, including me.

I'm so glad I have my earbuds. I plug them into my phone and resume listening to a sci-fi thriller starring Qa'hr, a kick-butt heroine who's been kidnapped and is trying to figure out how to escape from the kidnapper's spaceship. It feels oddly relatable, especially the part with the aliens howling outside her door like mutant werewolves.

The Emergent Enterprises Annual Report is full of graphs and charts and buzzwords. Scattered throughout are pictures from successful ad campaigns, including local restaurants I recognize from when we come downtown for plays at the

Denver Center for Performing Arts. Mom insists on an annual subscription to the theater to up our cultural IQ points.

As I flip through the pages, I pay more attention to the drama playing out in my earbuds than the words on the pages, until I come to the last page, when I groan out loud. There's a picture from last year's employee summer picnic—a close-up shot of me with a unicorn painted on one cheek, a sparkly rainbow on the other. Mom used me as the model for the face-painting table for little kids. The caption reads, "A Kristoff team member gets into the spirit at the company picnic."

Team member? Seriously? And why isn't there an equally incriminating photo of my sister? Probably because she's smarter than me and avoided being photographed. I glance up, wondering how many seconds of peace I have before everyone starts laughing at me.

Stupidly, I glance across the room at Carlos, who meets my gaze, his dangerous grin trained on me. He holds up his annual report and points to my photo, then gives me a thumbs-up. I roll my eyes, so he adjusts his thumb, pointing it down and frowning. I shake my head, embarrassed. He shrugs and moves his thumb so it's in the sideways neutral position. He makes his expression blank and I can't help but smile as I turn away, cheeks flaming.

A smattering of laughter breeches my earbuds, indicating everyone else has seen the incriminating photo. I open my notebook and make a note: *Bring camera and yarn to work tomorrow. And knitting needles for self-defense.* Knitting is one of my favorite stress busters; Mom taught me when I was young and over the years I've gotten pretty good at it. If I'm going to spend lunches by myself and generally be ignored by the interns, I might as well make something pretty.

And it won't hurt to be armed with a sharp weapon, just in case.

Chapter Five

I survive the rest of the day by keeping my head down and my earbuds in, except for the three o'clock meeting in which I begrudgingly deliver snacks and take notes as the interns discuss what clients' projects they hope to work on this summer.

Dad isn't ready to leave at five o'clock, which isn't a surprise. While I wait for him in Ms. Romero's empty outer office, I fire off a text to Lexi.

Is the water park hiring? I might need a job at the snack shack.

What happened?

I'm pondering my reply when a knock sounds on the doorway. I glance up, startled to see Jason standing there.

"Hey, Laura…el." His smile is tentative.

"Hi." I give him half a point for almost getting my name right this time.

He glances toward my dad's door, then back to me.

"Do you have a message for my dad?"

Jason runs a hand through his messy hair. "I…kind of

wanted to thank him for giving me a shot." He chews his lip. "Anyway, I'm sorry about earlier. You must think I'm an idiot."

"Why would I think you're an idiot?" I want him to keep talking so I can drink in his jocky yet dorky cuteness and decide whether or not to forgive him for not remembering me, or my name.

A rueful grin flits across his face. "We go to school together, but I didn't recognize you. I didn't put it together until I saw that picture in the annual report."

Oh, excellent—seeing me with a sparkly painted face brought it all home.

"It's okay," I say with false brightness. "I wouldn't expect you to notice me." Even though our private school isn't that big. And we've had classes together.

"Your sister Kendra goes to college in California, right?"

My stomach butterflies yawn and go back to sleep. They've figured out something that's just now dawning on me.

"Yeah, she's at UC San Diego. She stayed there for a summer internship."

Jason nods and glances toward my dad's door again. I wonder if he's trying to earn brownie points by staying late or if he really wanted to apologize.

"I'd love to go to school in California, but it'll never happen." His voice is hollow, defeated, and my heart squeezes. I can't believe the Manicotti wanted to fire him just for being late.

"I've gotta catch my bus." He forces a grim smile. "Guess I'll see you tomorrow."

"So, you didn't get scared off? I mean, you know, with the rules and the Mani—Mr. Mantoni."

"Oh." He darts another anxious glance at my dad's door. "Well…it's…I guess…this is how it works in the real world, right? That's what Coach always says. 'Jason, you have no idea how things work in the real world.'"

We laugh and I completely forgive him for not recognizing me. I also admit to myself that my infatuation might be winding down. He's a decent guy, but up close and personal, I don't feel the fireworks I'd always fantasized about.

Dad's office door opens, and he strides out, looking harried, briefcase in hand. He stops short when he sees us.

"Hey, Dad. Jason and I were just talking about how awesome today was." The lie flows easily because I want Dad to like Jason, and I want him to have a shot at the scholarship.

"I'm glad to hear it." He turns to me. "Ready to go, Laurel?"

Jason back-steps into the hallway. "See you later, Mr. Kristoff. Laurel." He gives a half wave, then hustles away. I guess he lost his nerve to thank my dad.

Dad doesn't look happy. "Was that young man flirting with you, Laurel?"

"*Dad*. No, not even." I choke-laugh. "He didn't even know…never mind."

"I should have thought of that complication," he mutters as he strides quickly toward the elevator. "I'll have to talk to Tom about this."

Panic rockets through me. "There's nothing to talk about. Especially not to the Manicotti."

Dad glares as he presses the elevator button. "Don't call him that, Laurel, especially in this office."

"Sorry." I tug at my hair. "Dad, it was no big deal. Jason goes to school with me. We were just catching up."

The elevator arrives, and we step in. "Laurel, you're… these boys…young men…" He's struggling for words, which never happens. I wait, but he goes silent until we reach the underground level. I almost have to run to keep up with his long strides as he heads toward his car, muttering under his breath.

Once we're out of the garage and driving in traffic, he resumes his train of thought. "You're only seventeen. This is no time to…to…"

"Get married?" I joke. "But back in the olden days, we'd be the perfect marrying age. Which one should I pick? You could have a grandchild by Easter if you're lucky."

He jerks his head to glare at me, his mouth an angry slash. "Do not joke about that, Laurel Anne. Ever."

I giggle. I can't help it. Sometimes I like to push the Vader's buttons.

"Dad, you know I'm kidding." I fiddle with my beaded bracelet. "Also, you don't have to worry about me, um, dating any of these guys or whatever." As the words tumble out, Carlos's dimpled grin pops into my mind. And stays.

"I would hope not, Laurel." I feel Dad's stare on me. "That would disqualify an intern from winning the scholarship."

It would? Holy crapoli. Rattled, I change the subject away from my nonexistent office romance to more important matters.

"So, Yoda. You have a rogue Jedi you need to rein in. Mr. Mantoni is not yet one with the Force. It's more like he's bashing everyone over the head with excessive force."

Dad grimaces as we race toward the highway on-ramp, passing the Pepsi Center concert venue and the Auraria campus of urban colleges, including CU Denver, which Carlos mentioned.

Why do I keep thinking about Carlos? I frown and tug at my gauzy skirt, trying to shut off my thoughts.

"What do you mean by excessive force?" Dad asks, skillfully maneuvering through traffic until we're in the far left lane.

"Rules, Dad. I thought companies today were all hip and flexible. Like Google, with napping pods and games. And slides." I side-eye him. "You could put a slide in, from the third floor down to the lobby. That would be sweet. Or maybe a fireman pole."

He gives me a look that reminds me why I usually give him a wide berth until he's had his after-work beer. I take a breath.

"I'm…well, I have some…concerns about the, uh, success of this project." Dad glances at me curiously. "Mr. Mantoni scared everyone today. He's like a dictator. And the worst part is he wants me to report back on rule breakers. Inappropriate behavior, cheating…whatever." I sigh, allowing my worries free rein. "I don't know if the interns will talk to me after today, let alone let me help them."

"That boy lingering in my office talked to you."

Oops. "That was…he was just…"

Jason's apology seemed genuine, but I know how much he needs the scholarship. I hope he wasn't sucking up to me because of my dad.

"Anyway, no one else talked to me after the Manicotti laid down the law."

Though Carlos did interact with me, with the thumbs-up stuff. That was funny. But he didn't speak to me the rest of the afternoon, and he'd been the first person to leave at five, without a backward glance.

"How about Trish? How's she holding up with her dad laying down the law?"

A question I couldn't answer. She had a giant chip on her shoulder that would either alienate everyone or earn their grudging respect. I just wanted to stay out of her line of fire.

"You two should be friends," Dad continues. "Both of you working with your dads." He shoots me a knowing smile. "The enemy of my enemy is my friend."

"Ha," I scoff. "That'll never happen. She treats me like

gum on the bottom of her shoe."

Dad frowns. "I'm sorry to hear that. Maybe I should talk to—"

"No. You should not talk to anyone, especially Mr. Mantoni. Trish and I will be fine. What's it called when enemies agree not to kill each other?

"Truce?"

"The French one."

"Détente."

"Yeah, that's what I'm hoping for."

We drive in silence, until I gather the courage to ask something that's been bugging me all day.

"So Dad…do you think…I mean…"

He downshifts and glances at me. "Go on."

"Did you hire me thinking I could help out? Or did I just wear you down?" As much as I want the chance to spend time with him, I don't want to be the daddy's girl with a fluff job, like Trish assumes.

Dad clears his throat. "You might be surprised. Stay open to the possibilities."

Why is he talking in riddles? "What possibilities, Yoda? You gonna train me in some new secret Force moves?"

He rolls his eyes, which makes me happy. I didn't think he knew how.

"We learn from all of our experiences. Even when we don't realize what we've learned until it's over."

"Do. Or do not. There is no try."

He fake glares. "Don't Yoda me, Padawan."

I smile out the window, but I'm still worried about my job. About the Manicotti. About Trish.

Traffic slows to a crawl and Dad runs a hand through his hair.

"Laurel… This scholarship program is a big deal. At first

I said no because I thought you working here would be a distraction. But the more I considered it, the more I realized it's a great opportunity for you." His fingers tighten around the steering wheel as we slow to ten miles per hour. "Tom may have gone a bit overboard today, but it's because he wants this program to succeed."

"That's what Ms. Romero said."

Dad nods. "She's right. As usual."

I wonder if I'll ever make a boss that happy, if I'll know just what to say or do, no matter the circumstance.

"Dad…this idea of me voting on the winner. I don't like it." I hold my breath.

"Two votes," Dad corrects.

"But why—"

Dad honks at a pickup truck who cuts us off. The guy flips Dad the bird. Dad doesn't return the gesture, though I suspect he would if I wasn't with him.

"Idiot," he mutters, then glances at me. "I thought you'd like that. You were the one who told me you could do a 'peer review.'"

"That doesn't mean I want to vote. I don't want to give somebody a rose while everyone else is disappointed."

"Rose?" Dad shoots me a confused glance. "What are you talking about?"

Clearly he doesn't watch reality TV. "I mean that I shouldn't vote. You should. You and Mr. Mantoni and whoever else. But not me."

We're silent for a bit, then he asks, "What do you think of the interns so far?"

Uh-oh. "They…" I stop. What should I say? I hardly know them. "I'm withholding judgment. It's only the first day."

"First impressions are important," he counters. "Sometimes you have to make snap decisions based on them."

"Dad, come on."

"Hypothetical question. You're stuck on a desert island. Which one of them do you want with you?"

I tense, then tell myself he doesn't mean this in a suggestive way; he's my dad, after all. He probably means it in the Yoda way—like when Luke was training on Dagobah.

"Uh…I can't answer that." Well, not entirely true. "Okay, so as of right now, definitely not Trish. She'd kill me and cook me over a campfire to survive."

Dad coughs, but he's hiding a laugh underneath.

"Anyway," I say, "it's too early for me answer that question. Let's table this question until Friday, okay?"

After a beat of silence, Dad speaks. "Table we will, until Friday it is."

One of Mom's inviolable rules is that we eat dinner as a family at least two nights a week. She'd prefer more but Dad works too late most days. It doesn't matter what we eat—fast food was acceptable when Kendra and I had after-school practices or whatever, but we have to sit at the table together.

So here we are, minus Kendra, and by the gleam in Mom's eyes she can't wait to pepper me with questions.

"Is Mr. Mantoni excited to have you working there again?"

Excited is not the word I'd choose. I take a long drink of iced tea to stall. I glance at Dad, whose attention is on his cell phone, violating another of Mom's rules. I point to Dad and Mom's expression transforms from anticipation to annoyance.

"Rhett. No phones at the dinner table."

Chastised, Dad gives her a sheepish grin and flips his phone screen-side down. I don't think anyone else on the planet could boss Dad Vader around except my mom.

My parents met in college, in a ridiculously romantic and dramatic way. Mom and a few of her friends went to a frat party to protest the "demeaning and sexist swimsuit contest." Instead of prancing around in a bikini to be ranked by a bunch of Neanderthals, Mom stayed fully clothed and led a protest chant, waving her giant poster and marching around the swimming pool.

A couple of the frat brothers grabbed Mom and tossed her into the pool. Unfortunately, she couldn't swim. Her friends freaked out, and while most of the frat guys ignored their pleas for help, Dad jumped into the pool and rescued her. The story has achieved legendary status over the years.

Dad didn't stay friends with the guys who threw Mom into the pool. The fraternity stopped hosting beauty contests years ago, because the protests continued until the fraternity dropped the whole thing. Mom considers this one of her biggest accomplishments, and she made Kendra promise to be very careful about the whole frat scene when she went off to college.

"So, tell me about your day," Mom prompts me. "How were the interns? Was Trish nice to you?"

Dad and I exchange a secret look.

"It was fine." I shrug and twirl spaghetti around my fork.

Mom frowns. "Fine?" She side-eyes Dad, who mirrors my shrug. "Laurel, I—we—have high hopes for this summer. This job's an opportunity for you to develop new skills. And use the ones you already have, of course." She smiles brightly. "You have so much to offer."

Like what? Snack delivery? Also, it sounds like she and Dad memorized talking points, which makes me suspicious.

"The job is fine, Mom. Don't worry. Once I get to know everyone I'm sure I'll, um, contribute a lot."

Dad nods. "I have no doubt. You have much more to offer than you realize."

I don't know if he means it, or if it's one of those parental platitudes that's supposed to make me feel better.

Mom asks more questions and I give her vague non-answers, deflecting and evading like a pro until dinner is finished and I can finally escape to meet Lexi.

"Tell me about the water park. Anything exciting happen?" Lexi licks icing off her cupcake like a kid. We've been friends since she transferred into Clarkson Academy in the second grade. Back then she reminded me of a fairy—petite and graceful with long black hair and golden-brown skin. She hasn't changed much—except now she has a foul mouth for someone who looks so sweet and innocent, but she keeps it under control since we're sitting outside, surrounded by families.

"Nothing special," she says. "Just like last summer—yelling at kids to stop running, burning my retinas because of old guys in Speedos. The usual."

I'm eating my cupcake with a fork because I'm weird like that, but my fork stops halfway to my mouth. "Guys don't really wear those anymore, do they?"

She laughs. "Those who do definitely shouldn't." She licks more icing and nods at me. "Go on. Tell me about your day at the evil empire."

I know where I have to start. "So…Jason Riggs is one of the interns."

Her mouth opens, then closes. I know she wants to say something R-rated, but a cute toddler has wandered close to our table.

"Sorry," his mom says, dragging him away and lecturing him about personal space.

Once they're out of earshot, Lexi asks, "So did you attack him in the supply closet?"

"Yeah, right. Like that would happen." I imagine the Manicotti's reaction to PDA and shudder. "Anyway, he didn't even remember me. He called me Laura, then he asked about Kendra, because of course he remembers her." I stab a huge bite of cupcake with my fork and shove it in my mouth.

"Anyway." I shrug, dismissing thoughts of Jason, which is easier than it used to be, especially when I remember Carlos's grin when he found my unicorn face. I poke at my cupcake. *No crushes on the job.* I can't risk it, especially if it means the guy would be disqualified from the competition.

I stare across the parking lot at the Apple store. Maybe I could get a job there.

"So far, my job is basically like working on a reality show, *Survivor*, intern edition. Remember the crazy guy who freaked out when I wore flip-flops to the office last summer? He's in charge."

Lexi's dark eyebrows shoot up. "You're voting people off the island? Firing them? I thought this was a good cause, for a scholarship."

"It is, but I think Mantoni just likes to stir up drama. The interns all do a summer project, and someone wins the full scholarship at the end."

Lexi studies me, eyes narrowed. "Tell me about the interns. Besides Jason."

I lift my hand, raising fingers as I speak. "One, supermodel artist girl. Two, smart and hot suit guy who wants to be an accountant. Three, Jason. Four, Trish, she's the crazy guy's daughter. She's already in college at Boulder." I fake shudder. "She's sort of scary."

Lexi nods. "I thought there were five."

"Right." I focus on the little kids chasing each other. If I make eye contact with Lexi, she'll read my expression too easily. "Last one is a guy named Carlos. Super smart. Knew a bunch of intel about my dad and his company." I continue to stare at the giggling kids until Lexi reaches across the table, turns my face toward hers, and grins.

"Carlos is cute, obviously. Or he did something to get your attention."

"He's okay." I shrug and stare at the orange and red striations of the sunset.

Lexi laughs and steals the rest of my cupcake. "Uh huh. Well, your gig sounds a lot better than mine. You might even score a few dates by the end of the summer."

My gaze locks on hers. "No way."

"Why not?"

Unbidden, Carlos's intense dark gaze pops to my mind. "No," I say firmly, more to myself than Lexi. "This is a job, not a dating game. I need to prove to my dad it was a good idea to hire me."

Lexi doesn't look convinced. "Why can't you do a good job *and* have fun?"

"Even if I wanted to, I can't. Dad said any guy I dated would be disqualified."

"Wow. That stinks."

Lexi's phone buzzes and her eyebrows knot as she reads. She looks up, her gaze unfocused as she stares across the parking lot.

"Lex? You okay?"

"Sorry I'm distracted. Stuff at home." She drags her finger through a bright pink glob of cupcake icing. "Lots of yelling between my brother and my parents."

That surprises me. Lexi's brother Scott is Mr. Responsible.

He graduated as valedictorian last year with a full scholarship to Gonzaga. I assumed her parents would be thrilled to have him home for the summer.

"What's going on?"

She shrugs and brushes a strand of hair from her face. "Let's go to the movie."

My skin prickles as I assess the worry in her eyes.

"Lex, you can tell me, whatever it is."

"I know." She bites her lip. "But I just want to escape, okay?"

"Sure." I stand up, wincing at the scrape of metal chair on the sidewalk. I offer her my pinkie. "No more boy talk or work talk. Pinkie promise. Just girl time for the rest of the night."

She smiles and locks her pinkie with mine.

"Deal."

Chapter Six

"Why do you always go into the office so early?" Leaving the house at seven a.m. on a summer day is criminal.

"Why do you think?" Dad's thumbs bounce on the steering wheel in time to a horrible eighties hair band.

"I'm not in a riddle mood, Yoda." I nibble on the granola bar I swiped on the way out of the house.

Dad chuckles and takes a sip from his coffee mug. He's always been a morning person—just one more sign he's from the dark side.

"Let me guess. Because you're running the Empire and your work never stops?"

"Exactly." He gives me an air cheers with his cup.

I grumble to myself, but softly so he can't make out the words. Unlike yesterday, we don't talk much on the way in. Dad listens to news on the radio and I put in my earbuds and resume my sci-fi audiobook.

Qa'hr has a plan to attack her alien captor with a metallic wall panel she's managed to loosen, but she can't decide when to do it. Part of me hopes a hot Captain Mal dude is going to show up and help save the day, but that's not how this story goes; she has to save herself. I'm sure that's important symbolism I should pay attention to in my own life, but I'd like at least one hot kissing scene before this book is over.

At the office, I make myself a cappuccino with the fancy one-cup machine and grab a donut from a box on the counter, silently thanking whoever brought them in.

Now it's time to put my win-over-Miss-Emmaline plan into action. Last night I pondered why her animosity bugs me so much. It's because she thinks I'm a slacker. She only busted me once last summer, but it colored her whole perception of me.

It's bad enough worrying the interns think I'm useless; I don't want Dad's staff thinking that, too. Plus, she looks like a sweet little old lady from a cookie commercial. Shouldn't she like everyone?

I approach her cautiously. She glances up but doesn't return my smile.

"Good morning, Miss Emmaline." I force extra enthusiasm into my voice.

"Laurel." Her gaze sweeps over me and I wonder what she thinks.

Today I'm wearing this funky crocheted top Mom made and a swishy skirt. My sandals are strappy gladiators. I don't think they're against the dress code, but I guess I'll find out. I decided not to fake it and dress like a mini-executive like Ashley. I'm going to be myself and not worry about impressing anyone. Including the guys.

"I see you found the donuts." Miss Emmaline frowns.

A bolt of panic jolts through me. "I hope it's okay that I took one."

She nods. "They're for everyone."

"Did you bring them?"

"No, Ms. Romero did. Your dad makes sure we have them."

Huh. Dad unleashes his sweet tooth at work, apparently. Donuts, brownies. I tuck that bit of info away for later use, then take a breath and launch phase one of my plan.

"Miss Emmaline, what do you call a pig that knows karate?"

Her frown deepens as I wait for her to play along. She doesn't.

"A pork chop!" I laugh like this is the funniest thing I've ever heard. A few employees crossing the lobby stare at me, but I keep the hilarity plastered on my face.

Miss Emmaline shakes her head and types on her keyboard, dismissing me. Sighing in resignation, I turn away. I take the elevator to the top floor, hoping my embarrassment at my failed joke will burn off by the time I reach my desk.

No surprise that I'm the first one in the intern wing; it's not even eight o'clock yet. A woman in the finance area glances up and nods. I sit at my empty desk and eat my donut, allowing myself a few moments of self-pity, then I think about Qa'hr, who managed to loosen a spaceship wall panel with just her fingernails. Convincing the interns that I'm here to help should be a lot easier than that.

My computer whirs to life. I have one email, from Miss Emmaline. She's sent it to the office distribution list, reminding everyone that next Friday is pizza day. Also, it's a foosball tournament and people are supposed to bring desserts.

It will be painfully awkward if I'm the odd one out at the pizza party. But that's assuming the worst—maybe by then I'll have connected with some of the interns. I try rousing myself with a pep talk.

"Today's a new day. Start fresh. Be the change." I take a big bite of donut.

"Sounds noble."

The voice startles me, and I jump, smearing chocolate

icing on my face. I scrub my face with a napkin, but not fast enough. Carlos appears in front of me, that cocky grin of his firmly in place.

"Sorry I startled you." He points to his nose. "You missed a spot."

Fantastic. I wipe my nose with the napkin and will him to disappear into thin air, but of course he doesn't. He's not wearing a tie today, but he still looks…good. Really good. I remind myself of the reasons I can't have a summer fling with an intern and add an extra reason just for him—he's too… *something* It's a swagger, an aura he gives off like he's got everything under control.

"Are there more donuts?" Carlos watches me warily, and I'm grateful mind reading isn't a thing.

"Yeah. In the kitchen."

He nods and heads for his desk. I watch as he unpacks his backpack. I shouldn't stare but I can't look away. He's wearing khaki pants and a pale yellow Oxford shirt, a leather belt, and Sperrys that are worn but not trashed. He looks like he went to a prep school, yet he's planning to attend the urban commuter college unless he wins the scholarship. An intriguing mystery.

No, I tell myself, *I'm not intrigued.*

"Want anything from the kitchen?" Carlos glances up and busts me staring at him.

Crud. I feel my cheeks heat as I wait for the smirk, but it stays hidden.

"Why'd you choose *that* desk?" I blurt.

"Why do you ask?" He crosses his arms over his chest and holds my gaze. I'm transfixed by his mouth, still hoping for the smirk. I think I spot a lip twitch, but it might be wishful imagining.

"Just making conversation." I shrug, then blunder ahead.

"It's just…the other interns all chose prime window seats. Except you."

This time his lips definitely twitch. "You didn't."

"I'm not an intern. I'm an assistant."

His eyes widen briefly, then dart toward the windows. "Top secret," he finally says. "You have your reasons and I have mine."

Way to shut me down, dude. I turn back to my computer, wishing I had a hundred emails to distract me. I hear his footsteps come closer, but I ignore him, clicking the new message button. I'm typing gibberish, but he doesn't need to know that.

"Last call for another donut." He stops in front of my desk, so close I can smell him. And he does not smell bad. The opposite, in fact.

"No thanks." My fingers fly over the keys like the survival of my dad's company depends on how fast I can type a nonsense string of letters. He looks ready to speak again, but he changes his mind and walks away quickly.

Even though my plan is to make friends with the interns and make myself useful, that plan sort of falls apart around Carlos.

My inbox pings with a new email from Mr. Mantoni and I spring to attention.

"Interns! Meet in the conference room at 9:00. Don't be late."

I take a deep breath and wish I'd asked Carlos to bring me a second donut.

By eight-thirty, everyone else has arrived. Today Ashley's wearing a red dress, which only highlights her fabulous blondness. Jason can't stop staring at her. He still looks slightly disheveled, though he's managed to comb his hair. Elijah ratcheted his junior exec look down a notch, ditching the tie like Carlos. When they do the dude-chin-nod, I realize Jason didn't acknowledge Carlos when he arrived. Interesting.

Trish is the last to arrive, wearing a long black skirt, a black blouse, black boots, a spider necklace, and dangling anarchy symbol earrings. I want to give her a thumbs-up, but I don't since she'd probably slice off my thumb with a hidden switchblade. Still, I have a healthy respect for a girl who's mastered the art of vicious compliance with dress codes.

The window view interns focus on their computers, keyboards clacking. I wonder if they're writing gibberish like me or surfing the internet. I glance at Carlos in the middle of the room. He's propped his head on his hand, elbow on his desk as he reads a book. He's polished off two donuts. Not that I'm spying.

My gaze shifts to Elijah, whose fingers flick over his phone screen. He glances up and smiles at me. Flustered, I turn back to my computer and resume typing nonsense.

There's movement and rustling as everyone stands up. It's almost nine o'clock. We all make our way down the stairs to the conference room, but we're quiet. This bothers me because I don't think Dad would want his interns to act like they're headed to an execution. I wish he'd listened to me when I brought up my worries about the Manicotti.

We file into the conference room, taking seats around the table. Mr. Mantoni is already there. On the whiteboard is a new rule, in all caps.

8. NO FRATERNIZING!!!

Three exclamation points. This must be big. Elijah leans over and whispers to Carlos, who glances at the board with a sly grin. They fist-bump and I'm dying to know what they just said.

"Any questions, interns?" booms Mr. Mantoni, making Ashley flinch.

Jason's hand shoots up. "By fraternizing do you mean, uh, well…what exactly do you mean?"

Ashley blushes prettily, Trish rolls her eyes, and Carlos and Elijah exchange wicked grins. I stare at Hello Kitty and start drawing whirlpools in my notebook.

"I mean no boy-girl stuff." Mr. Mantoni points at all of us, wagging a warning finger.

"What about girl-girl stuff?" Trish asks and Elijah chuckles. My pen digs into the paper as I color in my whirlpool. I glance up in time to see the Manicotti's neck vein bulge.

"You all know exactly what I mean. None of it on the premises."

Ashley tosses her hair over her shoulder. "But off-premises is okay? After work's over?"

I can't look at any of the guys because I know their eyes are bugging out. Other body parts might be, too, and I definitely don't want to know about that.

Mr. Mantoni folds his bulging arms, reminding me of a sumo wrestler. "Look, it's clear what I mean. No funny stuff on the job." He glances at me and I wonder if this new rule is because of Dad seeing Jason and me talking after work yesterday. Ugh.

"Our full-time employees have the same rule," Mr. Mantoni continues. "We don't allow romantic relationships between people in unequal power positions. For instance, a supervisor and his or her underling."

"Gross," Trish says. "No one here is interested in that, since you're the supervisor." Ashley's eyes widen in horror and Carlos does his cough-laugh.

I'm stuck on the word "underling." Who says that in real life?

"Part of working together is forming bonds," the Manicotti continues, ignoring Trish. "Teaming up on projects. But everything needs to stay professional, am I clear?"

"Crystal," I mutter under my breath.

I don't have to worry about this stupid rule, but Ashley does; I'm sure all the guys want to fraternize with her. I draw a girl with a giant F on her chest, yelling, "Help! I was caught fraternizing!" I smile to myself as I doodle. When I glance up, Carlos is watching me with an inscrutable look. He points to my notebook and gestures like he wants to see it.

No freaking way. I shake my head. We're across the table from each other so my doodles are safe from his prying eyes, but still…I shoot him a slit-eyed warning glare. Laughter dances in his eyes, eliciting butterfly swirls in my stomach. Evidently the butterflies are now on Team Carlos.

"We're starting with a brief presentation by our marketing director today." Mr. Mantoni scribbles **MARKETING** on the whiteboard. "She'll go over a few of our popular campaigns and talk about how we came up with them. Then we're going to turn you loose on a test project."

Everyone sits up straighter, except for Trish, who lounges in her chair, snapping gum. Carlos catches my eye again, a quizzical look in his eyes. I turn away.

A light knock sounds on the door, then it opens, and a tall, slim woman enters. She reminds me of Halle Berry, and I recognize her from past holiday parties at our house.

"Hello everyone, I'm Katherine Simmons. Please call me Ms. Simmons." She smiles around the table and nods with recognition when her gaze lands on me. Trish sighs in annoyance.

Ms. Simmons sets her laptop on the table and picks up a remote. Cheesy music wafts from the ceiling speakers. Mr. Mantoni leaves, and I breathe a sigh of relief.

"This is a presentation we use for prospective clients," Ms. Simmons says. "It's an overview of some of our most successful ad campaigns and gives a glimpse into our employee culture." She dims the overhead lights and we all focus on the screen.

"Where's the popcorn?" Elijah whispers. Ms. Simmons cocks a disapproving eyebrow in his direction, but a contradictory smile curves her lips.

We watch a slick mini-movie that includes my dad being pithy, Ms. Simmons talking about branding, and a few people I don't recognize extolling the awesomeness of Emergent Enterprises. Interspersed with these nuggets of wisdom are shots of magazine ads, social media ads, a couple of TV spots, and photos from events.

"Product launches," Ms. Simmons says as we study images from a fancy foodie event and a packed floor of trade booths at the convention center. The last few photos are from charity events—Emergent employees at the Race for the Cure, serving a holiday dinner at a homeless shelter, wrapping toys in Christmas paper.

I have to admit the propaganda movie makes my dad's company look cool…and him, too. An unexpected pulse of pride strums through me.

Ms. Simmons turns the lights back on and we all blink at each other.

"First, you're all going to work as a team. I want you to come up with a product launch campaign. Figure out your target audience, stay within a budget, and give me your best idea."

Ashley's grin is wide, her lips red and glossy to match her dress. Jason chews his lip, a nervous habit he's had since forever. Trish studies Ms. Simmons, actually looking interested, which surprises me. Elijah and Carlos take notes on their laptops.

Carlos looks up from his laptop. "Is this a real product or a fake one?"

"It's real, but not for a company we represent. It's a warm-up activity for you."

Ashley clears her throat. "What about each of us working on our own project? I thought we got to do that."

Ms. Simmons's responding smile is tight. "You will, eventually." She glances at me. "Don't forget that Laurel is part of your team, too. She'll be happy to assist however you need."

Whoa. Who told her to say that? I bet it was Dad. Ugh. Everyone glances at me, but no one smiles.

"Now, for the product," Ms. Simmons says dramatically. She reaches into her tote bag and pulls out a plain white box. Everyone shifts in their chairs, leaning forward. I fantasize about an oversized jack-in-the-box sprouting a maniacal clown.

But when Ms. Simmons opens the box, she pulls out...a miniature Death Star. We all look at each other—correction, *they* all look at each other. In my excitement, I try to make eye contact with someone, anyone. I wonder if this is my dad's private message to me. That would be epic, but I don't think he's that clever.

"What is that?" Carlos asks, frowning.

"You don't recognize it?" I'm disappointed. Even non-geeks should know it on sight.

"I know it's the Death Star." The smirk flashes. "But what does it *do*?"

Jason picks it up. "I think it's a speaker." He flips it over. "Yeah, Bluetooth connection."

"Let me see it." Ashley holds out her hand and Jason slides it toward her. She studies it like she's never seen the Death Star. I bet she hasn't ever seen *Star Wars*. I wonder if she's one of those people who dismisses all things geeky. "Is this for kids?"

Ms. Simmons shrugs. "That's for you all to figure out."

"Dude." Elijah glowers at Ashley. "*Star Wars* is for everyone. Not just kids."

Is Elijah part of my secret tribe? He must feel my worshipful stare because he graces me with a grin.

"What's our fake budget?" Carlos asks.

"Three thousand. It's a small start-up company," Ms. Simmons says. "Let's pretend they're based in a tiny town in North Dakota and this is their first product. They're passionate about it, but don't have money. They've set up a website but haven't sold much."

"Hey, this is a real thing." Jason waves his phone at us. "It's on Amazon for fifty bucks."

Note to self: buy Death Star speaker with first paycheck.

"Ah," says Ms. Simmons, "that reminds me. For this exercise I want you to pretend Amazon doesn't exist."

"What?" Jason yelps.

"I know it seems unfair." Ms. Simmons smiles apologetically. "Selling this on Amazon is the easy way out. I want to see how creative you can be without using the retail gorilla."

Carlos runs a hand over his mouth, hiding a smirk. I wonder why he finds this so amusing. He seems to find a lot of things amusing. Our gazes meet across the table and hold until I look away, my breathing coming faster than normal.

"Just sell it at Comic Con," Trish says, finally chiming in. "Travel around the country to all the comic cons."

"Genius," Elijah whispers, putting out his hand for a fist-bump. Trish complies, smug and triumphant.

I have to admit it's a great idea. I love Comic Con. Denver's is the third biggest in the country and I go every year. I'm almost done making my Qa'hr costume for this year.

"Interesting idea." Ms. Simmons closes her laptop and slides it into her tote bag. "Remember, the fake company is in the middle of nowhere, not close to any big comic con cities." She slings her tote bag over her shoulder. "I'll leave you to it. I look forward to your presentation." She hands me a stack of papers. "Laurel, please make copies of this for everyone."

I nod, even as my face burns. Copies. Snacks. *Great.* But I'm the one who offered to work as an assistant. I shouldn't complain. The room is quiet until she leaves, but as soon as she closes the door, everyone starts talking at once.

"This is dumb," Jason complains. "If we can't sell it on Amazon what are we supposed to do?"

"She's treating us like children," Ashley complains. "It's a toy, for goodness sake." She slides it down the table to Elijah, who picks it up with the reverence it deserves.

"This is *not* a toy." Elijah stares down Jason. "Dude. We're supposed to be creative. Amazon's too easy."

Carlos tilts his chin at Trish. "I like your idea. Let's see if there are any small comic cons within driving distance to Podunk, North Dakota." His fingers fly over his keyboard.

A hot current bursts through me as Trish smiles at Carlos. Reminding myself to focus on the project, I doodle a small Death Star in my notebook, with music notes wafting out of it. I love that Elijah's a nerd because at first glance he seems way too cool for geekdom.

I used to fantasize that Jason was secretly a geeky jock, and that someday we'd discover a shared love of dorky fandoms. But as he stares into space, his only idea to sell the speaker on Amazon, disappointment washes over me. Just because he looks like he might star on *The Big Bang Theory* meets *Friday Night Lights* doesn't make it real. I guess I shouldn't be surprised. My fantasies never come true.

As everyone chatters around me, I lean across the table to

pick up the Death Star. Whoever came up with it was brilliant; I'd like to meet him or her.

"I'm sure your dad will buy you one," Trish snarks.

The room goes quiet and I feel everyone's eyes on me. Heat crawls up my skin. I force a smile, pretending her statement was innocent rather than an insult.

"I'll buy it myself. After payday." I don't want everyone thinking what a spoiled daddy's girl I am.

"Seriously?" Ashley asks, her perfectly shaped eyebrows shooting up. "Why would you want it?"

"Because I love *Star Wars*. And it's portable, which is cool."

"How convenient," Trish says, her voice laden with sarcasm. "You could take it out to your swimming pool. Or your horse stables."

Apparently Trish hasn't forgotten anything from when she visited our house. I can't make eye contact with anyone. This is mortifying. She's made me look like a spoiled rich girl in a room full of people who are here because they need money for college.

I take a breath and turn the speaker over in my hands, determined to ignore Trish and act normal. "Anyone want anything from the kitchen?"

Everyone shakes their heads in unison, so I set the speaker on the table, grab the stack of papers from Ms. Simmons, and leave, closing the door behind me, but not quick enough to drown out Ashley's voice.

"She has horse stables? For real?"

I wish I was like Rey in *The Force Awakens*, brave and tough. Or Princess Leia, snarky and brilliant. But right now, I feel like a young Anakin Skywalker, when no one thought he was capable of piloting his own Podracer, let alone winning a race.

. . .

*T*he copier is in the supply room next to the kitchen. A couple of people stand around talking, but they don't pay any attention to me as I try to decipher the copier's touch screen.

"Need any help?"

I glance up, meeting the curious blue eyes of a guy who looks to be in his late twenties with curly red hair and a friendly smile.

"Uh, yeah." I return his smile, grateful for his offer. "I need to collate and staple this stuff."

He touches the screen and walks me through the steps, making me feel like an idiot because it's so simple.

"You one of the summer interns?" He leans against a large metal filing cabinet, watching me with friendly curiosity.

I shake my head and stare at the copier as it spits out papers. "No. I'm…assisting them, sort of." I glance at him, and he frowns. Then his expression clears.

"Oh, wait a minute," he says. "You're Mr. K's daughter, right?"

"Yeah, I'm Laurel."

The guy holds out his hand. "I'm Brian."

It takes me a second to realize I'm supposed to shake his hand. I do, feeling like an impostor in a world where I don't quite belong.

"Well, good luck, Laurel. This is a cool place to work, but I guess you already know that." He smiles again, and I feel off balance.

He's way too old for me, obviously, but he's friendly. I could use a friend around here. The copier continues to whir and make a weird chunking sound every time it staples a new stack of papers. Maybe I could move my desk in here and be the copy queen. Boring but safe.

"See you around, Laurel."

"It was nice meeting you."

He grins and flips me a wave as he leaves.

I take the elevator to the roof, hoping no one else is there. It's my favorite place at Emergent, surrounded by potted trees and plants, with small conversation areas set up in the corners. Fortunately, no one else is here. I beeline to the farthest corner and flop into a cushioned wicker chair.

I have to figure out a way to survive. I picture Trish's pinched face. Somewhere underneath that attitude is a girl like me. We shouldn't be enemies. Maybe I should try talking to her, even though the thought makes my stomach twist.

I lean back in the chair and let the warm sun beat down on my upturned face. Below me, traffic hums, horns honk, and a distant siren ramps up its volume. I love being downtown, so that's one thing I can do to cope—use my lunch break to explore. I can start shooting photos for the Faces of Denver photography contest I plan to enter. I pull my phone out of my skirt pocket but instead of texting Lexi I text my sister Kendra.

> *Can you talk?*
> *What's wrong?*
> *Summer job from hell.*
> *Ugh. Sorry.*
> *How's your job going?*
> *Great!*

I sigh as I stare at my phone. If Trish thought I led a charmed life, she should meet Kendra.

> *Is Dad being a pain?*
> *Not too bad. But it's weird with the interns. I'm supposed to be their "assistant" but I don't think they're going to let me.*

Let's talk tonight. Ten o'clock your time?
Sure.

She texts me a bunch of hearts and I shove my phone back in my pocket. I take the stairs down to the third floor, hoping none of the interns ever finds out about the rooftop. I'd like to have an escape pod no one else knows about.

The interns are at their desks. I drop off the copies, head down so I can avoid eye contact. When I flop into my desk chair, my Hello Kitty notebook winks up at me. Oh no; I left it on the conference table. Who brought it back? And did they look inside to see my stupid doodles and notes about everyone?

I open my notebook and discover to my horror that someone has not only read my notes but commented on them.

Note: *Jason, while adorable, is not very prepared.* Comment: He's definitely not prepared. You really think he's adorable?

Note: *Does Trish like Elijah?* Comment: Trish flirts with everyone.

Note: *Carlos is trouble.* Comment: True. Is Carlos adorable?

Note: *Too little, too late, Manicotti.* Comment: Who's the pasta?

Note: *Bring camera and yarn to work tomorrow. And knitting needles for self-defense.* Comment: Now you're scaring me. Do you take photos before or after you stab a person?

That one makes me laugh out loud. Who did this? I sneak glances around the room but no one's paying any attention to me. I expel a long sigh and stash my notebook in a drawer.

Note to self: never, ever leave private items unattended.

• • •

*D*uring my ride home with Dad, I quiz him about the Death Star.

"Who came up with the test project?"

"Ms. Simmons. Why?"

I study his profile for any signs of lying, but it's hard to tell since he's watching the road instead of me.

"So, it's just a coincidence that it's a *Star Wars* product?"

"Is it?" He glances at me, surprised, then grins. My dad has a great smile, but I don't see it very often when he's in work mode. "What is it?"

"A Death Star Bluetooth speaker."

He laughs, something else I don't hear too often. "You sure it wasn't *your* idea?"

"I wish." I sound irritable and his smile evaporates.

"What's wrong?"

"Nothing." I turn to stare out the window.

We're quiet for a bit, then he speaks again. "Well, it's a weird coincidence, but a good one. I'm sure you can help the interns with a lot of great ideas on how to market it."

Oh, yeah, Dad Vader. My geekspertise is in great demand.

After more silence, Dad turns on the radio to listen to droning stock market news, so I plug in my earbuds and listen to my book. The kidnapper alien brings Qa'hr food once a day, and this time when it opens the door to her cell, she's ready. She slices the jagged edge of the metallic wall panel across the alien's body and when it doubles over, oozing goop, she bolts to freedom.

*M*y sister Kendra calls me promptly at ten, as promised. I hear laughter and music in the background, then it fades away. I picture her leaving a party and moving to the balcony of her apartment. She lived in the dorms her first year, but now she's living off-campus with two friends. I try not to resent her freedom.

"Hey, Laurel-bell, how are you?"

When she uses my childhood nickname, my resentment fades. I love my sister, and I miss her.

"Laurel," she prompts, "are you okay?"

I lean back against my headboard and close my eyes. "Yeah. Just being whiny. It's my superpower."

She laughs in my ear. "No, it's not. What's up? Is working for Dad that bad?"

I sigh into the phone. "It's not him so much as the Manicotti, and…well, you know about the scholarship, right?"

"Yeah, it's awesome."

"It is, but I'm sort of freaking out because Dad wants me to vote on who wins. He says I get two votes."

"What?" Her voice pierces my eardrum. "Seriously?"

"I know. It's crazy. I mean, I offered to give him my feedback on the interns, but I don't want responsibility for the decision."

"No way. Besides, they probably all deserve it. What do you think of them so far?"

I pick at the crocheted afghan on my bed, made by Mom when I was five years old. "I don't know them yet. It's only the first week. But they all seem smart." I blow out a breath. "Jason Riggs is one of them."

"Ooh…you always had a thing for him, right?"

"He's okay. Not quite what I expected, up close and personal."

"I know just what you mean. When I dated Chris Hemsworth that's exactly what happened. He's not very cute with his shirt off."

"Shut up," I say through my laughter.

"Look," Kendra says, her voice now serious. "Dad has you there for a reason. You're smart, Laurel. And you read people well."

Maybe. I've managed to avoid a lot of drama and general assholery in school by being very picky about who I spend time with.

"Get to know them," Kendra continues. "Ask Dad if you can read their applications to get some insight. If you do have to make this decision, everyone should get a fair shot."

"Thanks, Ken. You're right, as much as I hate to admit it." She laughs softly in my ear and I wish she was flopped on the bed next to me. "I wish I could channel your friend-making skills. You always know how to win people over."

She huffs in my ear. "Not true. We have different styles, but people like you, too. Everyone thinks you're funny. And you're adorable, like I want to put you in my pocket adorable."

"Great. So, I'm a real-life Polly Pocket doll." I roll my eyes all the way San Diego.

"See what I mean? Funny and adorable. Use that."

"So far it's not working. I can't even get Miss Emmaline to laugh at my jokes."

"Really? I love Miss Emmy. She's all crusty on the outside but gooey on the inside."

"Like a pie, only filled with poison."

Kendra chuckles in my ear. "What about the girl interns? Start with them. Work up to the guys, if they make you nervous."

I picture scary Trish and beautiful Ashley. "Not sure that will work."

"Oh, come on, Laurel. Working women have to stick together. You can't believe how much sexism is still out there."

"Sure, I can." I tell her about Mantoni's sexist secretary remarks and she groans.

"I'm sure you can bond with the other girls. Women always have something in common with each other, even if it doesn't seem that way at first."

I close my eyes and burrow into my giant pile of pillows. Kendra always finds a way to bond with other girls, but it's not as easy for me. Not everyone appreciates my goofy ways when I try to be funny, or when I reveal too much of my nerdiness.

"I'll try."

"Good girl," Kendra says. "Report back to me later this week."

"Roger that."

"Over and out, sister."

We disconnect, and I stare at the ceiling, wishing I could channel even an ounce of my sister's charisma.

Chapter Seven

I've barely settled into my desk and turned on my computer the next morning when my inbox pings. **"Laurel, come to my office as soon as you read this."** My stomach hiccups when I see the email is from the Manicotti.

Am I fired already? But wait, how could Mr. Mantoni fire me if my dad owns the company? Besides, I haven't done anything.

Exactly, I think as I stand up to meet my summoner. I haven't done anything to help the interns yet. Crud.

I pass Carlos as I rush down the stairs.

"You going on a donut run?" His smile crinkles the skin around his eyes.

"No. I have a meeting with Mr. Mantoni."

His smile falters. "Good luck."

"Thanks, I need it."

Mr. Mantoni's head gleams under the industrial lighting in his office. He glances up as soon as I enter his peripheral vision. He doesn't smile, but he doesn't look ready to throw me overboard, either.

"Laurel. Come in. Shut the door behind you and take a seat."

Uh-oh. I close the door, feeling like Qa'hr trapped with the scary alien. I sit across from a desk piled high with stacks of papers.

"So." His eyes narrow behind the creepy rimless glasses. "How's it going so far?"

"It's, um, okay. Sort of quiet as everyone gets settled."

He studies me without blinking and it takes all my effort to keep my eyes wide and innocent, my lips forming what I hope is an "I love it here" smile.

He glances down at a stack of papers and straightens it, which seems futile.

"Your father and I have discussed your role here. We want your honest evaluation of all the interns. We want you to get to know them over the next couple of months."

I nod, recalling my convo with my sister. I clear my throat. "Um, do you think maybe I could see their applications?"

He frowns, rubbing a hand over his bald head. "Hmm. Those applications are confidential. Let me think about it." He pins with me a look that makes me grateful for Dad Vader. "You heard each of their introductions already."

"Yeah but...that's what they wanted us to hear." Not that they weren't honest, but those intros were like the cover of a book—shiny and enticing, but only a hint of what's inside.

"You can get to know them on a level that we can't, Laurel. You're their age, speak their language." He waves his hand around like he's talking about a magic formula he doesn't understand.

"But, um, what about Trish?" I dare to ask. "I'm not evaluating her, right?"

Mr. Mantoni's face closes up like a garage door. "No. Probably best if you give her a wide berth."

I can't ignore her. That will just make her dislike me even more.

"Check LinkedIn," he says gruffly. "We made them fill out online profiles as part of the application process." He picks up another messy stack of papers and shuffles it, then looks at me with a narrowed squint. "People are more than meets the eye, Laurel. Remember that. Each of them has something… big…they're dealing with."

He turns his attention back to his computer and jerks his head toward the door. I stand up and back away from his desk, escaping into the hallway. His words churn in my mind. How can I evaluate them if I don't know whatever their "something big" is?

I hope there are donuts again today because I desperately need sugar. I relax as I enter the cheery kitchen, a stark contrast to the weirdness I just escaped. A few employees are gathered around the espresso machine, including Brian, the copier tutor. He smiles and nods in my direction, then refocuses on the conversation.

No donuts today, but I spot a few brownies in one of the snack baskets, so I grab one. I'd love a cappuccino, but I don't want to interrupt the conversation, so I turn to leave, running smack into Jason and Trish.

"Hey, Laurel." Jason smiles at me, but I don't feel a swoon coming on.

Trish grunts as she moves past me. "'Scuse me, I need coffee," she says to the group gathered at the counter. They move out of her way.

"How's everything going?" Jason asks. We've spoken more in three days than our entire school tenure together. This should make me deliriously happy, but I still can't shake the feeling that the pedestal I've put him on for years was made of cotton.

"Okay." I shrug. "How about you? What do you think of the job so far?"

Why did I ask that? Considering who my dad is, I've just put him on the spot. And based on his flushing face, that's exactly how he feels.

"Uh, well, it's great. I'm grateful for the awesome opportunity." He answers like I'm a sports reporter at a game: "*We just got out there and executed. I'm grateful Coach gave me a chance to play.*"

"Yeah, I, um, hope it works out for you."

When his eyes widen, I wonder if I shouldn't have said that. Does it sound like I'm playing favorites? Argh.

My eyes flick toward the coffee machine. Trish is finished so I take her place, relieved to be interacting with an inanimate object. I expect her to leave as my cappuccino brews, but she doesn't. She watches me like a hawk stalking a baby rabbit. I hope she kills fast and painlessly.

Laughter bounces off the walls as the other interns enter the kitchen. Elijah heads straight for the coffee, flashing me a grin as he grabs an espresso pod.

"Mornin', Laurel. How's our personal assistant today?" There's a teasing lilt to his voice. I wonder if he's sucking up to the boss's kid or if he's just a decent guy being friendly.

I pick the second option, hoping it's true.

"I'm great," I lie. "How are you?" The coffee machine burbles and steams. My eyes flick toward everyone else. Jason is chattering animatedly to Ashley while Trish scowls at Carlos, who studies the brownie in his hand like it's the Rosetta Stone.

"I'm stupendous," Elijah says, recapturing my attention. "Ready to spread the awesome Death Star speaker far and wide." He winks, and I feel my cheeks flush. He takes a step closer and lowers his voice. "I'm the biggest *Star Wars* nerd around." His eyebrows lift in a question. "Except maybe for you?"

My blush deepens. "Uh, yeah." I swallow and decide to go for it. "You go to Comic Con?"

His grin is bone-melting. "Every year. Last year my girlfriend went as Rey and I went as Finn. I had to represent." He lowers his voice to a whisper. "How about you? Were you one of the awesome Reys I saw running around the con last year?"

I don't think I've ever been on the receiving end of attention from a guy as charming and fabulously nerdy as Elijah. He's going to be easy to get to know.

"Yeah," I manage to squeak out. "I made my costume."

I'd gone as Rey even though I knew a million other people would, too. I wonder if his girlfriend was one of the many Reys I'd asked to pose for a photo. Heck, I might even have a picture of both of them on my computer. Half the reason I loved Comic Con was photographing the amazing cosplayers.

Elijah raises his hand and I meet him halfway for a resounding high-five. The conversation among the other interns ceases as everyone turns to stare at us.

"Nothing to see here," Elijah says to our audience. "Move along."

I giggle at his *Star Wars* quote and he shoots me another wink, but now I know it's conspiratorial, not flirtatious. Honestly, I'm relieved he has a girlfriend. I appreciate his friendliness.

"We should head upstairs." Carlos's curious gaze slides between Elijah and me. "Before the big guy busts us." He freezes and turns to Trish. "Sorry. I, uh—"

Trish shrugs. "It's okay. I've heard him called worse. And you're right, he'll be pissed if he thinks we're just messing around instead of working."

She turns to leave the kitchen and a flicker of sympathy twinges in my chest. Maybe this gig is as hard for her as it is for me. Maybe worse, since her dad is so weird, and my dad's… well, possibly not nearly as bad as I assumed.

Ashley and Jason leave, but Carlos hangs back, waiting for Elijah, I assume.

I trail behind them, and Carlos pauses, glancing over his shoulder at me. "Elevator or stairs?"

So, he's including me? I'm surprised but try not to show it. "Either," I say as we walk down the hallway, but then remember I forgot to tell Miss Emmaline a joke this morning.

"You guys go ahead, I need to do something." I cross the lobby, putting my friendliest grin in place.

Miss Emmaline glances up. The intensity of her glare matches the intensity of my smile, which fuels my determination.

"Hi, Miss Emmaline." I rest my arms on the raised counter that surrounds her desk. "Did you hear about the pancake, fried egg, and strip of bacon that walked into a bar?" I wait, but she's silent as a stone. "The bartender said, 'Sorry, we don't serve breakfast.'"

Miss Emmaline's face remains frozen, but behind me I hear a groan and a laugh. Ugh. Why'd they have to follow me over here? I keep my smile in place and drum my fingers on the counter. "Have a fabulous day, Miss Emmaline. I'll see if I can do better tomorrow." I whirl around, heading for the elevator, Elijah and Carlos flanking me.

I stab the elevator button, wishing they hadn't overheard my stupid joke.

"What was that about?" Carlos asks, laughter dancing in his eyes.

I glance at him, but I can't maintain eye contact because a) I'm embarrassed and b) his deep brown gaze does all sorts of crazy stuff to my insides.

"You trying to suck up to Miss Emmaline?" Elijah asks

as we step into the elevator.

The doors slide shut and I stare at my feet. "Maybe," I mutter.

"Why?" they ask simultaneously.

I glance up. "Because she…"

No. I'm not going to confess my pathetic need for approval. I already look like a total dork, why make it worse?

"It's weird that she didn't laugh," Carlos says. "I mean, other than the fact it was a dumb joke. Usually she's friendly."

I glare at him. "Old people like corny jokes. And maybe she's friendly to you but not to me."

The elevator doors slide open and Elijah backs out, pointing to me as he walks backward. "Pro tip, Laurel. Never call old people 'old.'"

"Good point." Carlos laughs softly next to me. His arm brushes mine and a tingle zooms from my fingers to my heart.

"I'm not rude," I say, doing my best to ignore the tingle. "I'd never say that to her face. I just—"

"Hustle up, interns!" Mr. Mantoni looms in the doorway to the sky box.

Carlos and Elijah speed up, but I hang back to gather my composure.

When I enter the vast room, everyone is gathered by the windows at a round table, with the Death Star on display. I realize belatedly there isn't a chair for me at the table. I hesitate, then turn toward my desk.

"Jason, grab a chair for Laurel." Carlos's voice stops me in my tracks. Jason jumps up and follows orders. Ashley grumbles as he wedges the chair next to her. Carlos shoots Ashley a warning look, so she moves just enough for the chair to slide in. After all that commotion, I have no choice but to join them.

"All right," the Manicotti says. "You all know your task. I

expect good things." He tugs at his yellow tie. "Also, you're all invited to Friday Foosball. If you want to challenge the regular staff, a sign-up sheet is in the kitchen. We'll have beer but none of you are to touch it, understood?" He encompasses all of us with his glare.

We all nod, except for Trish, whose mouth twists in a defiant smirk. I wonder if she'll do a keg stand.

"I'll leave you to it." Mr. Mantoni steps away from the table. "You know where to find me or Ms. Simmons if you have questions. Email works, too." He glances at me. "Laurel, make sure everyone has whatever office supplies they need. Ask Miss Emmaline for the key to the valuables cabinet in the supply room if you need it."

Carlos and Elijah dart me amused glances, though Carlos's lingers longer than Elijah's.

"Oh, excellent," Ashley chirps. "I have a list of things I need."

Great.

As soon as the Manicotti is out of earshot, Trish leans forward.

"Look, guys. I know you all think my dad is crazy. Hell, I think he's certifiable. But I…" She takes a breath and I inhale with her, feeling like she's speaking for both of us. "If you could just…try to forget he's my dad, okay? Just think of me as one of you."

Envy and admiration pulse through me. Why didn't I think of saying that?

"Deal," Carlos says. He tilts his chin and grins at her, and everyone else chimes in their agreement. All eyes turn to me and I realize I haven't acknowledged her request. I take a deep breath as I meet Trish's suspicious gaze.

"Of course," I say. "I know just how you feel."

"It's different for you." Trish's voice is tight. "Everyone

likes your dad. Plus, he owns the place." Her lips curve, but not in a friendly way. "Anyway, you're not an intern so it doesn't matter."

I don't know what to say to that, so I spin my peace symbol ring around my finger. I sure don't feel peaceful right now, and I wish Carlos hadn't forced me to join them. Someone coughs. Jason shifts next to me on his chair and Ashley tosses her hair over her shoulder, a few shiny strands whacking me in the face.

"Okay," Trish says, sounding determined. "Let's get to work on selling this stupid toy."

"Hey," Elijah protests. "I told you before, this isn't a toy. This is a legit lifestyle accessory."

If I thought anyone would listen to me, I'd back up Elijah. The chattering fills my ears like a flock of hungry seagulls. I think about Qa'hr making repairs to the rickety spaceship she's hitched a ride on, finding a way to make herself useful. With a surge of determination, I stand up.

"Where are you going?" asks Trish, eyes narrowed.

I meet her challenging stare and channel my inner Qa'hr. "Paper clip emergency." I turn to Ashley. "Give me your list of supplies." She tears it out of her notebook.

Halfway to the door, I turn back. "I'm your only hope. If I don't come back with supplies, save yourselves." Then I flounce away, hoping I look more like a confident Leia than a stiff C-3PO.

Deep laughter rolls across the room, and I'm pretty sure it's Carlos who's laughing.

After I gather the supplies on Ashley's list and a few items for me, I swing by Ms. Romero's office for a confidence boost from a friendly ally.

"How's it going up there?" Her voice is warm, like she cares about my answer.

"Fine." I square my shoulders. I'm not going to complain anymore. I've got to make this work.

"How about Trish? You two getting along?" Ms. Romero's gaze is sharp, leaving no doubt she's pegged our dynamic.

"Sure." I reach up to push a curl behind my ear and smile brightly.

She looks skeptical, but before she can respond, the door to my dad's office opens and he steps out, adjusting his striped tie. He freezes mid-step when he sees me.

"Laurel. Do you need something?"

"No, I just stopped by to say hi to Ms. Romero."

Dad nods, then taps his watch. "I need to get to a meeting. See you back here after five, all right?"

"Sure." For a second, I hoped he might ask me to join him for lunch, but that's never going to happen. He has worlds to conquer.

Heaviness weighs me down as I trudge up the stairs to the sky box. I hoped I'd get more time with my dad by working here, but he's so busy I doubt I will. Maybe I should use a fake name and call Ms. Romero to get on his calendar.

Back in the sky box, the interns are still gathered around the table, having what my mom would euphemistically call a "healthy debate."

I settle at my desk, surprised to see a single-serving box of Special K cereal on my desk. A post-it note is stuck to the box: If your dad is Mr. K, then you must be Special K. I eye the interns suspiciously, wondering who did this.

With a sigh, I shove the box in a desk drawer, then put in my earbuds and check my email. Another all-employee message about the foosball event, bemoaning the lack of dessert signups. Maybe I'll make something, like a good little assistant.

Since I'm not allowed access to the interns' job applications, I decide to check them out on LinkedIn like the Manicotti suggested.

Candidate one, the supermodel. Ashley's face pops up, along with a résumé listing all of her fabulous volunteer activities, her volleyball stardom, her student advisory board service and her college major plans. Nothing surprises me— she's perfect on paper. And yet…something in her life isn't perfect or she wouldn't be here. I doodle a row of question marks in my notebook, then type Jason's name into the search box.

His profile picture reminds me of all of the yearbook photos I used to drool over. I glance at the table where the debate rages on. I wonder what it's about, but I don't want to look desperate to be included, so I return to Jason's profile. It's a lot like Ashley's, full of volunteer projects, sports, and of course, the plays.

I wonder what I'll put on my LinkedIn profile when it's time to make one. I suppose I can list this job, but I'll have to lie. "Advised interns on proper work attire and lunch options." I snicker to myself, then pull up Elijah's page.

Elijah's profile is dynamic, just like him. Activities and interests leap off the page. I wonder what his backstory is. Someday I might know him well enough to ask, since he's the friendliest of the bunch.

I realize I've saved Carlos for last. Was it intentional? I check the table to make sure everyone is still occupied. The interns have unearthed a pad of giant paper and affixed a sheet to the window. Carlos is standing, scribbling on the paper with a marker as everyone else talks and gestures.

On my computer screen, Carlos grins like whoever took

the photo was a friend. His eyes sparkle with humor and a dimple peeks out on the left side of his mouth. Like everyone else, his profile lists clubs, activities, and college major interests. For the past three years, he's worked at a restaurant called Encantado on the west side of town. He's done everything from washing dishes to cooking to waiting tables.

Curious, I look up the restaurant online. A website pops up with photos that are a bit fuzzy and out-of-focus. The interior shots of the colorful restaurant are fun, except for the focus issues. I click the "about us" button and strike gold.

"The Rubio family has owned Encantado for nineteen years. Encantado means 'charmed' and our restaurant reflects the warmth and love we share as a family. We love to welcome friends to our family table and hope you will be charmed by our people and our menu."

Nice ad copy. I wonder if Carlos wrote it? I study the family photo, wishing it was clearer. I assume the middle-aged couple are his parents. Carlos stands next to his mom. On his other side is a boy who looks about ten, and next to him are two younger girls who must be twins. Fanning out from the dad's side of the photo are several people who look to be in their twenties and thirties, and an older couple who might be grandparents.

Everyone has dark hair and beautiful eyes. And gorgeous smiles. My fingers itch to retake the photo so it does them justice. I'd like to reshoot the restaurant photos, too, at better angles and with better composition.

"Hey."

I almost jump out of my chair when Carlos appears at my desk, then fumble with my mouse to minimize my browser.

"What's up?" I try to look bored, not at all obsessed with retaking his photo.

He runs a hand through his dark hair, the hair I now know is a family trait. He's wearing khakis again today, and a pale blue dress shirt with the sleeves rolled up, revealing sinewy forearms.

"Sorry about how things went earlier." His gaze locks on mine and my oxygen levels plummet. "You're part of the team, too, Laurel." He glances toward the table. "Trish was… out of line."

"Maybe she just said what everyone else is thinking." I draw circles on my desk with my finger. "That I'm a spoiled rich girl who's only here because of her dad."

Carlos shoves his hands in his pockets. "That's not what I think." He sounds frustrated. "I don't know what's up with you and Trish, but not everyone is your enemy."

Guilt snakes through me. It was decent of him to try to make me feel better.

"Sorry, I just…I don't know." I force a half smile. "Even Miss Emmaline doesn't like me. I feel like the unwanted little sister everyone has to put up with."

He blinks, those chocolatey eyes wide and surprised. "But you're…" He clears his throat and glances away, then back again. "I guess it's hard being the boss's daughter. But that doesn't mean everyone hates you."

My pulse throbs in my ears and wrists, which is ridiculous because whatever this is, it's not flirting. It can't be.

"We're going to grab sandwiches at the deli," he says. "You want to come with us?"

"I…uh…" I remember my plan to take photos for the Faces of Denver contest. "I have plans. But thanks for asking." *Ask me again another day,* I want to say, *just you.*

He shrugs and steps back. "Maybe join us after lunch? We can't agree on a Death Star plan. Maybe you can be the deciding vote." His lips quirk up. "Again."

"Okay." I want him to like me. Not like *that*, because that's a pipe dream, but as a person with good ideas. An equal.

He slants me a quick smile, flashing the dimple, then heads back to the table as the eighth rule flashes like a scoreboard in my mind: *NO FRATERNIZING!!!*

Chapter Eight

The warm Colorado sun beats down as I merge with the lunch crowd filling the sidewalks. Out here, I'm just a girl with a camera, not a spoiled "daddy's girl" or a spy. Tension eases out of me as I pause to put on my rhinestone-studded sunglasses, a gift from Lexi.

LoDo, Denver's lower downtown area, is vibrant and diverse, full of historical buildings that have been repurposed and given new life. I have a long list of places to photograph. Today I'm starting with the oldest painted advertisement on a Denver building.

I head toward an alley off Fifteenth Street, where I find an entire building wall painted in old fashioned letters advertising Studebaker Carriages and Buggies. The letters are faded, but that's hardly surprising, considering they were painted in 1883.

As I select my lens and filter, adrenaline buzzes through me. I love photography because I forget about myself and become one with the camera. I become a giant lens, taking in what's in front of me, blinking and adjusting until I capture what I see with my heart as well as my eyes.

Time passes quickly as I fill my memory card with photos. My pace is quick as I head back to work, energy pulsing through me. That's what happens when I do what I love. Rounding a corner, my breath catches at the sight of an enormous sidewalk planter full of colorful blooms, but someone has graffitied the planter with an obscene phrase.

The contrast of the beautiful and the profane intrigues me, so I move closer, squatting down so I can zoom in.

"Hey, look, it's Jimmy Olsen. Where's Superman?"

Carlos and Elijah stare down at me, both of them wearing sunglasses so I can't read their expressions.

Flustered, I stand up and brush off my skirt. "Hi."

"Hi yourself," Elijah says, grinning. "Are you a professional paparazzi or what?"

Carlos's expression remains inscrutable, so I focus on Elijah and his mirrored sunglasses.

"Not exactly. It's just a hobby."

"Sweet setup for just a hobby." Elijah gestures to my camera, a Nikon D750. He's right. It was my Christmas present last year, after I was bitten by the shutterbug—Dad's dumb joke, not mine.

"Where's everyone else?" I want to change the subject from my expensive camera. I feel self-conscious, knowing that neither of them could probably afford it.

"We ditched them." Carlos finally speaks, a hint of a smile playing at his lips.

That makes me laugh. We head toward Dad's office and somehow I end up next to Carlos, which only amps up my adrenaline buzz.

"So, this was your 'other plans' for lunch?" Carlos asks. "Taking pictures?"

Ouch.

"Yeah." I take a breath. I owe him an explanation since he was so decent earlier. "Taking pictures makes me happy and I'm pretty good at it."

Neither of them speaks as we traverse the final block to Dad's office. When we reach the office, Carlos holds the door open, gesturing for me to go first. I pause inside the lobby, removing my backpack and stowing my camera.

"I'm grabbing a Coke from the kitchen," Elijah says. "See you upstairs."

I expect Carlos to follow Elijah, but he doesn't. Instead he falls into step next to me as we cross the lobby.

"Wanna try another joke on Miss E?" His teasing smile kick-starts my heart.

"No, that might tip her over the edge." I hope I sound unaffected by his smile. "Besides, I only do jokes in the mornings."

He laughs as we head upstairs. I wish I could change things so that it was just Carlos and me working here this summer. And maybe Elijah.

"How long have you been into photography?"

"About a year or so. It just sort of…grabbed me and wouldn't let go."

We start up the second flight of stairs and I wonder if he thinks I'm a dork.

"I know what you mean."

"You do?"

We've reached our floor. He glances down the hall to the sky box, then back at me.

"Yeah. I think everybody has something they're passionate about. Or if they don't, they're missing out."

He studies me, his expression thoughtful. I'd like to believe I see flickers of romantic interest in his eyes, but that's not it. I think he's trying to figure me out, or maybe he still feels obligated to be nice to me.

"You going to join us?" he asks. "I'd like your opinion on our Death Star strategy."

"I have a really bad feeling about this."

Carlos frowns.

"*Star Wars* quote, when the Ewoks capture Han Solo and are about to roast him for dinner. Also, when Han and Luke and Leia are about to be squashed in the trash compactor."

He cocks an eyebrow, but that doesn't stop my inner nerd from providing further clarification.

"Actually," I continue, "in all the movies somebody says that line, with slight variations."

The cocky smirk slides firmly into place and I shrug, embarrassed.

"Never mind."

"Now you definitely have to join us. We could use another expert."

He'd better not be mocking me.

"I should check my email first and, uh, do some…stuff." Like try to find you on Instagram. Snapchat. Tinder.

"Okay. I'll let you know when we need you, Sheldon."

I gasp. I don't know whether to be flattered or insulted. His grin is devilish as he saunters off, whistling.

Sinking into my desk chair, I make myself focus on non-Carlos related topics. Kendra texted me this morning with a reminder to work on female solidarity in the office.

Make friends with the girls! Ask how you can help them.

Trish and Ashley are both busy on their computers. Ashley has a vase of fresh flowers on her desk. *Star Wars* action figures are my desk decorations. I'd brought them in for fun but looking at Ashley's sophisticated bouquet I suddenly feel young. Sighing, I sweep the tiny plastic figures into a drawer and close it with a bang. Trish glances up at the loud noise and meets my gaze, frowning.

This hostility has to stop. What would Qa'hr do? Filled with determination, I cross the room.

"Hi." *Use the Force, Laurel.* "Do you want anything from the kitchen? I saw cupcakes in there earlier."

"Maybe an apple," Ashley says with a snowy white smile.

Trish twirls her nose stud. "I don't like cupcakes."

"Um, okay. Something else, then?"

Her eyes stay on mine, which is unnerving, but I don't blink.

"An espresso," she finally says. "No sugar."

"That fits." I wait for the smackdown, but it doesn't come. Instead, her pale lips twitch. Was that an almost smile?

"Be right back." I leave before I lose my nerve.

After I complete step one of my make-friends-with-the-girls plan, I resume my online investigating, starting with Facebook and Trish's name. Nothing, but that doesn't surprise me. Most people my age aren't on Facebook, or if they are, their pages are sanitized for grandparent viewing. I discover a locked-down page for Ashley, with a much sexier profile photo than the one on her LinkedIn page, and I also find a sanitized Elijah page.

I know all about Jason's page, since I've stalked it for years, but he hasn't posted anything for weeks.

Once again, I've saved Carlos for last. His cover photo is a family picture, full of all the people from the restaurant photo and then some. The younger kids wear cone-shaped birthday hats...and so does Carlos. He also wears a giant "18" button on his shirt. It's sweet that he's posted such a goofy family picture for everyone to see.

An audible sigh escapes me as I drink in Carlos's family photo and scroll down to check out his posts. He's disgustingly cute in all of his pictures, even the random, blurry ones his friends have tagged him in. Also, he's got a lot of girl friends. Girlfriends. Whatever.

I linger over one photo in particular—whoever took it was highly skilled, or maybe just lucky. Carlos sits on a bench in a church courtyard. He's wearing a suit and tie and he's flanked on either side by two little girls dressed in frilly white dresses. Maybe it was their First Communion or a wedding. They're clearly besotted with him, their adoring faces turned up like twin reflections. He grins down at one girl, while a hand rests protectively on the other girl's shoulder.

Nobody should be allowed to be so swoon-inducing. There should be a Facebook filter to protect girls like me from randomly stumbling upon such adorableness.

"Ready to join us?"

Gah! I grab my mouse, closing my browser. I need to be more careful. I have no idea what I'd say if he busted me cyber-stalking him.

"Uh, um." I'm incoherent, plus I'm blushing because my thoughts eagerly jumped to fantasizing about kissing him.

"Paper clip emergency?" he teases, one side of his mouth quirking up.

"You'd be surprised. There was a run on file folders and I almost got trampled to death."

His grin widens and I'm relieved I managed to come up with a joke in spite of my embarrassment.

"If this meeting blows up in my face, you owe me." I grab my Hello Kitty notebook.

"It won't."

I shrug as we walk toward the table. "It might," I mutter

under my breath.

He glances at me. "If it blows up, I owe you a Hello Kitty… something." He gestures to my notebook. "Obviously you're a fan of the feline."

That makes me blush, and I take a seat next to Elijah.

"Okay, back to work, everyone." Carlos moves toward the giant pieces of paper stuck to the window. He pulls a marker from his back pocket and taps a sheet of paper. "We need to vote on our marketing strategy. We've only got three grand and need to be smart about how we spend it."

"Which is why you should go with my idea." Elijah preens, his bright gaze sweeping around the table.

Trish rolls her eyes. "Sponsoring a podcast? I don't think so."

"Which podcast?" I ask.

"Geek Squeak." Elijah makes a fist and brushes it against his chest in an "I know I'm brilliant" gesture.

"That's perfect!" I squeal. "The hosts are hilarious—smart and nerdy and they love *Star Wars*. We could send them a speaker, and they'd rave about how great it is."

Everyone is quiet, staring at me like I'm crazy. Heat creeps up my neck. Enthusiasm is never cool, I need to remember that. Especially geeky enthusiasm.

"You do realize this is a *fake* campaign, right Laura?" Ashley asks.

"Laurel," I correct through gritted teeth. "And of course I know that. I just thought it was a great idea, that's all." I shrug at Elijah, who telegraphs me a *thank you* with his eyes.

"Nobody listens to podcasts, do they?" Jason asks. He doesn't say this in a mean way, more like he's confused.

"Sure, they do." Carlos's jaw tightens, and I try not to stare. Now that I've scrutinized his Facebook photos, I feel like I have a glimpse into who he is, and I might like that guy more than I should.

"Name one person you know who listens to them. Besides Elijah," Trish demands.

"My sister," Carlos responds, a defiant glint in his eyes. "My favorite AP teacher." His eyes flick to me, making my heart do an expert imitation of Thumper. "I like the idea," he tells Elijah, "but I'm not sure how broad their reach is."

"About three hundred thousand listeners each week." Elijah waves his phone in the air. "I just looked it up."

"Wow." Even Jason looks impressed. "That's weird. I don't know anyone who listens to podcasts."

Another chunk of Jason's imaginary pedestal crumbles. It's a good thing we never dated; I don't know what we'd have talked about.

Ashley tosses a shiny wave of blond hair over her shoulder. "Well, I like *my* idea," she purrs. "Everyone likes the Sharper Image catalog."

"I think my Comic Con idea is best." Trish pouts.

"It's a great idea," Carlos agrees, "except travel costs are high and booth space is expensive. We need something that hits a ton of people at once. Some way to get it into the pop culture zeitgeist."

Whoa, this dude is smart. And sexy. My pulse rate zings.

"*The Big Bang Theory*," I blurt out, and everyone turns to stare at me. I swallow and plunge ahead. "Imagine an episode where Sheldon gets one as a birthday present and tests it out. He'll love it. Maybe Leonard steals it." I decide to go for broke. "*Star Wars* is huge on that show. Remember when Amy and Bernadette made a Death Star cake? And when Sheldon builds the Lego Death Star?"

No one speaks. I wish for a hole in the floor to swallow me up. Then a slow grin spreads across Carlos's face and his eyes lock onto mine, like he's sending me a private replay of his earlier Sheldon comment.

"Genius," Elijah says. "I bow to you." And he does, leaning forward so his forehead smacks the table, making me laugh.

"Yeah, right," Trish snarks. "We'll just call Hollywood and make that happen."

I hesitate, because what I'm about to say might make her hate me even more. But it's also a chance for me to prove my value as more than a supply-fetching assistant.

"Okay, so the point of clients hiring a company like Emergent is for their expertise and connections, right?"

"Right." Carlos nods. "So how could Emergent make *The Big Bang Theory* happen?"

"Well…my dad went to college with one of the show's producers. They stay in touch."

"For real?" Elijah's whisper is reverent.

"You think he could get me in for a casting call?" Jason's whole face lights up with excitement. "If I somehow manage to go to college in Cali?"

"But I thought you wanted to study international business."

"Well, yeah, but that's a backup plan. I'd rather be an actor." He ducks his head, his cheeks reddening. "I don't know if I'm good enough for prime time, but maybe?"

Is this his big dream? My heart twists in sympathy. He's got the looks for it, but he can't really sing, or, um, act. He'd have way more luck going pro in the NFL than hitting it big in Hollywood.

I give myself a mental shake. Who am I to shoot down someone else's dream?

"I could take some headshots for you," I offer. "You know, for future casting calls. And for college apps, if you do major in theater." I smile, more to bolster my confidence than his. "I'll make it fun, promise."

"That'd be cool, Laurel." Jason grins. "Name the time and

I'm there. We could go—"

"Let's get back on track," Carlos interrupts. His eyes are frozen Fudgsicles, frosty and cold.

What's up with that?

"We need to take a vote." Carlos points to the paper. "Let's do it."

"We're each just going to vote for our own ideas." Trish tosses a paper clip in the air and Elijah reaches out to catch it.

"Except Jason and me, since we didn't suggest anything. We're the tiebreakers." Carlos points to the paper. "Who votes for the Sharper Image catalog?"

Ashley raises her hand and so does Jason. Surprisingly, it doesn't bother me; the guy has always been a sucker for pretty blondes. Carlos writes a "2" next to Ashley's idea.

"Comic Con booth."

Trish raises her hand but no one else does. Her glower has the force of a thousand Death Star explosions. As Carlos writes a "1" next to her idea, she mumbles something rude under her breath.

"Okay, Geek Squeak podcast." Carlos looks expectantly at Elijah, whose hand doesn't go up.

"Raise your hand," I whisper, but Elijah shakes his head.

"No votes for this one?" Carlos waits for a beat, then scrawls a "0." He clears his throat and is clearly avoiding eye contact with me. "*The Big Bang Theory*?"

Elijah's hand shoots up. I gape at him.

"It's the best idea," he says. "Even if it's not mine." He winks. "Raise your hand, Special K."

Did he give me that cereal box? I take a breath, then raise my hand because I believe in my idea. Now I'm tied with Ashley's Sharper Image idea. Everyone watches Carlos, who still won't look at me, even as he raises his hand.

"Boo-yah!" Elijah raises his other hand for a fist-bump

and I oblige, even though I'm embarrassed, and no one else is smiling. Carlos writes a "3" next to my idea and circles it.

"Congratulations, Laurel." His expression is blank, quashing my tiny thrill of victory. "So if this campaign were real, what would we do next?" He affixes a fresh sheet of paper to the window.

"Laurel would suck up to her daddy and wrap him around her little finger," Trish snaps.

I swallow, trying to come up with a response, but Ashley jumps in.

"Having connections is nothing to be ashamed of. That's what makes the world go 'round."

Jason nods. "Yeah. I mean, I'm totally gonna ask your dad about connecting me with his producer friend. Maybe you can send him some of the photos we'll take."

I've unleased a publicity hound. Elijah's leg bumps mine under the table, in sympathy I assume. Jason and I can talk later. Right now, I need to deal with Trish.

It's not easy for me to stand up to people, but I gather my courage, like Qa'hr when she told the pilot of her stowaway ship she can fix anything even though she can't. I meet Trish's challenging gaze.

"Look, Trish, I don't know why you…" I take a breath. I remember my sister's advice and start again. "If this scenario were real, I'd write something up, a proposal or whatever to present to my—to Mr. Kristoff—about why he should call in a favor."

Trish snorts, but I press on. "I bet your dad has contacts, too. Maybe for another type of client. It just so happens that the speaker is a natural fit for *TBBT*."

"Uh huh, and why is that? Did you tell Daddy Dearest what test product to give us so that you could be the—"

"That's enough." Carlos steps toward the table. I don't

think he means to threaten Trish, but she doesn't finish her sentence. "Picking fights is unproductive. And unprofessional." He taps his marker on the table. "We need to move on to our presentation. Who wants to be in charge of it? We can all contribute, but someone needs to take the lead." He looks at me expectantly and my stomach flips over.

I don't feel ready to take any kind of lead. I just want to participate, not be in charge of something.

"Do it, Laurel." Elijah grins. "I'll be your Huckleberry."

His old movie reference makes me smile, but I still don't want to do it. Still, what would Qa'hr do? Or Rey and Leia?

"I, uh, could come up with some ideas." I gesture to everyone else. "But everyone should help. We're supposed to be a team, right?"

Trish mutters under her breath again but I ignore her. "Also, if we went with the *Big Bang* strategy, it wouldn't cost any money for my dad to call the producer. We'd still have our budget to work with."

"You're right." Carlos's Fudgsicle eyes thaw slightly, which warms me to my toes.

A movement in the doorway catches our attention, and everyone freezes as my dad walks in. Carlos rolls down his shirt sleeves and smooths his hair. I wish I could send him a psychic message. *Relax. You're doing great. Also, that shirt makes your eye color pop.*

"How's everyone doing?" Dad grabs a chair from a nearby desk. Jason and Trish scoot over so Dad can squeeze in between them. Trish darts me a suspicious look and I shrug, hoping to communicate I have no idea why he's here.

"So, I hear you've been given your test product to market as a team." Dad studies us, steepling his fingers. "What's your strategy?"

Everyone's gaze shifts to Carlos, our de facto leader.

My dad notices, of course, and turns to Carlos, a smile transforming his face from scary CEO to nice guy. The thing with Darth Vader was you never knew if he smiled, because of the mask, though I doubt he ever did. Dad Vader, however, is approachable today, even friendly.

Carlos clears his throat and rolls the marker between his hands. *Relax*, I will him with my Jedi mind, but he doesn't get the message. He looks frozen, like he's been left on the surface of Hoth for too long.

"We just voted on our ideas," Elijah pipes up, so Dad focuses on him.

"Tell me more."

Crud. I want Carlos to get credit, since he took the lead and got everyone focused.

"Can I ask you something, Mr. Kristoff?" Trish tugs on her spider necklace and my skin prickles with apprehension.

"Of course."

"So, who chose the product for us to market? Was it you?" She points to the Death Star speaker like it's poisonous.

Dad shrugs. "Ms. Simmons must have chosen it, or someone on her team." He studies Trish. "I didn't select it, if that's what you're wondering."

Dad Vader isn't an idiot.

"It was a good choice," Carlos says. "It generated a lot of creative ideas."

I'm practically giddy that he found his voice.

"Such as?" Dad leans back in his chair and pins Carlos with an intense stare. I hold my breath, but Carlos doesn't flinch. Instead, he steps toward the window and points to the papers affixed to the glass.

"Everyone pitched their ideas, then we took a vote." His voice is steady and confident. I release the breath I was holding. "Since our number one choice doesn't cost anything, we're deciding which other strategy we can use, too."

"Mr. K, I have a question." I wince at the nickname but Elijah plunges ahead. "Do you really know a producer on *The Big Bang Theory*?"

Dad tilts his head, surprised. "Yes. Why do you ask?"

"It's part of our marketing strategy." Carlos's eyes flick to me, then back to my dad.

"Do you stay in touch with him?" Jason pipes up.

Oh no. I refocus my Jedi mind control powers on Jason, willing him to be quiet.

Dad locks eyes with me, transmitting his own Jedi message: *We'll discuss this later, Laurel.*

"I've got a meeting, but I look forward to seeing your presentation next week." He stands and nods at us. "Sounds like you're making good progress."

I hum the Darth Vader theme song under my breath as he leaves and Elijah snort-laughs. Once he's out of sight, everyone turns to me, making me squirm.

"Did you tell *Daddy* to check up on us?" Trish's voice is harsh, making my stomach churn.

"What? No. I didn't know he was coming up here."

"It's his company," Carlos says to Trish. "Of course he's going to check in with us." His eyes narrow. "Just like your dad does."

Trish flushes and drops her gaze to the table.

I swallow and place my hands on the table. I have to fix this. I can't let my dad's scholarship dream project go off the rails.

"Let's leave the dads out of this, okay? We all need to work together. Everyone has great ideas. Let's not argue."

"She's right," Carlos agrees. "Besides, Mr. Kristoff and Mr. Mantoni are our bosses."

"Suck up." Elijah tosses a crumpled paper at Carlos, who bats it away.

He's obviously frustrated. I wonder if it's with the job, or

Trish, or all of us. Maybe he wishes he'd never signed up for this internship. He's obviously smart and a great leader, even though he had a momentary freeze-up with my dad.

He sounded so passionate and sincere during his introduction the first day. I hope he still feels that way, even though things are a bit wacky with the Manicotti's rules and two "daddy's girls" engaged in a weird feud. A feud I'm going to stop, one way or another.

Carlos tosses his marker in the air and catches it behind his back. "You know what? Let's all take a break. We can figure this out later."

Definitely a smart leader.

Dad and I take opposite corners in the elevator at the end of the day.

"We need to talk, Laurel."

"Can it wait 'til we're in the car?" I'm all about procrastinating when I'm in trouble.

Dad's frustrated Vader energy seeps into me, enhancing the creepiness of the garage. I can't name one movie where the parking garage scene doesn't end with somebody kidnapped or dead. A horrible screeching noise makes me jump. The mechanical goat bleating originates from an older sedan with the hood up.

A figure leans over the engine, one hand gripping the raised hood. A very familiar figure.

"Try it again!" Carlos calls out.

"Come on," Dad says. I follow him, because what else can I do? As we get closer, Dad calls out, "Need some help?"

Carlos steps out from under the hood and brushes his hands together. His dark gaze can't seem to decide whether to focus on Dad or me.

"We need to jump it. Any chance you have cables in your car?" Now his gaze is fixed on my dad.

"I have something even better. Be right back." Dad leans down to peek in the driver side window. "We'll get you on the road in just a few minutes, Emmy."

Miss Emmaline gives him a grateful smile. I wonder what would happen if I called her Emmy? Nothing good.

Dad jogs to our car and Carlos finally looks at me.

"You're a mechanic in your spare time?" I try to joke.

He shrugs. "Not really, but I know enough."

Miss Emmaline's watching me. Maybe she'll crack a smile since we're off the clock. I squat to look her in the eye.

"Miss Emmaline, do you know how many tickles it takes to make an octopus laugh?"

As usual, I get the scowl, but I can't leave a punchline unsaid. "Ten tickles. Tentacles. Get it?"

Behind me, Carlos snorts. "That's worse than this morning's joke. Where do you find these?"

"Online." I smile at Miss Emmaline as I stand, willing her to at least blink, but she sighs and turns away like I'm trying to sell her a magazine subscription.

My dad returns, carrying a fancy battery-powered gadget that does everything—inflates tires, charges batteries, and who knows what else.

Carlos checks out the all-in-one-save-your-car appliance. "Sweet. Where'd you get this, Mr. K?"

Dad and Carlos devolve into caveman car talk and my eyes glaze over. I lean down and smile at Miss Emmaline again. "They're about to get you on the road again. Once they stop grunting."

She nods and taps her fingers on the steering wheel. "Your father always takes care of me."

I'm shocked she actually responded.

"How long have you worked for him?"

"Since the beginning. Fifteen years this August."

"Wow, that's amazing. He should throw you a party."

She sniffs and looks down her nose at me, even though she's sitting down. "He most certainly should not. I'm just doing my job. I don't need to be celebrated."

No matter what I say, it somehow offends.

"Start your engines, Emmy!" Dad calls out, and this time she chuckles at the corny joke, because it came from my dad. She turns the key and the engine roars to life. Carlos lowers the hood back into place after my dad unhooks the magical car gadget and they share victorious grins, like they just hunted down a mastodon with spears.

We step away from the car as Miss Emmaline drives away. She lifts a hand from the wheel to wave, but keeps her gaze focused straight ahead. I bet she never runs yellow lights.

"Thanks for helping her out," Dad says to Carlos. He clears his throat. "Sorry, I forget—are you Jason?"

Nice one, Dad. Way to make your interns feel special.

Carlos shakes his head and his mouth curves in that delicious smile, the one that shows the dimple. "I'm Carlos."

"Oh, right. Jason's the one who goes to school with Laurel." His mischievous expression sends panic streaking through me. "The guy you had a crush on, right?"

Oh. My. God.

This is worse than if he choked me with his thoughts like Darth Vader, but it has the same effect, rendering me unable to speak.

Carlos turns the dangerous dimple on me. "Oh yeah? Interesting."

Interesting? More like humiliating. Mortifying. Life-ending.

"Dad." My voice is a strangled gurgle. "Stop. Please." I can't look at Carlos, but I know he's laughing on the inside. I can feel it.

Mortified, I march toward our SUV, not caring that I'm acting like a kid throwing a tantrum. All I *do* care about is escaping mortification.

I don't have a remote for the car, so I'm unable to hide behind the tinted windows. I watch Dad say goodbye to Carlos, shaking his hand and clapping him on the back. What has gotten into Dad Vader, cracking dumb jokes and humiliating his daughter?

The unlock beep startles me into action. I slide into the car and slam the door closed. Dad slides into the driver seat and lets out a sigh.

"I'm guessing I said too much." He starts the engine.

"You think?" My voice drips with sarcasm.

He puts the car in reverse and doesn't say anything until we've exited the garage. It's hard to believe that a few hours ago I was enjoying a gorgeous sunny afternoon and taking photographs. Now I want to curl up in a hole.

"I was…" he begins and clears his throat. I glance at his profile, which is chiseled and boss-like. Not at all the face of someone who jokes about crushes.

"Maybe it wasn't the best strategy." His fingers tap restlessly on the steering wheel as we wait at a red light. "But I know the interns haven't been as…welcoming to you as I'd hoped, so I thought—"

"Who told you that?"

He glances at me, guilt clouding his face. "Uh, I don't—"

"Ms. Romero? The Manicotti?"

Guilt gives way to disapproval. "You know I don't approve of that nickname."

I shrug. "Whatever. Anyway, so you heard right. But that

doesn't mean I want you to try to fix it or whatever. Because what you just did made it worse, not better."

Dad focuses on the road when the light changes. "Carlos seems like a good kid. I thought maybe if I joked about you and Jason, it would make you seem…I don't know. Like one of them, I guess."

I glare out the window. "How do you even know about that stuff?" It's not like I ever told my dad about my crush drama.

Dad clears his throat. "Your mom and I talked about it. She looked at the applications when I decided to start the scholarship program. She recognized Jason's name and told me about, uh, your…feelings." He glances at me. "I almost didn't hire him because I didn't want any drama this summer, but your mom assured me there wouldn't be. She said you'd probably moved on from that, uh, infatuation." He looks as embarrassed as I feel.

My mind reels as I try to process this information. Since when does Mom evaluate my infatuation levels? "I didn't think Mom was involved in your business."

"Your mom always has input. I trust her opinion, especially when it comes to people. She was the one who told me to hire Emmy. And Tom—Mr. Mantoni."

In other words, Mom stinks at reading people. I love my mom, but what was she thinking?

"So explain to me how my producer friend is now on the interns' radar," Dad says, deftly changing the subject. Vader doesn't want to talk about my secret crushes any more than I do.

"Um, yeah. Sorry about that. We were brainstorming ideas for the Death Star speaker, and I realized how well it would fit in a *Big Bang* episode. Sheldon would love the speaker and Jason apparently wants to be actor and—"

"I appreciate your enthusiasm." Dad glances at me and his lips quirk. "But I'm not calling in a favor for Jason. I don't care how good of an actor he is, I'm saving my big-time favors for something special."

"Big-time favors?"

Dad revs his engine as he rockets us into the far left lane. "Sure. When you have friends in powerful positions, you don't ask for random favors. You choose wisely, holding onto the big-time favor until it's something important, for someone special." Apparently he's given this a lot of thought. "That's the type of favor I hold close to my vest." He reaches over and takes my hand, surprising me. "Remember this, Laurel. Good friends aren't to be taken advantage of, especially when they achieve a high level of success."

There's a whole subtext here, and I'm pretty sure I get it. He squeezes my hand.

"So tell me, Vader, if this was a real project, and I was the real account manager, and I came to you with my brilliant idea, would you call in your favor?"

Dad grins. "I thought Princess Leia didn't need to call in favors."

"Of course she did. Look at Obi-Wan—that was the biggest beg of all time."

Dad's shoulders stiffen. "I'd say taking down an evil dictator is worthy of calling in a favor."

"Okay, but in my boring world, let's pretend this is my first real job and I'm being tested and if I fail, I lose my job and have to move home and live in the basement. Are you calling your friend or not?"

Dad laughs and shakes his head. "You sure you don't want to be an actress? I know a guy."

That makes me laugh, but I still want his answer. "Come on, Dad. Yes or no?"

He turns to me, and I'm startled by the darkened hue of his gray eyes. "There are three people on this planet I'd do anything for, and you're one of them."

My heart squeezes. Dad's not a sentimental guy, but what he just said is like giving me a lifetime of hugs in one sentence.

"So that's a yes?"

Dad grins and presses the accelerator, leaving the other cars in the dust, and I have my answer.

After dinner, I corner Mom in the kitchen while Dad takes a bin of veggies out to our backyard composter.

"Why did you talk to Dad about my…my…about Jason Riggs?"

She freezes mid–dish scrub and pivots to face me. "Uh-oh. Problems on the job?"

I squeeze my eyes shut. *So many problems*, I think.

"Yeah," I admit. "But I'm never going to confide in you again." I realize I sound about five years old, but I can't stop picturing Carlos laughing in the garage.

Mom grimaces. "I'm sorry, honey. Maybe I should've told your dad not to hire him, but he has"—she breaks off, glancing away from me—"he deserves a chance at the scholarship." Her forehead crinkles with worry. "What's going on?"

I lean against the counter, thoughts careening through my mind. "It's nothing." Dad's teasing isn't a big deal, in the scheme of things. Yeah, it embarrassed me in front of Carlos, but I'll survive.

"Can you tell me what was on the applications? They had to write an essay, right? About why they need the scholarship?"

Mom shakes her head. "I can't tell you about the essays, hon."

"But if I'm supposed to vote I need to know the full picture."

She sighs and tosses the wet sponge in the sink. "Ask your dad and Mr. Mantoni."

"I already did. They said the apps are confidential. The Manicotti told me to check out LinkedIn, which I did, but it's not helpful."

Mom brushes a few curls out of her eyes. "You have the rest of the summer to get to know them. I'm sure they're all great kids and will open up to you." Her expression relaxes into a knowing smile. "You're easy to talk to."

Right.

Chapter Nine

*B*y the following Friday, the interns and I have settled into a rhythm. Elijah is funny and cool, and we share secret geek-outs together, debating superheroes and fantasy novels. Ashley is nice enough, but brittle. I'm starting to think her perfect facade is wafer thin and could crack at any moment.

Jason's clueless and cute, like a Golden Retriever puppy. I know now we'd never work as a couple, but I still have a soft spot for him. Trish is still sporting the chip on her shoulder, but I'm hopeful I can knock it off, eventually.

And Carlos…he's different than the rest. Polite and friendly. Smart and funny. Curious and charming. Genuine. He hasn't brought up the mortifying garage scene, and for that alone he deserves a medal. It's hard working with him every day and pretending disinterest, but I remember what my dad said about interns being disqualified for "fraternizing."

As Dad and I drive into downtown, the spicy sweet aroma of the pumpkin chocolate chip cookies I made fills the car. He's already eaten two cookies.

"Maybe you should have let me drive while you stuff your face," I tease.

"Not on your life." He steals a third cookie, keeping his eyes on the road. "Your Prius drives like a granny car."

"You could let me drive the SUV once in a while."

Dad snorts, then chokes on cookie crumbs. Serves him right for dissing my car. He chugs some coffee and gets himself together.

"So it's been two weeks," Dad says. "Give me your feedback."

My stomach shrinks and cowers. "About what?"

"The job, Laurel. My company. The interns. All of it."

Oh boy. I suck in a breath, then let it out. "It's been... interesting." I imagine the earful Princess Leia would give Dad if asked the same question. "Okay, so, the truth is, it's been tough."

Dad nods, keeping his eyes on the road. "Most jobs are, especially at first."

So much for sympathy.

"Trish still hates me."

Dad's lips twitch, which annoys me. "What about the other interns?"

"They're okay. I'm, uh, getting to know them." Trying to, anyway.

"Any bad apples?" Dad pins me with the Vader stare, so I know he wants the truth.

"Not that I can tell." Except maybe Trish, but I'm not ready to write her off yet.

I tighten the plastic wrap on my cookie tray.

He doesn't say anything, but I know he wants more intel.

"I forgot to tell you I'm staying in town late tonight," he says around a bit of cookie. "Your mom's taking the light rail down to join me after work and we're going to dinner and a concert, so you'll need to take the train home."

"Why didn't you tell me before we left? I'd have driven my granny car." And why didn't Mom tell me? She's the social organizer; I can't believe she forgot about her date.

He shoots me a guilty glance. "Sorry, honey. It's a surprise for your mom. I haven't told her yet. Ms. Romero is going to call her and ask her to come to the office for a fake meeting."

"Why is it a surprise?"

"We're going to see Duran Duran, one of her favorite eighties bands. She asked me about going months ago and I told her I'd cut off my hand before seeing that pathetic boy band."

That sounds more like the Dad Vader I know and love.

"So it was a deflection tactic. Good strategy, Vader."

He chuckles next to me. "Clever I am. Surprised she will be."

"Dad, you're not Yoda. How many times do we have to go over this?"

"Give me another cookie," he commands. "They're terrible. I'm going to have to eat all of them so you don't poison my employees."

I quash my laughter so he won't gloat, then hand him another cookie. I'd never admit it, but even when he's being Vader, our drives are turning into the best parts of my day.

Once we arrive, Dad books it to his office, worried he's late for a meeting. I take my time leaving the parking garage, awkwardly juggling my camera bag, messenger bag, and tray of cookies.

"Let me get the door for you."

Carlos. Where did he come from?

"Thanks."

I move through the doorway, covertly ogling Carlos. He's wearing a white dress shirt today, with pale blue stripes, and jeans. It looks soft and comfortable, not stiff and starched like my dad's shirts. I catch a whiff of his soap or cologne and tell myself to get a grip and keep moving. He hurries ahead of me to push the elevator button.

"Whatever you baked smells good. Are you going to share or are they all for you?"

I look up in time to catch the laughter dancing in his eyes. My stomach does an Olympian back flip.

"They're for the foosball tournament."

He holds the elevator door for me and I head for a corner. Being in a confined space with him is unsettling.

"Excellent. You playing in the tournament?"

I *should* play. I kill at foosball. But I don't want any weird attention, like *Aww, how cute, Mr. K's daughter is playing in the tournament. We should let her win.*

"No. Are you?"

Carlos shrugs. "Maybe. I need to suss out the competition first."

"Is that because you're good or terrible?" I blurt the question before my stupidity filter kicks in. Fortunately, he laughs.

"You'll have to wait and see."

I don't reply because the elevator doors slide open, which gives me the excuse I need to escape. As I start toward Miss Emmaline's desk, Carlos's voice stops me.

"What's today's joke?"

I glance over my shoulder. He's smirking, which doesn't help my nerves, but I shrug like I'm unaffected. "It's for her ears only."

He tilts his chin up. "Fine. But I bet I can make her laugh even if you can't."

"Because you helped fix her car," I grumble. "You have an unfair advantage." So much for my filter. As the elevator doors close, Carlos is still grinning.

I beeline to Miss Emmaline, who's already giving me the stink eye. I'm going to make this woman like me if it kills me.

"Good morning, Miss Emmaline." I balance the cookie platter on her counter. "Would you like a cookie? Homemade."

She glances at my fabulous pastries and I can tell she wants one but won't admit it. I lift the plastic wrap and hand one to her. Reluctantly, she accepts my offering.

"How much does a pirate pay for corn?"

Her eyes narrow behind her glasses.

"A buccaneer." This stupid joke actually made me laugh when I read it online.

Miss Emmaline adjusts her glasses on her nose and sighs. I take that as my cue to leave.

*U*p in the sky box, the finance employees buzz in their corner, industrious and focused. Carlos sits at his desk, reading whatever mysterious book captures his attention every morning. I've tried to identify it from afar, but I can't make out the cover or title on the spine. I could use my telephoto camera lens, but that would be creepy.

I settle in at my desk and check my email. Just one—another reminder about the foosball tournament from Miss Emmaline.

"Did she laugh?" Carlos's voice jars me from my thoughts. He's turned his book upside down on his desk to mark his page.

I shake my head, and he grins. He stands and quickly closes the distance between us, my heartbeat racing as each step brings him closer.

"What was today's joke?"

"It was a classic. Only someone determined to hate me wouldn't laugh."

He cocks an eyebrow. "Let's hear it."

Leaning back in my chair, I cross my arms over my chest, like somehow that can protect me from the intensity of his chocolate eyes.

"How much does a pirate pay for an ear of corn?"

"No wonder she doesn't like you."

"You don't even know the punchline!"

"A buccaneer." He rolls his eyes. "You need better material."

"Like what?" I'm indignant, but my body is also buzzing from the adrenaline of this…this whatever we're doing. Are we just joking around? Or are we flirting? Whatever it is, I don't want it to stop. But it has to. I'd never forgive myself if he was disqualified because of me.

"You need jokes that are actually funny."

"How do you know the punchline to that one, anyway?" I try to fake annoyance, but I fail. I'm about as good an actor as Jason.

He leans a hip against my desk. His grin is an arrow piercing my heart. Must. Not. Swoon.

"I live with little people, so I hear a lot of dumb jokes."

"Little people?"

"My sibs. They're constantly trying to outdo each other with dumb jokes."

I recall the restaurant website and the family photo. I'm dying to know more about him and his family, but I don't dare ask, since that would reveal my cyber stalking.

"The best jokes are situational. Improvisational." He says this like he's given it a lot of thought.

"I thought you were interested in pre-law, not stand-up."

He points at me. "See, that's what you should focus on—spontaneous humor, not premade jokes."

"But that only works if the other person talks to me."

"I'm talking to you right now, aren't I?"

A weighted, expectant silence blooms between us as his eyes lock on mine. I swallow, my brain scrambling for a reply that doesn't betray my true feelings.

The sound of laughter distracts us. The rest of the crew has arrived. Carlos steps away from my desk, quickly moving toward his own. My stomach drops. Is he embarrassed to be seen talking to me? All of the buzzy tingles evaporate.

"Yo, Rubio." Elijah raises his hand for a high-five as Carlos passes him.

Elijah tilts his chin at me. "Yo, Jedi. What's up?"

Trish rolls her eyes and shoulders past Elijah. Today she's wearing a short black leather skirt with black leather boots, even though it's Friday and everyone else is wearing jeans. Her blouse is red and looks like she met Edward Scissorhands in a dark alley.

"Don't call me Jedi," I whisper to Elijah. He frowns and lets Jason and Ashley move past him, chattering like birds, oblivious to everyone else.

"You ashamed of the Force?" Elijah points an accusing finger, but he's grinning.

I motion for him to lower his voice. He glances around, then back to me. "You can't worry about what other people think, Laurel. Besides, geeks are the new black, didn't anyone tell you that?" He gestures to himself. "And as a black geek, that means I'm twice as cool. But you already knew that."

"I'll never be as cool as you. Just don't call me Jedi. Please."

His gaze sweeps my desk, then a frown wrinkles his brow. "Where are they?"

"What?"

He steps closer, glaring down at me for real. "Han. Leia. Chewie."

I dart a nervous glance across the room. Carlos is watching us, a ghost of a frown flitting across his face. My pulse rate speeds up when his intense gaze connects with mine.

"They're in a drawer. For safekeeping."

Elijah rolls his eyes. "Whatever you say, *Lando*."

"I'm not a traitor." I return his glare, but I'm not mad— mostly I'm embarrassed.

"Interns!"

The Manicotti looms in the doorway, bald head gleaming, beefy arms puffed up across his chest. He points to the table by the windows. The Rocky Mountains are gorgeous this morning, the peaks looming in the distance like immovable sentries.

Everyone stands and moves toward the table, including Elijah and me.

"A few pieces of silver and you hide your true nature, Judas," Elijah goads, shoulder-bumping me.

"Shut up," I hiss. "Nobody paid me to hide them."

Carlos catches up to us. "What are you two arguing about?"

"Nothing," I snap at the same time Elijah says, "Laurel denying her true nature."

Carlos's curious gaze shifts from Elijah to me.

"He's just kidding around." I slide into a chair at the far end of the table. Elijah and Carlos sit down on either side of me. Great. I won't be making any funny notes or doodles with these two flanking me.

"All right," Mr. Mantoni says, "it's Friday. You've survived your first two weeks at Emergent. Don't forget you're presenting to Ms. Simmons, Mr. Kristoff and me next week."

Like we'd forget. I want to share an eye roll with someone, but don't dare.

"You'll also be assigned your individual projects for the

remainder of the summer. Final approval will be granted by myself and Mr. Kristoff."

My fingers itch to doodle the Manicotti spouting rules and bestowing favors like a king, but I don't because of the prying eyes on either side of me.

"So today's our quarterly foosball tournament," Mr. Mantoni continues. "One of our core values at Emergent is fun with a capital *F*. It's built into our culture, starting from the top with Mr. Kristoff."

A snort escapes me. My dad, the embodiment of fun? Everyone stares at me, including the Manicotti, and I feel my cheeks burn. Trish's smirk is triumphant, probably because I've just accidentally mocked my dad in front of everyone.

Mr. Mantoni clears his throat. "As I was saying, we value fun here at Emergent, and you'll see that in action today. We'll have pizza and beer at noon—not for you, of course, but sodas will be available. Tournament starts after lunch." He pauses, his beady eyes scanning us. "Any of you planning to play? We've got some real competitors on our staff, but they'll go easy on you."

I snort again, annoyed at the suggestion that none of us could keep up with the great Emergent foosball champions. But as everyone's gaze shifts to me, I want to slide under the table and disappear.

The Manicotti glares at me. "Laurel, do you have something to add to the discussion?"

"No." My voice is barely above a whisper.

"Good." His beady eyes lock onto mine. "Please follow me to my office." He turns and stalks away.

Called to the principal's office in front of the class. Embarrassed, I follow him, refusing to make eye contact with anyone. Miss Emmaline watches me suspiciously as I cross the lobby several paces behind the Manicotti. *You're right,* I want to call out. *I'm busted again.*

"Close the door, Laurel," Mr. Manicotti commands. I comply, then sit in a chair, fiddling with my notebook. At least I was smart enough not to leave it behind this time.

He adjusts his glasses, then tugs at his tie, a horrible tie-dye pattern. I wonder if Trish picks them out, intentionally choosing the ugliest ones she can find.

"Your dad and I discussed your request to read the interns' applications."

I perk up.

"Our first decision stands."

"But that's—I mean—how am I supposed to…" My voice trails away.

Mr. Mantoni shrugs. "We want you to get to know them, Laurel. See beyond the surface. If you read the essays, it's the easy way out."

That sounds like something my dad would say. And why isn't my dad having this conversation with me? Is he too busy to spend ten minutes with his own daughter?

"You've got plenty of time to figure out who deserves your vote."

"What if they all do?" My stomach is jumpy with nerves, but it's a question that constantly weighs on my mind. "What if everyone deserves the scholarship? Then what?"

He blinks at me from behind his glasses. The only noise in the room is the faint sound of downtown traffic filtering through the windows.

"There's always a winner, Laurel. That's how life works."

Maybe in your world, I want to say, but instead I stand up to leave.

"See you at foosball?" he asks as I open the door.

"Sure." Maybe I will play, since I feel like crushing someone.

. . .

I stop in the kitchen for a sugar hit before heading upstairs. The room bustles with employees dropping off desserts, and a group of people gather around a poster mounted to the wall. "Foosball fanatics sign up here!" I start to back out of the room when Brian spots me. He waves and smiles.

"Hey, Laurel. You here to sign up for the tournament?" A few people turn to glance at me, curious.

"I'll think about." I turn to leave, almost crashing into Ms. Romero, who's carrying a large platter of cookies.

"Laurel, how are you? Your dad told me your cookies are delicious. I can't wait to try them." She beams at me, then sets her platter on the overflowing table. "I guess Miss Emmaline's pleas for desserts worked."

I force a smile but I'm dying to get out of here.

"Are you okay, honey? You look pale."

Because I have to quash three dreams, I want to say, *and pick one winner.* "I'm okay."

Mrs. Romero reaches out to brush hair off my face, then appears to think better of it and drops her hand to her side. "Sorry. I wouldn't do that to any other employee. I just feel protective of you." She looks chagrined. "You're like my office daughter," she whispers.

If I were Trish I might karate chop her, but since I'm not, I smile for real this time. "It's okay. I sort of like the idea of a work mom." It's true, even though it makes me sound ten years old. And I have an *actual* parent just down the hall.

"You need to talk? We can go to my office."

"I need to get back to my desk." Even though it's the last place I want to go, I can't keep hiding out.

Chapter Ten

The rooftop is full of chattering Emergent employees clustered in groups, most of them juggling bottles of local microbrews and slices of pizza. The hot Colorado sun beats down on us, but a few canopies are set up to provide shade.

I hang back until everyone else grabs food and drinks. Most of the pizza is picked over, but I don't care. I grab a slice of veggie and a soda and make my way to a far corner of the rooftop. My camera dangles from my neck strap. I can always hide behind it if no one wants to talk to me.

Ms. Romero spots me and purposefully heads my way. It's sweet of her, but also slightly pathetic that the only person willing to talk to me is my dad's assistant.

"How's the pizza?" She smiles, and I notice the lines around her eyes and her lips. Her eyes are always so full of warmth. I decide to take a photo of her later, preferably when she's laughing.

"It's great." I take a swig of soda from my warm can and try to look enthusiastic.

Ms. Romero glances around the rooftop, then turns back

to me. "Why aren't you with the interns?"

The interns cluster in a group, wearing sunglasses, no shade umbrellas for them. They laugh together like besties, making me feel like the unwanted guest invited by the popular kid's mom. I try to ignore Carlos and Ashley standing close together, his head tilted toward her as she flashes her pearly whites.

It doesn't matter, I tell myself. It's not like I can do anything about my stupid crush.

"Have you met many other employees yet?" Ms. Romero asks, jarring me back to the rooftop. She takes my arm and steers me toward the group closest to us. Their faces light up for Ms. Romero, no doubt because of her role as Dad's lieutenant. No way will I remember all of these names, but it's clear they're all making mental notes that I'm Mr. K's daughter.

We continue around the rooftop, me in her shadow as she makes introductions. I glance toward the interns and see Trish squinting, her sunglasses on her head as she tracks me with dagger eyes. I think Carlos might be watching me, too, but I can't tell because he's still wearing his shades.

Finally, we complete the circuit, ending at a small group consisting of my dad, the Manicotti, and Ms. Simmons. I want to run the other direction.

"Hi." I snatch a cookie off my dad's plate and shove half of it in my mouth so I don't have to say anything else. He cocks a disapproving eyebrow, but I don't care. It's self-preservation.

"We were just talking about you," Ms. Simmons says. She reminds me of a cat, regal and proud. Dread fills me as I wonder what they were saying.

I choke on the last bit of cookie, crumbs flying out of my mouth. I cover my mouth and do that awful choke-breathing where you can't get your breath and feel like you're going to die. Dad pounds me on the back while Ms. Romero runs off for a water bottle. I'm dimly aware that I'm causing a scene and most people in our vicinity have stopped talking to stare at me.

"Should someone do the Heimlich?" Ms. Simmons asks, her feline features contorted with worry. I shake my head and grab the water bottle Ms. Romero thrusts in my face. I take a few swigs and finally stop the desperate gasping for air. Now I'm sweaty and mortified. I wonder if Dad would care if I snuck out, but before I can try it, copier dude Brian clangs two beer bottles together to get everyone's attention.

"Yo! It's time for the tournament! We've got two tables. First up on table one is Todd vs. Amy!" A smattering of cheers and applause echoes across the rooftop. "Table two is Malik and Carlos the intern!" More cheers and applause.

Everyone gathers around the two tables that have been wheeled to the center of the rooftop under shade canopies. I sneak a peek at Carlos. He's removed his sunglasses and his dress shirt, revealing a form-fitting black T-shirt. It's a good look on him.

Who am I kidding? Everything's a good look on him.

I scan the crowd and spot the other interns huddled together. Elijah removes his shades and meets my gaze, motioning me over, but I shake my head. Since my choking attack, I want to draw as little attention as possible.

A raucous crowd surrounds Todd and Amy, drowning out the clatter of their spinning foosball rods. A smaller group watches Carlos and Malik. Carlos moves quickly, brow furrowed in concentration, then his face splits with a grin and a few cheers sound, so I assume he scored. Miss Emmaline clinks her beer bottle with another Carlos fan, making me smile.

"You gonna show 'em how it's done?"

Surprised, I face my dad, who's leaned in close. There's a hint of emotion in his eyes. Is that worry?

"I don't think so." My earlier desire to crush someone faded after my choking attack and being ignored by the interns.

He frowns. "Why not? I'd put my money on you."

"Just because I can beat all my friends doesn't mean I can take on these guys."

Dad sips from his beer bottle. "The fear of loss is a path to the dark side."

I narrow my eyes. "You did not just quote Yoda."

"Quote him I did."

"You need to stop, Vader."

"You need to compete, Padawan."

Another whoop from Carlos's table draws our attention. Elijah high-fives him. So does Ashley. *Whatever*. Dad and I watch the next few rounds. Brian updates the brackets poster after each game, and every time Carlos moves up a round, Dad nudges me.

"Bet you could beat another intern," he says.

"Not. An. Intern," I growl. "Just an assistant."

Dad's eyes widen, then he laughs. "I keep forgetting that."

Someone taps him on the shoulder, so I wander away to snap a few photos of employees at the dessert table and of a guy leaning over the rooftop yelling "Go Rockies!" to the baseball fans on the street below. I snag a Rice Krispies Treat and when I turn around, Dad's talking to Brian, who glances my way and points to the poster.

Uh-oh.

"You in, Laurel? I can slot you in for the next round, since Victor dropped out. He had to go pick up his kid from school." Brian smiles encouragingly while my dad tries to use Jedi mind control on me. I can feel it wafting across the rooftop.

"Uh, I don't know."

Brian uncaps his marker and crosses out Victor's name. His hand hovers over the paper as he glances between Dad and me.

"There is no try—" Dad begins.

"I'll do it." Dad grins as Brian scribbles my name, clearly pleased with himself.

I'm going in cold against a big guy named Lewis. He looks like a defensive back, complete with sleeve tattoos. He glances at my dad, then me, as I take my place at the table.

"You're Mr. K's kid?"

Just call me Special K. "Yup. You're Lewis?"

He frowns. "I guess I'll go easy on you. Don't wanna upset your dad."

Just like that, my competitive streak is activated. "Don't go easy on me. I can handle it. My dad wouldn't want you to cheat."

Lewis looks like he's torn. "I dunno, kid."

"If you call me kid again, I'll have no choice but to destroy you." I smile sweetly.

A few people in our audience laugh and somebody slaps me on the back.

"Your funeral, kid," Lewis growls, getting into position on his side of the table. He crouches down in a horse stance and grasps two rods, glaring at me menacingly across the table.

Adrenaline rockets through me as I grasp my own rods. I can't believe I talked smack to this giant, but it's too late to take it back. I close my eyes and take a deep breath, pretending I'm Qa'hr, Leia, and Rey all rolled into one fierce foosball competitor.

"Everybody give a hand to Lewis and Laurel! Ready?" Brian calls out. Lewis and I nod, our eyes fixed on the table.

"Go!"

The next few minutes are a frenzy as I acclimate to the table, the pace, the yelling and smack-talking surrounding me. I score first and hear a cheer, which surprises me, but I ignore it, focusing on defending Lewis's attempts to score. I steal a glance at him and see sweat beading on his brow. Guess he's not taking it easy on me after all. Good.

My palms get sweaty, and my left hand slips off the goalie rod at the exact wrong time, allowing Lewis to score. He yells like he just won the freaking Super Bowl. I wipe my hands on my jeans.

"Go Laurel! Go Laurel!" The chant echoes behind me and I wonder who it is, but I can't focus on that. I pretend I'm channeling the Force. And it works. I feel myself leap into the zone, blocking all of Lewis's shots and scoring two more times. It's three to one, and we're playing to five for the win. Lewis thumps the table in frustration, jarring the ball loose from where my three-rod has trapped it.

"No hitting the table!" I shoot Lewis a glare, then glance around for Brian, our de facto referee. He's busy slugging a beer, so I turn back to the table, deciding not to raise a stink. I can beat this guy whether he follows the rules or not.

My hair is hot on my neck; I wish I'd tied it back in a ponytail. My eyes track the ball, my hands anticipating Lewis's every move as I twist my five-rod, timing it perfectly so the ball zooms between his plastic players and into the goal.

"Four to one. Hot damn, Laurel!" Brian yells, clinking a beer bottle with my dad. I grin at my dad and nod at Lewis, whose face is beet red. He looks like he wants to kill me.

We pause for a water break. "Kick his ass," a voice mutters close behind me as I swig from my water bottle. Trish is next to me, her eyes dark slits aimed at Lewis. She leans in closer. "I hate that guy. Rip off his nuts."

It takes me a second to process that she's on my side,

for once. She shoulder-bumps me. "You're doing great, *kid*. Keep it up."

I wince when she calls me "kid" but she disarms me with a grin, the first one I've ever received from her.

Jason and Ashley lean against the roof ledge, watching the street action below, but Elijah and Carlos focus on me, giving me matching thumbs-ups. Then Carlos does that "eyes on you" thing, pointing two fingers at his eyes, then at me. I look down, because if anything's going to rattle my composure it's the thought of Carlos's eyes. On me.

"Don't let her win just cuz she's the boss's kid, dude," says another big guy, who's lumbered way too close to the table.

"He's not," Trish snaps from behind me. "She's legit kicking his ass!"

"Hey. Knock it off, Cruz," Brian commands. "And back off. You're too close to the table." He points to Lewis. "Your serve."

Lewis grunts as he drops the ball onto the table with excessive force. Not cool, but I don't care. Just one more point and he's done. Except this time he surprises me, sneaking in a goal when I least expect it. Four to two. Crud. The obnoxious guy, Cruz, starts to yell in my face until Trish jumps between us, poking him in the chest.

"Penalty!" she yells. "Get off the field!"

Brian laughs as he drags both of them away from us. "Everybody simmer down."

Now everyone has gathered around our table. My hands grow sweaty again, especially when I notice Carlos has moved so he's standing behind Lewis. I make the mistake of eye contact, and his lips ease into a sexy grin, flashing the deadly dimple. He points at Lewis, then twists his hands like he's crushing a can. I bite back a nervous laugh and refocus on the table. *You can do it*, I tell myself.

"Laurel! Laurel!" A chant goes up and increases in volume,

freaking me out. I make myself tune it out, determined to crush Lewis. He's putting his full weight on the table, which is not okay, but there's no time to argue rules. *Crush him.*

He takes a shot, sending the ball sliding under my players, but I rotate my goalie rod just in time to send the ball flying back the other direction. He fires back but I stop the ball with my five-rod and line up my shot, then take it. He tries to defend it, but his timing is off and the ball slides into his goal pocket.

"Yes!" I raise my hands in victory. Trish grabs me around the waist and screams in my ear. Elijah and Carlos move in with high-fives. I don't even have time to enjoy the slam of Carlos's skin on mine before Ashley smothers me with an overly affectionate hug.

Jason tilts his chin. "Way to work it, Laurel."

I'm swarmed by a huge group of people who want to congratulate me. I look around to shake Lewis's hand or fist-bump him in a good sport gesture, but he's stormed off to grab a beer with his obnoxious friend.

Giddy with victory, I accept everyone's congratulations, including Miss Emmaline, who shocks me by acknowledging me with a lip twitch that almost looks like a smile. Dad waits until everyone else drifts off before he moves in. He glances around, then slips me a low-five.

"Knew you could do it, hotshot." He grins like a little kid, then quickly composes himself. "But I can't show favoritism."

I roll my eyes. "It's the only thing I've got going for me here, Dad." I nod to the corner where Lewis is still pouting, a beer in each hand. "That guy's kind of a jerk."

Dad's grin fades. "We'll discuss that later." He motions Brian over. "Who's in the final bracket?"

"Your daughter," Brian says with a grin, "and Carlos. It's an intern showdown."

I start to remind him I'm not an intern, but what's the point?

"Knock 'em dead, kid," Dad says with an evil grin.

Carlos ambles over and my mouth goes dry at the sight of him. His T-shirt reveals tanned and sculpted arms. I wish I had someone to share my ogling with, but I don't. Even though Trish was my champion for a few minutes, I can't trust her with secret lust data.

"Ready to throw down, Special K?" There's a teasing challenge in his eyes and it sparks a fire inside of me, heating me from head to toe.

"Did you put that cereal box on my desk?"

He shrugs and flashes his dimple. I feel like a middle-school girl who dug through a shoebox of identical, store-bought valentines only to discover a gaudy homemade valentine from her secret crush.

Instead of swooning, I square my shoulders and put on my Qa'hr face, because I want that cheesy trophy. Winning first, then swooning. But in secret, because he can't know.

"I'm always ready to throw down," I say. "What about you? You're not going to let me win because of my dad, are you?"

Carlos looks across the rooftop toward my dad and I notice a hint of stubble on his jaw. I've never crushed on someone who stubbled before. It's…exhilarating. His gaze slides back to me and I become painfully aware of my sweaty armpits. Could I be more gross right now?

"I play to win." He steps close, his dark eyes brimming with…something. "Don't hold back, Laurel," he says, his voice low and urgent, "show me your best game."

Where's a bucket of ice when I need one? Do his words hold a double meaning or am I delusional? Though I know I shouldn't, I eyeball our potential kissing logistics. Depending on what shoes I wore, he might not have to bend down too much, but I—

"Deal?"

"Huh?" I blink, forcing myself to stop fantasizing. "I mean, yeah, deal. I won't hold back."

"Good." He smiles, like he guessed exactly what I was daydreaming about.

I need to get a grip. Qa'hr doesn't zone out about kissing the pilot of the supply spaceship. Leia didn't get all gooey about Han, at least not until he was about to be frozen in carbonite. And Rey has no time for romance. Not yet, anyway.

"We've got five minutes before our game starts." His gaze sweeps me up and down. "You want a water or something? You look hot."

My stomach does a backflip and he takes a step back, wincing.

"I mean hot like it's a hundred degrees up here, not hot like…I mean, I don't…"

Ugh. I should save us from this mutual mortification but I don't know how. Fortunately, Elijah chooses that moment to crash our party.

"Yo, foosball fanatics. Who should I put my money on?" He strokes his chin. "I'm leaning toward Laurel, since she took down that monster." He punches Carlos on the shoulder. "You only had to beat that tiny Asian chick in the last round."

Carlos recovers quickly from his embarrassment. "Are you being a racist?"

Elijah rolls his eyes. "I'm just comparing the competition."

"Just because she was, uh, petite doesn't mean she wasn't good. And what does being Asian have to do with it? Do you call me the Mexican?"

"Dude. Are you colorblind?" Elijah gestures to himself. "You really think I'm gonna do that?"

Carlos huffs out a breath and runs a hand through his hair. "Sorry. I'm just…I'm grabbing waters. You want anything?"

Elijah shakes his head, then turns to me as Carlos practically sprints away.

"What'd you say to freak him out, Special K?"

"Did *you* put that cereal box on my desk?"

"Me? Nah. But the nickname fits you." He tilts his head as he studies me. "Seriously, what'd you say to send him running off?"

My heartbeat is still racing, but I try to pull off casual. "We were just smack talking each other. Maybe he has the pregame jitters."

Elijah's eyes narrow. "Uh huh." He glances toward the drink table, then back at me. "That guy doesn't get the jitters."

Of course Carlos hadn't meant to say I was *hot* hot. He meant I was a sweaty mess. And his challenge to bring my best game only meant foosball. Why do I let myself get carried away? I reach into the back pocket of my jeans for a hair tie, then pull my hair into a ponytail. I can't afford to be distracted by anything if I want to win.

And I want to win this whole thing. I want to take home that cheesy trophy Brian stuck on the dessert table. I want another low-five from my dad.

Carlos returns with water bottles but doesn't make eye contact when he hands mine over. I take a long swig, wishing for a towel to wipe my face and neck, but that would only draw attention to my sweatiness.

"Final round!" Brian yells. "Everybody gather around!"

"May the best foosballer win." Elijah reaches out to shake both of our hands with mock solemnity.

I follow Carlos to the table, pushing through the crowd, which has grown louder as the afternoon has worn on and more beers have been consumed. We take our places on either side of the table. I notice the other interns gathered in a tight knot, watching us, and I wonder who they'll cheer for. Who am I kidding? *Go Carlos go!*

"Ladies and gentlemen, this is the first time we've had interns as our final competitors." Brian pauses. "It's also the first time Emergent has ever hired interns, so…" A few people laugh.

"Carlos and Laurel will play until one of them wins five points. Whoever wins gets the trophy, bragging rights, and their name added to the Foosball Hall of Fame plaque."

There's a plaque? For real?

"You guys ready?" Brian asks. We nod.

Carlos gives me the chin tilt, which I interpret to mean good luck. Or maybe, *I'm going to crush you.* I guess if I'm going to be crushed by anyone, I'd like it to be him. But that makes me think of bodies crushing together and—

"Go!" Brian yells, and I jerk my attention to the table.

Playing Carlos is way different than playing Lewis. Whereas Lewis was frenetic and impulsive, Carlos is deliberate and strategic. He lines up his shots carefully and figures out my style of play quickly. The scoring goes back and forth, and before I know it we're tied at three.

A loud cheer goes up after he scores his third goal, and I notice the interns are especially raucous. Way more than they were when I scored. Except for Elijah, who shows the same enthusiasm for each of us. Lewis and his beefy friend stand off to the side, cheering loudly for Carlos. Their obvious sexism irritates me, so I channel my frustration into the game, scoring a fourth point quickly with a move that catches Carlos off guard.

He glances up, setting me off balance with a smirk. "Nice shot."

I nod my thanks but don't say anything. He serves and

we're back in the groove, shooting and blocking. We enter a rhythm, both of us predicting the other's moves and responding accordingly. In any other circumstance I might say we're compatible. Well-matched.

My cheeks heat at the direction my thoughts are going and I remind myself to focus, but in the few seconds I'm distracted, Carlos takes advantage and scores, tying us at four.

"Nice shot."

"Loser buys donuts for the winner." The skin around his eyes crinkles and the butterflies in my stomach swirl like a tornado.

"Deal." It's my turn to serve, so I do, intending to score quickly and end this. But Carlos surprises me, switching up his game and transforming into a whirling dervish instead of the measured competitor he's been for the past four points. I try to match his play, but I'm a beat too slow, and he scores the game-winning point to a deafening roar of cheers.

Go, Carlos, go.

He's swarmed by fans, and I step back from the table, stunned at how he tricked me. If I'd watched him to do it to someone else, I'd have been impressed. Sighing, I wipe a sheen of perspiration from my forehead. Why is it no one swarms the loser after a game?

Brian presents the trophy to Carlos, who grins and takes an exaggerated bow as the crowd applauds. I scan the clumps of people for my dad. I spot him, and he gives me a thumbs-up, but even from a distance I can tell he feels bad for me.

I'm anxious to get home, maybe join Lexi at the pool, but then I remember I don't have a ride home thanks to Dad's surprise date for Mom. *Great.* Now I have a long, hot train ride to look forward to. I sneak toward the exit.

"How about a round of applause for Laurel?" Carlos calls out, making me freeze mid-escape.

I flatten myself against the wall as everyone turns toward me, since Carlos has helpfully pointed me out. Ugh. The crowd claps and a few people whistle. I assume it's pity cheering because I'm Mr. K's daughter, which stings even worse than losing. I offer a pathetic half wave and refuse to make eye contact with the winner. Fortunately, my time in the spotlight is short-lived as everyone turns back to Carlos or grabs more beer and soda.

Ms. Romero, ever my champion, appears next to me and hands me a water bottle. "Great game, Laurel. You made him fight for it."

Not really. I suspect he had me figured out from the beginning. I wonder if he let me score on purpose, waiting until the very end to destroy me. If he did, that sucks. I hate when people don't play their best, reeling others in and then revealing their true skills. And he told *me* not to hold back?

"We leave early on pizza Fridays," Ms. Romero says. "I need to clean up so I can get out of here. Enjoy your weekend, hon." She gives my shoulder a squeeze and heads to a nearby table littered with empty beer bottles, gathering them up.

I frown, wondering why people don't clean up after themselves, when Carlos swoops in, quickly gathering bottles and empty plates.

"You don't have to do that," Ms. Romero protests, but she looks grateful.

Carlos grins. "I'm a professional. Years of experience." He moves quickly to the other tables, bussing like a pro because of his family restaurant, I assume. I head to the dessert table, stacking up empty platters, trying to make myself useful. A few other people join in and the mess is cleared quickly.

Ready to leave, I head for the stairs carrying empty dessert trays, but a hand on my shoulder stops me. I know who it is before I turn around.

"It was a great game, Laurel." Carlos reaches for the platters. "I'd shake your hand but you're making it tough. Let me help you carry that stuff."

I shake my head like a stubborn child. "I've got it." Then I remember what a sore loser Lewis was. I don't want to be like that. I force a smile. "You played great. Congrats." I want to brush the stray hairs from my face but can't because my hands are full. "Uh, what kind of donuts do you like?" I know he likes chocolate, but it's easier to ask *that* than ask if he let me score.

His expression shifts. "I was just kidding about that. Trying to, uh, stoke the competitive fires or whatever."

"We made a deal. Loser buys donuts. So tell me what you like or I might show up with something awful, like plain donuts."

"I'm a traditionalist. Plain is perfect," Carlos jokes. When I don't laugh, he frowns. "Are you upset about the game? You played great, Laurel. You almost beat me."

Flustered, I shift my stance and the plates wobble. Carlos reaches out again, taking the stack from me. His fingers brush mine and launch another butterfly party in my stomach.

"I just…" I begin, then stare at the ground. Do I really want to know if he gave me the go-easy-on-Mr.-K's-daughter treatment?

"What?" he prompts.

We stare at each other. It's not one of those Hollywood omigod-we're-going-to-kiss moments. Instead it's awkward and uncomfortable. I glance around, noticing we're the last ones on the rooftop. How did that happen?

"Did you let me almost win?"

He looks as shocked as I am at the words tumbling out of my mouth.

"Are you kidding me?" His grip tightens on the plates.

"Why would you even ask that?"

"Because at the end you shifted to a whole new style of play. It was almost like you held back the rest of the game." I take another breath and bite my lip. His gaze darts to my mouth, then he frowns and glances away. "Also," I continue, "I'm the boss's daughter. It's hard to know who's being… genuine…or whatever, and who's not."

He flinches like I've slapped him.

"I don't cheat," he says, his jaw tight. "And I don't suck up to people because of their connections." He shifts his stance and bites out the next words. "Sorry you thought I did."

And then he's gone, disappearing through the doorway, the sound of his footsteps rocketing down the stairs.

Way to go, Laurel.

Way. To. Go.

Chapter Eleven

Lexi and I meet at the pool after I get home. The water feels amazing after burning up on Emergent's rooftop, then riding home on the light rail. I spent the entire train ride cringing as I replayed how I'd insulted Carlos.

"So do you still want to quit your job?" Lexi asks. We're treading water in the deep end, ignoring the crazy kids splashing around us.

"No."

Her eyebrows lift in surprise, then she swims off to the edge after a rambunctious boy splashes her in the face. I follow her and we perch on the ledge, our sparkling rainbow fingernails grasping the smooth lip of the pool deck.

"So what changed your mind? I thought you hated working for the evil empire." She blinks her dark lashes and tosses wet hair over her shoulder, a few wet strands sticking to her chest. Lexi fills out a bikini top impressively. Me, not so much.

"Yeah, well…turns out it's not so evil."

"Interesting." She leans back, balancing on her elbows. "Maybe Kendra is right. Try to make friends with the girls, at least one of them. That will make it more fun." Her lips curve into a Cheshire grin. "Plus, three cute guys? Come on, you ought to be able to hook up with one of them this summer."

There's only one guy I'm interested in, but I managed to insult him today, so I've killed any chance I had. Not to mention it's against the rules.

"Hey, my mom said you're working the church carnival, so now I have to." Lexi doesn't sound thrilled about this.

I shrug. "I don't mind doing it. It's for a good cause."

She rolls her eyes. "I know that. Don't make me feel like a jerk."

"So don't do it if you don't want to. You could donate money instead. Buy a fake brick."

Our church sells fake bricks at the carnival every year. People pay crazy sums of money for a cardboard rectangle, and the little kids decorate them. Then we stack the bricks in the reception hall until next year's carnival rolls around.

Lexi exudes annoyance, and I realize we're not really talking about the carnival.

"Something up with you and Brayden?" I ask. I hope not, because even though I don't like him, I want her to be happy. She shrugs and turns away, watching the kids playing Marco Polo. "Lexi, what's up?"

"My brother. My parents are so freaked about the way he bombed out of school that they've got us both on lockdown. I had to beg them just to hang out with you tonight."

"But that doesn't make sense. You haven't done anything wrong."

"You don't have to tell me." She sighs and closes her eyes. "I just wanted a normal summer, you know? Working, hanging out with you, seeing Brayden. But I'm not allowed to see him unless he comes over while my parents are home."

I wince. "Ugh. It's like you're in middle school."

"I know, right?" She twirls a strand of wet hair around her index finger. "I'm so mad at Scott for messing up, but I'm worried about him, too."

I push myself up to sit next to her. I can't imagine how she feels because I can't picture Kendra messing up. Ever. When she'd told me he'd flunked out, I couldn't believe it.

"Is there anything I can do?"

She shrugs. "Maybe not complain so much. Your life's not that bad, you know?"

Her words cut, but instead of getting defensive I stay quiet, because deep down I know she's right.

"We should do something fun." I want to make her laugh, or at least smile.

"Like what?"

"Watch a movie with me tonight. I made cookies yesterday." Lexi likes my cookies almost as much as Dad does.

"Okay." She doesn't look excited, but I hope I can cheer her up. Maybe she's right and I need to stop focusing on my own problems.

Unfortunately Lexi leaves after the movie instead of spending the night.

"No sleepovers," she grouses, staring at her phone.

"Not even with me?" I can't believe her parents are being this strict.

I hug Lexi goodbye and wave from the front door as she climbs into her SUV. This summer is going to stink if her parents keep her on lockdown, but I'm hoping they'll relent soon.

My parents will be out late, so I curl up on the family room sofa with my laptop. After wasting time on a few YouTube videos, I give in to my true desire and pull up Carlos's restaurant website. I may have looked at it a few times this week, late at night while lying in bed. Maybe more than a few times. An idea bubbles in my mind, but I try to quash it. I am not stalking Carlos at his restaurant.

No way.

"Encantado, may I help you?" The voice is familiar, even over the cacophony of laughter and music in the background.

My throat constricts as I debate what to do. Disguise my voice and ask how late they're open? Tell him I'm sorry for what I said on the rooftop?

"Hello? May I help you?" Carlos is unfailingly polite, even to a prank caller.

I disconnect and toss my phone aside like it burns my hand. The last time I phone-stalked a guy was in the eighth grade. And it was Jason. What is *wrong* with me?

Eventually I drift to sleep in front of the TV, dreaming of my parents' soft voices and the warmth of a blanket being tucked around my body.

"She lost the foosball tournament today," my dad whispers. "But she was a good sport about it."

Maybe I'm not dreaming. Mom's cool hand smooths hair from my forehead. "Of course she was. Sounds to me like she's being a trooper with this job, Rhett. I hope it works out the way you hope."

Even though I'm 99 percent asleep, my ears prick up.

"It will," Dad says. "I'm sure of it."

Chapter Twelve

On Monday, my own personal Dementor fog shrouds me. I dread facing Carlos after the way I accused him of cheating at foosball

Dad chats me up as we drive, saying he's proud of the way I'm "hanging in there" and of how I almost kicked Carlos's butt at foosball, though he doesn't phrase it quite like that. Vader is a mood reader.

"I noticed you took photos on Friday. May I see them?"

Suspicion pricks at me like thorns. "Maybe."

"Laurel, don't be stubborn. I'd like to see how they turned out."

"It's not like I'm a professional."

He blows out an exasperated breath. "Come to my office. I have an idea."

"Does this idea involve you embarrassing me in any way?"

"What? No."

"Can we have lunch together today?" I ask. "I can run out and bring us back sandwiches if you're too busy to go to a restaurant."

Dad glances at me, brow furrowed. "Sorry, kiddo. I'm meeting with a client for lunch today."

"How about tomorrow?"

"Not sure. My lunches are usually booked up far in advance." He keeps his focus on the traffic.

I slump in my seat, as deflated as the tires on my old tricycle rusting in our shed.

"Maybe I'll check with Ms. Romero. See if there's room to squeeze me into your schedule."

"She would know."

Does he even want to spend time with me? I know he's running the empire, but can't he eke out twenty minutes to have a sandwich with me?

*D*ad checks out my photos while Ms. Romero stacks files on his desk. She does it every morning, with color-coded notes and instructions. I wish I had a Ms. Romero to organize my homework.

"Fantastic, Laurel." Dad looks up from my camera, his grin wide and genuine. "I want you to show these to Brian and Jiang." His enthusiasm takes away some of the sting of no lunch date.

"Really? Where do I find them?" I'm kind of excited. If the marketing people like my photos, maybe they'll show up on Emergent's social media, which would be cool.

"Second floor. Look for the life-sized King Kong cutout."

"Later, Vader."

"Later, Leibovitz."

"I wish." I can only dream of someday being as accomplished as the famous Annie Leibovitz.

On my way to meet with the social media crew, I swing by

Miss Emmaline's desk. Sighing heavily, she folds her hands on her desk, waiting.

"Morning, Miss Emmaline." I take a sour apple Crazy Cowboy candy from the bowl on her counter. Crazy Cowboy is a local Colorado company and one of Dad's clients, so those little candies are everywhere in our office. More fuel for Dad's sweet tooth.

"Why couldn't the toilet paper cross the road?" I unwrap the candy and pop it in my mouth, sour apple flooding my taste buds.

She grimaces and doesn't respond.

"It got stuck in the crack."

Her lips pucker like she's sucking on the same candy as me. I should've known she wasn't a butt joke aficionado.

"Have a great day, Miss Emmaline." I spin around and head for the steel staircase.

The second floor buzzes with energy and laughter. I spot the King Kong cutout right away. Colorful Hawaiian leis dangle from its neck and a Barbie doll is taped to Kong's clenched fist.

Brian glances up from his cubicle, which is full of toys and I mean, *full*. Nerf guns, a Velcro dart board, a miniature corn hole set. And a Lego *Millennium Falcon*. My eyes roam the ship. I have a few completed *Star Wars* Lego kits in my bedroom, but that's top-secret information.

"Hey, Laurel. You here to hang with the cool kids?" Brian grins and tosses a hacky sack in the air, catches it, then tosses it up again. I watch him the same way Lexi's dog watches anyone with a tennis ball.

Jiang rounds the corner and stops when she sees us. "Hi. You're Mr. K's daughter, right? I'm Jiang." She holds out her hand and I shake it. She's dressed in a trendy outfit that makes me feel like a gawky twelve-year-old.

"What's up, Laurel?" Brian plops the hacky sack on his desk.

"I, um." I tug at my blouse. Brian's a decent guy; this should be easy. "My dad suggested I show you some of the photos I took on Friday. To see if you might want to use them on social media."

He shoots Jiang a cryptic glance and I flush. Maybe I shouldn't have mentioned my dad. Now they'll pretend to like my photos even if they don't. Crud.

"Let's see them." An encouraging smile lights up Jiang's face. "I noticed you with your camera on Friday. Have you been into photography for a while?"

"About a year or so." I hand over my camera, biting the inside of my lip. I need to relax. This isn't a big deal. If they don't like—

"Whoa. Check this out, Bri." Jiang hands my camera to Brian, then glances at me with new respect.

Brian grabs eyeglasses from his desk, puts them on, and studies my camera's viewer. He grins, then cycles through the photos as I wait, holding my breath. Finally he looks up, removing his glasses.

"Awesome. Candids are hard to pull off, but you've got a knack for it." He hands my camera to Jiang. "Let's use the one of Mr. K laughing with Mr. Mantoni, and the one of you battling the intern kid. Carlos, right?" He glances at me for confirmation and I nod. "And the one where people are fighting over the last slice of pizza. That's golden."

That picture is one of my favorites. The lighting was just right, making the pizza warriors look like they're lit by a spotlight against the brick rooftop wall. The photo of Jiang and Carlos is also a favorite; they both look so fierce and focused, and the contrast of Jiang's yellow sundress and Carlos in his black T-shirt works well.

I may have cropped the photo so I could enjoy a close-up of Carlos's face for later viewing. Like, way too many viewings.

Grinning, Brian reaches out to fist-bump me. Jiang gives me a thumbs-up. I wonder if I can convince my dad and Mr. Mantoni that this department is where I need to be, not spying on interns.

Jiang disappears with my memory card to make copies of the photos.

"You do Instagram?" asks Brian.

I hesitate. "Yeah."

"And?" He cocks an eyebrow and I shrug, embarrassed, but I know what he wants.

"Nikonik." I spell it out as he writes on a scratch pad. I'd wanted Nikonic, but someone beat me to it, plus it's a hashtag used by photographers.

"Clever." He nods approvingly.

Jiang reappears with my memory card. "I copied all of them; hope you don't mind." She glances at Brian. "What do you think about giving her access to our Twitter?" She studies me, her gaze assessing. "I assume you're good at phone photos, too."

I nod, surprised by how well this is going. I hope it's not special treatment because of my dad.

Brian hesitates. "I don't know." His eyes are full of apology as he turns to me. "It's not that I don't trust you, and you've clearly got skills, but we have to be careful about who we give access to. If anything…off…was tweeted, it'd be a disaster. We're role models for a lot of our clients, you know? We direct them to our social media as an example when they screw up—" He clears his throat. "I mean, when they need pointers."

I understand his reluctance. I wouldn't want to give a teenager access to my Twitter if I were in his shoes. Even if said teenager was the daughter of the president of the company.

"It's fine," I say quickly.

Jiang smooths her silky dark hair. "Maybe you could do some stealth photography for us."

"Stealth photography?" Goose bumps rise on my arms. I'm already supposed to be reporting rule violations to the Manicotti, now Jiang's asking me to sneak photos of people?

She must sense my anxiety because she pats my arm. "Nothing creepy or weird, I promise."

"Not creepy," Brian agrees, then retrieves a huge battery-powered Nerf gun from underneath his desk

"We're planning a surprise for your dad," Jiang whispers. "Just a few people are in on it, for now. We'll tell more people when we get closer."

"Closer to what?" I keep my voice soft like hers.

"To Emergent's anniversary. Fifteen years this August." She glances at Brian, who squints at his gun, checking its ammo status.

"We're making a mini movie and planning a surprise party," Jiang says. "I've found a ton of older photos, but we need photos of the current staff." Jiang tilts her head to study me. "Candids like the ones you took on the rooftop. Those are perfect."

"That sounds great." And it does, except I'm not sure how I'll pull off slinking around the office and snapping photos without drawing people's attention. "But I—"

Brian raises his Nerf blaster and fires off a round of foam ammo. A startled yelp sounds behind me. I whirl to see Lewis, the big guy I beat at foosball, staring down at a pile of orange foam bullets on the floor. His buddy Cruz pokes his head out from his cube and glares as he assesses the situation.

"Son of a—" Lewis begins, then stops when he sees me.

He looks like he wants to do bodily harm to Brian, who's snort-laughing in his chair, his gun propped on his thigh like a cocky Bruce Willis.

Yeah, I definitely need to transfer to this department.

"Yo, Lewis," Brian says. "Bring me a donut, would ya? I know you're headed to the kitchen to stuff your face."

Lewis's cheeks puff out like a blowfish and I wonder if Brian will pay for his sneak attack later. Then something Brian said tugs at the edges of my memory as Lewis storms off.

Donut.

Oh no. I was supposed to bring donuts to Carlos since I lost the foosball game. He'd said he was kidding about the wager, but as I recall the hurt expression on his face when I accused him of cheating, I know I have to pay up.

"I'm sorry, but I have to go. Maybe we can meet later?"

Jiang nods. "How about lunch today?"

"Uh, sure." I might as well, since my dad's too busy and the interns never invite me. A bubble of apprehension pops in my stomach. Is she hoping I'll tell Dad how nice she is? I grit my teeth. I've got to stop questioning everyone's motives or I'll go insane.

Brian slides his Nerf weapon under his desk and grins, still gloating over his sneak attack.

"Meet us back here at noon." Jiang points to Brian. "You're buying."

His eyebrows shoot up. "Me? Why me?"

As their conversation devolves into friendly bickering, I rush off, hoping I can pull off an express donut run.

I rush up the last flight of stairs to the third floor office, breathing heavily because I ran all the way. Unfortunately for me, it's five after nine and the interns are already gathered around the meeting table. With the Manicotti.

At my less-than-graceful entrance, everyone turns to stare. A blush burns a path from my neck to my cheeks. I approach the table warily, pastry bag in my hand.

"Laurel, what's rule number two?" demands Mr. Mantoni as I sink into the only open chair, between Trish and Elijah. I shove my messenger bag under my chair and set the pastry bag on the table.

"Don't be late." I brush loose strands of hair behind my ears and refuse to let my gaze stray to Carlos, who sits on the other side of Elijah.

"And why are you late? I know your father's been here for at least an hour."

My blush spreads all over my body and I feel like a child being called out by a snarky teacher.

"I needed to pay up on a bet."

Mr. Mantoni's beady eyes squint skeptically. I don't dare look at Carlos.

"Donuts." I slide the bag toward Carlos, but Elijah snatches it off the table and peers inside.

"There's two in here, dude." Elijah clutches the bag to his chest. "You gotta share."

"You didn't need to do that," Carlos says to me when I make eye contact. "I told you the bet was just a joke."

"Excellent." Elijah grins. "They're mine, then." He opens the bag wider, but Carlos's hand jets out, snatching the bag before Elijah can dig in.

"Tomorrow, be on time, understood?" Mr. Mantoni stands up, clearly annoyed with my disruption, then storms off.

Carlos takes a bite of donut and my stomach does a happy twirl. I'd been half afraid he'd toss them in the trash. Still chewing, he lifts his chin in what I hope is a gesture of thanks.

Elijah leans over to whisper in Carlos's ear. Carlos glances at me, glares at Elijah, then takes another bite of donut.

"Put your tongue back in your mouth," Trish mutters. I must look stunned, because she flicks a hand in exasperation. "I only speak the truth." Now her expression wavers between teasing and intimidating.

Embarrassed, I check to make sure Carlos and Elijah aren't listening. Fortunately, they're arguing over the last donut.

"You're the one with tongue issues," I mumble, then I tense, waiting for her attack. Instead, she laughs.

"Yeah, well." Her black-lined lips curve into a knowing grin. "I've had lots of practice. I'm guessing you haven't."

Jason has joined the guys in the donut argument, so Ashley scoots her chair closer to Trish and me, her blue eyes sparkling with interest. "Are we talking tongue action? Cuz I've got tips if you girls need them."

Omigod.

"I hate it when guys go there right away," Ashley whispers conspiratorially. "Like, give me time to assess your dental hygiene situation first, right?"

Trish barks out a laugh and the guys pause their jabbering to glance at us.

"We're all fine here." I lock eyes with Elijah, who grins in appreciation of my *Star Wars* quote, then grabs for Carlos's bag again. Carlos deflects his move and waves the bag above his head.

"They're such dorks," Ashley says. "But they're cute."

"Eh, I've seen better." Trish shrugs.

Ashley twirls a strand of hair around her finger. "If I didn't have a boyfriend in college I might have to make a move." She glances at Trish. "After hours, of course. Rule number eight."

Trish scowls and I wince sympathetically.

"I'm kidding," Ashley says. "I understand why your dad made the rule." Her gaze shifts to me. "Which guy would you pick? If you could."

I can't tell if that's an insult or not. She's still beaming at me, so I give her the benefit of the doubt since this is the nicest she's ever been to me. I keep my eyes on the girls instead of the guys, but it doesn't work—my cheeks still heat, betraying me.

"Ah ha!" Ashley bounces in her chair. "I knew it." She turns to Trish. "How about you?"

Trish leans her head back, eyes rolling to the back of her head. "Not interested."

Ashley shrugs and aims her curiosity at me again. "So come on, Laurel. Which guy is making you blush?"

Silence washes over us, and I'm painfully aware the donut argument has ceased and all eyes are on me. Good God. How much did the guys overhear? I pull my messenger bag out from under my chair, keeping my gaze lowered.

"We should work on our Death Star presentation." My voice is shaking and so are my hands as I open my Hello Kitty notebook. I'd decided to stick with her, no matter how unprofessional.

"I thought each of you could prepare slides on your idea, then I'll pull them all together into one presentation." I point at Trish. "Comic Con for you." I nod at Ashley. "Sharper Image catalog." I clear my throat. "I'll do one on *The Big Bang Theory* and Elijah—"

"Podcast. I'm on it." Elijah swipes the empty bag from Carlos and tilts it up, dumping the crumbs into his mouth. Carlos shakes his head at Elijah, then glances at me, a hint of a flush creeping up his neck. Is that good or bad?

"What about me?" Jason looks at me hopefully, and I chew the inside of my lip. I don't want to hurt his feelings. I've spent considerable time contemplating what task he could handle, given his limited appreciation of nerd-dom.

"We need some iconic shots from *Star Wars* movies. Grab some off the internet. But the original trilogy only. No Jar Jar Binks or Padmé."

Elijah nods approvingly and we exchange inside joke smiles.

Jason's floppy blond hair falls into his eyes. "Iconic? You mean like, uh, Dark Vader and—"

Elijah gasps, clutching his chest. "Did you say *Dark Vader*?" He stares at Jason in mock horror, then shakes his head. "Dude, are you for real?"

A hint of a blush tinges Jason's cheeks, and I'm surprised by my desire to defend him. Apparently six years of hardcore crushing don't disappear overnight without leaving a shadow of…something.

"Hey, Elijah. Come on. Not everybody's a certified geek like us."

"Special K, you're killing me here." Elijah continues clutching his chest like he's dying. "Let's give that task to our man Carlos. He might not be a nerd, but I think we can trust he knows who *Darth* Vader is."

Silence settles over our table as I struggle for words to defuse the situation.

"I think Jason should do it," Carlos says, breaking the silence. "I'm guessing Laurel has another job for me, right?"

Just like in a cheesy movie, our gazes meet across the table. But unlike in a cheesy romance movie, his eyes don't light up with affection. Instead, they darken, and his eyebrows meet in a slash over his nose.

Here goes nothing.

"I do have a job for you. Presenter. Once the slides are put together, you should be the emcee or whatever."

Carlos's eyes darken even more, and his chin juts out. "Why me?"

"Yeah," Trish snaps, "why him?"

I swallow and try to remain calm, keeping my attention on Carlos. "Because you organized us. You ran the meetings. You're the project leader so you should present."

"True," agrees Elijah. He points at Jason. "Run all your *Star Wars* photos by Special K or me first, okay?"

Jason shrugs, embarrassment oozing off of him like a rain cloud. "Since when is Carlos the leader? It's not like we voted on that. He just took over."

Carlos huffs out a frustrated breath and stands abruptly, crumpling the empty donut bag. "Somebody had to, so I did. I don't care about the presentation. Go ahead and do it if you want."

"I'm wondering why a woman wasn't suggested as presenter." Trish surveys me through narrowed eyes.

"Maybe Laurel had *other* reasons for picking Carlos," Ashley says suggestively. She waggles her eyebrows between us.

This can't be happening. All I'd meant to do was reward Carlos because he took over the project so smoothly. Yeah, maybe I have a thing for him, but that didn't influence my decision. Did it?

"If you're all gonna waste time arguing, I'll be the presenter," Elijah says. "I'll make everyone look good."

"But I'm an actor," Jason argues. "I have more experience than—"

"Stop!" someone yelps and everyone freezes, and I realize that I'm the yelper. I panic, grasping for words, but I'm coming up empty.

Carlos backs away from the table. "I'm taking a break." He's scowling, and I wonder if Ashley's innuendo embarrassed him, or if he thinks I'm crazy, or if he thinks I gave him donuts because I'm a dork with a crush.

Maybe all of the above.

Everyone else scatters, while I stay at the table, gazing at the mountains, wondering how I managed to mess everything up. I'm dimly aware of the finance employees in the other corner watching me, but I try to block them out.

I feel terrible. I didn't mean to upset anyone or cause drama. The last thing I want to do is ruin the internship, but I have no idea how to fix this.

*L*unch with Jiang and Brian cheers me up somewhat. They make me laugh and include me like I'm one of them. We discuss my dad's upcoming surprise party and I make a mental note to let Mom know about it so she can attend.

"We should do something for Miss Emmaline, too. It will be her fifteen-year anniversary with Emergent," I suggest.

"Great idea," says Jiang. "I found some fun old pictures of her and your dad when they worked out of a tiny two-person office together."

"She's like the office grandma," Brian slurs around a bite of sandwich.

"More like a wolf in grandma's clothing." I sip from my iced tea, glancing out the window at the busy street crowded with office workers enjoying their lunch break. I wonder where the interns went, then tell myself I don't care.

"She's not so bad," Brian says, eyeing me curiously.

I shouldn't say anything negative about Emergent employees. Dad wouldn't like it, and it makes me look a spoiled daddy's girl, the last thing I want.

When the bill arrives, Brian glances at Jiang. "You still think I'm buying?"

She grins and raises her glass toward him in a "cheers" gesture. He sighs and shakes his head, but a smile plays at his lips.

"Well, since I'm going to be promoted as your boss any day now, I guess it's the least I can do."

Jiang's grin fades as Brian pulls his wallet from his pants pocket.

I clear my throat. "I can pay for my lunch."

Brian shakes his head. "No way am I letting Mr. K's daughter buy her own lunch."

Whether I want to or not, I'm getting "Special K" treatment.

"Thanks." I force a smile, but just once I'd like everyone to forget who my dad is.

As we walk back to the office, Jiang says she'll email everyone that I'm taking photos for a "school project," and to ignore me if they see me snapping photos.

"Hopefully you'll become invisible and can get some good candids."

"No problem there. I excel at invisibility."

When we enter the office lobby we encounter the interns, who've returned at the same time.

"Yo, foosball champ!" Brian calls out. Carlos turns, a surprised look on his face when he sees us. His gaze darts to me, then back to Brian.

"Hey." He steps away from the group. The other interns swarm toward the elevator, buzzing like bees.

"You put your foosball trophy on display?" Brian slugs him playfully on the shoulder. "I bet you're one of those guys with a whole shelf of trophies. You look like a jock."

Ugh. I'm cringing right along with Carlos, who's contemplating the airspace above Brian's head. I wouldn't say he looks like a stereotypical jock, but he's definitely…fit.

"I could've taken you," Jiang teases, "but I'm out of practice."

Carlos smiles at her and it's like the sun appearing from behind a dark cloud.

"We've got a one o'clock meeting." Brian sucks the last bit of soda from his straw, then crumples the to-go cup.

"Thanks for lunch. It was fun." I smile at Brian and Jiang, expecting Carlos to leave, but he doesn't.

"You bet. We'll do it again sometime." Brian shoots me a cocky grin.

"Good luck on your *school project*." Jiang winks as she exaggerates the last two words, then she and Brian cross the lobby together.

I stay put, hopeful that Carlos and I will head upstairs together, but he turns abruptly and leaves me standing alone. My heart heavy, I glance at Miss Emmaline, whose sharp eyes have missed nothing.

I trudge up the stairs, wondering if I should quit this job before I make things any worse.

Chapter Thirteen

The rest of the week is a slog. The interns work on their presentation tasks, but don't speak to me much, except for Elijah. Carlos is polite but distant, like he's put up an invisible wall between us.

On Friday, we've barely settled in after lunch when Mr. Mantoni marches into the sky box, a determined look on his face, and we all freeze, hands poised over our keyboards.

"I'd like a status update on your team project."

We sneak furtive glances at each other, and mine lingers on Trish, wondering if she told her dad everyone's mad that I assigned Carlos to presenter duty.

He gestures to the table and we all slink toward it like we're headed to a guillotine. I sit at one end and everyone else clusters at the other end. The Manicotti's gaze sweeps around the table and I'm sure he notices the odd seating arrangement.

"Everything going okay? Duties equitably assigned?"

Trish rolls her eyes, Jason snorts, and Ashley tosses her hair over shoulder, but doesn't make eye contact with him. Elijah runs a hand over his face while Carlos stares stonily into space.

Fantastic. I open my mouth, ready to confess this is all my fault, but I don't get the chance.

"Unacceptable," Mr. Mantoni says. "You all have to learn to work as a team. It's one of the skills you'll be rated on at the end of summer. Based on your attitudes, you're all looking at goose eggs."

Trish drums her fingers on the table and pins me with her scary stare. I try to telegraph a silent apology with my eyes, but her expression doesn't change.

"Since you can't seem to figure out teamwork voluntarily, I'm going to make sure it happens." The Manicotti folds his arms over his chest and trepidation creeps up my spine. "We've got a basement full of old files that need to be scanned. The files are a mess and need to be organized."

No. No no *no*.

He hooks a thumb toward me. "Laurel got a start on it last summer but left a lot unfinished."

What is he talking about? Dad had told me I'd finished what he needed, that it was just a short-term job. Had he lied to me? Had I complained so much he'd decided it was easier to leave me at home? Humiliation burns through me as I absorb the heat of everyone's glares.

"As of now, you're all on file duty. Follow me."

My body is wound tight as a rubber band stretched to its limit. I wait until everyone leaves, then I follow, dragging way behind. How has my idea of a fun job, a way to spend time with my dad and help out the interns, turned into this?

We take the stairs down three flights to a steel door marked "Basement." Mr. Mantoni punches a code into an electronic keypad mounted on the wall, then grunts as he opens the heavy, windowless door.

As we trudge down a steel staircase, our footsteps clang

like hammers on pipes. The basement is dingy, with peeling brick walls. A damp, moldy smell fills my nose.

Two hallways fan out from the bottom of the stairs in an L shape. The Manicotti leads us down the shorter one, lit only by a couple of dim wall-mounted bulbs. He pushes open the door of a storeroom and flicks a switch. Two fluorescent light fixtures overhead flicker to life as we file in behind him. He's right. It's a disorganized mess. Last summer, the file boxes were delivered to my cube; I hadn't even seen the basement. He can't possibly mean for us to stay and work in this hellhole. This must violate OSHA or humane working conditions laws or *something*.

"See all these boxes?" He points to leaning stacks of boxes lined along one wall, piled nearly to the ceiling. "The five of you ought to be able to get through these, even if it takes all day and all night. I want them alphabetized by client and organized by date."

"What?" Trish yelps. "Dad, you can't. You're violating a ton of labor laws. You can't make us—"

"You all are a team, whether you want to be or not," Mr. Mantoni interrupts, ignoring Trish. "I assume you've all had experience on teams—sports, debate club, whatever. But the work world is different. The consequences are bigger. Often there's no end in sight—no final game or match. You have to figure out how to work with people you don't necessarily like or have anything in common with. Indefinitely."

He pins Trish with a dark look. "And in the real world sometimes you have to work overtime. I've pulled all-nighters for clients before. It won't kill you." He nods and steps toward the door. "How you handle this is up to you."

And then he's gone, the door banging shut behind him, echoing off the brick walls. No one speaks for at least a full minute.

"I'll do it," I say softly. "This is my fault, my problem. You guys can leave." I hate that my voice is wobbly, but I'm not letting everyone else pay for my mistake.

"Nice try at playing the martyr card, princess, but it won't work. We all have to do this." Trish shakes her head, clearly disgusted. "They're the ones who need the scholarship, not you, Laurel, so they're screwed if they don't pull this off." She kicks at the floor with her boot. "I'm sorry, guys. My dad can be a righteous prick sometimes."

Her words land like a volley of punches and I feel bruised, not to mention ashamed, because she's right—the interns need the scholarship money and I don't. They risk a lot by walking out.

"It's a waste of time to blame Laurel or your dad," Carlos says to Trish, his words clipped. He shoves his hands in his pockets and tosses his head like a prize horse ready to race. "We need to jam through this crap. I've got to work my other job tonight. I can't stay here all day and night." As he speaks, he looks at everyone but me, and that hurts even more than what Trish said.

"Maybe this was the real reason they hired us," Ashley says, "to clean up this mess. Maybe the scholarship is just a front."

I can't tell if she's joking, but Jason huffs a laugh, so maybe she is.

"Don't be stupid, Ash," Elijah says. "Of course there's a scholarship. We just screwed up today and he heard about it."

"How did he find out about our argument?" I ask Trish. "Did you tell him?"

Not the best way to get everyone's attention, but it works since they all turn to me, eyes wide. Trish's shoulders stiffen as she stares me down.

"No, I didn't. I don't go running to my dad over every little thing."

"Like I do? Come on, Trish, that's not fair. I haven't complained to my dad about anything." My breathing is short and fast. I hate confrontation, but it seems to be the only way to get through to her.

"You don't have to. He gives you everything you want, doesn't he? Private school, whatever college you want to go to, a cake summer job that you don't even—"

"Catfight!" Jason grins as he says it and Trish turns her ire on him.

"Are you kidding me, dude? You really wanna throw out that sexist demeaning bullshit just because two girls are having a healthy disagreement?"

Healthy disagreement? I wonder what level of attack she considers a real argument?

"Knock it off. All of you." Carlos's eyes are stormy, going even darker as they skim over me. "Just get to work, all right?" He stalks toward the boxes and glares at the looming stacks like he wants to knock them down.

"Here." Elijah appears at his side with a ladder that was leaning against another wall. "You climb, I'll take stuff from you." Ashley rushes over to hold the ladder while Carlos climbs.

As they snap into action, the rest of us watch. Whether they meant to or not, they got us to stop arguing. Trish, Jason, and I give each other sheepish looks.

"Come on," Trish says with a sigh. "Let's do this."

Jason and I follow her, and he leans in to whisper in my ear. "I didn't know catfight was a bad thing. I thought it was funny. I was trying to make you guys chill out." His green eyes are full of sincerity and I believe him.

"It's okay. Just, uh, maybe be more careful next time."

He nods vigorously, darting a wide-eyed, fake scared look at Trish's back that makes me giggle. From the top of the ladder, Carlos glances at me, box in his hands, and my stomach twists because he looks pissed, like I think this is all a big joke. All the donuts in the world can't make up for the predicament I've put him in.

Chagrined, I move quickly, clearing off a long table stacked with random junk. "Let's put the boxes here." I try to sound all business. "I can sort through them while you and Jason keep passing them over to us."

"Hold on." Trish raises her hand. "Let's be logical about this. How about we empty some of the boxes first so we can use them to alphabetize the files?"

"Good idea," Carlos says from his pedestal. I nod at Trish, because he's right. It's a good idea.

We make an assembly line to deliver the boxes from the stacks to the table. After we've emptied about a dozen boxes, Trish unearths a Sharpie from somewhere and labels the boxes: *A*, *B*, *C*, etc.

"We need twenty-six empty boxes," Elijah says.

"Probably more than that," Ashley points out. "We'll have a lot more *M* files than *Z* files, for instance."

I work silently, but I'm keenly aware that we're working as a team. Everyone has helpful ideas, and eventually we find a rhythm. It's like we're allies in a battle, working together for a greater good, even if that good seems like pointless busywork.

After a long stretch of quiet, ant-like assembly work, Elijah takes a break from helping Carlos and balances his phone on a file cabinet. Dance music sounds through the tinny phone speakers and Ashley spins in a circle.

"Dance break!" she calls out with a laugh and Elijah joins her, followed by Jason. I smile as I watch them but I'm too shy to join in. I glance up at Carlos, still on top of the ladder. A hint of a dimple appears on his face as he watches the frenetic dancing.

"Omigod," Trish groans. "It's the freaking *Breakfast Club*."

I laugh at her reference to the iconic dance scene. "Not even close." I point at Carlos. "He's no Judd Nelson dancing on top of the statue."

Trish flashes a grin. "You're obviously the Molly Ringwald. Shouldn't you be showing off your moves?"

"If I'm the Molly, then you're Ally Sheedy." I gesture to her all-black outfit. "Obviously."

Her grin widens. "Except I'm the smart one, not the crazy one." Her gaze slides to Carlos, then back to me. "Too bad he doesn't have a pierced ear. You could give him a diamond stud like Molly did to Judd at the end of the movie."

That makes me blush and want to laugh and shove her all at once. "Not gonna happen."

"Only because he doesn't wear an earring. Otherwise we're looking at the same basic dynamic. Dude from the other side of the tracks. Pretty rich girl. Yada yada."

"Except he's not a troublemaker. Not even close." I sneak a glance, only to find him watching us from his perch on the ladder. Well, watching me. Even though I know he can't hear us over the music, my cheeks burn and I focus on Trish, wondering if I dare say what I'm thinking. I decide to go for it. "You know, if we follow this analogy all the way through…"

"My dad is the dick principal. Believe me, I know." She does a great imitation of her dad's scowl and tosses out a quote from the movie. "'Don't mess with the bull, young man, you'll get the horns.'"

We laugh with each other, stupidly, genuinely, neither of us noticing Carlos until he clears his throat. He's climbed down the ladder and is now within sniffing distance.

"You two aren't dancing?" he asks, then he takes a slug from a water bottle. I wish I'd thought to bring one with me. I also wish I could stop staring at his mouth.

"Nope." Trish turns and yells, "Dance break's over, people. Back to work!"

Somehow, between the working together and the dance music, the mood has shifted. We're chattering now, joking about some of the faded photos and ads in the old files, and mocking each other about music choices as Elijah cycles through his playlists.

It's hard to tell how much time has passed since we're in a windowless basement, but eventually my stomach tells me it must be close to five o'clock. I check my phone and I'm right, it's 4:55 p.m. I wonder if I can convince the Manicotti to let us go home at our normal time since we've done such a good job, even though we're only about halfway finished.

"I'm going to go find your dad," I tell Trish. "To see if he'll release us from prison." I brace for impact, but she doesn't freak out.

"Want me to come with you?"

"No. I still feel like this whole mess started because of me, so I'll go." I flash her a quick grin. "If I'm not back in ten minutes, send a rescue crew."

She rolls her eyes, but she's almost smiling.

In the dimly lit hallway, I blink to adjust my eyesight. It's sort of creepy out here by myself. When I hear a rustling noise around the corner, I freeze, terrified it's a rat, or worse. The rustling starts up again and I realize it's footsteps.

Chill out, I tell myself. Maybe it's the Manicotti coming to release us. Cautiously, I creep forward, grateful my shoes aren't heavy boots like Trish's. I peek around the corner and spot a tall, hefty figure at the far end of the deserted hallway. This longer hallway has only one dim bulb to light it, and it's only firing at about twenty watts. A creepy haunted house noise wails as a door creaks open, and the silhouetted figure disappears into a room.

Holy crapoli. What's going on? Who is that? And just like a dumb TSTL character in a horror movie, I start to tiptoe down the hall toward the creaky door, telling myself it has to be the Manicotti. I take only a few steps before an arm wraps around my waist from behind and a hand covers my mouth.

I start to scream, in spite of the hand on my mouth, but I'm pulled against a tall, solid body and a voice whispers in my ear.

"Quiet, Laurel. It's just me."

Carlos.

My heart races, but not from fear; it's because Carlos is pressed up against my back like, well, like we're way more than coworkers. I wonder if he can hear my pulse thudding through my skin, because I sure can.

And why is he still holding me?

"Don't move," he whispers, his breath hot on my neck, and I shiver. The hand that was on my mouth now rests on my shoulder, and his other arm is still wrapped around my waist.

"What do you think you're doing?" he whispers in my ear. "Spying?"

"What are *you* doing?" I hiss, annoyed and yet also secretly thrilled at our full body contact.

"Watching out for you." He loosens his grip on my waist and puts some space between us, much to my disappointment. "Let's get out of here."

"No." I turn to face him, swallowing hard as I look up at him. It's so dark I can't make out his facial expression. Since my face is burning hot, I'm relieved he can't see me clearly, either. "I think it's Mr. Mantoni and I need to talk to him."

"It's not." Carlos's response is quick and frustrated. "And we don't—"

The wail of the creaky door snakes down the hallway and Carlos grabs me again, tugging me around the corner.

He reaches up to pull the lightbulb string, shrouding us in darkness. We flatten our backs against the wall, breathing heavily. He grasps my hand, his warm and strong; mine, sweaty and shaky.

The footsteps grow louder. I hold my breath as the figure lumbers around the corner toward the staircase. Whoever it is doesn't even glance our way. It's a big guy, bigger than the Manicotti. He's carrying something, but I can't tell what it is. His heavy footfalls clang as he trudges up the metal stairs. The door opens, then slams shut behind him.

Carlos and I blow out relieved breaths and he lets go of my hand.

"What just happened?" I whisper, then wonder why I'm bothering to whisper.

"I don't know," Carlos whispers back.

"Why did you think I was in danger?"

"I'm not sure." He yanks the lightbulb string, bathing us in dim yellow light.

"I wanted to go upstairs to get cell service. But when I saw you creeping around the corner I got a weird vibe."

Bolstered by the concern I hear in his voice, I seize my chance to apologize.

"Look, I'm so sorry about this stupid punishment. I shouldn't have decided you should be the presenter." I glance at the concrete floor. "I didn't know it would kick up such a storm."

He shrugs. "It's a done deal now, and it ended up all right. Nobody wants to kill each other. At least not at the moment."

"I probably owe you more donuts to make up for all this."

He leans against the wall, crossing his arms over his chest. "I bet you can come up with something better than donuts." His eyes are definitely back into melty territory. My pulse hums.

"Let's, uh, go upstairs." No time for melting. "You can make your call and I'll track down Mr. Mantoni to ask if we can be released from captivity."

We take the metal stairs two at a time, but when we push the door, it doesn't open. We try again, but the door is locked, trapping us inside.

"Damn," Carlos mutters under his breath. "Now what?"

Panicked, I stare at my cell, which still shows "no service."

Carlos pounds on the door, making me jump.

"What are you doing?"

"Maybe whoever that guy was will hear us, if he's still out there."

We wait, but nothing happens.

"Hey! What's going on out here?" Trish's booming voice shoots down the hallway and up the stairs.

"Come on. Maybe somebody else has a better idea." I rush down the stairs, Carlos at my heels. My panic is rising. If we can't get cell service, and nobody can hear us pounding on the door, then what? But the Manicotti has to come back, doesn't he? He's not going to leave us down here to rot, right?

Trish meets us halfway down the hall, and when she catches sight of Carlos, she raises her eyebrows at me.

"Should've known I'd find you two together."

I ignore her insinuation. We've got more important things to worry about.

"We're locked in here." Frustration deepens Carlos's voice. He brushes past her into the file room. Trish runs down the hallway and up the stairs. I hear her struggling to open the door, then the sound of her stomping back down stairs.

"This sucks." Her face contorts with more worry than anger. "I can't believe my dad did this."

Back in the file room, Carlos issues commands.

"Turn off your music," Carlos orders Elijah, who's pitching

crumpled paper balls to Jason, who's swinging at them with a ruler.

"Come on, guys." Carlos's words snap like firecracker poppers. "Now."

Ashley, perched on a step stool to watch the impromptu baseball game, jumps up and rushes to Elijah's phone, silencing the music.

"What the hell, man?" Elijah hurls a crumpled paper at Carlos, who catches it, then chucks it into a trashcan.

"Bad news. We're locked in. And no cell service."

Everyone gapes at him, then grabs their phones to confirm.

"Damn," Jason grumbles. "I can't stay here all night." He glances at Trish. "Your dad wasn't serious about that, was he? He didn't lock us in here on purpose, right?"

Trish bites her lip, looking unsure. I wish I could hug her, but I don't want to lose an arm.

"Maybe there's a landline," I suggest. "Let's look."

Everyone launches into search mode, checking out all the walls and dark corners of the room, but no luck.

"I'll check the hallway." Footsteps trail behind me and I expect it to be Carlos, but when I glance over my shoulder, it's Trish.

"You okay?" I ask. She looks worried and angry.

"Hell no. I can't believe my dad did this. What if there was a fire down here? We'd all die."

"Way to go to the dark side, girl."

She scowls at me, then her lips quirk. "Whatever." She shoulder-bumps me and I wonder if this is how she shows affection. We round the corner, heading down the long, dark hallway, and my heart rate picks up even though I know the mystery man is gone.

"Do you know what's in these rooms?" I ask as we try a couple of locked doors.

"Dead bodies?"

I laugh nervously as my hand jiggles another door handle and almost stumble when the door swings open. The room is dark and musty, and I shriek when sticky cobwebs attack my face. Leia and Rey would be so disgusted with me.

"Relax, princess." Trish pushes past me and runs her hand along the wall, looking for a light switch, I assume. She finds one, but nothing happens when she flips it up and down. "Crap." She pulls out her phone and turns on the flashlight feature, sweeping the light around the room, which is even more cluttered than the file room.

"What *is* all this stuff?" I pick my way through a maze of boxes and unidentifiable objects covered with blankets. "Point that light over here." I yank a blanket off the closest object, which stands taller than Carlos.

We both scream, then gape at each other, then back at the…thing…that was under the blanket.

"Don't touch it," I warn her, though I step closer to get a better look.

"What the actual f—" Trish begins, but the thud of pounding footsteps stops us in our tracks.

Carlos bursts through the door first. Trish flashes her phone light on him, blinding him and making him swear.

"What the frack?" Elijah steps around Carlos.

"Are you guys okay?" Carlos asks, but his eyes are on me, not Trish.

"Yeah, just freaked out. Show them," I tell Trish. She shines the light on the object and Elijah gasps, then dissolves into hysterical laughter.

Carlos steps closer, brushing my arm with his. "Wow." His laughter is soft and rumbly.

"This isn't funny. It's creepy." No matter how good he smells or how close he's standing to me, I'm still freaked out.

"This thing is going to give me nightmares."

Elijah has stopped laughing and leans in close to the mannequin, wrapping his arm around her like she's his inanimate date. "Somebody take my picture. This is going on my Instagram."

Carlos starts to comply but I bat his hand down. "Are you crazy? This is super weird! We don't want it on social media."

"She's got a point," Trish says. "People will think you're deranged, Elijah." She trains her phone light on the mannequin again.

I take a backward step, but Carlos stops me, putting his hand on my back and sending hot tingles rocketing through me.

"It's not real," he whispers. "It can't hurt you."

"Do you see that knife? Whoever did this is nuts."

I watch his lovely brown eyes go wide and I'd bet money he just remembered the guy we saw in this hallway earlier.

"Crap," he mutters. "You don't think…" He runs a hand through that messy, thick hair I desperately want to touch.

"I don't know what to think." I let myself lean into him because he feels safe and I'm seriously creeped out by this thing. Also, it's a good excuse to get closer to him. His hand slides across my back and squeezes my waist. His touch does more than reassure. It sends inappropriate images rocketing through my mental camera as we face down this mutant mannequin.

The mannequin is a she, based on its curves. Its face is garishly made up with black-and-white clown makeup. A spiky silver wig perches on its head, and the torso wears an Insane Clown Posse T-shirt. Someone has taped a knife to its hand and drawn blood dripping down the arm.

"What the hell is *that*?" Elijah asks, pointing to the mouth.

Trish moves in close and puts her phone up to shine on

the mannequin's face.

"Eek!" I scream like a terrified, locked-in-the-basement-in-the-dark girl. What kind of freak tapes a dead mouse to a mannequin's mouth?

"I'm surprised they let you out of the suburbs, princess." Trish knocks the dead mouse to the ground and Elijah kicks it across the room.

"Hey, cut her some slack." Carlos's hand squeezes my waist again. "I'm freaked out by this, too."

Trish side-eyes him. "Liar. You're just trying to make her feel better." She shines her phone light on us. "Or maybe cop a feel."

Carlos drops his hand from my waist. I wish I were brave enough to throw the mouse at Trish.

"I say we get the hell out of here," Elijah says. "This feels like a bad horror movie." He deepens his voice and makes it wobble, like a creepy Vincent Price. "Trapped in a basement! With an armed mannequin." He spins and points to the mannequin. "That's really…ALIVE!" He screeches the last word and lurches toward me with his hands curled in the air like a zombie. I stumble backward, but Carlos's warm hand returns to my back, so I don't fall.

"Dude," Carlos warns. "Don't make me hurt you."

A scuffle sounds in the doorway. Jason and Ashley join us, rumpled and flustered. What exactly have they been doing?

"Hey, we told you guys to stay put." Elijah attempts a bossy scowl, but Trish pulls it off much better.

"We were worried," Ashley says in her breathy voice. "All that screaming, then quiet, then another scream."

Trish slants me a mocking smirk. So I screamed, so what?

"What the heck is that?" Jason asks, aiming his flashlight at the mannequin. Ashley lets out a tiny shriek when the light illuminates the creepy face, and I feel vindicated. If I didn't want to stay in the warm cocoon of Carlos, whose arm is now wrapped around my shoulders, I'd fist-bump her.

Jason examines the mannequin. "Twisted." He glances at me. "I can see why you screamed."

"How do you know it was me?"

He tilts his head toward Trish. "She wouldn't scream."

"I'll take that as a compliment." Trish crosses her arms over her chest, grinning.

"Let's get out of here," Carlos says. "We've got to get out of this basement. I'm already late for my other job."

His words sober us and we quickly exit the room. I tug the door closed behind us. Carlos reaches around me to mess with the latch.

"Someone broke the lock." Our eyes meet in the dim light of the hallway. A shiver runs up my spine. "Let's go." Carlos takes my hand, leading me back to the file room. I'm not sure what is happening between us. Maybe he'd do this for anyone who was scared. He does have little sisters, after all.

Back in the file room, we all frantically try to use our phones without success.

"My dad's not going to forget us," Trish declares, but I hear a thread of anxiety underneath the defiance.

"I'm sure he won't." I hope my voice doesn't betray my own anxiety.

"Even if Mr. Mantoni forgets, your dad will come looking for you, right Laurel?" Ashley says. "Because you carpool to work?"

Ugh. Way to reactivate the dad feud, Ashley.

"Um, no. He went to the Rockies game this afternoon. I'm taking the light rail home." If I get out of this dungeon.

"Great." Carlos groans and runs a hand through his hair.

"What about security?" Jason asks. "Isn't there a security guard who checks stuff after hours?"

Everyone looks at me, like I know everything about this business.

"Yeah," Trish pipes up. Everyone swivels their head toward her. "I saw a guard one night when I stayed late waiting for my dad."

"Do you remember how late?" Carlos asks.

Trish shakes her head. "Not sure. Maybe seven or eight?"

Carlos blows out a frustrated breath and mutters something under his breath in Spanish.

"Truth or dare," Elijah says.

We all stare at him like he's crazy, but he shrugs and gives us his most disarming smile.

"Might as well entertain ourselves while we're waiting. But we need music."

He fires up a new playlist on his phone, then sits cross-legged on the floor, leaning against a filing cabinet.

"Hit me with your best dare."

Chapter Fourteen

"No way," Trish says. "I'm going to pound on the door again. Somebody's got to be around to hear us." She sprints for the door, Carlos close behind her. The sound of their footsteps echoes in the hallway.

"Those two have no sense of fun." Elijah lifts his shoulders in disgust and focuses in on me. "Come on, Jedi, don't leave me hanging. Hit me with a truth or dare."

Jason sits on the floor, his back against the wall, and stretches his legs out. "If we're gonna do this, I need food. I'm starving."

Considering he's a football player, I'm not surprised he's hungry. Those guys consume twice their weight in food.

"Nobody has food," Ashley pouts. "We all came down here without our backpacks or anything."

She's right. I glance around the room, wondering if there's a secret stash of bomb shelter food. Maybe we'll get lucky and find ancient granola bars or something.

"I'll look." I make my way down a narrow aisle with floor-to-ceiling shelves. I use my phone's flashlight to scope out the shelves, which are full of ancient computers and monitors, old printers, and broken desk lamps. Why doesn't my dad get rid of this stuff?

I move farther down the aisle, pausing when I see a box marked "Two-year Anniversary Party." I open it, revealing a big stash of Pixy Stix. What the heck? I root around, but that's all there is. I scan the last few shelves, but all the boxes are labeled "Old Brochures."

Pixy Stix it is.

Carlos and Trish have returned. Based on their scowls, pounding on the door didn't elicit a rescuer.

"I have food," I announce. I set the box on the table and chuck packages of Pixy Stix at everyone.

"Is this it?" Jason sounds grouchy. I can't blame him; straws full of sugar aren't going to sate his jock appetite.

"Sorry. It was all I could find."

"It's almost six-thirty." Carlos looks defeated. "I hope a guard will be here soon."

"Um," Ashley says hesitantly, "what if the guard doesn't come down here? What if he only checks the main office areas?"

"She." Trish tears off the end of a Pixy Stix with her teeth. Ashley blinks at her and Trish rolls her eyes. "Why do you assume the guard is a guy? Plenty of women are security guards, and cops and firefighters and—"

"Okay, okay." Jason puts up a hand. "We get the message. Women can do anything. Fly to the moon, brain surgery, run for president. Whatever."

"Don't be a dick, Justin." Carlos tears into his own Pixy Stix, dumping two straws' worth of sugar into his mouth.

"My name is Jason." Jason glares at Carlos, whose lips are purple from the grape Pixy Stix.

Carlos flutters his ridiculous eyelashes. "Sorry. Forgot." He sends me a sideways glance and his purple lips twist in a smirk. I can't look away, especially when he licks the purple sugar off his lips.

"Okay, people." Elijah brushes red sugar off his hands. "Truth or dare. I'll go first." He points at me. "I choose dare. Jedi, proceed."

He's got the right idea. We need to reclaim our earlier dance party vibe to survive the wait.

"Okay, let me think." I take a moment to suck down two straws of blueberry sugar, pondering my question. "I dare you to go back to the mannequin room without your phone and sit there in the dark with the door closed for ten minutes."

Everyone laughs and smack-talks him. Maybe we'll get past the cranky, hungry, we'll-never-get-out-of-here stage.

Elijah shakes his head slowly. "You disappoint me, Jedi. I shall return, victorious." He jumps up and grabs a package of Pixy Stix from the box. "See y'all in ten minutes."

Carlos stands up to follow him. "I'll guard the door to make sure he doesn't cheat. Anybody else wanna come?" His gaze sweeps the group of us, but lands on me.

"It's scarier for him if we all stay here." Trish's eyes hold a challenge.

A hint of panic flits across Elijah's face. "Fine," he says. "But if I'm found murdered, you're all taking the blame."

"Deal," Carlos agrees. "I'll make sure he goes in there, then I'll come back."

As they leave, everyone grabs more Pixy Stix.

"I haven't had these since I was a kid." Trish smiles as she examines the package. "My dad used to buy them for me when we went to the movies together."

I have a hard time picturing the Manicotti and a young Trish at a movie theater, sharing candy like a normal family.

"What was your favorite movie when you were a kid?" I assume she'll answer with a horror movie, but she surprises me.

"*Charlie and the Chocolate Factory*."

"Original or Johnny Depp?"

"Depp, of course."

I hope my expression conveys my disgust. "No way. The original is way better."

"I dunno," Jason says. "My mom made me watch both and I agree with Trish. I liked how weird Depp was. And when the bratty girl spun down the drain—that was awesome."

Ashley shudders. "That movie freaked me out. I think my favorite was *Madagascar*. Or *Happy Feet*. I loved that little penguin."

"Aww," Trish coos. I can't tell if she's being sarcastic or not.

"*Sharkboy and Lavagirl*," Carlos says from the doorway. I jump, wondering how long he's been standing there. He crosses the room and sits on the floor next to me. I reach for another Pixy Stix to distract myself.

"That movie was epic," Jason agrees. "I bet I watched it a hundred times."

Carlos laughs. "Me, too."

"Sharkboy made stuff happen by dreaming, right?" I ask. My memories of that movie are hazy.

"Yeah." Jason sighs and leans back against the cinderblock wall, closing his eyes. "I wanted that to be true so bad. To close my eyes and change reality."

Pounding footsteps thud down the hallway and we all turn to see Elijah rushing toward us. He stops just inside the doorway and grins.

"Dare accomplished. Who's next?"

Carlos glances at his phone. "That was only seven minutes. You failed." He grins and as I study his profile, I wish it was just him and me trapped down here. All sorts of things might happen.

Yeah, right. Now I sound like Sharkboy, trying to dream

my secret fantasy to life.

"Close enough." Elijah joins our circle on the floor and grabs more Pixy Stix.

"Favorite movie?" I ask him. "And it can't be *Star Wars*. Something that came out when we were kids."

"Hmm." He narrows his eyes, considering.

"We already said *Sharkboy and Lavagirl*," Jason says.

Elijah grins. "Damn, I loved that movie."

Trish shakes her head. "I don't usually say this, but it must be a guy thing. I thought that movie was dumb."

Ashley and I raise our hands for high-fives and Trish slams her palms on ours.

"Oh! How about *Night at the Museum*?" Elijah's eyes dance with excitement.

Jason heaves another wistful sigh. "Another one I wished was real."

"That was the best thing about being a kid," I say. "It all seemed possible. A talking pig and a spider who loved him, squirrels hopped up on caffeine in the Ice Age, race cars that talked, a board game that sends you into outer space. It felt like we could do anything we could imagine."

It's quiet for a few moments and I wonder if anyone else is secretly wishing to be six years old again, like I am. I feel Carlos watching me and heat spreads across my face.

"Remember *Zathura*?" Elijah breaks the silence. "My dad bought me the board game and I was mad when I didn't end up floating next to Saturn like in the movie."

"I loved that movie." It was scary, but I watched it over and over.

"Because you have excellent taste," Elijah says.

"Remember *Narnia*?" Ashley asks. "Every day I checked all the closets in our apartment for a secret door into another world."

Trish's eyes soften as she looks at Ashley. "I was sure the secret passage was in my dad's closet, but I wasn't allowed in his room. It was torture, believing the magic was there but I wasn't allowed to see it."

"I still feel that way sometimes," Ashley says quietly, "like there's a secret door somewhere that will lead me to a better place. I just can't find it."

Her words tug at my heart, peeling away some of my jealousy.

"Whose turn for truth or dare?" asks Jason.

He's such a dude. Just a hint of girly emotion and he panics.

"I have a better idea." Trish clears her throat. Is that the shine of unshed tears in her eyes?

"What's better than truth or dare?" Elijah sounds indignant.

"Two truths and a lie. But one of the truths has to be what you thought of this job on the first day."

I suck in a breath. Is she trying to ruin the tenuous truce we've all achieved?

"And the other truth should be something funny or weird about you that none of us knows."

"Who put you in charge?" Jason grumbles, echoing the complaint that started this whole mess. I wish I could make him a protein shake to improve his mood.

"Come on. It'll be fun." Trish grins and I'm struck by how much it morphs her into a different person. I'd love to take a ton of photos of her, in all of her moods.

"I'm in," Elijah says.

"Sure, why not," Carlos says next to me. "I'll go first."

My heart stutters. What's he going to say about his first day here?

He shifts next to me, raising his arms up in a stretch. I catch a whiff of his soap or whatever that is that makes me want to kiss him. Heat floods my face as I try to banish the thought, but now all I can think of is kissing his neck.

Carlos states his supposed truths in a monotone. "The first day here, I thought I was the only one who'd last the whole summer. I dated a skier who's competing in the next winter Olympics. My first day here, I wondered if Trish's dad was on crack."

After a few seconds of silence, everyone laughs, even Trish. Everyone except me, that is, because I'm stuck on his second statement. It can't be true, can it? And if it is, who am I to think I could interest him?

"Can we ask questions to help decide?" Ashley asks. Trish shakes her head and Ashley frowns, studying Carlos curiously with her big blue eyes.

"I got this," Elijah says with a cocky grin. "The lie is that you thought Mr. Mantoni was on crack."

I peek at Carlos. I'm at a disadvantage viewing his profile. His eyes reveal his emotions so clearly, if I could see them I'd know for sure what's true.

"No way." Jason still sounds cranky. "The lie is that he dated an Olympic skier. In your dreams, dude."

God, I hope Jason's right.

"I think the lie is that he thought he was the only who'd last all summer. Half the people in the office think my dad's on something. You wouldn't be the first." Trish smirks and I really wish I could see Carlos's eyes. Trish glances at Ashley. "Your turn."

Ashley licks her glossy lips. She must have brought lip gloss with her; too bad she didn't think to bring food. "Okay, I think…" She pauses, searching his face for clues, I assume. I wonder if he enjoys her scrutiny. "You lied about Mr. Mantoni." She tosses her hair over her shoulder. "I can totally see you dating a hot skier."

Everyone laughs, except me, and Jason, who rolls his eyes.

So Jason's the only one who thinks he didn't date an Olympian? Crud. Considering his cluelessness about a lot of things, my heart sinks. That's not the lie, I can feel it in my bones.

"Laurel, wrap it up and bring it home." Trish grabs another Pixy Stix from the pile and tosses it to me. I reach to catch it, but I miss, and it lands on Carlos's lap. He turns and hands me the straw.

We stare at each other and my mouth goes dry. I can tell he's trying to keep his face impassive, but, as always, his eyes give him away. A sigh escapes me, and I tear open the sugar straw.

"Truth, you thought you'd outlast everyone. And you dated…are dating?…a skier."

"Dated," he says. "Past tense." His eyes remain locked on mine.

"Ha! I knew it," Elijah gloats. "So do you ski?"

"I do now."

Even Jason laughs at that statement. I dump the grape-flavored sugar in my mouth, focusing on the sticky sweet powder. I always hated this game at sleepovers, and now I remember why. I always found out something I wished I didn't know.

"I didn't think your dad was smoking crack," Carlos says to Trish.

Trish cocks an eyebrow. "Well done, Rubio. Who's next?"

"I'll go." Jason crosses his legs. "First day, I was sure you guys would vote me out when I was late. First day I worried I wasn't gonna last all summer. If I don't win this scholarship or get a football scholarship, I'm gonna have to get a full-time job after I graduate."

Nobody laughs. Nobody moves. I'm pretty sure he

misunderstood the rules and just told us three truths, but I don't want to point it out since everything he said makes me cringe with sympathy pains.

"You'll get a football scholarship," I say to reassure him. "We've been to state twice because of you, Jason." Everyone looks between Jason and me, except Carlos, whose attention is solely on me.

"I wish." Jason gives me a sad smile. "But if that happens, then my dad's gonna want me to go pro. I'm not *that* good. And even if I was, I don't wanna end up with CTE." He picks at the seam on his pants. "That's why I want this scholarship. I don't want to have to suffer through four more years of concussions just to get a degree."

His words suck the energy out of the room.

"At least you play quarterback," Elijah says. "You don't get as many knocks to the head as other players."

Jason scowls, still picking at the thread. I shoot Elijah a frustrated look and he mouths "What?" but I ignore him.

"You play any other sports?" Carlos asks. "Anything else that could get you a scholarship?"

Jason shrugs. "I used to, but then I focused in on football. I, uh, didn't have much choice. It's what my dad wanted. He'd kill me if I quit playing."

Omigod. I want to launch myself across the room and hug him, and not because of my old crush. I feel terrible for him. I always thought he loved being king of the football team.

"That's hard," Ashley says, her voice so quiet I can barely hear her. "I can relate. My mom says the only way I'll go to college is if I get a scholarship. She says college is for rich kids. Not people like us." She stares at the floor and a single tear trickles down her cheek, making me regret every snarky thought I've had about her. "She says I can always get a job as a model or find some rich guy to marry." She swipes away the tear and lifts her head, her jaw clenched with determination. "But that's not what I want. It's not the fifties. I'm not just gonna sit around and look pretty until some guy saves me. I have my own dreams. I just have to figure out how to make them happen."

Now I want to hug Ashley, too, but Trish beats me to it. She scoots next to her and wraps her arm around Ashley's shoulders. "You can make it happen, Ashley. I'd bet on you."

Elijah blows out a long breath. "Okay, if we're doing true confessions, I guess I'm next."

My eyes snap to him, and anxiety floods my nervous system. He's such a great guy, I'm almost afraid to hear his secret.

"Sooo…I grew up thinking I could go to whatever college I wanted, right? My dad had a great job and we lived in a nice house and my sister and I pretty much got whatever we wanted."

He stops, and we all wait. Next to me, Carlos turns and leans a shoulder against the wall so he can face Elijah directly. Which means I'm in his direct line of sight, too. Flustered, I follow his lead and turn to face Elijah. At least Carlos is staring at my back now.

Elijah's lips pucker in a rueful smile. "But when I was a freshman, it all came crashing down. My dad lost his job and then we had to sell our house. My mom went back to work—got a job as a secretary, but that doesn't pay much. Not enough to live like we used to, that's for sure. My dad just… checked out." He closes his eyes and leans back against a file box. "We're poor enough I can probably get some scholarship money, but my grades tanked when all that crap was going down. I pulled them up last year, but I know it hurts my chances." He opens his eyes and his gaze lands on me. "That's the cool thing about this scholarship. Your dad made it so we don't have to be superstar students to have a shot."

He did? I'm embarrassed to realize I don't even know the scholarship criteria. On top of that, I feel like a spoiled princess listening to how hard it is for everyone. Dad was right when he said I didn't realize how fortunate I am. I thought I did, but listening to everyone else, I realize how clueless I've been.

How does Elijah stay so upbeat when his home life has cratered? His energy and humor always make me laugh. I'd never have guessed his backstory.

But I whined to Ms. Romero because my dad is too busy to have lunch with me? I'm pathetic. Dad's the one who makes it possible for me to go after my dreams. What's that saying about being born on third base making it easy to hit a home run? That's me.

"You're gonna conquer the world, dude." Carlos's breath tickles my neck from behind. "You're one of the smartest people I know."

"And the funniest," I say.

Elijah rolls his eyes. "Just because I can make people laugh doesn't mean I'm gonna be successful." When he speaks again, his voice is low. "My dad used to be a laugh riot. Not anymore."

Ouch. I duck my head, embarrassed that I spoke up.

"It's okay, Laurel." Carlos's whisper is so quiet and so close to my ear that I wonder if it's my imagination.

"My dream is to get myself through college, then find a good enough job I can put my little sister through college," Elijah says. "She's only ten. That gives me eight years to get my act together, right?" He flashes his familiar grin and I wonder if it's as much to assuage our anxiety as his own.

"You'll do it," Ashley says with conviction. "I believe in you."

I believe in all of them. Maybe I should say that.

"I guess it's my turn," Carlos says from behind me. Everyone shifts their attention to him. I take a breath and force myself to turn around.

He glances at me, then focuses across the room. "So I really did think I'd outlast all of you on that first day, but now I see how wrong I was. You're all tougher than me. Honestly, I'm lucky. My family's awesome. There's just too many of us." He laughs and shakes his head. "I'm kidding. But that's partly why there's not much money for college. I'm one of five kids. We own a restaurant. It does okay, but not well enough to put five kids through college."

The pictures from his family website pop to mind. One of these days I want to meet them. The way he talks, I can tell he loves them. And if the rest of them are half as amazing as him, I have to meet them. Someday, somehow.

"I almost feel like I should drop out of this competition," Carlos says, and my heart stops. "I mean, you all honestly need this more than me. I can work my way through CU Denver if I have to and live at home." He glances at me again, his mouth curving into a smile I want to nibble. "That's what Laurel's dad did and look how he turned out."

"Word," says Elijah. "I guess I could do that, too. But I kinda want to get out of my house, ya know?"

"Hell yeah," Jason pipes up. "I've gotta get away from my dad." His gaze sweeps around the room. "You know why I was late the first day? My dad was drunk the night before and I had to pick him up at the bar. We got home and he grabbed my keys and chucked them out the window. Said if he couldn't drive, then neither could I."

Oh God.

"So I took the bus, but it was late, and I missed my transfer by like two minutes." He glances at me sheepishly. "Good thing Laurel voted for me to stay." He shoots embarrassed smiles at Ashley and Trish. "You, too."

Carlos coughs next to me. I wonder if he's remembering how he stared Jason down and refused to raise his hand for him to stay.

"You're all amazing," Trish says. "I'm sorry I've been such a bitch to everyone." She tugs at her blue hair. "I've been in a pissy mood because the internship I'd lined up in DC fell through at the last minute. My dad said I could work here instead." She snorts. "I wasn't happy. It felt like such a comedown, after almost interning in DC."

She looks at each intern, taking her time to go around the circle. "But you all put me to shame. I mean, yeah, my dad's a nutcase, but he's not like, well, like some of your situations. And I'm lucky that I only have to do small student loans."

I'm surprised she has to take out any loans. Does this mean my dad doesn't pay her dad well enough? I can't imagine that, but I squirm restlessly.

"I'm a sucker for bitchy girls," Elijah leers at Trish. "Total turn-on." She winks at him and licks her lips.

No matter where he goes to school he's going to kick butt.

"So." Trish turns to me. "I guess it's your turn. Any deep dark secrets you want to share?" She hesitates. "Only if you want to." Coming from Trish, that's like a giant, squishy hug.

I wilt under everyone's attention. What can I possibly say? I even have a freaking pony, for God's sake. I have my own car. I don't have to work my way through college. My parents love me. So does my sister.

"If anyone doesn't deserve to be here, it's me," I say. My voice sounds wobbly and I hate it. I wish for some of Trish's confidence and bluster.

Ashley clears her throat and looks me in the eye. "Um, if you don't mind me asking, why are you? You said you aren't competing for the scholarship." She sounds nervous, and I wonder what she thinks of me.

It's my turn to stare at my lap and worry a loose thread. "I wanted to. I had to beg my dad to hire me." I laugh, but it sounds bitter. "He didn't want me to do this, and I can see why." I shrug. "It's not like I'm useful around here. But I guess I wore him down." I shrug, still toying with a loose thread. "I don't see him much at home. He works all the time." I look up and meet Elijah's dark gaze. "And I'm grateful for that. I can't imagine him not working."

My reasons seem so petty and ridiculous in the face of what I've learned. But I owe them honesty, after all they've shared with me. I swallow and look Ashley in the eye. "It sounds dumb, but I wanted to spend time with my dad. I figured at least we'd spend our carpool time together." I squeeze my eyes shut but keep talking. "You know what's stupid? I've been upset because my dad's been too busy to have lunch with me since I started this job." I open my eyes. "I know how pathetic that sounds." I blow out a breath. "I wish you could all win the scholarship. You all deserve it."

As soon as the words are out, my gut twists. How can I possibly pick a winner now that I know all of their backstories? The room is quiet, and I assume everyone is thinking what a spoiled brat I am, but they're too kind to say it out loud.

The clang of a door slamming startles us. We all jump and race down the hallway. Footsteps clomp down the steel staircase and a shadowed figure approaches us, then freezes when she spots us. She reaches for her holster.

"Everybody freeze!"

"Don't shoot!" I push to the front of the group. "I'm Mr. Kristoff's daughter. We all work here, but accidentally got locked in."

Trish steps up next to me. "I'm Mr. Mantoni's daughter. He's the one who brought us down here to work in the file room. Go ahead and check with him, but let us out of here first."

The guard steps closer and sweeps her flashlight over us. She must decide we're harmless, because her next words are what we've been waiting for.

"All right. Grab your stuff and let's go upstairs."

In the blink of an eye, we grab cell phones and all the Pixy Stix, for some reason, and rush up the stairs. We emerge into the main lobby, blinking like newborn kittens.

Mr. Mantoni joins us, summoned by the security guard. He looks even more stressed than usual. He apologizes to us for "the incident." He didn't realize he'd locked the door behind him, and he assumed we'd all left at five o'clock, in spite of his threats. He said he was preoccupied by a "pressing issue" and didn't think to come check on us.

Everyone laughs and chatters like we just came off a roller coaster. Everything's back to normal, yet everything has shifted. I step away from the group and pretend to read a text as I compose myself. I breathe in and out, counting to twenty to calm my nerves. I glance up at the laughing group and wonder what my place is with them.

Or if I even have a place.

Chapter
Fifteen

The weekend passes like I'm trapped in a jar of molasses, or caught in a dream where I'm trying to outrun someone, but can't find my footing. The person I'm trying to outrun is myself.

This morning at church we listened to the story of Paul's conversion on the road to Damascus, how he fell to the ground as a blinding light surrounded him and he heard the voice of God. As corny as it sounds, I feel like something similar happened during my time in the basement with the interns. I didn't hear the voice of God, but the experience changed how I perceive everyone, including myself.

Now, standing at the sink washing the breakfast dishes, I'm weighed down with the responsibility of casting not one but two votes for the scholarship. I've no idea how to choose since I want everyone to win. Also, I'm certain that my ridiculous "true confession" made me sound whiny and privileged, both of which are true. I doubt anyone will even talk to me tomorrow.

On top of all that, last night I checked Carlos's Facebook

page—because I'm an idiot, obviously—and struck gold. He was tagged in a new photo by Rose Rubio, his sister, I realized by checking her page. It's a fantastic shot taken at a park. Carlos holds a soccer ball in the crook of his arm, wearing a soccer uniform like the other guys in the photo. But on him, the uniform makes him look like the real deal, like one of those unbelievably fast and athletic guys on the European teams my dad watches every summer during the World Cup.

"**Carlos does it again**," his sister Rose said in the post. "**Goooallll!!**"

As perfect as the photo was, it also packed a sucker punch because although he held a soccer ball in one arm, his other arm was draped over the shoulders of a pretty girl who smiled up at him like she knew him very, very well.

I'd closed my browser and vowed to never check his page again.

"Want me to dry?" Dad asks, sidling up to the counter.

Surprised by his offer, I give him a grateful smile and hand over a towel. Usually he holes up in his home office on Sunday afternoons. He's been solicitous this weekend, asking me how I'm doing at least half a dozen times. He apologized profusely for the basement incident and promised to talk to the interns about it tomorrow.

"Why are you washing dishes instead of just loading the dishwasher?" he asks as he dries the omelet pan.

"It's a Zen thing. Helps me process stuff." All of my friends hate dish duty, but I love it. Weird, I know.

"Wax on, wax off," he jokes, and I flick soapy water at him. His old movie references are never-ending.

Mom enters the kitchen, laden with a stack of handmade clothes. She's participating in a fashion show in Fort Collins this afternoon, focused on trendy and organic items, made from hemp and other organic fibers. Wealthy granola women love my mom's line of clothes. Dad sets down the pan and hurries to take them from her. I flash on Carlos, how he's always the guy holding the door open or helping people jumpstart their car.

"Good luck, Mom," I say. "Break a leg. Sell a bunch of stuff."

Mom hugs me from behind since my hands are occupied. She tugs one of my curls like I'm five. "You and your dad stay out of trouble today, okay?"

"We'll try." When I was young that phrase was our cue to watch movies and eat junk food together, but we haven't done that in ages.

Through the kitchen window, I watch my parents after Dad loads up his SUV with Mom's garment bags and plastic tubs. Dad pulls Mom into a hug and she beams up at him like, I don't know, it's their first date or something. It's sort of weird. And sort of adorable. When he bends down to kiss her, I turn away because it feels like I'm spying. And I refuse to do that, even on people I love. Especially them.

Also, since when did Vader turn up the PDA? Has he always been this way and I've been oblivious, like I was with the interns and their struggles? Like I was with Emergent, which I always assumed was a corporate monster, crushing people like an elephant? How much of my resentment is built on false assumptions, or cluelessness?

After Mom drives away, Dad resumes his drying job. "Yoda I am, dry dishes I will."

"Dad, please. Give it up." I laugh, which is a relief because I'm desperate to shake myself out of my funk. "How was the game on Friday? Did the Rockies win?" I don't follow baseball, much to my dad's disappointment.

"Eight to three. I took some of the staff with me to thank them for putting in so many extra hours lately."

"Oh yeah? Who'd you take?"

"The social media crew. Brian had a great time. He's as obsessed with baseball as I am.

"Brian's cool."

Dad nods. "Great guy." He side-eyes me. "But way too old for you."

Heat floods my body. "Dad! *God*. Of course he is. Don't be gross."

He grins sheepishly. "Sorry. I just…worry about you."

"Then maybe I should work somewhere else. Away from tempting older men." I waggle my eyebrows and he snaps the dishtowel at me. I'm only half kidding. Part of me wants to quit so I don't have to face the interns again.

"You're working where I can keep tabs on you. It's bad enough I have to worry about your sister living on her own and meeting God knows who."

"Apparently she had a date with Thor and it went well."

"What?" Confusion clouds Dad's eyes.

"Chris Hemsworth. She says he looks awesome without his shirt."

Dad looks ready to freak, so I squeeze his arm with a soapy hand. "Kidding, Vader. Take a chill pill."

"You girls are going to send me to an early grave." He closes his eyes, pinching the bridge of his nose.

"Dad. Don't even joke about that." A rush of affection for him washes over me and I blurt out an idea. "*The Force Awakens*?"

He rubs his chin like this is a difficult decision. "Maybe. Do I get popcorn with M&M's?"

"Ewok's honor." I hold up three fingers. "Last one to the TV is a rotten tauntaun."

And for the next couple of hours, it's just me and my dad basking in the glow of our shared dorky obsession, gorging on junk food, not worrying about what tomorrow will bring.

Chapter Sixteen

On Monday morning, I hang out in Ms. Romero's office until the last possible second, then rush upstairs, entering the sky box at exactly eight-thirty. Everyone glances up at my entrance, but to my surprise, no one shoots me eye daggers. They smile. All of them, even Trish. A thin layer of my anxiety slips away.

"Good thing you got here before my dad," she jokes when I sit down. "Rule number two."

Everyone laughs, and my shoulders relax. Maybe I was right about everything shifting Friday night. I guess sharing hard truths can create unexpected bonds between people.

Movement in the doorway grabs our attention. It's Dad and Mr. Mantoni, both wearing solemn expressions. Mr. Mantoni carries a stack of folders.

"Good morning," says my dad. "Let's everyone move to the table so we can chat."

We do as he says, though I hang back, waiting for everyone else to sit. I'm not the only one. Carlos joins me.

"How was your weekend?" His voice is low and quiet, for

my ears only.

"Fine." I bite my lip and stare out the windows to the mountains. What if I look at him and he reads my thoughts and discovers I spied on his Facebook page? And that I can't stop fantasizing about kissing him.

Dad glances at us. "Come on over, you two." His gaze narrows slightly, tracking Carlos's progress. I hope he's not morphing into protect-my-daughter-from-all-males mode.

I take a seat and Carlos sits next to me. Unnerved, I grab a stray paper clip from the table and twist it into an unrecognizable shape.

"What did that paper clip ever do to you?" Carlos whispers. I hear the laughter in his voice, but I still refuse to make eye contact.

Fortunately, my dad starts the meeting, leading with an apology like he promised.

"First, I want to apologize for what happened Friday night. It's inexcusable and won't happen again. We're having an alarm put in that will ring upstairs if anyone ever gets trapped down there again."

Mr. Mantoni reddens, from embarrassment or frustration, I can't tell which. I sneak a glance at Trish, who watches them intently, arms folded across her chest.

"However, you made good headway on the files, according to what Ms. Romero tells me, so thanks for that." Dad grins. "And apparently I'm not the only one who likes Pixy Stix."

Everyone laughs, and I wonder how many empty sugar straws we left behind.

"So." Dad leans back in his chair and loosens his tie slightly. "Time for your individual assignments." He glances at the Manicotti, who nods and picks up the top folder from his stack.

Mr. Mantoni's gaze settles on Ashley. "As you requested,

Ms. Goodsen, you've been assigned to work on the art gallery project."

Ashley's face lights up as Mr. Mantoni tells her the name of the staff person who will mentor her. I'm thrilled for her, especially since I know it's her dream to work in the art world, in spite of her mom's lack of encouragement.

The Manicotti slides the next folder to Elijah. "You're working with a couple of our finance team members who are setting up funding for two minority-owned businesses, as you requested. They're up here, too, so you have a short commute." He tilts his head toward the far corner of the office and grins like this is hilarious.

Elijah nods, eyes shining. "This is perfect. Thank you."

I grin at him across the table, and he shoots me a thumbs-up.

Mr. Mantoni turns his attention to Carlos, who sits up straighter. "Carlos, you're working with the local restaurant chain, as you requested. They're looking to expand regionally and you'll be in on the early planning stages this summer."

I finally sneak a peek at Carlos in time to see a dimple flash. I wonder if he wanted that project so he could help Encantado expand. I'd bet my summer paycheck he did. I love that he's using his internship to help his family.

Mr. Mantoni slides a folder toward Jason. "Jason, we were able to place you on the Cal Stockwell project. You may even have a chance to meet him. But no sampling the wares." Mr. Mantoni wags a warning finger in Jason's direction.

Jason lights up at the mention of the recently-retired basketball player and his new venture, a microbrewery called Stockwell Suds. Maybe working with another jock will help him realize football isn't his only career choice. I Googled CTE over the weekend and was shocked at the stats.

Mr. Mantoni rubs a hand over his shiny head as he focuses

on his daughter. "Patricia. We've assigned you to assist with some pro bono fundraising work we're doing for a couple of nonprofits."

When he slides her folder over, I see apprehension in his eyes as he waits for her response. She doesn't say anything as she opens the folder and scans the contents. Then she looks up and actually beams at her dad.

"Thanks, Dad. This is awesome."

Mr. Mantoni looks as relieved as I feel.

Dad stands up. "Good luck, everyone," he says. "We hope you're pleased with your assignments and we look forward to your final projects." Dad gestures to me. "Don't forget that Laurel's here to assist you however you need."

For the first time, I don't feel embarrassed by my role. Instead, I want to help them—all of them—so that by the end of the summer they each have fantastic projects to present.

Once the dads are gone, the interns chatter excitedly about their projects. Carlos and Jason lean toward each other, voices pitched low, but I don't sense their usual animosity. Ashley, Trish, and Elijah huddle together, gesturing animatedly.

As I take in the new and improved atmosphere in our corner of the office, I make a decision. Before I can chicken out, I stand up and rush out of the sky box, hoping to catch up to my dad and Mr. Mantoni. I hurry down the stairs, waving as I run past Miss Emmaline, who shakes her head, lips pursed. I'll wow her with a new joke later.

My dad and the Manicotti have disappeared. I glance in the conference room windows as I head for my dad's office, but the room is empty.

Ms. Romero greets me with a smile when I enter her outer office.

"How are you, hon? Recovered from your experience Friday night?"

"Yeah. It was weird but it all worked out okay."

She nods and purses her lips. "Well, no one was more surprised than me. I'm so sorry I didn't know you were all trapped down there." She spins her chair around and grabs a box from the credenza behind her. "Here."

I step closer to her desk, recognizing the logo from the gourmet bakery where I purchased Carlos's donuts.

"These are for you and the interns. They can't make up for what happened, but it's something. Take them upstairs with you, okay?"

"Sure, but I need to talk to my dad first. Is he available?

She sets the box on her desk and frowns. "He's with Mr. Mantoni. I don't think they're interruptible."

"Perfect. I need to talk to both of them. It's important." I give her a pleading look.

"Sweetheart, I don't think—"

I cross the office and knock on my dad's closed office door. Ms. Romero's mouth rounds in surprise. I shrug an apology just as my dad yanks open the door, scowling. He stops short when he sees me.

"Laurel? What is it? Is something wrong?"

I peek around him and spot the Manicotti sitting in one of the guest chairs. Excellent.

Gathering my courage, I push past my dad, who stares at me like I've lost my mind.

"This won't take long," I say. "But I have to talk to both of you." I sit down next to Mr. Mantoni, ignoring his glare as I wait for my dad to take his seat.

As I study the cluster of framed family photos hanging on the wall, all of them showcasing our happy family, my stomach lurches. I replay what Jason told us about his dad's drinking, and Ashley's mom's low expectations of her daughter. And Elijah, putting on a brave face in spite of his circumstances.

"What's going on, Laurel?" Dad sits down and leans his elbows on his desk, bouncing his fingertips against each other.

I clear my throat and straighten my spine. *Be Qa'hr*, I tell myself.

"After my experience Friday night," I begin, side-eyeing Mr. Mantoni, "I've decided I can't possibly vote twice on the scholarship."

"Why not?" Dad asks, fingertips still tapping out a rhythmic pattern. He's in Vader mode, eyes narrowed and flinty, but I'm not intimidated. After all, this is the same guy who dried dishes for me yesterday. And fought me for the last M&M's in our popcorn bowl.

"So Friday night was weird." I dare to make a judgy face at the Manicotti, who grunts and lowers his bald head. "But it was also very…revealing. I learned a lot about the interns and why they're here. I bet I know more than if I read their application essays, which you won't let me do anyway."

My dad opens his mouth to say something, but I put up my hand.

"They all deserve that scholarship. No way am I picking just one of them." I can do a Vader death stare, too.

Dad heaves a sigh and leans back in his chair, gripping the armrests. Mr. Mantoni shifts next to me, muttering under his breath.

"You're the one who wanted to work here," Dad reminds me.

"I know. And I still do. But I don't want to judge my friends." As soon as I say the "f" word, I lose focus. Are we friends? Maybe if I work with them for the rest of the summer, and we don't have more drama, maybe by then we'll be friends. Even Trish. *Or more than friends,* a tiny voice whispers in my mind when I picture Carlos.

I blink, snapping myself back to the present.

"You're in a position we aren't," Dad insists. "You can observe daily behavior and decisions. How they interact with each other, and you."

My attention pivots to Mr. Mantoni. "What about Trish? Have her do it."

He shakes his head. "She can't. She's interning, too. She's one of them."

"But she's not competing for the money, so she's not really one of them."

My dad and the Manicotti share a mysterious look.

"I hate feeling like a spy. Is this what people mean by corporate espionage?"

Mr. Mantoni snorts and my dad chuckles. "Not exactly. Look, kiddo, this scholarship is a big deal. We want the most deserving intern to win."

Frustrated, I stand up. "That's the problem. They all deserve it." Then I spin on my heels and storm out of the office, slamming the door behind me.

Ms. Romero jumps in her chair, sloshing the coffee in her mug.

"Sorry."

"Never mind." She hands me the donut box. "Have some sugar, you'll feel better. Take it upstairs and share it with your friends."

There's that "f" word again.

"Thanks." I take the box, then escape before my dad and the Manicotti decide to chase me down.

The interns gobble up the donuts, even Ashley, who I assumed was one of those girls who subsists on air and water. One more blown assumption on my part. When we both reach for the last donut, we agree to split it, laughing as we argue over who gets the biggest piece, since I didn't cut it into equal halves.

Our Death Star presentation goes well, and the rest of the morning passes quickly as everyone dives into their new projects, doing research on their computers and reading through their thick folders. I don't want to interrupt anyone, so I put in my earbuds and am rewarded with Qa'hr and the pilot's first kiss. It's super steamy and definitely worth the wait. I hope no one hears my muffled giggle as I replay the scene in my earbuds. Five times.

I don't like how my meeting with the dads went, but I'm not giving up. After all, they can't force me to vote, can they? But what if it comes down to a tie, like on the first day with Jason, and I have to be the tiebreaker? Ugh. I refuse to think about it.

Once lunchtime rolls around, the interns exit noisily, laughing and talking, except for Elijah and Carlos. I grab my camera bag, ready for my loner photographer lunch, but Carlos's voice stops me.

"Laurel. How about lunch with Elijah and me?"

Mayday! Mayday!

"Yeah, Special K," Elijah chimes in as they approach my desk, "take a break from your secret lunchtime lover and hang out with us for a change."

"Dude." Carlos's voice holds a warning.

Elijah grins and punches him on the arm. "Save your scary eyes for somebody else."

To go or not to go? It's just lunch, says one voice in my brain, while another voice warns me not to spend any more time with Carlos than necessary. I don't dare break rule number eight.

"I'm craving pho," Elijah announces.

"Too hot for pho." Carlos heads toward the door, Elijah falling into step next to him while I remain at my desk, immobile.

"Street tacos?" Elijah suggests.

"No way. Nothing around here tastes as good as my mom's cooking." Carlos hesitates in the doorway, glancing at me over his shoulder. "Are you joining us or not?"

There's something about the tone of his voice—a dash of challenge mixed with an undercurrent of something else. Hope? Desperation? Or is he just hungry?

Oh, what the heck. A girl needs to eat, right?

We compromise on an Asian fusion restaurant where Elijah orders pho, Carlos orders sushi, and I order rice with shrimp and vegetables. The restaurant is packed, so we squeeze around a small table meant for two. My back is against the wall and I face the two of them like a firing squad.

Or maybe I'm paranoid.

"So, Jedi. We have questions." Elijah whips open his napkin with an exaggerated flourish.

So I was right to be paranoid. Anxiety skips up and down my nerve endings.

"Wow, that's your strategy, Sampson?" Carlos sighs. His face contorts with embarrassment. "We just wondered, um, what your plans are for the rest of the summer. At the office, I mean."

Elijah snorts as Carlos's neck reddens. Carlos shoots him a glare.

"You've been observed meeting with your dad and Mr. Mantoni. On your own." Elijah lowers his voice conspiratorially. "Trish thinks you're spying on us. I think her dad just likes to give you a hard time." He glances at Carlos. "And Rubio isn't sure what to think."

Carlos shrugs. "I have my theories, but I prefer to go straight to the source rather than make assumptions." His gaze locks on mine and my lungs forget how to do their job for a few seconds. "What's with the school project? Is that really why you're sneaking around taking photos in the office?"

I want to leap over the table and escape, but since I'm not Wonder Woman, I sip from my water glass and stare down Elijah. It's easier than eye contact with Chocolate Eyes. For a long moment, I consider spilling the truth about how I'm supposed to evaluate them and vote, but I don't. I decide to tell one truth to make up for the lie of omission.

"The photos aren't for a school project."

They tilt their heads like twin puppies listening for a whistle, surprise widening their eyes.

"It's a fun project for the company, nothing to be worried about. But I can't say what it is." I blow out a breath and plunge ahead. "I'm trusting you guys." I point a chopstick at them.

"We're totally trustworthy." Elijah flutters his dark eyelashes. I roll my eyes and glance at Carlos.

"I won't say anything." His eyes stay on mine, and I believe him.

"So what about Mantoni?" Elijah says around a spoonful of broth. "You aren't reporting on us like a tattletale, are you?"

I squeeze my eyes shut. How to answer this? "No. I wouldn't have anything to report, anyway, since you're all so fabulous." I mimic Elijah's eyelash fluttering. "Especially you, *Finn*."

Elijah grins at the *Star Wars* nickname. From the corner of my eye, I see Carlos's lips thin.

"Anyway, as for my plans for the rest of the summer, I'm supposed to be your assistant, right? Even though I bet none of you will ask for my help."

"Wrong." Elijah takes another slurp of pho. "I'm always up for free help. I'll put you to work, Special K."

Carlos says nothing, then pops a piece of sushi in his mouth, which tells me he has no intention of asking for my assistance.

"Uh-oh." Elijah's brow furrows as he glances at his phone, which is buzzing with a rapid string of text messages. "Sorry guys, I've gotta make a call." He winds his way through the crowded restaurant and out to the sidewalk.

Carlos leans back in his chair and crosses his arms over his chest, pinning me with such an intense expression I pause with my fork halfway to my mouth.

"What?" I'm so rattled by his attention, I barely get out one word.

"Are you going to ignore me the rest of the summer? Or do I have to file a complaint with HR?"

I lower my fork to my plate and wipe my mouth with my napkin. He tracks every movement, his gaze lingering on my lips. I swallow, telling myself I'm hallucinating.

"What could you possibly complain to HR about?"

The stupid dimple reappears, and I'm flustered because I haven't seen it since Friday.

"I could complain about your lack of…fraternization."

"*What*?" Surely he doesn't mean what I hope he means. "But we're not supposed to fraternize. Rule number eight. Remember all the exclamation points?"

He takes a long sip of water, so I take the opportunity to stare at his mouth.

"I see rules as suggestions." He sets his glass on the table and his lips take their sweet time curving into a tempting smile.

Flustered, I focus on my half-empty plate, taking a deep

breath and wishing Elijah would hurry up with his phone call already and get back here.

"Besides, there are degrees of fraternization," Carlos continues. "I'm sure he didn't mean to ban *all* of them."

I force myself to resume eye contact, which is a mistake because his dance with mischief.

"Degrees?"

He nods and takes a pen from his pocket, then writes on a clean napkin.

"Number one: introduction." He glances up and grins. "We did that on the first day, in case you forgot. I even got your name right, unlike some interns."

I roll my eyes and try not to reward him with a smile. He can sense victory, though, because his grin deepens in a way I've never seen. Wait—does he have *two* dimples? This is completely unfair.

His pen scrawls across the napkin. "Number two: shared interests." He shrugs. "That's obvious. We work together. We both think your dad is cool."

I narrow my eyes. "Who says I think he's cool?"

"Number three," he continues, ignoring my comment. "Joint projects. Teamwork." He looks up. "Duh."

"Duh," I agree. "Where are you going with this?"

"Pay attention, Miss Kristoff."

Stupid dimples. I take a big slurp of water and notice my hand is trembling.

"Number four: friendly banter." He surveys me critically. "I sense potential for this, but you have to work with me, Special K. A man cannot banter with himself."

"He can if he's crazy."

"Which I am not. Besides, half the fun is not knowing what the other person will say."

It's like I've left my body and am watching an alternate

version of myself. We stare at each other as I try to remember how to breathe. In. Out. Don't look into his eyes.

"Did anyone ever tell you your eyes look just like Hershey's Kisses?"

Omigod. That was my outside voice.

He blinks, then a slow grin reappears as he points his pen at me. "You just proved my point. I definitely wasn't expecting you to compare me to a food product."

"A *dessert*," I clarify. "Not just any food product."

"See how much progress we're making? We just leapt ahead to number five."

"What's number five?"

He props his hands on the table, resting his chin on his hands. "Nicknames. You can't expect me to do everything, Dobby."

"Don't call me Dobby. That's a horrible nickname."

"Hermione?"

I shake my head and mirror his posture, propping my chin on my hands as my elbows rest on the table.

"Special K?"

I shrug. "Did you give me the cereal box?"

"Affirmative."

"Hmm. Maybe I'll allow it."

I'm rewarded with both dimples and it's a good thing I'm sitting down, because my knees are jelly.

"How about Jedi?" he asks. "Or is that one reserved for Elijah?"

"Correct. Only fellow *Star Wars* geeks can use it."

We gaze into each other's eyes, oblivious to the busy restaurant noise surrounding us. If eyes can laugh, his are. Now I hope Elijah's phone call lasts as long as every painful *Star Wars* scene with Jar Jar Binks.

"Your eyes don't look like candy," he says, but before I

have time to register disappointment, his voice drops low. "They remind me of the water in the Caribbean. Sparkling, and like I can see for miles. Not hiding anything."

Whoa. We just jumped from bantering to something else entirely. Something that's making my pulse throb in my wrists, in my ears, in my chest. Everywhere.

"What number are we on?" I whisper.

"I've lost track. But we're not at ten yet."

"What's number ten?"

"It's—"

But before he can finish, Elijah reappears, sliding into his seat and killing the crackling electricity arcing between Carlos and me. We sit up straight, acting like nothing happened. Well, Carlos does. I'm not as successful, knocking my knife onto the floor and fumbling for my napkin, which somehow follows the knife to the floor.

"Yo." Elijah glances back and forth between us, then at our plates of food, which we haven't touched since he left. "Ookaay. Want me to leave again?" He cocks an eyebrow at Carlos, then has the nerve to wink at me.

"Nope. We should head back." Carlos grabs the incriminating napkin from the table, folds it carefully, then slides it into his shirt pocket. He flashes me a dimple—just one this time.

"We'll finish this later, Special K."

*A*fter lunch I sit at my desk, still buzzing from my time with Carlos. I distract myself by browsing through Twitter and experience the extreme horror of finding my dad on a #CEOHotties thread. More than once.

"Vader has a fan club," I mutter to myself. I switch to my

email because I can only handle so many tweet squees about my dad's movie star hair.

"**IMPORTANT ANNOUNCEMENT!**" jumps out at me from my office email. I open the message.

"**Emergent Employees, please join me in congratulating Jiang Chen on her promotion to Director of Social Media. Jiang has served as a Client Social Media Specialist for three years and proven herself to be a true leader and visionary. Her tenure as Director officially begins on Monday. Congratulations, Jiang!**"

The email lists my dad's name and Ms. Simmons's name as senders. That's cool. I like Jiang. I wonder if she and Brian are celebrating by showering her cube with Nerf bullets, or maybe dancing with the King Kong cutout.

I fire off a quick email: "**Congrats, Jiang! Good luck in your new job.**" I add a GIF of a rabbit dancing with balloons.

As soon as I hit send I panic. Does "good luck" imply that I don't think she can do the job? Was the dancing rabbit too childish? I groan. I can't even get an email right.

I decide to burn off my nervous energy by snapping candids for Dad's surprise party. I try a few shots of the interns by the window, but the glare from the windows washes out the photos.

"Whoa." Elijah's head snaps up like a gopher's. "Paparazzi alert."

I'll get photos of the interns some other time. As I leave the room, I sneak a glance at Carlos, who flashes me a secretive smile. I could spend all day taking photos of him, but no way will I do that.

I wander into the kitchen to take a few snaps of people as they come in for snacks and drinks.

One guy gives me a surfer wave and another lifts his

soda to his forehead in a salute, which makes up for the pinched face I get from Ms. Simmons as she peels an apple. She removes the shiny red skin in one long strip, which makes for a great photo, but her scowl ruins the effect. I'll crop her out and zoom in on the apple, then get a better picture of her later.

Jason wanders in and gives me a chin bob, but doesn't say anything, just grabs a Coke from the fridge and snaps it open. Lewis, the foosball Neanderthal, walks in and grunts at Jason.

"We got cleared for a tour of Stockwell Suds," Lewis says "Don't screw up."

I remember the Manicotti's warnings about not sampling the wares. Jason wouldn't do that; he's not a partier. After our *Breakfast Club* night, I know why. I raise my camera and click, catching Lewis's scowl.

"Just taking photos for my school project." My squeaky voice sounds like I'm hopped up on helium. Jason grins, but Lewis glowers at me, so I book it out of there for friendlier territory.

I stop by Ms. Romero's office and take photos of her working, then one of her sharing a laugh with my dad when he comes out of his office and asks if she brought brownies today.

"Dad, I had no idea you were such a sugar addict. I need to let Mom know, or else I can bake more."

He smiles like a kid who's been caught sneaking cookies. "Your mom knows all about my sweet tooth. That's why I have to get my fix here." He points to my camera. "Are you getting some good photos for your school project?"

"So far, so good." I don't mind this white lie, because it's for something fun to celebrate him and his company.

"Don't forget the Manicotti," Dad calls after me. I whirl

around, surprised at his use of the nickname. He widens his eyes innocently and Ms. Romero glances between us, confused.

Laughing softly to myself, I wave to my dad then head for the stairs. I should be able to get a fantastic photo of Jiang since she'll be happy about her promotion.

I'm halfway up the stairs when Brian rushes past me, his face grim. He barely glances at me as he speeds by. In the fun wing of the office, the King Kong cutout now wears a red sash that says, "Congratulations!"

Lewis and Cruz huddle in a corner, whispering and shooting glares toward the rest of their team. Why are these two such jerks? I wonder if they're jealous of Jiang. I spot her talking to a few other staff members and move closer to take a few pictures, capturing her smile and animated hand gestures. She notices and waves me over.

"Congratulations on your promotion." I wonder if I should shake her hand, but that feels dorky so I don't.

"Thanks!" She gestures to the other employees. "You all know Laurel, Mr. K's daughter, right?" They nod and smile at me, so I act like I remember them.

"We're going for ice cream to celebrate," Jiang says. "Want to join us?"

"No thanks. I need to take more photos and get back to uh, assistant stuff." I wince. Way to sound idiotic, Laurel.

Jiang nods like my reply was normal. "Sure, I understand. We'll do it another time."

"Could I take a photo of you? Posing by King Kong?"

Everyone eggs her on as she strikes funny poses and I snap away. After I'm finished, the group heads out for ice cream and I traipse back downstairs. I flash on Brian brushing past me earlier and wonder why he looked so upset, and why he's not joining his team for ice cream. Oh, wait...when we had lunch, he said that soon he'd be Jiang's boss.

Does that mean she got the promotion he was expecting? Ugh. I hope he's not the type of guy to hold a grudge.

Before I go back to the sky box, I might as well take a few photos of Mr. Mantoni. I try to sneak up on him, camera raised, but he must have super hearing because his head snaps up, suspicious squint firmly in place.

"What are you doing, Laurel?"

"Umm…school project," I mumble, anxiously clutching my camera strap.

"Well, hurry up and take my picture." He gestures to my Nikon, so I quickly snap a few photos of his unsmiling face. These definitely aren't going in my contest entry and probably not in the anniversary slide show, either.

I head back to the lobby, my steps light and quick because taking pictures is my happy place, even when the subject is a scowler. In the lobby, Carlos leans on the reception desk, laughing as he unwraps a Crazy Cowboy candy. Miss Emmaline beams up at him like he's her favorite grandchild. I sneak behind the plant again and snap away. Even though I'm ridiculously jealous of her response to Carlos, the photos are fantastic.

"Boo," whispers a voice in my ear.

"Aah!" Heart racing, I jump and whirl around to see Brian. "You scared me. Don't ever do that again."

He shrugs and grins, then his attention focuses over my shoulder, and I realize I've blown my cover. Crud. Slowly, I turn to see Carlos watching me with a knowing smirk. Miss Emmaline's face is pinched.

"Good strategy, hiding to take the candids," Brian says.

I look away from Carlos and Miss Emmaline. "Uh, thanks." I hesitate and clear my throat. "I took some good ones of Jiang with King Kong, celebrating her promotion."

"Excellent." He flashes a genuine grin and relief washes over me. Looks like he's not upset about her promotion after all.

Footsteps sound behind me but I keep my focus on Brian.

"Yo, Carlos, how's it going?" Brian lifts his chin in the universal dude greeting.

"Great," Carlos replies, his voice closer to my ear than it should be.

I could take one backward step and we'd be in full body contact again. I flash back to that night in the basement, when he pulled me close and I felt the warmth of his body, both reassuring and exciting. No way can I turn around now.

"I've gotta get back to work," Brian says. "Catch you kids later." He flicks us a peace sign and heads for the stairs. I'm so focused on Carlos's proximity I don't even care that Brian called us "kids."

Still avoiding Carlos, I cross the lobby for the elevator, but he matches my stride.

"Did you get some good photos?" he asks.

"Thanks to you, I got one of Miss Emmaline smiling." I dart him a frustrated glance. "I don't know why she dislikes me so much."

The elevator doors open and we step inside. Every elevator kiss I've seen in movies tumbles through my brain, so I examine my shoes, face burning.

"She doesn't dislike you," Carlos says. "I bet she's harder on you because you're the boss's kid."

My head whips up. "Did she say that?"

Carlos shrugs, a quick grin lighting his face. "No, but I used to go to school with a kid whose mom was the principal. He suffered more than anybody else because his mom didn't want to show favorites."

"Whatever," I grumble. Now *I* feel like a little kid.

When we reach our floor, I practically sprint to the sky box. Carlos follows me, drops something on my desk, then crosses the room to talk to Elijah. I glance at my desk to see what he gave me. A handful of bright red cherry Crazy Cowboy candies shines up at me.

"Pucker up!" say the labels. "Cherry kisses are the best!"

Chapter Seventeen

My dad's distracted and irritable when we drive into work the next day, so he's having a hard time reining in his NASCAR tendencies.

"What's up, Dad? You're usually a morning person."

He frowns, then runs a hand through his hair. "It's nothing."

"Liar."

"Hmph." He shoots me a curious look. "You spend a lot of time on Twitter, right?"

"Sometimes. Why?"

He practically growls as a car cuts him off, then slows down. Dad roars around him and I wonder what our odds are of getting a speeding ticket today.

"Some jerk tweeted about Jiang's promotion yesterday and it wasn't a compliment. I hope it's just a fluke, but I'm concerned it might be coming from inside the company."

"What? Nobody at Emergent would say anything bad about her." Would they? I pull my phone out of my messenger bag and open the Twitter app.

"Who tweeted?"

Dad grimaces. "Somebody going by @PRTruth."

I search for the account. Whoever it is only has about four hundred followers and hasn't been tweeting for long. The profile picture is a question mark.

"#Fail @Emergent. Promoting an unqualified chick over a qualified dude? Way to be PC @KristoffRhett. Enjoy your lucky break @Jiang93."

Omigod. The tweet has over two hundred likes, and a lot of comments from chauvinist idiots making rude comments about tokenism and the hazards of being male in today's world. Trish will flip when she sees this.

"This is awful."

"Agreed." Dad's jaw tightens with anger.

"Maybe it's someone outside the company, like a competitor." I can't believe anyone who works for my dad would do this.

"I wish, but I don't think so." His hands clutch the steering wheel so tightly his knuckles go white.

I scroll the other @PRTruth tweets, which are mostly critical take-downs of bigtime marketing campaigns. When I read the tweets criticizing Apple, I laugh.

"This guy's an idiot, whoever he is." Everyone likes the Apple commercials.

Dad nods. "Whoever it is has an axe to grind. With me in particular."

Goose bumps make me shiver, followed by a rush of adrenaline that makes me feel overheated. I've seen Twitstorms destroy some of my favorite celebrities. I can't watch that happen to my dad.

"We have to find out who it is."

"No, *we* don't. This isn't your issue, Laurel. Tom and I will track down whoever this is."

I don't have much faith in the Manicotti as a social media

sleuth. And my dad shouldn't have to waste his time on this. A jolt of excitement makes me sit up straight. Maybe I can figure it out.

"What if I—"

Dad cuts me off. "Stay out of this, Laurel. You've got enough on your plate helping the interns."

"Okay," I lie. A recent text from Lexi floats to mind: it's better to ask for forgiveness than ask for permission.

Once at my desk, I open my drawer and retrieve the *Star Wars* trinity from my drawer, placing Leia, Chewie, and Han on my desk where they belong. I've decided not to hide my dorkiness. Plus, it seems appropriate, since I'm determined to figure out who's trying to take down Dad Vader and his empire.

Before I start my sleuthing, I need to check in with all the interns to ask if they need help today. I start with Elijah.

"Yo, Special K." He grins as I approach. "What's up?"

"You tell me. How can I help with your project today?"

He blinks, surprise lighting his features. "You mean it?"

"Of course I do. That's why I'm here."

"Sweet. Except I don't have a plan yet." He picks up a pen and taps it on his desk. "I have a meeting later today with my project mentors, so I'll check in with you after that, cool?"

I nod and he reaches out for a fist-bump. One down, four to go. I take a breath and walk to Ashley's desk. She looks up, all bright-eyed and glossy-lipped.

"Hi!" Her entire face beams like a tiny sun.

I wonder if she wakes up like that, or if she chugs energy drinks to generate that type of buzz.

"Hi." I tuck an errant curl behind my ear. "I wanted to, uh, offer my services." Whoa. That sounds weird. Almost dirty. At least I didn't say it to one of the guys. I cough and start over. "What can I do to help you with the art gallery project?"

"Oh! That's so sweet of you." Ashley swirls her hair in a fluid move. I wonder if her mom taught her how and I try not to cringe. "So, do you know much about art?"

That's a broad question, but I'm happy to answer. "My mom is an artist. A fiber artist."

Ashley tilts her head. "She knits?"

"Yes. And crochets and hand weaves and dyes her own yarn and sews and—"

"Wow." Her cheeks turn pink. "I never thought about crafts as art."

I power up an imaginary lightsaber, but keep it sheathed because I want to make friends with Ashley. My mom has fought this battle her whole life.

"Women's art is always diminished, Laurel," she's told me a hundred times. "Especially when it's also functional."

To my surprise, Trish pipes up from her desk. "I remember your mom's loom," she says. "That thing's wicked cool."

Ashley and I turn to her. Trish must've seen the loom at a company holiday party, back when she attended them and ignored me. My mom has a beautiful studio lit by huge windows and skylights, and Dad loves to show it off because he's so proud of her. He probably took everyone on a tour during the party.

"Yeah," I agree. "It is."

"You ever try it out?" Trish asks. She's curious, not hostile. I like this new and improved Trish. Also, I want to tell her about @PRTruth, but I need to do that in private.

"I've tried it. It's fun, but tough to get the rhythm down. I do better with knitting needles since they're easier to control. Plus they remind me of swords." I sweep my hand in the air, brandishing an imaginary weapon.

"You're such a dork." Trish's mouth pulls up into a grin.

"You're just now figuring that out?" A bubble of hope blooms inside of me. Maybe friendship isn't an impossibility. I turn back to Ashley. "You should check out my mom's website. I'll send you the link. Her work has won a lot of awards."

"Women have coded secret messages in textiles forever," Trish tells Ashley. "It's traditional *and* subversive. That's why it's awesome." She studies me, curiosity lighting up her dark eyes. "Does your mom put secret messages in any of her work?"

I'm embarrassed that I don't know the answer. "She might. I'll ask her and let you know."

Ashley nods, then stands up quickly. "I need caffeine. Anybody else want anything?"

Trish and I decline. As soon as Ashley is gone, Trish fixes her determined gaze on me.

"Yes, you can help me. I'm going to visit my nonprofit projects later this week. Come with me. Bring your camera." She grabs a post-it and scribbles on it. "Here's the nonprofits. Do some Googling, like Encyclopedia Brown over there." She tilts her chin toward Carlos, and I embarrass myself by giggling, which earns me an eye roll, but also another quick grin.

"Okay." I clear my throat. "Sounds great."

Next, I force myself to approach Carlos's desk, where he waits, arms crossed over his chest, watching me in his intense way. Slowly, he opens a desk drawer and retrieves something. He unfolds it and I recognize his fraternization list from our lunch. My carefully rehearsed offer to help with his project flies right out of my brain.

"Let's see where helping me on my project falls on this list." He picks up a pen and clicks it, eyeing me from underneath ridiculously long lashes.

Cautiously, I take a tiny step toward his desk so I can read the list.

"Number three." I point to the napkin. "Teamwork."

He nods and underlines the word. I notice he's added numbers six through ten. Nothing is written next to those numbers, except for ten, next to which he's drawn a smiley face.

"What's that for?" I point to the smiley face. He leans back in his desk chair and grins up at me.

"Not sure yet."

My heart throbs in my chest and my imagination is off and running, fantasizing about number ten.

Carlos points to number five: nicknames. "I think this is where we left off at lunch." He clicks his pen repeatedly and I resist the urge to snatch it out of his hand. "I'd prefer not to be nicknamed for a pasta, but I gave you a cereal nickname, so..." He shrugs but keeps his eyes on mine.

"I...pasta...what?" He's not making sense.

He bites his bottom lip, and I have no trouble picturing what will make *me* "smiley face" if we ever make it to number ten. Also, I'm pretty sure he's a mind reader because his gaze drifts down to my lips, then back up to my eyes.

"The Manicotti. Who is it?" He glances across the room. "Elijah? He can be sort of cheesy."

My mind analyzes his words, sliding them around like one of those puzzles where you have to move a string through twisted metal. And then it clicks.

"You read my notebook! You're the one who—" Panic zings through me as I remember what I wrote about him, Carlos is trouble, and his editorial comment. True. Is Carlos adorable?

Apparently I'm not the only spy around here.

"Why'd you pick this desk?" I'm desperate to change the subject.

"I like the view."

"But it's better by the windows."

"Depends on which view we're talking about." He gives me a cryptic smile, one that makes my stomach dip. "Anyway, I *saved* your notebook. You're lucky no one else read your notes."

Mortified and defiant, I cross my arms over my chest. "You didn't have to read it. You could've just returned it."

"I was just checking to make sure you'd listed all of Mr. Mantoni's rules."

"Uh huh."

Across the room, Elijah stands up and stretches. He glances at us, an amused smirk twisting his lips like he knows something I don't.

Carlos writes on the napkin again. Number six: healthy disagreement.

"You're kidding, right?" Isn't that what Trish called our "catfight"?

His responding grin packs more heat than it should.

"I think we've gone offtrack." I'm proud of how calm I sound, even though my nerve endings are exploding like firecrackers. "We're supposed to talk about how I can assist on your project."

Carlos's grin vanishes, and he rolls his chair away from me. The micro-climate surrounding us plummets from blazing to freezing.

"My project…it's…" He tugs at his hair and stares out the windows. "It's almost more important than the scholarship. I'd already started researching restaurant expansion before I even got this gig." He blows out a breath and turns back to me, his eyes cloudy instead of warm and melty. "My family owns a restaurant. The food is fantastic. We've got a loyal local following. But I think we can do more—*should* do more. There's a ton of crappy restaurants doing better than ours, and it drives me nuts. My family deserves more success."

He frowns down at his desk, clicking his pen.

"Encantado," I say so quietly I'm not sure he's heard me.

His head snaps up. "How did you—"

"Research. It's part of my job to know everyone's background. So that I'm, uh, a more helpful assistant." It's not *exactly* a lie.

He taps his pen on the napkin, but his eyes have a distant, faraway look. Funny, flirty Carlos is gone, replaced by someone much more serious. I debate whether to tell him about my idea to revamp his family's website, but before I can work up the nerve, he opens his desk drawer and tosses the napkin inside, then slams it shut.

"We should get back to work." His voice is clipped and his eyes are on his computer screen. "I'm sure the other interns will keep you busy, so don't worry about helping me." His eyes cut toward me, then back to his screen. He may as well have shut me in the drawer, too.

Reeling, I attempt to decipher his sudden mood change. "So you're saying you don't need my help. Or anyone's."

"No, that's not…" He sighs and glances across the room at Elijah, whose shoulders lift in a shrug.

Carlos drums his fingers on his desk, watching me through hooded eyes. "Look, I'll think about it, okay? I'm not saying I don't want your help, but—"

"It's okay. I'll work with everyone else." My gaze slides to Elijah's empty desk then back to Carlos. "You're in a league of your own, anyway. Definitely un-helpable." I can't believe I said that out loud, but my feelings are hurt so I let my inner ten-year-old take over.

He blinks in surprise. "What?"

"Never mind." I scurry back to my desk like the big chicken I am. Leia and Rey would be disgusted with me, and they'd be right.

After my weird interaction with Carlos, I spend my lunch at the Sixteenth Street Mall, a pedestrian-friendly street lined with shops and restaurants. The only vehicles allowed are the electric hybrid shuttle buses that transport people from one end of the mall to the other and the occasional police motorcycle. Small water fountains spurt out of the ground at periodic intervals, so I take photos of laughing children and one over-excited dog running in and out of the water.

As I head back to the office, I spy Lewis and Brian engaged in a heated exchange on a street corner. They look angry, their hands flying around while they speak. I hope their argument doesn't devolve into a physical fight. My stomach twists and I wonder if I should mention it to my dad.

But wouldn't that make me a spy? Exactly what I don't want to be? Anyway, maybe they're arguing about baseball or a girl or something not work-related at all. I duck across the street so they won't see me and almost crash into Trish.

"Running away from something, princess?" She surveys me curiously, then takes a slurp from her Big Gulp cup.

Reflexively, my gaze darts to the arguing guys, then back to her. She follows my gaze and frowns.

"Weird." She glances at me, and I can tell she's debating whether or not to say something. "Lewis hates my dad." Her shoulders stiffen defensively. "I mean, obviously my dad's not Mr. Popular like yours, but Lewis sort of…takes it to another level."

I'm so surprised she confided in me I'm not sure how to respond. "Wow. That sucks." I tug at my camera strap. "What did he do?"

She shrugs and I swear I see an actual chip materialize on her shoulder. "I've overheard him talking a lot of crap." She darts me a wary glance, then appears to remember we're not enemies anymore and her face relaxes. "Anyway. We should get back."

As we walk toward Emergent, dodging lunchtime office workers and dawdling tourists, I decide to tell her about @ PRTruth.

"So my dad told me some jerk is tweeting anti-Emergent stuff. He thinks it's coming from the inside."

"Seriously?" She stops to stare at me, then resumes her quick stride. "What did they tweet?"

"Stupid stuff about Jiang's promotion. The tweeter is a guy, and a sexist pig."

Her mouth twists in disgust and her shoulders hunch. "I'll check it out."

"I can't imagine it coming from anyone on the inside." I come to a halt in front of our building. "Except maybe..."

"Lewis," we say in unison.

Trish tugs at her Smurf hair. "Let's talk after I check out the tweets."

I feel relieved and energized. Having an inside ally will make it easier to track down the troll. If we catch the guy, my dad will be so proud. I hope.

When we enter Emergent's lobby, Carlos and Elijah are engaged in their own intense convo as they wait for the elevator.

"What's with all the dude drama today?" Trish jokes, and my responding laugh echoes across the lobby.

Both guys glance at us, then away. Elijah shoots a mocking

smirk at Carlos. I hope those two aren't arguing, too, because I think their bromance is adorable.

"Wanna catch the elevator with the—"

"No." I bite the word out and Trish cocks an eyebrow.

"Trouble in geekville?"

"No trouble." I cross the lobby quickly, ignoring Elijah holding the elevator door for us. Trish follows me up the stairs.

"Anyway, Carlos isn't a geek," I mutter and Trish snorts next to me.

"Sure he is. In his own way. We're all geeks about something."

We pause at the second floor landing to size each other up.

"Don't forget to research my nonprofits."

"I won't. And don't forget to check out Twitter."

We head up the second flight of stairs and I'm seized by a crazy urge to ask Trish for advice. Maybe I have sunstroke from taking pictures under the blazing sun. Or maybe it's because she's offered to help me find the troll.

"Can I ask you something?" I hesitate at the doorway. At least I know she won't sugarcoat her answer.

"Hit me." She slurps noisily from her Big Gulp.

I blow out a breath. "Okay, so, I'm supposed to assist you guys, right? But Carlos blew me off. And I think you'd agree he's been nicer to me than anyone, except maybe Elijah. But Carlos doesn't want my help."

I've just revealed my biggest vulnerability to the person who was my mortal enemy just last week. Qa'hr and Leia would be appalled, but I'm going to trust our new alliance.

Trish's eyes turn flinty, assessing me like a hardcore detective. "What happened before he blew you off?"

"Nothing." I glance at a framed photo of my dad on the wall rather than look her in the eye. "I mean, we were sort of…joking around…and then he said his internship was more important than the scholarship, that he needs to help his family—"

She puts up a hand. "The 'joking around' part. By that I assume you mean flirting?" Her eyes narrow to slits. "Be straight with me, princess. I can't help you if you lie."

"Uh..."

Her eyes pop wide open, so that she can roll them skyward. "Okay, so there was flirting, then he backed off. Got all serious about his job." She shakes her head. "Your cluelessness is astounding, but anyway—if you want to help him, come up with something special. Don't just offer to make copies or whatever, because that's lame. And it's easy for him to say no."

"I...wow." This isn't the type of girl talk I'm used to with Lexi or my sister. Trish isn't pulling any punches.

"Got any ideas to help his project?" She slurps her drink again, then quirks her lips when a passing employee shoots her a disapproving scowl. "Bad habit. I do it to annoy my dad."

I do have an idea—a great one. I just need to act on it.

"Yeah."

Her eyebrows arch. "Well then, Jedi, fire up your X-wing starfighter and go save your Boy Scout."

And with that she turns on her heel and leaves me standing alone in the hallway, speechless.

Chapter Eighteen

"I'm hungry." Lexi's pink sunglasses embellished with fake rhinestones sparkle in the bright sunlight. It's a gorgeous Saturday afternoon and we've just left our church carnival planning meeting. "You promised to feed me, so where are we going?"

"How about Mexican food?" I keep my voice light and casual.

"Sounds great."

"It's, um, kind of a far drive, but the food is supposed to be awesome." I haven't confessed my secret plan yet. I'm waiting until we get there.

"I've got nowhere to be. I was lucky to get a Saturday off work, and Mom's let me off my leash, so whatever we do is good with me." Lexi slides into the passenger seat and takes control of the music, starting one of her favorite playlists.

Carlos's family restaurant is already plugged into my car's GPS. My heart rate skips jerkily as I head toward the highway. This may be the dumbest idea ever, but I'm still doing it.

Today's visit is undercover. The woman who answered

the phone this morning said Carlos isn't working today, so it's a good day for recon. After spending the past two weeks helping all the interns except Carlos, I'm following Trish's advice to do something specific, whether he wants it or not. Visiting Encantado will make my website redesign authentic instead of abstract.

And yeah, I also want to check it out because the restaurant is a big part of who Carlos is, since it's entwined with his family.

Besides, these past couple of weeks I've visited museums with Ashley, helped Elijah with budgeting spreadsheets, taught Jason the rule of thirds in photography and how to take a decent iPhone photo, and spent a couple of days with Trish visiting her nonprofits.

Carlos is the lone holdout.

Not that he's ignoring me. He's back to friendly bordering on flirty, and last week we had a foosball rematch on the roof, just the two of us taking a late afternoon break. I won fair and square, and when he slammed my hand for a congratulatory high-five, he held onto it, lacing his fingers through mine. He reeled me in with his deadly Hershey's eyes and I was simultaneously thrilled and terrified he was about to kiss me.

So I pulled away, because I couldn't be responsible for him being disqualified for the scholarship. But the rest of the day, I imagined all sorts of ways we could break rule number eight.

"How's everything with your brother?" I ask as we merge onto the highway. Time to stop daydreaming about Carlos and focus on my friend. Lexi clammed up via text earlier this week when I probed for details.

"He's making progress, I guess. He's seeing a counselor and going to those recovery meetings. My parents made me go to one." She shudders and a sympathetic wave of sympathy slides through me.

Lexi stops the current song mid-screech. "Everyone spilled their guts and told crazy stories. Some people cried, but they laughed at stuff, too. Stuff I didn't think was funny, but…I don't know… Mom says the meetings work and he's going to them every day, so I guess that's good."

We drive without speaking for a while. I'm grateful when Lexi restarts the loud music to fill the silence. Scott was always Mr. Responsible—the designated driver at parties, the guy you knew would do the right thing. It's unsettling to imagine him on the other side of the coin.

"It used to bug me, how my brother was always the perfect one and I couldn't live up to his example." Lexi twists the hem of her shirt. "But now…I hate seeing my parents treat him like he's a huge failure."

"Maybe it's because they're scared to see their perfect son not so perfect anymore." I glance at her. "He's not a failure, Lex. He's still brilliant and driven. I bet a year from now he'll be a pain in your butt again, back at college and earning straight As."

"You really think so?"

"Of course. And we both know I'm never wrong."

Lexi laughs, and I relax, as much as I can considering where we're headed.

The restaurant is tucked away on a side street off of Federal Boulevard, a main thoroughfare on the west side of Denver. It looks like one of those restaurants that used to be something else, like an old IHOP, but has been repurposed. The sign on the roof spells out ENCANTADO in bright turquoise swirling cursive.

The small parking lot is full, which I assume is a good

sign, so we park a few blocks away on a neighborhood street.

Lexi hesitates on the sidewalk. "This isn't exactly our usual scene."

"Don't be a snob, Lex. Come on."

She falls into step next to me as we walk past tiny brick houses, many of them overflowing with toys and bikes in the yards, bordered by flower and vegetable gardens. Some of the houses are better tended than others. My hands itch to take photos.

The scent of delicious food wafts over us as we approach the restaurant, drawing us in like we're captives to a magical hunger spell.

"Sooo hungry. Must eat." Lexi clutches her stomach and I pretend to push her toward the restaurant door.

Once we're inside, the smells are even more mouth-watering. A friendly cacophony of laughter and conversation washes over us as we approach the hostess stand, where several people wait in line ahead of us.

A group of men perch on barstools, watching a soccer game on TV. Fabric-covered booths line the walls of the restaurant, and fully occupied tables fill the space between the booths and the bar. A shelf mounted over the hostess desk displays a small Madonna statue, postcards of famous Mexican landmarks, a framed one-dollar bill, and photos of the Rubio family. I spot a young Carlos in one of them. He's maybe nine or ten, but I recognize the dimpled grin.

Standing in this place where Carlos spends so much time is like being close to him by proxy. I wonder what number "stalking your family restaurant" is on Carlos's napkin fraternization list.

"Welcome, *amigas*." A pretty middle-aged woman who I suspect is Carlos's mom greets us with a wide smile. "Table for two?"

I nod, because I've lost my voice. Lexi squints suspiciously like she can tell something is up. We follow Mrs. Rubio as she snakes between tables and end up at a booth in the far corner. I relax slightly. It's safer to spy from a corner booth than a table where everyone can watch us. We slide onto the padded seats and she hands us menus.

"Water? Soda?"

"Diet Coke," we say simultaneously, and Carlos's mom smiles warmly.

"Coming right up, girls. Your waiter will be right over."

I blow out a breath and relax against the booth.

Lexi points a finger at me. "Okay, girl. Spill."

"What?" I try to sound innocent but fail miserably.

"Come on, Laurel. I know you better than I know myself. Why are we here?" She stabs her finger on the table. "*This* restaurant."

From my seat, I can glimpse the kitchen. Dark pants and shoes shuffle like a choreographed dance as bodies hustle back and forth. The sounds of clanging pans and laughter, mixed in with rapid-fire Spanish conversations, rise and fall like stadium cheers. I open my mouth to tell Lexi the truth, but our waiter arrives, carrying a basket of tortilla chips and a small bowl of salsa.

"Welcome to…Laurel? What are you doing here?"

Everything happens in slow motion, the way Carlos freezes and slowly unfreezes, setting the chips and salsa on the table. He wears black pants and a white dress shirt with the sleeves rolled up, a black half apron tied around his waist. His dark hair is slightly disheveled, but the dimples are definitely in working order and on full display.

"I…uh…" I've got nothing. Zero. Nada. Zilch. I dart a glance at Lexi, whose eyes are wide with appreciation as she takes him in. She slants me a sly look that says way too much.

"I guess I should be flattered," Carlos says, his eyes full of mischief. "It's been a while since I've been stalked."

Lexi collapses into giggles and I grasp for a witty response.

"Uh, we're not...I'm not...stalking you." *Omigod*. Why didn't I have a contingency plan in case he was working today?

He cocks a disbelieving eyebrow. "So you just had a craving for Mexican food and ended up here?"

"Yes." Lexi comes to my rescue. "You guys have great reviews on Yelp. And we were in the neighborhood."

"She's right." I nod vigorously, hoping he'll buy it.

He bestows his flirty smirk on Lexi, then turns back to me. "Whatever you say, Special K."

"Special K?" Lexi asks.

"It's a dumb nickname from work." I grip my straw like it can morph into a lightsaber and blast my way out of here.

"I thought you liked the nickname." Carlos crosses his arms over his chest.

My cheeks burn. Of course I do, because he came up with it.

"Maybe I need to revise number five." The Hershey's eyes are fixed on me, but now they're Special Dark instead of milk chocolate. "I can come up with a better nickname."

I stare at the basket of chips, unable to absorb the heat blazing out of his eyes.

Lexi clears her throat. "We're on a photography field trip," she says in a valiant attempt to save me, "not stalking you."

I want to kiss her. Maybe kick her. Not sure which.

Carlos looks doubtful. "Field trip?"

She nods, tossing her hair. I guess I can't blame her for going into automatic flirt mode. He's impossible to resist.

"Yeah, it's this thing Laurel does with her camera. She drags me all over town to take photos for this contest she's entering. And today we ended up here because of a church she wants to check out."

That's a half-truth. I told her about the church as we drove here, and I did want to photograph it, after the restaurant.

Carlos's sardonic gaze slides back to me, taking in my side of the booth. "Looks like you forgot your camera."

Crud. I swallow as a slow burn works its way up my face. I can't believe I left my camera in the car.

"You dork," Lexi says.

If God were listening to my prayers right now, he'd zap me straight up to heaven and spare me any further mortification, but I guess he's got bigger problems. Or maybe he's getting a laugh out of this, too.

A young dark-haired woman who looks to be in her early twenties emerges from the kitchen balancing plates of steaming food. It's Rose, his sister. I recognize her from Facebook.

She leans into Carlos and says, "Stop flirting, *hermanito*, and get to work." Then she winks at us and hurries off.

Carlos shoots a glare at her retreating back, then pulls an order pad and pen from his apron.

"Do you know what you want?"

You, I think, my blush so hot I want to dump ice water on my face. I glance at Lexi, who's clearly read my mind, judging by her Cheshire grin.

"Not yet." My voice cracks. *Way to go, princess. Qa'hr would kick your butt, and so would Leia.*

"Yeah, maybe give us a few minutes," Lexi says. "I'm Lexi, by the way. Laurel's best friend."

"Oh, sorry. I'm Carlos. Laurel and I work together. Not here, obviously, but at—"

"Her dad's company," Lexi finishes. "I've heard all about the interns."

I kick her under the table.

"All about us, huh?" Carlos smirks, then shoves the pad and pen back in his apron pocket. "I'll be back in a few minutes to take your order, ladies." And then he's gone, leaving me holding my breath until I'm sure he's out of earshot.

"Oh. My. God." Lexi leans over the table, her eyes dancing with laughter. "He's freaking adorable. Why didn't you tell me—"

She stops talking when an older man appears at our table with our sodas. We thank him, and as soon as he's gone, Lexi opens her mouth to continue ranting.

"Shh!" I put my finger to my lips. My eyes dart around the room, but Carlos is on the far side of the restaurant now, clearing empty plates and glasses from a table.

Lexi leans back against the booth. "Tell me what's going on, Laurel. Now."

I give her the CliffsNotes version, including Trish's advice to do something proactive rather than wait around for him to give me a boring task.

"Wow," Lexi says when I finish. "Your job is way more interesting than mine, that's for sure." She grins and grabs a handful of chips. "You need to tell him why you're here."

I nod, twirling my straw around my glass. "I know. And I will…just not right this minute."

Lexi snorts. "And you totally need to explore this 'friendly almost flirty' thing and see where it goes. Maybe take some close-up shots of him. For the website." She does air quotes around "website," making me cringe.

"Stop. Please."

"Dude, you get to spend all summer with that guy. I don't want to hear any more whining from you."

I let out a long sigh. "I know. Maybe we should go," I whisper urgently as my earlier courage evaporates. "We can sneak out of here before he—"

Carlos chooses this exact moment to reappear at the table. His sister whooshes by again, giving him a knowing eyebrow waggle. He narrows his eyes at her and mutters something in Spanish I don't understand, but whatever it is, it makes her laugh. He turns back to us and taps his pen on the order pad.

"So do you want food? Or is your stalking mission accomplished?"

"I'm starving," Lexi says. "I'll have the relleno and enchilada plate."

He scribbles on his notepad then pivots to me. "And for the Jedi warrior?" His smile levels up his dimple game so much that I choke on my soda.

Is he making fun of me? Or is this...flirting?

I'll have you, with that side of sass. I get the feeling he's reading my mind, because his grin deepens and he does something melty with his eyes that makes me tingle in all the wrong places.

"Same for me," I manage to say.

He clicks his pen, then rushes off, speaking curtly in Spanish to one of the busboys doing a lackluster job of clearing a table.

"Give me your keys." Lexi holds out her hand.

"Why?"

"So I can get your camera and make you look legit. Otherwise he'll know you're a stalker." She grins. "Like he hasn't figured it out already."

Sighing, I hand over my keys, then stare at my phone so I don't have to look around the restaurant and accidentally make eye contact with Carlos. That lasts about ten seconds, because he's back at the table, picking up our glasses for refills.

"So you really had nothing better to do on a Saturday than show up on my side of town?"

I force myself to meet his gaze, which is determined.

Curious. And something else I'm not sure of. *Be honest with him*. I think it's Qa'hr talking because the voice in my head is growly and insistent. I take a breath and speak.

"So, I, um, thought about what you said. How the job is more than just an internship for you." I pause and Qa'hr gives me a mental kick to keep going. "From what you said, your family wants to open more restaurants and you want to help them do it right. So I thought maybe if I saw this place firsthand I could help you and your family. With my idea."

His eyes are locked on mine and his expression is completely unreadable. Not even a hint of his cocky smirk.

"So tell me your idea." He's moved close to the table and looms over me. Being this close to him, the energy between us suddenly feels pressurized, like a gathering storm, or a ball of lightning hovering on the edge of exploding.

"Your website." I chew my lip nervously. "For the restaurant. I can update it, especially the photos. They're pixelated, but if I shoot with raw film, the quality will be so much better. And I was thinking it would be fun to do a 'first bite' collage of customers. You know, like, here's someone taking their first bite of a chimichanga, and they'd look all blissed out because it tastes so good. I'd do about a dozen of them. If you think it's a good idea."

I pause for a breath. I cannot believe I just spewed all that dorkiness at him. He can't believe it, either, based on the way he's fast-blinking.

"Uh, wow." He runs a hand through his mussed hair. "You've, um, given this a lot of thought."

In other words, *You're a scarier stalker than I realized. I'm going to file a restraining order*. Or at least file a complaint with the Manicotti.

"I…" What can I say? *Why, yes, I have spent an inordinate amount of time studying your website. And your Facebook.*

Your Instagram, too, if only I knew what it was. But my internal Qa'hr kicks me in the shins and I square my shoulders. "I'm helping everyone else. I'd like to help you, too. I took a website design class last year and I learned a lot."

"Okay." His Adam's apple bobs up and down as he swallows. He doesn't look convinced.

"Do you want to see what I've done so far?

His eyes widen in surprise, then he nods. I pull up the mobile version of the mock site on my phone and hand it to him.

"You definitely want a mobile version," I say, "because everyone looks up stuff on their phone, especially places to eat, like when they're out driving and say, 'Hey, let's get Mexican food. Where's a good place?' and then if they link to your website from Yelp—"

Why doesn't my guardian angel push my mute button? Carlos glances up from my phone, and I nearly sag with relief when he quirks a smile.

"You've been busy, Special K."

"I…yeah." My whole body sags and I shove a handful of chips into my mouth.

Lexi rushes up to our table, slides into the booth with my camera backpack, then chucks my keys across the table.

"You're welcome." She grins and takes a long drink from her soda.

Carlos returns my phone. "So my sister will freak out about her hair and makeup or whatever, but other than that I can round up everyone for photos. If you can stick around for a while after you eat."

"Really?" Nervous adrenaline arcs through me. "You don't think it's a terrible idea?"

He studies me, and I crumple the napkin on my lap because there's just so *much* in his eyes. It's like a whole parade of emotions, but they're shifting so quickly I can't latch on to any of them.

"I don't think it's a terrible idea." His gaze stays fixed on mine. "I want to check it out on a bigger screen but—"

"Carlos!" Rose calls out, glaring at him, hands on her hips.

"Gotta check on my other tables. We'll figure out the pictures later." He rushes off to help a large party that's just been seated.

"So." Lexi stirs the bowl of salsa with a chip. "Apparently you've been holding out on me."

"Holding out on what?" I stuff my mouth with more chips, then bat my eyes like I don't know what she means.

She rolls her eyes. "Your personal interest in this particular intern." She hesitates, holding the overflowing chip halfway to her mouth. "Unless you're planning on visiting all the other interns, and this is our first stop."

"Of course I'm not visiting everyone. I don't care about—" I stop myself but it's too late. She grins, reaching for more chips. "I mean, I don't need to visit them, there's no reason…" I give up and focus on the hot salsa burning my tongue because it hurts less than my embarrassment.

"So what is it about Carlos that intrigues you so much?" She glances across the restaurant where he's laughing as he takes orders from the big crowd crammed around two tables. An older guy, maybe the dad of the group, says something that makes everyone laugh, and Carlos's responding grin makes my stomach flip over.

"Besides the obvious, of course." Lexi watches him, then turns to me with an impish smile.

I let out a long sigh and grasp my spoon, running my thumb over its curved surface. "He's…he's smart. And funny. And he's treated me like an equal since the first day."

"What about that other guy? Elijah? You said he's funny and a nerd like you."

"Yeah, he's awesome. But he's got a girlfriend." I take a drink of soda. "Which is just as well. It's nice to have a guy friend at work who doesn't make me all jittery when I talk to him."

"What about Jason?" she probes.

It's my turn to bat my eyelashes. "Jason who?"

Lexi laughs. "What happened to the girl who swore off summer flings?"

Heat suffuses my cheeks and neck. "I'm still swearing them off." I have to, if I want Carlos to have a fair shot at the scholarship. I shrug helplessly. "You know how it is. Sometimes you get overly curious or whatever about someone."

Carlos's sister Rose appears at our table with two steaming plates. I inhale deeply and my stomach growls in anticipation as she sets our food on the table.

"Can I get you girls anything else?" She grins, the bright curiosity dancing in her eyes reminding me of Carlos.

"Looks great." Lexi grabs her fork and digs in.

I shake my head. "No thanks."

She studies me, then puts a hand on her hip. "You know my brother, right? I'm Rose, his sister."

Anxiety streaks through me. Does she think I'm a weirdo stalker, too? I reach for my glass and take a long drink.

"How do you know Carlos? School?" A speculative smile plays at the corners of her lips and I wonder how many infatuated girls she's quizzed. Probably a lot.

"No, I, uh...we're working together this summer. At Emergent Enterprises." Lexi's foot bumps mine under the table but I ignore her.

Rose's eyebrows shoot up. "Oh! You're one of the interns?" Before I can correct her, she plunges ahead, eyeing me up and down. "You're not the scary one, so you must be the pretty one, who wants to study art or something, right?" Her voice is triumphant like she just won a round of Jeopardy.

My whole body deflates as reality douses me like a cold downpour. I peek across the table at Lexi, whose face twists with sympathy.

"I'm, uh, not—" I begin, but Carlos rushes up to the table before I can finish.

"Table four needs their waitress," he tells Rose, his face conveying a "get lost" message.

Rose smirks. I'm sure she tortured him when they were younger, but I bet he gave it right back to her. I glance at Lexi, whose eyes are full of "this sucks" empathy. I shrug, sending her a silent "it figures" message and take a big bite of enchilada.

Rose shoots Carlos one final withering glance, then flounces away. Carlos runs a hand through his dark hair. I'm surprised by how rattled he looks.

"How's the food?" he asks me, but I can't answer because I'm still chewing. I nod and give him a thumbs-up, feeling like a dork. His lips quirk, then he turns to Lexi.

"It's delicious, Carlos."

He looks relieved. "Can I get you anything else?" he asks me, but he's frowning, and all the embarrassment of the day floods through me.

I can't believe I showed up here with my crazy "let me be your Steve Jobs" plan. And now that it sounds like he's interested in Ashley? Ugh.

But then why does he flirt with me? Is he one of *those* guys?

"No thanks." I focus on the chip basket, avoiding eye contact until he walks away.

Lexi nudges my foot under the table and I raise my eyes to hers. She's genuinely disappointed for me. I can read her like a book.

"Remind me never to stalk again, okay?" I try to plaster a self-deprecating smile on my face, like it's all a big joke.

Because she's a loyal friend, she goes along with my facade. "Deal. And you remind me never to go skinny-dipping with Brayden, okay?"

"What?" My voice is a high-pitched squeak, causing a busboy to stumble as he hurries by with a plastic tub. "When did that happen? Why didn't you tell me?"

"Last night." She drops her gaze and two spots of pink bloom on her cheeks.

I lean back against the cushioned booth. Lexi's always been more daring than me, but this still throws me for a loop. "Did he make you do it?"

"Well…I just took my bikini top off." She stares at her half-eaten chicken relleno like she wants to stab it. "But Brayden was, you know, persistent."

That's a euphemism if I ever heard one, and one more reason I don't like the guy. "So what happened?"

My disappointment about Carlos evaporates as I focus on my friend, worry coursing through me. We're whispering now that our conversation has taken a serious turn, and neither of us is eating. From the corner of my eye I notice Carlos head toward us, then hesitate. He must be a pro at deciphering customer vibes, because he pivots and heads to another table, leaving us in peace.

"We snuck into the club pool. Hopped the wall. It was fun, sort of daring but not actually dangerous, you know? At first we just swam and messed around, then he, uh…wanted to get naked."

She glances at me, wary of my reaction. She's way more experienced than I am with guys. I'm not going to judge her, but I'm terrified that whatever happened wasn't consensual. If he forced her—

She takes a breath. "He kept pressuring me, and I said no. Like a bunch of times." She raises her stormy eyes to mine. "I guess we were yelling pretty loud, then all of a sudden Scott showed up and — "

"Your brother? What was he doing there?"

Lexi shrugs. "I don't know. I yelled at him later for following me, but he said he was out walking because he was sick of being cooped up in the house. Our parents finally left us alone for a night and I think we were both relieved."

She sighs and pushes a pile of rice around her plate. "Anyway, Scott heard us yelling and he came to check because it didn't sound like, you know, normal skinny-dipping. When he saw it was me and Brayden, he freaked. Said he was going to hunt Brayden down and, uh, remove body parts."

"Did Scott hop the wall to rescue you?" I could easily picture her big brother on a mission to castrate Brayden.

"He started to, but Brayden took off. What a jerk." She gives me a wobbly smile. "Also a big chicken, apparently." She closes her eyes and groans. "The worst part was my own brother seeing me topless. I think we're both scarred for life."

Ugh. I wince, trying to shove that image out of my mind.

"Thank God you're okay." I scowl into my soda. "I never liked Brayden."

She takes a big bite of relleno. "I know," she mumbles around her food. "Next time maybe I'll listen to you."

She chews and swallows, then huffs out a sigh. "Maybe I'll be like you for the rest of summer. No flings or dating or whatever. I should spend more time with my brother, anyway." Her eyes are cloudy with worry as they meet mine. "He needs to get back to the land of the living. Like last night. Even though it was weird, it was good to see him out of the house and being an obnoxious big brother, you know?"

I nod. "It was probably great for him, too, coming to your

rescue." My stomach knots. "I hate to think about what could have happened if he didn't show up."

Lexi shakes her head. "Brayden was backing off, but he was mad. He seemed to think just because we'd been dating awhile that entitled him to…you know." Her face scrunches in disgust. "But I think he got the message that's not how it works." She taps her phone resting on the table. "He sent me a million texts today but I'm ignoring him. We're so done."

"Good." I blow out a relieved breath and smile at my friend. Lexi and I have been through a lot together and I've always admired how she stands up for herself. It's something I hope to do a better job of in my own life.

Lexi's expression shifts, humor lighting her eyes. "So how's it going with that crabby old lady at the office? She laugh at any of your silly jokes yet?"

"Ha. I wish. I'm determined to get on her good side, but she's making it tough." I point my fork at Lexi. "What do you call a pile of cats?"

"Do I even want to guess?"

"A meown-tain."

"Ugh." She groans, but her lips quirk.

Carlos approaches our table hesitantly, so I offer him a tentative smile to let him know we're past the serious convo.

He surveys the table. "More refills?"

"Yeah, I need something to wash away the awful taste of Laurel's bad joke." Lexi grins.

Carlos's lips slide from smirk to laughter. "I bet. I keep telling her she needs better material to crack Miss Emmaline."

"That's for sure," Lexi says, laughing. I shoot fake glares at both of them. Carlos takes our empty glasses and heads for the bar. Lexi slants me an assessing look.

"You're sure about that no fling rule?"

I nod. "Sounds like he has a thing for Ashley, based on what his sister said. Anyway, he's too...*everything*." I snap a tortilla chip in half. "I'm too dorky for someone like him."

Lexi starts to argue, but instead clears her throat as Carlos returns with our sodas. He sets them down, then pins me with a penetrating stare that makes my heart thump hopefully. Stupid heart.

"What do you call an unpredictable camera?" he asks, and it takes me a few seconds to realize he's telling a joke. A stupid one, just like mine.

Lexi's foot does some sort of foot Morse code under the table, tapping out an urgent message on my shoe, which I ignore.

"I don't know."

The skin around his eyes crinkles when he smiles. It's hard to breathe when he steps closer to the table. "A loose Canon."

Lexi's foot is apparently having a seizure as it repeatedly slams into mine. I shoot her a glare.

He gestures to our empty plates. "How about dessert? Sopapillas, churros, or flan? On the house." He tilts his head and a few loose strands of hair fall across his forehead. I ache to push the hair back and just...*argh*...

"Surprise us," Lexi says with a pointed glance at me.

Carlos turns to me, his eyes darkening. "You like surprises, Special K?"

"If you keep calling me Special K, you're definitely in for a surprise."

A slow, sexy grin lights up his face, heating my insides like honey melting in hot tea. He leans over the table for our empty plates, then speaks, his voice a low rumble close to my ear. "Note to self: Laurel is trouble."

Then he does the unthinkable and shoots me a wink,

straightens, and heads to the kitchen while I try to catch my breath.

Lexi fans her face. "Damn. His sister was right."

I blink, confused. "About what?"

Lexi grins. "She told him you two could start a fire with all the sparks shooting between you."

Chapter Nineteen

After Lexi and I eat way too many sopapillas, we pay our bill—leaving Carlos a very generous tip—and stop by the restroom to wash honey off our sticky hands.

"Excellent restaurant choice," Lexi says as she applies lip gloss. "Delicious food." She winks at me in the mirror. "And a hot waiter. Definitely worth a repeat experience."

I scrub a rough paper towel over my damp hands. It was a stressful meal, but it was also fun, when I wasn't freaking out about Carlos. A stall door opens and to my horror Rose emerges, a smug grin splitting her cherry-red lips. She moves to the sink and washes her hands, her eyes meeting mine in the mirror.

"So I'm guessing you're the one who called this morning to ask if Carlos was working today."

I glance at her reflection then watch my own reflection turn pink as I realize she's the one who answered the phone. And lied.

"Uh, yeah."

She straightens and nods, then yanks a paper towel from

the dispenser. "I figured." She glances over her shoulder at me and smiles. "Sorry for the little white lie, but I was curious to check out Carlos's latest stalker." She turns and crosses her arms over her chest as I wish for the floor to swallow me up. "Also, I love to torture my little brother."

"So he has a lot of stalkers?" Lexi asks. I want to mute her.

Rose snorts. "Since he was about twelve years old. I thought my mom was going to put bars on the windows when he was in high school, so many girls were always coming by the house." She shakes her head, smiling.

"Wow." Lexi's hip bumps mine none too subtly. "So does he have a girlfriend?"

Rose's expression is wary as she looks from Lexi to me and back to Lexi. "Who wants to know?"

"No one," I say at the same time Lexi says, "Everyone."

"I don't think so, but he tries to keep that part of his life private, which is tough in a big family like ours." Her gaze settles on me. "He's obsessed with that internship. He's always doing research at home on the computer, and he goes to the library or the coffee shop to work when the house gets too noisy." She lifts an eyebrow. "Though maybe he's meeting a girl, who knows?"

"It's really none of our business if he has a girlfriend." I glare at Lexi, then force myself to resume eye contact with Rose, whose expression softens like she approves of my response.

"So if you win the scholarship, where do you want to go to college?" she asks, jolting me with the reminder that she thinks I'm Ashley.

"Oh, I, um, I'm not competing." I clear my throat. "Emergent is my dad's company. I'm just working there this summer. Assisting the interns." I should get a scarlet *A* for assistant on all my shirts.

Rose's dark eyes widen, and her pretty lips form an *O*. "So you're…" She hesitates, like she's holding something back. "You're the girl he beat at foosball?"

He told her about that? "I thought you said he keeps his personal life private."

"He does, mostly. But I'm good at cracking him open." The new intensity in her eyes reminds me of her brother. "He felt so bad that day. He said you almost won the game. You beat some Neanderthal dude, right?"

Note to self: Carlos is a blabbermouth when interrogated by his big sister.

"Yeah, but it was no big deal. That Carlos won, I mean." I shrug. "He's good. And now he has a cheesy trophy for his collection." I smile, hoping it looks casual and not panicky, because I desperately need to get out of this tiny space and breathe.

"He put it with all his soccer trophies." Rose grins. "Sounds like you have a lot of fun at your dad's company. It's cool working with your family, isn't it? I love working with mine, even when they drive me crazy." She wipes her hands on her waitress apron. "Speaking of working, I need to get back out there before my mom yells at me." She grins and opens the door, waving at us over her shoulder.

Lexi and I stay put until the door closes, then we both exhale.

"Wow. So she's the direct pipeline to Carlos data." Lexi points at me. "You need to mind meld with her."

"Absolutely not." I like Rose, but she's a bit intimidating. She's gorgeous like her brother, and funny, and not at all shy. And clearly protective of Carlos. Kind of like my own big sister, now that I think about it.

Lexi reaches for the door handle. "So do I really have to wait around while you take pictures?"

"Yeah, you really do." Unless Carlos has changed his mind. But when we emerge into the restaurant, it's clear that he hasn't.

"Why didn't you warn me?" Rose rushes past us. "I need more lipstick, and I don't want to pose in this horrible uniform but I..." Her voice fades as she rushes back into the bathroom.

Carlos gestures us to the hostess stand, where his mom and several people have gathered.

Lexi trails behind me, and suddenly I'm face-to-face with what I assume is the Rubio clan, or at least most of them.

"Mom, this is Laurel Kristoff," Carlos says formally. "Her dad owns the company where I'm interning."

Mrs. Rubio's face lights up as she steps forward and grasps my hands. "So nice to meet you, Laurel. Carlos loves that job. He was so happy to get it."

Carlos grimaces, clearly embarrassed.

"This is my Uncle Javier." He nods to the older man who served our drinks earlier. "And these are my cousins Samson and Denise." I recognize the busboy from earlier, and Denise wears a white chef's coat.

Everyone talks at once, reaching out to shake hands, and I'm a bit overwhelmed by the warmth everyone exudes. His family is just like I hoped they'd be when I studied their website photos.

"This is my friend, Lexi," I say, realizing she's still hanging back.

"*Encantada*, Lexi." Mrs. Rubio's easy smile encompasses both of us, then she turns away to answer the phone.

Encantada...like the restaurant name, Encantado?

"It means 'delighted to meet you,'" Lexi clarifies. "If Carlos said it to you, he'd say '*encantado*,' since he's a guy." She waggles her eyebrows.

Showoff, I think, but secretly I'm pleased. Lexi takes

Spanish. I take French, which Lexi says is pretentious. At this moment, I wish I could borrow her language brain.

"Carlos! Carlos!" Two tiny bodies burst through the front door and launch themselves at his legs, wrapping around him like barnacles. It's the girls from the church bench photo. Today they're dressed in shorts and T-shirts instead of frilly white dresses, but the adoration in their eyes is the same as in the photo.

He groans as he detaches them from his legs. "You two are gonna kill me someday, you know that?" The girls giggle, then run to the gumball machine, arguing over who gets to put her quarter in first.

A tall, lanky man wearing a cowboy hat follows the girls into the restaurant. I take one look at his smile and know it's Carlos's dad. Nothing like meeting your secret crush's entire family all at once.

"What's going on? Family meeting I wasn't invited to?" Mr. Rubio's voice is deep and authoritative, but a familiar twinkle glints in his dark eyes.

"Yeah, we just voted to close early on Saturdays." Carlos grins at his dad. "So, I don't know about the rest of you, but I'm outta here."

Mr. Rubio laughs, deep and rumbly, and then he notices Lexi and me.

"Hello." He glances curiously at his wife, but before she can speak, Carlos does.

"Dad, this is Laurel Kristoff. Her dad runs the company where I'm interning. And this is her friend Lexi."

I hold out my hand, pretending I'm Princess Leia meeting a royal ambassador. "It's so nice to meet you, Mr. Rubio. My dad is so pleased to have Carlos working for him this summer." Dad Vader would be so proud.

"The pleasure is mine, Miss Kristoff." Mr. Rubio shakes

my hand and grins, dimpling like his son. Among them, the Rubios hoard a ridiculous number of dimples. I can hardly wait to start taking photos.

"Hi." Lexi lets her hand be gripped by Mr. Rubio next and giggles nervously.

"Laurel's working on a new website design for us," Carlos says casually, like he didn't just find out about it twenty minutes ago. "She came by to take photos of the restaurant. And of us."

"Is that right?" Mr. Rubio cocks an eyebrow.

I nod, telling myself to exude confidence instead of panic.

"God, I can't believe this!" Rose joins us, wearing fresh lipstick and mascara, her dark curls shiny and perfect. "There's a coffee stain on my shirt. Can't I just put on civilian clothes for this picture?"

To my surprise, Carlos and his mom look to me for an answer.

"Uh…sure. Everyone doesn't have to be in uniform." I glance at Mr. Rubio, who's dressed in a plaid western shirt, dark jeans, and cowboy boots.

"Oh, thank God. I'll be right back." Rose rushes off again, and the little girls run toward us laughing, each clutching a small plastic cube. I smile at them, remembering how I used to love those prize machines, especially when they spewed out cheap, shiny jewelry.

"I got a ring!" squeals the girl wearing a yellow T-shirt.

"Mine's prettier." The girl in a blue shirt beams up at me. "Who are you?"

"Marisa, that's not how you introduce yourself to someone." Carlos shoots me an apologetic smile. "This is my friend Laurel. We work together at my other job. And this is her friend Lexi." He puts a hand on each girl's head. "These are my sisters, Marisa and Teresa."

Marisa studies me, her smile giving way to a serious assessment. "Are you Carlos's new girlfriend? Because I know he likes someone. I heard him talking to Rose—"

"Marisa, that's enough." Carlos's voice is sharp as he glowers at his little sister.

My fizzy excitement about meeting the Rubios evaporates, but I pretend like I don't care if he has a harem of girlfriends.

"So where should we pose?" Carlos asks.

"Let's take some outside first." I glance toward the full restaurant. "Are you sure you have time? It's so busy right now." I bite my lip. This isn't the most professional way to handle this. I should have planned ahead—made an appointment and scheduled this during a slow time.

"We're always busy, unless we're closed," Mr. Rubio says with a proud grin. "Besides, our customers will understand." He takes a few steps into the restaurant and claps his hands for attention. "*Amigos!* We're going to spend a few minutes outside taking family photographs." He glances at Carlos and I catch a glimpse of the Rubio smirk I've come to know quite well.

"Apparently we're updating our website and need new photos. We want to show what it looks like on a busy day here at Encantado." He doffs his cowboy hat and bows. "Thanks for your patience. Drinks are on the house as soon as we're done."

A few appreciative hoots and applause sound from the barstools and Mr. Rubio grins. I, on the other hand, am mortified. Now they have to give away free stuff because of me? Ugh. I sneak a peek at Carlos, who's watching his dad the same way he watches my dad—like he's taking mental notes.

"It's okay," Lexi whispers in my ear. "You got this."

Mr. Rubio turns to me and gestures to the door. "We're

in your hands, Miss Kristoff." He and his wife walk outside together, holding hands like newlyweds. I wish I'd had my camera ready for that.

Carlos's little sisters paw at him like eager puppies as they head outside. Rose hurries up to Lexi and me, wearing a beautiful red blouse that complements her dark hair and eyes.

"How do I look?"

"Beautiful," I tell her. "Your whole family is beautiful." As soon as the words pop out, heat floods my cheeks. I hope Carlos didn't hear me. The gleam in Rose's eyes tells me she knows exactly what I meant.

Taking a breath, I push through the door into the bright sunshine, hoping I can pull off my crazy scheme to win over Carlos. Not in a romantic way, in a professional way.

I'm such a liar.

The Rubios are perfect models. They laugh and joke and mug for the camera. I take bursts of photos, close-ups and wide angles, anxiously aware of the customers waiting inside.

"Okay, everyone back to work." I point to the restaurant and Mr. Rubio gives me a thumbs-up. "I'll take more photos of you and your customers inside. And maybe a few in the kitchen?"

"Great idea." Carlos steers his little sisters back inside, but not before tossing me a bone-melting grin over his shoulder.

"Are you dying inside?" Lexi whispers as we wait for everyone else to go inside. "Because I'm dying for you. He's amazing. I refuse to believe he has a girlfriend or that he likes Ashley when he smiles at you like that. What do his sisters know, anyway?"

"It doesn't matter. What matters is taking these photos, then finishing the website." I hold the door for her. "I'm not destined for a summer fling, Lex. It's just not meant to be."

• • •

*A*n hour later, I've photographed everyone in the restaurant, including the Rubios at work and customers enjoying their meals. I hope to use some of those photos for the "first bite" collage I suggested to Carlos. I've got a memory card full of photos and can't wait to get home and start editing them.

"You girls come back and see us again, soon, okay?" Mrs. Rubio squeezes my hands in hers when I say goodbye.

"We will." I hope it's not a white lie. I'd love to come back.

Mrs. Rubio releases my hands. Lexi and I are almost out the door when a voice stops me in my tracks.

"Laurel, wait up."

Carlos. He's removed his apron and if I'm not mistaken, he's combed his hair, something he didn't bother with for the photos I took. My pulse thrums.

"I'm taking a break. Rose, you've got my tables," he says to his sister, ignoring her raised eyebrows. He shifts his gaze to me. "Ready?"

Lexi jabs me in the back, so I move, following Carlos out the door. I hear giggling, then two small bodies push past me, running toward Carlos.

"Wait for us!"

Carlos turns around, eyes narrowed, and points to the door. "Go back inside."

Undeterred, they stand their ground. "Where are you going? Can we come?"

He glances at me, frustration and embarrassment in his eyes. "I'm going for a walk, and no you can't come." The girls pivot to Lexi and me.

"So you have *two* girlfriends?" asks Marisa. "Is that allowed?"

Carlos pins his sisters with a glare. "You two need to go back inside. Now."

Their tiny bodies lock into place, hands on hips, unmoved by his command.

"Uh-uh," pipes up Teresa. "We're going with you and your girlfriends."

"We're not his girlfriends," I say. "We're just friends." I feel like an idiot, clarifying our relationship status to small children.

Marisa mimics Rose's speculative assessment posture. "Carlos has lots of those. Girl friends."

My lips quirk. "So I've heard."

His eyes widen in surprise, but he recovers quickly, rewarding me with a sly grin. He puts a hand on each girl's head and marches them toward the door, their faces contorted into pouts. He releases them to yank the door open, then shoves them gently inside. "I'll see you later, troublemakers."

"Carlos has two girlfriends! Carlos has two—" He slams the door, cutting off their singsong voices as Lexi and I dissolve into giggles. He runs a hand through his hair, ruining his earlier combing efforts, a resigned smile tugging at his lips.

"This is my life," he says with a shrug, his intense brown eyes fixed on mine. "Just one thrill after another." I feel like there's a hidden meaning to his words, but I'm not sure what it is. "So you still want to take pictures of the church?"

I nod and he tilts his head toward the street. "Let's go."

The three of us fall into step together, me in between Carlos and Lexi. We've only walked half a block when Lexi pulls her phone from her pocket.

"I have to call my mom. She's texting me and freaking out, wondering where I am."

I'm about to say we can skip the photos, but when I turn to Lexi, a devious gleam sparkles in her eyes. I hope Carlos can't read her the way I can.

"You guys go on ahead. I'll catch up."

She's not subtle, but Carlos doesn't seem to realize she's faking.

"Walk three blocks," he tells her, pointing straight ahead, "then cut across the park. The church is on the other side of the park. You can't miss it."

Lexi nods and waves us on, then makes a show of putting her phone to ear. I wonder how far she's going to take her charade, and as Carlos and I resume walking I get my answer.

"God, Mom. Relax, okay? I'm just hanging out with Laurel."

I have to smash my lips together to hold in my laughter. I'm keenly aware of the tiny bit of space between Carlos and me. His arm brushes mine as we walk. More than once.

"So." He huffs the word like an exhale. "What did you think of the restaurant? And my crazy family?" He cuts me a sideways glance and I bite the inside of my lip, wondering how honest I dare to be. I don't want to scare him away with borderline stalker behavior.

"They're great." I clear my throat and focus on a riotous garden of wildflowers instead of him. The colors momentarily distract me. "Hold on for a sec."

I set my camera bag on the ground and retrieve my camera, then put all of my energy into capturing the garden in my lens. I take a few wide shots of the whole garden, then zoom in on the frail blue-and-white beauty of a single columbine. I'm dimly aware that Carlos waits patiently and quietly. I'm grateful he's not asking questions while I shoot. It's like he knows he shouldn't.

Satisfied with my shots, I lower the camera and see that Carlos has slung my bag over his shoulder. The small gesture makes my heart squeeze.

We fall into step together and I answer his question. "Your family is fantastic. Your little sisters are adorable. Rose is friendly, and funny." We glance at each other and I wonder if he's worried that she revealed secret data.

"Yeah. She's cool, but she's a pain in the butt sometimes."

I kick at a rock on the sidewalk, sending it skittering ahead of us. "I can relate. I have an older sister, too. I love her but she drives me crazy."

He chuckles softly next to me. "I guess all older sisters are a pain sometimes."

"Yeah. Like parents." I blush as I realize my faux pas. "Your parents are great. I meant mine."

"Your dad's awesome. He's built a great business."

"Yeah, I guess."

"How about your mom?" he asks. "What's she like?"

Is it normal for a guy to actually show interest in a girl's parents? It's sweet, but unexpected.

"My mom's a weird mash-up of a hippie and an entrepreneur, but I think her business savvy was cultivated by Dad."

Carlos grins. "My mom's the business genius in our family. My dad's great at working the bar and making people laugh, but Mom's the brains."

We've reached an intersection and he gestures for us to cross the street. We enter a small pocket park, lush with greenery and colorful flower beds. A playground full of laughing kids is the focal point. Parents sit on surrounding benches, chatting, sipping from to-go cups, and occasionally calling out to their kids.

"This was my favorite park when I was a kid." Carlos kicks a stray soccer ball toward an enormous pine tree. It's a powerful kick, and perfectly aimed.

I hesitate just for a second, then run after the ball, landing a solid push kick that sends the ball right under the tree. "Goal!" I throw up my hands in victory and hear Carlos's deep laughter behind me.

"Nice shot. You play soccer?" He sounds surprised, smiling as he jogs to catch up to me.

"Yeah, I play."

His gaze turns speculative. "Me, too."

"As well as you play foosball?" I challenge.

"Better." His trademark smirk appears, making my pulse flutter.

I'm not sure why I'm able to tease him right now. Maybe it's because we're not at work with the Manicotti looming over us. Maybe it's because I saw another side of him working at the restaurant and with his little sisters. Whatever the reason, I like how this feels between us—friendly with a definite side of flirty.

"That figures." I tilt my head back so I can look directly into his eyes. We're standing in the shade of the enormous tree, so I don't have to squint, and neither does he, allowing us a long moment to just…drink each other in.

"Maybe we need another rematch," he says, taking a step toward me. "On the soccer field instead of foosball."

He's standing so close that my brain short-circuits as I struggle for a clever comeback. What would Qa'hr say? I swallow as I continue staring into his eyes, then my gaze drifts down to his mouth, which is a bad idea, because if I think about kissing him, I'll never come up with a witty response. My focus shifts back to his eyes, which spark with a new intensity, and he mirrors me, his gaze darting to my mouth, then back to my eyes.

"I…uh…wouldn't want to show you up," I stammer. I don't think I'm imagining the energy crackling between us, especially when he steps even closer, leaving just inches between us.

"I think I can handle whatever you throw down, Special K." His voice is low and threaded with a husky undertone that makes my legs wobble. He reaches out to tuck a strand of my hair behind my ear and I shiver as his fingers brush my skin.

"I'm about to make a bad decision, Laurel. Or maybe a good one." His Hershey's Special Dark eyes are riveted on mine. "I'm about to break a rule."

"Rule number eight?" My heart stutters like an engine that can't decide whether to start or stall.

He grasps my waist, pulling me in close. His hands feel like fire, burning through my thin cotton shirt. "I'm not a fan of arbitrary rules," he says, his voice even lower, "and we're not on the clock."

My body arches toward him like a sunflower reaching for the sun, but I have to ask a question. "B-but don't you have a girlfriend?"

His eyebrows dip in a V over his nose. "No. Do you really think I'd...oh...my little sisters." He rolls his eyes skyward. "They watch too many princess movies and think I'm, uh, dating every girl they meet."

"What about Ashley?" I don't want to ask, but I have to. As much as I want this kiss, if he's a player, I'm out of here.

"What?" He blinks, a quizzical expression transforming his expression.

"I, uh, thought..." I shrug helplessly, afraid I just killed our moment.

Smiling down at me, he shakes his head. "Nope. There's only one girl at Emergent who distracts me." His gaze locks on mine. "I'm not seeing anyone. Not interested in Ashley. But I'm keeping my options open. One option in particular."

Holy wow. With courage I didn't know I had, I place a hand on his chest, feeling him suck in a breath. "Are you sure you want to kiss the boss's daughter? I hear that's a firing offense."

Oh crap, why'd I say that? Now all I can think of is rule number eight and him being disqualified and—

"I'm willing to risk it." His voice is rough as he pulls me even closer. "I've wanted to kiss the boss's daughter since the first day I met her."

The heat we're generating swirls all the way to my toes. If he weren't holding me, I might collapse from shock. And happiness. And kissing him here doesn't count as a rule violation, does it? We're not at work. No one from Emergent will see us.

My body buzzes and crackles like an electrical current. His heart beats through the fabric of his shirt against the palm of my hand. My other hand tentatively makes its way up to his hair, my fingers hesitant at first, then plunging in fearlessly. The strands are silky smooth and messy and...perfect.

"You're going to be a lot more trouble than I thought you'd be, Special K." Carlos's voice drops a whole octave.

"I'm not troub—" But I don't get to argue because his lips are finally, *finally* on mine.

And it's fantastic.

Our bodies meld together—curves and muscle, heat and desperation—like this is our only chance to steal a kiss and we both want to make it count. Carlos kisses with the same confident intensity he uses at work, taking charge like a kickass Rebel pilot. His hands move from my waist, sliding up my back, to my neck, cupping my face briefly, and then his fingers are in my hair, tugging gently at first, then with more urgency. His mouth is hot and demanding, and I do my best to match his urgent pace.

"Hey, Carlos! That's my soccer ball."

Startled, I start to pull away, but Carlos keeps a hand

locked on my waist as he turns and kicks the ball out of the tree's shadow. A young boy stops it with his foot and waves at us.

"Kids," Carlos mutters. "Why are they everywhere?"

I should crack a joke, or if I was brave, pull him into another kiss, but now I'm in shock.

Carlos kissed me.

Expertly. Thoroughly. Who knows how long we would have kept it up if it weren't for that kid? My legs are jelly and my pulse pounds in my ear like an erratic drumbeat.

"Y-you probably should go back to work."

Carlos cocks an eyebrow. "You're kicking me to the curb already? Guess I need to work on my technique."

"I...that's not...you don't...your technique is, uh, fine... better than fine..." Babbling is my new superpower, which is a shame, because I'd much prefer invisibility at this moment.

"I do need to get back to work. Rose is gonna kill me." He grins down at me. "Totally worth it, though."

All I can do is nod.

"You still want pictures of the church?"

I nod again, like an idiot.

"Come on." He takes my hand in his and we cut diagonally across the park until we're standing in front of a beautiful old church made of red sandstone.

"Wish I could stay, but I've gotta get back." He squeezes my hand.

"I understand. I'll, um, see you later."

He gives me one last high-voltage grin, then releases my hand and jogs across the park. He sneaks up on the kid who interrupted our kissing session and kicks the ball out from under him, making me laugh.

Lexi's at the church already, and she pumps me for details as I take photos. It almost feels sacrilegious talking about kissing while I take photos of a church, but I tell her everything.

"Wow," she breathes. "He must have amazing skills."

"Not that I have a lot of experience, but yeah…amazing."

When we return to my car, a paper flutters under the windshield wiper. Slanted cursive scrawls across a page torn from a restaurant order pad.

"Special K—thanks for stopping by with your friend. Hope you got great photos of St. Pete's. Call me if you want a rematch. Maybe with fireworks? — C." Followed by ten digits.

I read the note several times. Is he referring to Fourth of July fireworks or kissing fireworks? My finger traces the *C* like I'm a pining heroine in an old novel who just received a love letter.

Lexi reaches out and takes the paper, scanning it quickly. She huffs out a small laugh. "This, my friend, is flirting. Expert level. Put it in your scrapbook for when you're old and gray. But call him first."

"Shut up." I unlock the car and she sticks her tongue out like one of Carlos's young sisters, making me laugh.

Carefully, I fold the note and tuck it into a zippered pouch of my camera bag. I'm not putting the note in a scrapbook, but I'm definitely not throwing it away, either.

As for a rematch, I'm not sure my heart can handle it.

Chapter Twenty

I don't text Carlos over the long holiday weekend. However, I do put his number in my phone's contact list, code name Poe from *The Force Awakens*. And I *think* about texting him, a lot. But I never actually do it because I spend the weekend worrying about him being disqualified for "fraternizing."

As Dad and I pull into the parking garage, I send up a quick prayer that Carlos arrives late so we don't have our usual morning "alone time" up in the sky box. Instead, Carlos is waiting for the elevator when my dad and I push through the steel doors. My heart beats so loudly I wonder if he can hear it; no way can I make eye contact.

"Good morning, Mr. K," Carlos says to my dad. He glances at me, but I keep my focus on the elevator doors.

"Good morning, Carlos."

I'm secretly pleased Dad remembers who Carlos is. Technically he should know all of the interns by name, but he is the big kahuna, after all, with more important things on his mind, like who's trying to destroy Emergent on social media.

Today I'm supposed to meet Jiang for lunch, and I hope

to pump her for info. She and Brian planned to spend the weekend digging deep, hoping to find a trail of breadcrumbs leading to the jerk. My money's still on Lewis.

When the elevator doors slide open, I move to a corner and so does Carlos, parking himself next to me, which is both horrifying and thrilling.

"Hi, Laurel," he says, and now I'm stuck.

"Hi." I barely glance at him but my whole body amps up, every sense hyper-aware of him.

Dad leans against the opposite wall of the elevator and studies us. "Did you have a good weekend, Carlos?"

My eyes narrow suspiciously. It's this type of random yet pointed inquiry that makes me suspect he truly has Darth Vader spying abilities, even though his expression is bland. I don't dare look at Carlos, whose arm brushes mine as he raises it to run a hand through his hair.

"Yeah, it was great." I hear the grin in his voice. "Full of surprises."

My face flames as I stare at the numbers above the elevator doors, willing us to speed up. Dad glances down at his phone and his shoulders tense.

Uh-oh. Has @PRTruth struck again? The elevator dings as we reach the first floor of Emergent and Dad steps out, so distracted by whatever is on his phone he doesn't say goodbye. The doors slide closed, leaving Carlos and me alone together in the metal box. I sneak a glance at the chocolate eyes, which look especially melty today.

Carlos clears his throat. "So. We should talk about what happened on Saturday."

Since when do guys want to talk? Oh wait, that's what this is—the sorry-if-you-got-the-wrong-idea-it-was-just-a-kiss speech.

"We don't have to talk. It was no big deal." Each word

rips out a piece of my heart, but it's for the best. I won't be the reason he loses his shot at the money.

"You're a lousy liar, Special K." His gaze narrows. "Why didn't you text me?"

"I—uh—don't know."

"Look, if you're not interested just be straight up and tell me, okay?" There's a surprising hint of defensiveness in his voice.

Not interested? *Not interested?*

The elevator doors slide open to reveal Trish, arms crossed over her chest, who studies us suspiciously. "Did I interrupt something?"

"Nope." Carlos adjusts his backpack strap and stalks away, leaving me alone with Trish.

"What'd you do to piss off your Boy Scout, princess?"

I stare after Carlos, wishing I were brave enough to call after him. "I'm an idiot," I mutter under my breath.

"Agreed." Trish steps into the elevator as I exit. "You want a donut?"

I blink, surprised by her offer. "Okay. Chocolate. Please."

She nods, and right before the doors close she flashes me a sympathetic half smile.

I spend the morning on to-do tasks for Elijah and Ashley, then sit with Jason to show him a few basics of Photoshop. He struggles to keep up. Dark circles shadow his eyes and he can't stop yawning.

"Big party weekend?" I ask, immediately regretting my drinking joke.

"Not for me, but my dad had a hell of a weekend." He tries to smile but fails.

Jason ducks his head, and red blotches of embarrassment bloom on his neck and cheeks…and that's when I notice the makeup. He did a good job applying it, blending it into his skin as thoroughly as a makeup salesperson at Ulta, or someone who's familiar with stage makeup. I examine it more closely and have to swallow my gasp.

I didn't just miss the makeup earlier, I missed the mottled purple and blue bruising underneath it.

Oh God. Why am I so stupid?

"I'm sorry," I whisper. "My party weekend joke was insensitive. Feel free to ignore my idiot self the rest of the summer."

He glances up, flashing a quick, shy smile. "You're not an idiot, but sometimes I think I am." He points to his computer screen. "This software stuff kills me. Sometimes I think all I'm good at is throwing footballs and cleaning up my dad's puke." He winces and darts me an apologetic look. "See what I mean? I can't even have a normal conversation."

Tentatively, I place my hand over his, which is gripping the computer mouse. "It's okay, Jason. You're dealing with a lot. I'm impressed you're here every day, with all that's going on."

His hand relaxes its death grip on the mouse, so I remove my hand from his. He blows out a long, slow breath, then turns to me.

"Thanks, Laurel. That means a lot." He pushes back his overgrown blond hair that used to captivate me. "I know I don't have a shot at the scholarship compared to everyone else, but working here is pretty cool." He flashes me another quick grin. "Except for getting locked in the basement."

It's my turn to wince. "Yeah…that stunk…except for the Pixy Stix."

Jason laughs, and the sound lifts my heart. He deserves so much more than life has dealt him.

"Let's try this again." I reach for the mouse and take him

through the basics, but slower this time. We crack dumb jokes about our practice photo of two dogs playing tug-of-war. His fatigue appears to lessen, and this time around he remembers what I show him.

A reminder pops up on his screen: "**Stockwell Suds tour in one hour.**"

"I've gotta go meet Lewis." He rubs his palms across his khakis. "Do I, um, look okay?" He stands up and straightens his tie, which must be his dad's, based on the boring pattern and faded colors.

I've always thought he looked more than okay, but I try to be objective, viewing him as Cal Stockwell might. His creamy button-down shirt is decent; he must've ironed it, which makes my heart crack a tiny bit. His khaki pants are fine. Most people won't notice the frayed edges on the pant cuffs.

He looks like who he is—a nice guy who wants to make a good impression.

"You look great." I hope my smile conveys that I mean it. I hesitate, then point to my cheek. "Maybe touch that up just a bit."

He startles like a skittish deer, then hunches his shoulders. "Okay. Thanks." He won't look me in the eye, so I stand up to face him.

"Jason, I meant what I said." I touch his shoulder, grateful he doesn't flinch. "You look great, but more important, you're a smart guy. Don't forget it."

He nods, raising his head and meeting my gaze. "Do you think it's weird, me working on a brewery project?" He chews his lip. "Since my dad is, you know?"

"No. I assume you chose it because Cal's a pro athlete who started his own business. And you're hoping someday to do the same."

He nods, relief shining in his eyes. "That's exactly why. If acting doesn't work out, and I have to play pro ball, I don't want to do it for long." He taps the side of his head and grins. "I don't have extra brain cells to lose to concussions."

"You have plenty of brain cells. Now, get going; you don't want to be late. Lewis could make your day miserable." I shoo him away, and he waves, looking much happier than earlier.

My stomach twists with worry for Jason. I wonder if I should tell someone about the bruising. But who? Eyes downcast, I make my way to my desk, sneaking a peek at Carlos.

That's a mistake, because though he sits as stiffly as a mannequin, his wounded expression looks like someone just punched him in the gut.

And I'm afraid that someone is me.

I'd do anything to take away the hurt in Carlos's eyes. I'm worried he took my elevator silence as a rejection, and that he misinterpreted my interactions with Jason. As much as I want a chance with him once this internship ends, maybe it's not in the cards.

Frustrated, I shift my energy to the Rubios' website. I worked on it over the weekend, tweaking the photos and putting them into a new website template. Even though my stomach twists every time I glance at Carlos at his desk, I still want to do this for him, and for his family.

After a few font changes, I decide it's ready for feedback. I take a breath and email the test site link to Trish, putting "Boy Scout" in the subject line. I know she'll be honest and for whatever reason, I'm starting to trust her.

A few minutes later my inbox pings with a new message.

"It pains me to admit you do have a brain, princess. Good

work. Send it to the Boy Scout."

I glance at Trish, whose lips twist in a grudging smile. She tilts her head toward Carlos, whose brow is furrowed as he hunches over his computer. She's right, of course. The final say is up to him and even if he hates it, and me, maybe the website will drive more people to Encantado.

I glance at the *Star Wars* figures on my desk. "May the Force be with us," I whisper, touching Leia's head for luck. Holding my breath, I email the test site link to Carlos, then grab my camera bag, eager to escape for lunch.

In the lobby, I approach Miss Emmaline's desk, since I was thrown off my morning joke routine by my elevator ride with Carlos.

"Hi, Miss Emmaline."

She folds her hands on her desk and waits.

"Why did the skeleton go to the party by himself?"

She responds with one slow blink.

"He had no body to go with him."

A single silver eyebrow arches, but she says nothing. Somehow our familiar, stubborn exchange puts me in better spirits.

"One of these days you're going to crack, Miss Emmaline. I can feel it."

Once outside, the hour speeds by. There's a baseball game today, so I take tons of photos of fans—families decked out in Colorado Rockies gear, a group of loud guys wearing San Diego Padres T-shirts engaging in friendly heckling with Rockies fans, and street vendors selling burritos and bottled water outside the stadium. It's a glorious afternoon and I hope my pictures capture the crackling energy. On a whim, I buy my dad a Rockies bobblehead figure from a street vendor.

Back at work, I stop by Dad's office, but Ms. Romero tells me he's out to lunch with a client. I put the bobblehead on his desk with a note, drawing an *X* and *O*, and a Vader helmet.

Upstairs, everyone is back at work except Jason, who's at the brewery, and Elijah, who is daringly breaking the one-hour lunch rule. More power to him.

When I sit, I sneak a glance at Carlos, who's watching me like he's trying just as hard to figure me out as I am him. He stands up and strides purposefully across the room. He presents me with a battered book with a sun-faded cover. *Cornball Jokes to Annoy Your Friends, Volume Two.*

"There's more than one volume?" I'm proud of myself for joking, because I was sure he'd never speak to me again after this morning. I can't believe he brought me a gift—a super dorky one, yet something that's specific to me.

Carlos grins. "Four, actually. I thought this might help you with Miss Emmaline."

We stare at each other, and I feel the energy crackling between us again. I wonder if he's giving me another chance, but how do I just blurt out that *of course* I'm freaking interested in him; we just have to wait four more weeks until the internship is over.

I open the joke book to a random page. "Why does the seagull fly over the sea?"

He shrugs, but the way he's smiling at me is so distracting I have to look at the book again for the punchline.

"Because if it flew over the bay, it would be a bay-gull."

Carlos groans, but his flirty smile doesn't waver.

"Thanks for this." I close the book. "I'll try out the seagull joke tomorrow."

Carlos nods and pushes a lock of hair out of his eyes. His eyelashes are stupidly long for a guy and I wish he'd stop blinking them so wantonly, like a Hershey's Kisses eye slut.

"So." He perches on the edge of my desk. "I checked out the website link."

I reach out to clutch my Princess Leia figure for luck.

"It's great." He picks up my Chewbacca figure and rolls him between his palms.

"So you like it?" My eyes dart to Chewie. He's been in my collection since I was eight years old and I don't want him damaged.

"I do. So does my dad—I sent him the link while you were at lunch. Rose loves it. Just need to see what my mom says. She's the boss." He flashes both dimples, and I almost forget about Chewie. Almost.

I hold out my hand and clear my throat. "Could you, um, please give me Chewbacca?"

Carlos blinks like he's not quite sure he heard right, then hands him over. I breathe a tiny sigh of relief and return Chewie to his place of honor. I have my priorities, after all, one of which is keeping the holy trinity together. I glance at Carlos, wondering if he's sorry he kissed such a dork.

"So, uh, how'd it go with Jason this morning?" Carlos is still perched on my desk, and I get the feeling he's not leaving until he knows where he stands with me, which puts me in a painfully awkward situation.

"Good. I showed him some Photoshop tips."

Carlos waits for me to say more, using his hypnotic eyes to break through my flimsy barricade. Unable to resist, I babble like a prisoner bartering secret intel for freedom.

"He had a rough weekend, so he was tired. He was worried about touring the brewery with Lewis, and making a good impression on Cal Stockwell, and he doesn't want to lose any brain cells to concussions, and he's a great guy, you know? But he's stuck in a horrible situation with his dad and he doesn't deserve it and…"

I run out of steam, but I hope Carlos got the unspoken message underneath my babbling. I grasp my tiny Han Solo, squeezing him as if he can somehow send me some of his cocky bravado.

Frowning, Carlos crosses his arms over his chest. His someday-I'll-be-a-lawyer persona analyzes my words.

"Rough weekend." His voice is clipped, his eyes frosty. "As in he partied too hard?"

"No," I snap. Carlos has no business judging Jason. "As in his *dad* partied too hard and Jason had to deal with the fallout." I hope my eyes are as frosty as his.

Carlos reels like I've slapped him. He drops his gaze and is quiet for an uncomfortably long moment. When he finally looks up, the frostiness is gone.

"You cheered him up." Carlos states this as a fact. "Gave him a shot of confidence before he went to the brewery."

My defensiveness cracks. "I hope so. He needs all the support he can get."

Carlos ducks his head, dark hair falling across his forehead. I'm not going to tell him any more about the situation. Maybe I should be flattered he was jealous, but what I want is for him to be kind to Jason.

The awkward silence between us stretches like a rubber band about to snap, but we're saved by Elijah, who slides into the room like somebody cued him for a rescue.

"Dudes!"

Carlos looks as grateful as I am for our one-man distraction.

Elijah turns his manic energy on me. "Special K, is your costume ready? Comic Con is almost here. Wait 'til you see this." He yanks his phone from his back pocket. "Prepare to be amazed."

He hands the phone to me, and yes, I am amazed. He's wearing a complete Star-Lord getup from *Guardians of the Galaxy*, including the long duster coat and leather boots. And a vintage Sony Walkman exactly like the one in the movie.

"Where'd you get that?" I ask, excitement pitching my voice higher. "Not Target."

"I know, right?" Elijah shakes his head in disgust. "Those toys are for kids." A proud grin stretches across his face. "My mom insisted I keep some of my paycheck for me this time, so I bought it on eBay."

He's so excited about the Walkman, I don't think he realizes he revealed that he's giving up his salary to help his family. Carlos and I share a meaningful look, and my insides go gooey at the warmth and compassion in those chocolate eyes. If only he'd show Jason the same.

"Well?" Elijah prompts. "Say something, Special K."

I stand up in an effort to match Elijah's enthusiasm. "You're right—it's amazing." I grin. "So's your costume."

"Told you." He takes his phone from me and scrolls to another photo, this one of his girlfriend Alisha as Gamora, looking sexy in a skintight leather outfit, long dark wig, and green skin makeup.

He shows Carlos, whose eyes go wide, clearly appreciating the costume. "Who's she supposed to be?"

Elijah and I share an appalled look, and Carlos sighs. "I bet if I showed you a picture of Kaká you wouldn't recognize him."

"Brazilian soccer star," I say. Carlos grins appreciatively.

"Whatever." Elijah points to his phone. "Dude, don't you go to the movies? How can you not recognize her? And my costume?"

"I'm more of a John Wick guy."

"Star-Lord's like the John Wick of the galaxy," Elijah tells Carlos. "I can't believe you haven't seen *Guardians*."

"I don't think I'd use a John Wick analogy. He's more of a—" I'm ready to engage in a nerd debate with Elijah, but the quizzical expression on Carlos's face stops me.

This is where the cute guy finally realizes what a super nerd I am and wonders why he ever kissed me. I've been here before, at the Winter Dance when my date walked away from me and never looked back after I geeked out about a graphic novel.

"Wait," Carlos says. "Is that the movie with the talking tree?"

Elijah rolls his eyes. "Groot. And he's not a tree. He's an extraterrestrial badass who *looks* like a tree. He can regenerate over and over."

"Okay, okay." Carlos laughs, but not in a mean way. "So maybe my sci-fi knowledge is lacking. But a guy can learn, right?" He glances at me and all I can do is nod. I'm still absorbing the fact that he hasn't walked away.

"It's possible to learn, with the right teacher." Elijah side-eyes me, eyes glinting. "Like Laurel, for instance."

I start to protest, but Elijah's faster. "Is your costume ready, Special K?"

Carlos's interest level perks up considerably. No way am I showing them the picture of me in my Qa'hr outfit. I'm worried it's too sexy, by my standards, but Lexi insists it's not.

"Yeah," I say reluctantly. "It's ready."

"And?" Elijah's eyebrows raise expectantly.

"And it's ready." My cheeks flush and I wish someone else would interrupt us. Even the Manicotti would be welcome right now.

"What's your costume?" Carlos asks, a flash of something bright and intrigued in those dark eyes.

I hope he's not wondering if I'm going to look as hot as Elijah's girlfriend, because that's impossible. Or maybe he's wondering if I'm going as something esoteric and unwieldy, like the Tardis on rolling wheels. Then again, he's never been to Comic Con so he has no idea of the possibilities.

"It's a character from a book series," I tell them.

"Huh." Carlos frowns. "So how do you know how she dresses?"

Elijah shakes his head in mock disgust. "This Padawan has so much to learn."

"We all start somewhere." I smile shyly at Carlos. "I'm lucky these books have fantastic covers and a few interior illustrations, so that's my reference." I hesitate. "Plus, fan art can be really inspiring."

"So people will recognize a character from a book? Even if it hasn't been made into a movie?" He sounds genuinely curious.

"Fans of the books will. It's sort of like a secret club."

"With a secret handshake." Carlos grins. "That's cool."

"You don't think it's stupid?"

"My little brother spends half his life in costume. I don't think he's stupid."

Elijah puts up a hand. "Whoa. Cosplay is not childish. It's serious business." He darts me an amused glance. "Want me to kick his butt? I'm sure it's breaking one of Mantoni's rules, but whatever."

"I didn't mean it as an insult." Carlos glances anxiously between us. "I'm trying to…I just…crap. Never mind. I'll just say the wrong thing again." He tugs at his hair, clearly frustrated.

"It's okay," Elijah says like he's granting a huge favor. "You're a noob nerd. You're allowed stupid statements—one per day." He turns to me. "So are you gonna tell us which book?"

"Nope." No way. They'll both Google it and once they see Qa'hr, I'll be way too self-conscious.

Qa'hr isn't bursting out of her clothes like some comic book females, but her battle-worn pants are shredded, revealing some skin, and she does rock killer thigh-high boots. Her silvery shirt is a sleeveless turtleneck with a cut-out infinity symbol over each shoulder. The best part is her weaponry, a selection of awesome knives, but since Denver Comic Con has a strict policy about weapons, I'm going to skip those.

"I bet I'll know it when I see it." Elijah's grin is smug.

"I'll be impressed if you do."

"Can I still get tickets?" Carlos asks. "For my brother. And I'd have to bring him, since he's only ten."

My stomach hits the floor. Carlos at the con? I don't know if I can handle my worlds colliding like that. "It's sold out." This isn't a lie—it sells out early every year.

Carlos's hopeful smile falters.

"Check out the online ticket resellers," Elijah says, making me want to practice Qa'hr's self-defense moves on him. "I bet you can score two tickets. Might be pricey, though."

The office phone on my desk rings, making all of us jump.

"Hello? This is Laurel."

"Laurel! In my office now!" The Manicotti sounds apoplectic.

"Um, okay. I'll be right down." I grab my Hello Kitty notebook. "Duty calls."

"I could hear him screaming all the way over here." Carlos sounds concerned.

"We got your back, Jedi. Light up the Bat-Signal if you need backup." Elijah gives me a fist-bump as I leave.

As soon as I knock on his door, Mr. Mantoni points to his guest chair.

"Close the door."

I do as he commands and perch anxiously on the edge of the chair. He spins his monitor around and points to his twitter feed.

"Look at this."

Goose bumps chill my skin. @PRTruth has struck again.

"Underage drinking by paid interns? Way to go @ Emergent @KristoffRhett. Make your clients proud. @StockwellSuds."

The tweet is posted with a picture of Jason leaning against a bar drinking amber liquid from a pint glass. A slew of tweeters has already weighed in. It's just a matter of minutes before the client calls my dad.

My stomach twists as my mind whirs with questions and conspiracies. Lewis isn't in the photo, but I assume he encouraged Jason to drink. Maybe even forced him. Jason wouldn't do this voluntarily, not with his dad being an alcoholic.

Or did he think it would be rude not to have a sip, if Cal was there? But who would tweet this, and why? My whirling thoughts return again and again to Lewis.

I face the Manicotti. "I think Lewis tweeted this."

He scowls. "What if it was Jason?"

"He wouldn't," I insist. "He doesn't drink."

Mr. Mantoni's lips purse and his eyes disappear into a squint.

"It's true!" I exclaim. "I don't know what he said in his essay but—" I stop. What if Jason didn't reveal his family troubles in his essay? Maybe he only told us.

The Manicotti stabs his computer screen. "Photographic evidence, Laurel. Pictures don't lie."

"Of course they do." Doesn't he know what Photoshop can do?

My scalp tingles, sending a chill down to my neck. Wait a minute. What if—

"Maybe it was another intern." Mr. Mantoni interrupts my thoughts. "Trying to get rid of the competition?"

He's crazy. How does Trish stand it?

"But that's…I mean, how would another intern get the photo? That had to come from Lewis."

He rubs a hand over his bald head, clearly frustrated. The door bursts open and my dad stalks in, followed by Jiang and Brian, who look panicked. Dad stops short when he sees me.

"What is my daughter doing here, Tom?"

Jiang and Brian take seats at the small meeting table, darting each other nervous glances.

"I think she can help," Mr. Mantoni said. "These tweets from @PRTruth started the week the interns started." His face twists with suspicion. "Coincidence? Or clue?"

Dad Vader looks murderous. He yanks out a chair and tilts his chin toward the door.

"Time to leave, Laurel."

"I think I'll stay." I cross the office and sit next to Jiang, whose face is tight with stress.

"This is a professional meet—" Dad begins, but I cut him off.

"Dad, I need you to listen to me. There is no way Jason drank at that brewery." I stare him down. "You have to believe me." I swallow. "Please." I glance at the Manicotti. "None of the interns would do this, but maybe I can help you figure out who it is."

Dad and the Manicotti share a scowly, meaningful look full of all sorts of coded messages. I'd put my money on Dad winning this battle.

Mr. Mantoni heaves a resigned sigh. "Maybe she can check their social media. But that's all."

"We already did that," Brian says. "Nothing incriminating."

Dad taps a pen on the table. "I just got off the phone with Cal Stockwell. He's furious. He wants Lewis fired, or at least off the account." He surveys everyone at the table except me. "And he wants to know why we put an underage intern on his account."

Ouch. Maybe I should leave.

"You two figure out who's doing this." Dad orders Jiang and Brian. "Where's Katherine?"

Jiang clears her throat. "On her way to the airport, but she said she'll cancel her trip if—"

Dad waves a hand dismissively. "No. I'll call her." He stands abruptly, jarring the table and knocking over an empty water glass. "As soon as Jason and Lewis are back, send them to my office."

My stomach shrinks in on itself, imagining the upcoming storm. Dad shoots me a slightly less intense glare. "Go back to your job, Laurel, and stay out of this. It's not your problem."

He storms out, and I can practically see the black Vader cape billowing behind him. Jiang and Brian share worried looks while Mr. Mantoni tugs on his tie.

"You heard your father, Laurel," Mr. Mantoni says. "Go back to work."

He doesn't need to tell me twice.

"If you feel like something's off with any of the interns, please let us know," Jiang calls after me.

I nod at Jiang and close the door behind me, wondering how long until my dad explodes. And Jason…omigod, poor Jason. I can't let him be the victim of whoever is sabotaging my dad. If anyone should be fired, it's Lewis, I'm sure of it.

But what if my dad does fire Jason? What will his dad do to him? Panic grips me by the throat and I change course, rushing to my dad's office.

"Laurel, honey, not now." Ms. Romero stands up from her desk like she's ready to body block me.

"Sorry," I mouth, then I barge into Dad's office. He's on the phone, firing words like bullets. The look he shoots my direction has probably annihilated worthier opponents than me. But I'm not backing down.

He points to me, then the door. I shake my head and stand my ground.

"Katherine, give me a minute." He presses the mute button on his phone and glares at me. "Laurel, I know you have feelings for this boy, but you cannot—"

"No, I don't," I interrupt. "Not the way you think." I approach his desk, my hands twisting nervously. "Dad, I'm begging you to listen to me. Jason does. Not. Drink. I know it."

"Every teenager tries booze, Laurel. I'm not an idiot," He scrubs a hand down his face. "This is partly my fault, putting him in a situation where beer is flowing and he's surrounded by athletes he admires. I should've known   "

"Dad, listen to me! Jason doesn't drink because his dad does. Way too much." I silently beg Jason for forgiveness as I reveal his secret. "Look at his face." My voice is a ragged whisper. "Look at the shadows under his eyes. Look at the bruise on his cheek he tried to hide with makeup today."

My dad's flinty gray eyes blink rapidly, anger quickly replaced by shock. He presses the button on his phone. "Katherine, I'll have to call you back." He lowers the phone to the cradle and folds his hands on his desk.

"Tell me what you know, Laurel Anne."

Chapter Twenty-One

*T*witter was a nightmare last night, with people tearing into my dad and Stockwell Suds for "endorsing" teenage drinking. Emergent issued a press release early this morning apologizing for the incident, and so did Cal Stockwell, on behalf of his brewery. Dad drove in early today and I took the light rail, which was just as well. I couldn't handle his Vader energy for a long car ride.

I begged Dad to tell me if he fired Jason, but his lips were sealed. I'd desperately wanted to text or call Trish last night, but I don't have her number. After today, I will.

As I make my espresso in the Emergent kitchen, I overhear whispered rumors that Stockwell Suds fired Emergent. If that's true, Dad Vader will probably destroy an entire galaxy. I hope his wrath spares Jason. It better, after what I told him yesterday.

Dad had listened to me, then quietly but firmly told me to take the rest of the day off. I hadn't argued. I'd spent the late afternoon at the historic Union Station taking photos, then Lexi picked me up on her way home from the water park.

I don't bother to tell Miss Emmaline a joke. I cross the lobby to the elevator, my hot coffee cup warming my cold hand. I didn't sleep well last night, between my worries about Dad and him storming around yelling into his cell. Mom and I went for a late-night swim, hoping he'd calm down, but he was still fuming when we returned.

Kendra and I talked late into the night. She listened and consoled me, and told me Dad would do the right thing.

"He always does," she said.

I hope my sister is right.

The elevator doors open to reveal Brian and Carlos standing in opposite corners. Brian's face is drawn tight with stress, and he's droopy with fatigue. I assume he was on the receiving end of Dad's ranting last night. Carlos graces me with a chin lift but doesn't say anything. As the doors close I stare at our mirrored reflections. Maybe Brian is mad at all the interns now—guilt by association.

Brian exits on the second floor, and it's just Carlos and me for the quick ride to the third floor. I'm a tangled mess of worries—about Dad, about Jason, about Emergent's reputation.

"We still haven't talked about what happened at the park," Carlos says softly. "And you still haven't texted me."

I take a deep breath. "I almost did. Does that count?"

He smiles down at me. "A guy's gotta know where he stands, Special K. Almost doesn't count."

Holy wow… My body feels like somebody set a match to it. I wish we could sneak up to the rooftop and pick up where we left off at the park. But as much as I want to tell Carlos exactly where he stands, and ask him to wait just a few more weeks, my worries tamp down my giddiness.

"What happened?" Carlos asks, his voice sharp.

My head jerks up. "What do you mean?"

His gaze is penetrating, assessing. How can he know stuff just by looking at me?

"Something's wrong. I can tell." His hand tightens on the strap of his backpack and his eyebrows dip over his nose. "Brian acted like I spit on his grandma and you look like you want to be anywhere but here."

"You sure you don't want to be a journalist? Or maybe a detective?"

The elevator doors open and we step out, but Carlos puts a hand on my arm to stop me. "Tell me." He drops his hand and clears his throat. "Please."

"It's easier to show you." I pull my phone from my bag and scroll through Twitter, trying not to think about how warm his hand felt on my skin, like the sheer fabric of my peasant blouse wasn't even there.

"Here." I hand him my phone. No sense hiding it; everyone will know soon enough.

The Hershey's eyes widen in shock as he scrolls the tweets. He looks up, clearly appalled. "Is this for real?"

What can I say? I nod, and he turns his attention back to my phone, fingers flying across the screen. His panicked expression amps up my own anxiety.

"This is bad," he whispers. "Really bad."

"I know."

We've moved to a corner of the hallway without me even realizing it. In any other circumstances, I'd find our proximity thrilling, but I can't let myself get distracted.

"Your dad must be furious." Carlos returns my phone and I tuck it in my bag.

"I didn't ride to work with him this morning, thank goodness. His car probably left a trail of fire on the highway."

Carlos's lips twitch briefly, then compress into a tight line. I could watch his mouth for hours. God, I'm pathetic.

Emergent is in crisis mode and I'm obsessing over lips.

"So is Jason…gone?" Carlos shoves a loose strand of hair behind his ear.

"I hope not." I look into his eyes, willing him to trust me. "He didn't drink, Carlos. You know he didn't, not with the way his dad is."

His gaze locks on mine. "I hope you're right. And I hope this doesn't ruin things for the rest of us."

His response frustrates me. I wish I could reassure him this won't impact the other interns, but I can't. God only knows what the Manicotti will do. We might all be fired by lunchtime. Unless my dad believes what I told him and gives Jason a second chance.

"I don't know what's going to happen, Carlos, but I trust Jason."

In case this is the last time we're this close to each other, I reach up and squeeze his shoulder. "I'm sorry about all of this." Through the soft fabric of his shirt, a muscle flexes underneath my touch, and I let go. A heated blush colors my cheeks as his dark unreadable eyes lock on mine.

Elijah's laughter echoes in the hallway, saving us once again from an awkward silence.

"Yo, Jedi. Rubio." Elijah's ready grin is blissfully ignorant of our drama. "What's up, my Rebels? Are we storming the Death Star today or what?"

"Not so much," Carlos mutters, pushing past us.

Elijah stares after him. "What's up with Padawan?"

Should I tell Elijah? Tell all the interns? Wait for Mantoni to burst in and fire us all?

"Hey, move it, nerds," Trish says from behind us. I glance over my shoulder. Even though she sounds snarky, there's a weariness in her eyes that throws me for a loop.

Elijah and I move aside, and Trish drops her gaze as she

passes. Her dad must have been in on the screaming calls last night, too.

"Trish, wait," I call out. She stops and turns around.

"Can I talk to you for a sec?"

Elijah cocks his head. "You need backup?"

"No." I roll my eyes at him. "Don't you have a crazy raccoon to rein in, Star-Lord?"

Elijah takes the hint and leaves.

Trish tilts her head. "Let's go."

She drags me toward the same corner where Carlos and I huddled. She's wearing her spider pendant again, and an octopus-patterned blouse that reminds me of the steampunk costumes I see at Comic Con.

"I assume this is about Jason."

"Did your dad show you the tweets?"

"Yeah." She grimaces. "I know Jason's the object of your childhood affections, princess. And his home situation sucks." Her eyes dart down the hallway then back to me. "But maybe the apple didn't fall far from the tree. I hate to say it, but—"

I put up my hand. "Hold up, queen of darkness. First, how do you know he was the object of my childhood affections?"

"He said you go to school together. You voted for him to stay that first day when he was late, then spent the first week making sexy eyes at him. I'm not an idiot."

Sexy eyes? I don't even know how to do that.

Trish nods toward the sky box. "Though it's obvious you've moved on. Don't need to be a queen of darkness to figure that out."

"Okay, maybe I used to like Jason, but not anymore. And that's not the issue."

"Agreed. The real issue is whether my dad and yours totally lose their minds and fire all of us, or if we can convince them not to."

We?

"We have to prove Jason's innocence." I fill my voice with all the conviction I feel deep inside. "He's innocent, I know he is. I've been at parties with him and he never drinks." I'd thought it was sweet when I'd been in the throes of my crush, but now that I know the real reason…

"You sure about that?" Trish still doesn't look convinced.

Before I can answer, Ashley appears, gliding down the hall in a shimmery green dress that makes her look like a sixties Barbie doll. I should ask her which secondhand shops are her favorites.

Trish bobs her head at Ashley. "Morning, Marcia."

Ashley pauses. "Marcia?"

"You know, like *The Brady Bunch*. 'Marcia, Marcia, Marcia.'"

Ashley's expression clears and she laughs. "Oh right I haven't heard that one in a while." She shifts her leather portfolio bag on her shoulder. "Are we having a secret girls-only meeting?"

"No. We're having a secret Trish and Laurel meeting." Trish gestures toward the office. "Catch you later, blondie."

Ashley frowns, but she leaves us in peace.

"That was mean." I hate to see Trish backslide to bitchy.

"Sorry." She tugs at her spiky blue hair. "I'm stressed and exhausted. I'll fall on my sword later and bring her some air to snack on."

"She's not like that. We fight over donuts and she always wins the biggest half."

Trish changes the subject. "Was your dad totally unhinged last night? Mine was. I wanted to grab his phone out of his hand and smash it."

"Uh, yeah. He was on the phone for hours."

"I bet your dad called Stockwell to try to talk him off the

ledge and keep the account here." She hesitates. "Your dad's a lot better at schmoozing clients than mine." A flush tints her cheeks. "My dad's…you know…not good at, uh, diplomacy."

She's revealed another crack in her facade, a hint of vulnerability.

"Your dad has his strengths, too."

She snorts. "Like what? Scaring the crap out of people?"

"Exactly." A smile pulls at my lips. "He's the guy you want on your side in a battle."

Trish's gaze darts up and down the hall, then she whispers, "My dad wants to can all the interns—no surprise."

"Seriously?" My stomach drops as I imagine how upset everyone will be. And how upset I'll be on their behalf.

"Your dad talked mine out of it. For now. But I think Jason's the sacrificial lamb."

My hand flies to my mouth. I thought my dad believed me.

She squints at me. "You really don't think he was drinking?"

"Would you, if your dad was an alcoholic you had to rescue him from binges? And put up with his abuse?" Crud. I said too much.

"Abuse?"

I gesture for her to step closer. "We got off to a bad start, Trish, but here's the thing. I'm going to trust you."

"Why?" She leans against the wall, eyes narrowed.

"You're passionate about causes you care about. And you don't BS."

"And you're a lot smarter than I thought you were." An ironic smile curves her lips. "You're still a princess, but you're more of a Fiona than a Sleeping Beauty."

"Now *that* is high praise." And it is; I love Fiona and Shrek.

"So spill, ogre princess. What do you mean by abuse?"

My body shivers, but I have to tell someone. "Yesterday

I helped Jason with computer stuff. And I noticed he was wearing makeup."

"What?" Her eyebrows shoot up in disbelief.

"He was covering a bruise. His dad hit him."

Trish's mouth drops open, then snaps shut. "Crap."

"I know." The stupid tears are back, but I blink them away. "Imagine what his dad might do if he loses this job."

Trish steps away from the wall, full of righteous indignation. "So we won't let it happen. We tell our dads and—"

"I already told my dad."

She frowns, considering. "It's that picture. My dad can't stop talking about it."

"I'd bet money it was Photoshopped."

"Can you prove it?"

"I hope so. But I need to talk to Jason."

"You don't have his number?" She looks skeptical.

"He never said two words to me before this summer."

The elevator pings. Mr. Mantoni emerges and we both suck in our breath.

"Here we go," Trish mutters. Her shoulder bumps mine. "Ready to go down fighting, Jedi princess?"

We've moved way past détente. I imagine us fighting Stormtroopers together, flying X-wings and performing crazy aerial maneuvers to take down Dad Vader and the Manicotti. We won't kill them, of course. Just take away their powers.

"I've been training my whole life for this."

She snorts, then steps out of our hidden corner and I join her.

The Manicotti's heavy footfalls echo on the tiled floor as he approaches us. He hesitates when he spots us, then resumes his determined march.

"Girls." He nods at us, then frowns at Trish. "I mean ladies. Women."

"How about just calling us by name?" Trish snaps.

His forehead vein throbs. "Go inside, gir—Patricia. Laurel."

We follow him into the office. I wish I'd had a chance to warn Elijah and Ashley. Maybe we could have strategized a united front.

"Interns!" he barks. "At the table. Now."

Carlos makes his way to us rather than the conference table, where Ashley and Elijah wait.

"So is this it?" he whispers, his voice threaded with anxiety and something harder, something more like anger. "Are we all getting fired?"

I square my shoulders. "Nobody's getting fired."

"Trish! Get over here!" The Manicotti points at Carlos and me. "You, too!"

Mr. Mantoni stands with his back to the window, arms crossed over his puffy chest. The finance employees huddle in the far corner of the room, whispering. I wonder if the whole office is speculating on the Twitter debacle.

We sit at the table, Carlos on one side of me, Trish on the other. I'm oddly comforted by this.

"We have a situation," the Manicotti booms. "Does everyone know what I'm talking about?"

Elijah and Ashley gape at each other, baffled, while Carlos clenches his jaw.

"Your compatriot Jason was photographed drinking beer at our client Stockwell Suds," says Mr. Mantoni. "The photo is all over Twitter. We're under fire, as is our client. But this isn't the first Twitter storm we've weathered. Since the beginning of summer—in fact, the week you all started here—there've been several damaging tweets that had to come from in-house."

Time to Leia up. "I told you before. Jason doesn't drink. Something about that tweet isn't right."

The Manicotti braces his hands on the table and tries to shoot an eyeball laser beam into my skull. At least that's what it feels like, but I refuse to back down.

"Did you ask Jason about it?" I demand.

Mr. Mantoni puffs up like the Hulk, ready to blow.

"We have photographic evidence. It doesn't matter what Jason said."

"So Jason denied it? And you didn't believe him?"

Trish clears her throat. I appreciate her warning, but this is my moment—just like when Rey battled Kylo Ren. Right now, I can bolt from this room and run to my dad and ask him to fight my battles for me. Or I can power up my own lightsaber and tap into my own Force.

"Why don't you believe Jason?" I fling my hands out in frustration. "You can't fire him without cause, and you don't have one." I lean forward. "My dad believes in second chances. What about you?"

Carlos squeezes my knee under the table. I don't know if he's encouraging me to keep talking or trying to shut me up, but his touch startles me.

"What did the other tweets say?" Carlos asks. I wonder if he's trying to misdirect the Manicotti's attention away from me, like throwing rocks at a grizzly bear.

"One disparaged Jiang Chen's promotion," Mr. Mantoni says, his angry eyes still on me. "We had another this morning that revealed client info that could only come from in-house."

Trish and I share a surprised look; neither of us knew about that one. It must have happened after we got here. My dad must be going crazy.

"Mr. Mantoni." I take a deep breath, hoping my voice doesn't come out shaky. "Did you—is Jason—does he still work here?"

He narrows his beady eyes and runs a hand over his chin.

"You don't need to know the answer to that."

"Yes I do! We all do." I gesture around the table. "We're a team." I picture Jason's agonized face when he told us about his dad. He'd trusted us. We can't let him down.

The Manicotti scowls and looks out the window toward the mountains.

"Laurel's right," Elijah says. "We *are* a team. And I think Jason's innocent."

I give Elijah a grateful smile.

The Manicotti's sharp gaze darts around the table. "All right. Remember the first day? Only two of you voted to let Jason stay when he was late. How many of you would vote for him to stay now?"

My body tenses. This isn't something to be decided by a vote. Either he's innocent or he isn't.

"I agree with Laurel," Trish says. "Jason needs this chance. He was thrilled to work at Stockwell Suds. I don't think he'd mess it up." She glances at me, then at her dad. "He has good reasons not to drink.

I turn my grateful smile on her. She nods, but keeps her eyes fixed on her dad.

"So that's three in favor." He lifts his chin at Ashley. "What you do think?"

Ashley's gaze sweeps the table nervously. "I...yes. I'd vote for him stay."

Mr. Mantoni isn't happy. He turns his glower on Carlos. "I suppose you agree."

Next to me, Carlos shifts in his chair. He removes his hand from my knee and looks out the window, then at the Manicotti.

"I'm not sure. I understand why everyone wants to believe him, but—" He stops and clears his throat. "But I'm not convinced he should stay."

Stunned, I whirl to face him. "What the heck, Carlos?"

His lips compress, and his eyes are distant, not warm and empathetic like I expected.

Emotions roar through me like a tornado—anger, frustration, desperation. And raw, jagged hurt. How could he do this to Jason? To me? I shove my chair back from the table and stand up.

Time to storm the Death Star.

Mr. Mantoni calls after me, but I ignore him, running out of the sky box, down the hall, then down the stairs. I rush past Ms. Romero's desk and pound on Dad's closed door.

"Laurel!" Ms. Romero exclaims. She stands up and crosses the office. "Sweetheart, stop. You can't keep— "

The door flies open and my dad towers over me, glaring. "Now's not the time, Laurel."

"It is," I say, pushing past him. I slam the door behind us, then belatedly look around the room. Ms. Simmons sits at his conference table, along with two men I don't recognize. Oh wait—one of them is Cal Stockwell. I recognize him from Denver Nuggets games.

My determination dims briefly, but I need to be Luke Skywalker and finish my mission, even though I'm flying blind.

"Laurel, you need to leave." Dad is in full Vader mode. Even his voice sounds scary. He glances at his guests. "I apologize for my daughter's behavior."

"I'm sorry to burst in here," I say breathlessly. "I assume you're meeting about Jason Riggs." I square my shoulders. "I'm here to defend him."

My dad groans and squeezes his eyes shut. Ms. Simmons cocks an eyebrow. Cal Stockwell glances at the other man, who shrugs.

I take a breath and plunge ahead. "I've known Jason since we were kids. He's a good guy. He'd never do something to risk this internship. He needs it." I glance at my dad, who looks apoplectic, then at Cal Stockwell. "And he worships you."

Cal leans back, crossing his arms over his chest. "Sure didn't act like it."

I swallow and chew on my lip. My confidence is fading by the second. What was I thinking storming in here? My dad is going to kill me.

"The thing is, I know Jason doesn't drink. I've been to parties with him. He always drinks soda or water." I shoot a nervous glance at my dad, whose steely gray eyes flick around the table, then back to me. Yep, definitely gonna kill me later.

"Also, he...he..." I glance at Dad. "Did you tell them?"

Everyone turns to Dad, who grits his teeth. "No." His eyes bore into mine as he bites out the next words. "What you shared with me was private, Laurel. Stop and think."

His words are an ice bucket dousing what's left of my righteous fire. Dad's right. I can't tell strangers about Jason and his dad. Maybe if I bake Dad one hundred brownies he'll forgive me. Maybe.

"You had something to say," Cal says in his lazy drawl. "What is it?

What can I say that won't violate Jason's privacy, but still communicate his innocence?

"He has good reasons not to drink." I blow out a breath. "I've known him for years and I can promise you he doesn't drink beer, Mr. Stockwell. He wants to learn from you. He doesn't want concussions from going pro and he'll never make it in Hollywood but he doesn't realize how smart he is and he..." I trail off.

I'm a lousy witness, a babbling dork who just did more damage than good. I hang my head in shame. "I'm sorry. I'll leave." Mortified, I slink to the door, but to my surprise Dad follows me, closing the door behind us.

"That was unacceptable," his whisper is furious, way scarier than if he yelled. Not to mention his eyes are glaciers.

"I know. I'm sorry." I bite my lip and sneak a glance at Ms. Romero, who's pretending to ignore us as she types on her computer.

Dad leans back against the door, squeezing his forehead. "Laurel, honey. You're killing me here. I'm trying to get to the bottom of this." He scowls. "*Without* revealing Jason's family situation."

My sister's words come back to me. "*Dad always does the right thing.*"

Dad sighs, shaking his head. "Lewis claims he left Jason alone for a few minutes to talk to a few Stockwell employees, and when he returned Jason was swilling a beer."

Lewis is lying. I know it; I just have to prove it.

"So did you…did you…fire Jason?" The last two words are a whisper. Tears fill my eyes as the images hit me like a volley of punches—my dad firing sweet, goofy Jason. How Jason's dad will punish him. How he's lost a shot at the scholarship because of Lewis.

"Not yet," Dad says. "I told him to stay home today while I assess the situation."

Relief floods through me and I launch myself at my dad, enfolding him in a hug and burying my tear-streaked face in his chest.

"Thank you," I mumble into his starched shirt. He heaves an exasperated sigh and gives me a quick squeeze.

"I need to go back in there and do damage control." He pulls out of the hug and pins me with a stern look, but his glacier eyes have thawed. "Don't ever do that again."

I nod vigorously. "Promise." I swipe at my tears. "The Manicotti says you always give people second chances."

Dad's eyes narrow. "Don't call him that."

"Sorry. Forgot." I'm not sorry.

Dad puts his hand on the doorknob. "Ms. Romero, will you please make sure we don't have any more interruptions?"

She stands, her face full of apology. "Of course. I'm so sorry but—"

"It's all right," Dad says. "Apparently my daughter is unstoppable." His lips twitch, but he turns away before I can confirm he almost smiled.

"The tweets," I speak in an urgent whisper to the interns. "It has to be Lewis. We just have to prove it."

We're on the rooftop, huddled under an umbrella table. All of us except Carlos, who went to lunch by himself. I'm furious with him, and sad, and just…just… I can't even put my feelings into words.

Trish nods. "It has to be him. He's always bitching about the intern program."

"And the tweet about Jiang," I continue. "He was probably jealous of her promotion."

Elijah looks grim. "Can you show us the other tweets?"

"Yeah." Trish's fingers fly across her phone screen, then she hands it to Elijah.

"Whoa. These are harsh." He glances at me, a deep frown slashing across his forehead, then passes the phone to Ashley.

"Oh my gosh," she says, her blue eyes wide with shock. "No wonder Mr. Mantoni's so upset."

"I know." We have to stop @PRTruth. "Do you guys want to help me save Jason's job?"

Trish's lips quirk. "Like Scooby-Doo and the Gang? I call Velma." She smirks at Ashley. "Obviously you're Daphne."

Ashley shrugs and smiles. "I'll take that as a compliment."

I point at my chest. "I thought *I* was Velma. I'm the nerd, after all."

Trish grins. "True."

"Well, I'm not Shaggy," Elijah says. "I guess I can be Fred, except he wasn't very smart."

Trish's eyes dance with mischief. "My dad's gonna hate us sticking our noses in this." Her grin is devious. "You meddling kids!"

We laugh at her Scooby reference and Elijah waggles his eyebrows "He doesn't have to know."

"I don't care if he finds out," I say. "No offense, but I'm sick of trying to pacify him."

"Join the club," Trish mutters.

"Jason's more important than getting yelled at," Ashley says, and my respect for her skyrockets.

"The Resistance will not be intimidated," Elijah announces solemnly, and Trish stretches out her arms for fist-bumps from both Elijah and me.

"They wanted teamwork?" I say. "They're going to get it."

But I refuse to think about the one guy I never dreamed would bail on our team.

*N*obody gets much intern work done after lunch. Carlos returns, but he doesn't speak or make eye contact with any of us. My heart feels like it's squeezed in a vise, but I can't let that distract me.

Ashley and Trish have a whispered conversation while scouring Twitter, looking for clues and breadcrumbs. Ashley hurries to my desk with a post-it that says "Jason" and ten digits. So she has his cell number? Not surprising. I smile in gratitude and text him immediately.

Are you ok? We have to talk asap.

Elijah dives into the dark web, looking for anything related to @PRTruth.

Jason texts me back, then I sneak out to the hallway to call him.

"I didn't do this, Laurel, I swear." He sounds like he's choking back tears and my heart aches for him. "I'm hanging out at a friend's house. My dad thinks I'm at Emergent. He'd… well, you know what he'd do if knew I was about to get fired."

"You're not getting fired. Tell me what happened."

"It was a great day, meeting everyone at Stockwell. Cal was cool, asked me about my football team and stuff. Then everyone went into the tasting room, it's like a real bar, and started drinking beer. I ordered a Sprite. I was just hanging out talking to some of the people who work there."

"Did you see Lewis take a picture of you with his phone?"

He pauses. "Maybe. I don't know. He was taking a lot of photos. He did selfies with all the ex-ball players hanging out with Cal."

Of course he did.

"I swear, Laurel. Sprite is all I drank."

"I believe you, Jason. Hang in there."

Back at my desk, I download the incriminating photo from Twitter, determined to prove it's fake. I stare and stare, and finally I see it. I can't believe no one else has noticed, or that it took me so long.

In the photo, Jason's sitting sideways at the bar, holding a beer glass in his right hand as he talks to someone. But when I look closely, I see that his fingers are too narrow; they look almost feminine. Not at all like a quarterback's hand. Lewis must have colored the liquid in the glass, then tried to Photoshop fingers back on the glass.

My pulse pounds in my throat as I triple check to make

sure I'm not crazy. I'm about to run downstairs to show my dad when Carlos appears at my desk.

He picks up my Han Solo figurine. "Too bad I'm not more like this guy."

"What do you mean?" My voice comes out harsher than I intended, but I'm distracted. I need to find my dad.

He glances up, his eyes troubled. "I know you're pissed at me, and I don't blame you. But I had to be honest, Laurel. And the truth is I'm not sure about Jason."

"But I am." Especially now. "Why don't you trust me? Why are you ignoring what he confided to us?"

He doesn't say anything for a long minute. I'm about to demand Han's return when he speaks, not meeting my eyes. "Maybe your feelings for him have clouded your judgment."

"Feelings?!" I yelp. "What feelings?"

He finally looks me in the eye. "You know what I mean."

We stare at each other as I struggle to breathe, to speak. Does he think I still like Jason?

"But...but I don't...feel that way, not anymore." I need to set Carlos straight, but more importantly I have to get out of here.

He shrugs. "I don't know. The way you defended him today, it sure looked like you still have pretty strong feelings for the guy." There's a stubborn tilt to his jaw and he won't look at me. Is he jealous? This is ridiculous.

"I would've done the same for you, Carlos." I gesture across the room where everyone is pretending not to eavesdrop. "For any of them."

He sets Han on my desk. "I hope that's true," he says, turning away.

I want to chuck Han Solo at the back of his head but instead I sprint past Carlos and down to my dad's office.

"He's out for the afternoon, sweetheart, with Mr. Mantoni."

She smiles slyly. "Can't bust down his door today."

No, but I *can* blow up his phone with texts, so that's what I do for the next hour. He must have his phone in Do Not Disturb. Or maybe he's blocked my number.

I've shown the photos to everyone except Carlos, because he left early. Not that it would've changed his mind.

"This will end tomorrow," I tell everyone. "Lewis will be fired and Jason can come back. As soon as I see my dad, I'll show him the proof."

After everyone else has left, giving me props for my discovery, I open my Hello Kitty notebook to doodle my frustrations while I wait for Dad to return. I flip through the pages for a clean piece of paper and freeze when I spy tiny print scrawled under a sketch of me with Princess Leia hair rolls eating a donut.

"I kissed a nerd and I liked it." Followed by the 10 digits that are programmed into my phone—numbers I've never texted, and never will.

I can't believe I missed seeing this. It makes what happened between us today all the more painful. Sighing deeply, I stand and walk to windows. I gaze at the Rocky Mountains in the distance, immovable and awe-inspiring. After this internship gig is over, I'm going to spend time in the mountains with my camera to re-center myself.

But that can wait.

Chapter Twenty-Two

*D*ad and I spend most of the evening arguing. I manage to convince him the photo is fake, but he says we still can't prove it was Lewis. Exhausted and worn out, I go to bed, vowing to hammer him again in the morning.

Unfortunately, Dad leaves before I do the next morning. Mom hugs me and says he's stressed out, that I should take the light rail to work. While I'm on the train, Trish sends a group text to the Scooby Gang.

Check Twitter. Don't freak out, princess.

Dread fills the pit of my stomach as I open the app.

@RockiesRoast Don't go with @Emergent. Just ask @StockwellSuds. Local yokel @KristoffRhett can ruin your image.

This is bad. So, so bad. My dad's been testing different blends of Rockies Roast coffee at home and is excited about wooing them as a client. Bad as it is, the next tweet sends me reeling.

@KristoffRhett keeps his daughter & beer-chugging intern on staff. #paperclipprincess

#paidfornothing #nepotism #drunkintern

I panic when I read this, so much that Trish forbids any more texting until we meet in person at the bakery. None of us cares if we get to work late this morning.

"Jason's not fired yet," Elijah reassures me as he swoops into the bakery. "This guy just wants him to be."

"That's total crap what he said about you." Trish's eyes are as dark as her steaming espresso.

"We have to do recon today and stop this guy." Elijah looks determined. "All these tweets prove it's someone in-house." He frowns. "Heck, I could be blamed, since I can get access to financial data if I poke around, but you guys know it's not me, right?"

"Of course we do." Trish rolls her eyes. "You're a Boy Scout, just like Carlos."

"I wouldn't be caught dead in one of those uniforms," Elijah insists.

"Even when you were little?" I tease, and he glances away, embarrassed. "Ah ha!"

We laugh, then refocus on our mission, planning to hide out on the roof terrace after work, then snoop around the office. I have no idea what we'll find, if anything, but doing something feels better than doing nothing.

Back in the office, the finance crew glances at us curiously. Carlos's eyes stay on me as I turn on my computer. I feel heat spread up my cheeks, but I don't look at him.

When I open the urgent email Dad has sent to the entire company, I struggle to breathe.

Emergent Employees—I'm sure you're all aware of the social media problems we're experiencing on Twitter. Unfortunately the tweets have not stopped, and have turned personal, attacking my daughter. I won't stand for this and I urge anyone who knows anything—and

I mean anything—to come forward. We will get to the bottom of this, and if anyone is hiding information, that's just as bad as sending the tweets yourself.

Whoa. Vader's on a roll.

We've built a strong company with a collegial environment. I want to believe everyone likes their job and believes in our mission. If you don't, and if you're expressing that via social media and trying to harm this company, know that I won't stand for that, either. No one attacks my company, my clients, or my family without repercussions.

Wow. I glance up and meet Trish's wide-eyed gaze.

"I want your dad leading me into battle if we ever take on the Empire," Elijah calls out from across the room, and the employees in the finance corner give him a thumbs-up.

My desk phone rings. "This is Laurel."

"Laurel." Dad's voice sounds relieved. "Please come to my office." He hesitates. "Why didn't you come see me as soon as you got here?"

"Oh…I guess I…thought you'd be too busy."

"Why would you—" His exasperated sigh whooshes into my ear. "I'm not too busy for you. Get down here. Please."

I expect Dad to be sitting behind his desk, but instead he's waiting in Ms. Romero's outer office and pulls me into a one-armed hug. "You okay, kiddo?"

"Not bad for a paperclip princess."

"Don't say that." The shadows under his eyes remind me of Jason. I can't imagine the toll this is taking on him. But I have to ask him again.

"Dad, the photo—"

"We're close, Laurel. So I'm asking you—no, *telling* you—please stay out of this—you and your little posse. I don't want anyone getting hurt or impeding our investigation."

I grin up at him. "I have a posse?"

"I'm starting to think so."

"Okay, we'll stay out of it." I cross my fingers behind my back. "Oh, and, uh, Lexi's meeting me here after work. We're going to a movie at the Pavilions. She'll drive me home."

"What?" Dad's distracted, his mind already elsewhere. "Oh—Lexi. Fine. I don't know how late I'll be here, anyway."

Ruh Roh. I don't want him around when we're doing our Scooby thing. "You should go home at five, Dad. Get some rest, or at least work sitting by the pool."

Muttering under his breath, he gives my shoulder a squeeze, then heads into his inner sanctum, closing the door behind him.

Carlos heads my direction as soon as I'm back at my desk. "I saw the tweet." His voice is low and gravelly.

I nod but keep my eyes on my Hello Kitty notebook as I run my finger down the spiral coil.

"Laurel, please look at me." His voice is urgent, with frustration or desperation, I'm not sure which. Slowly, I look up and meet his inscrutable gaze.

"That tweet about you was BS. You know that, right?"

"What about the troll's swipe at Jason? Do you think that's BS, too?"

Carlos rubs a hand across the back of his neck, but says nothing. I flip open my Hello Kitty notebook to his sketch and get to work while he watches me. I finish quickly, rip out the page, and hand it to him.

I've underlined his message to me, and added my own:

"I kissed a soccer star/pre-law/waiter and I liked it. A lot." I've drawn Princess Leia with hearts for eyes and

blushing cheeks. Next to that, I've drawn a heart with a jagged crack down the middle. Two letters flank the crack: an *L* and a *C*.

Without a doubt, it's the most dramatic thing I've ever done to a guy, but I want him—*need* him—to know how heartbroken I am today…and how happy I was until he threw Jason under the bus.

As soon as Carlos and the finance employees leave for the day, my Scooby Gang sneaks upstairs. We take our backpacks with us so it looks like we've left for the day and stash them under a patio table. I worried other employees might be up here enjoying the warm summer evening, but we're the only ones on the roof.

"How will we know when everyone else has left?" Elijah asks.

"We'll have to wing it," Trish says. "Most people are out of here by six." She glances at me. "Except for our dads, especially with the Twitstorm. But they're usually closed up in their offices."

We've come up with a cover story for why we're here late—working together on my "school project"—but I hope we don't have to sell it. We sit on the ground behind large potted plants in case anyone else shows up on the roof.

"Comic Con is this weekend," Elijah says, grinning. "I can't believe they moved the date to July this year. I feel like I've been waiting for years."

Trish snorts. "You guys are such dorks." She side-eyes me. "Is it better than Christmas for you?"

"Absolutely."

We all laugh, even Ashley, who's nervously braiding her

long hair and darting anxious looks across the rooftop.

"Holy crap!" Trish exclaims, staring down at her phone. She holds it up so we can all see it.

@PRTruth has tweeted a photo of the basement mannequin. It's even creepier now, with a strip of duct tape across its mouth. "Do clients know how deranged you are @ KristoffRhett @Mantoni411? Or is this your interns' handiwork? #DontBringYourDaughtersToWorkDay."

We stare at each other, our faces reflecting shock and panic.

"When was the tweet?" I ask.

Trish checks her phone. "Five minutes ago."

Elijah exhales a curse. "I bet he's in the basement right now." Ashley pales and I squeeze her shoulder reassuringly.

"Maybe not. Maybe it's an old picture and he just now decided to tweet it." I'm freaking out on the inside, but I know what we have to do. I take a deep breath. "Are we ready?"

"As ready as we'll ever be." Elijah raises a hand and we all high-five him, then creep across the rooftop like cat burglars.

We sneak down the stairs to the main floor. As we tiptoe past my dad's office and approach Ms. Simmons's office, we hear a rattle and flatten ourselves against the wall. My heart races and Trish squeezes my hand. We wait until there's nothing but silence, then resume our tiptoeing.

Ms. Simmons's door swings open. Panic shoots through me, but I breathe a sigh of relief when I see Brian.

"Oh, thank God it's you," I whisper. Trish, Ashley, and Elijah stand right behind me, so close I can hear them breathing. "Are you working late?"

Brian eyes us warily, clutching a folder in his hand. "What are you doing here?" He grips his phone tightly.

Crud. Maybe he thinks we're the Twitter trolls, slinking around after hours for dirt to tweet. I hope he's not going to call security. That guard already thinks we're nuts.

"We could ask you the same thing," Trish says. I shoot her a glare. Brian's a good guy; we need him on our side. He scowls at her and I realize I need to talk fast.

"We want to help," I say. "With catching @PRTruth. We thought maybe if we poked around—"

"He just tweeted something creepy from the basement," Elijah interrupts. "Now's our chance to catch him red-handed. Wanna help us?"

Brian's eyes widen in surprise. "Seriously?" His fingers fly across his phone. His body tenses when he reads the tweet, then he peers at us through narrowed eyes "Are you responsible for this mannequin?"

"Gimme a break," Trish snaps. "That thing has 'designed by sicko dude' written all over it." Her chin juts out as she stares him down. "We all know it's Lewis. Or Cruz. Maybe both."

Brian squeezes his eyes shut briefly, then blows out a breath and regards us warily. "Maybe we should call security and have the guard check out the basement."

"There's four of us and one security guard," I say. "Five if you come with us." I turn and head down the hall, knowing my Scooby Gang has my back even if Brian doesn't.

It's like Qa'hr has inhabited my body. I'm not usually brave, but her kick-ass attitude has seeped into me, maybe because I've moved on to the second book in the series. She's even tougher in that one. Also, there's a lot more kissing in that book, which earns no complaints from me.

"Crud," I whisper when we reach the door to the basement. "We need the code to open the door."

Brian steps forward, his lips twisting to the side in an almost-smile. "Good thing you ran into me." He punches at the keypad, then pins us with a stern glare. "I think you should stay here. Let me handle this. I can't risk any of you getting hurt. You're just kids."

Trish shoves her way to the front of the pack. "You did not just say that. It's either all of us or none of us."

His gaze sweeps over us and his shoulders heave in resignation. "Fine. But be quiet and stay behind me."

Trish opens her mouth to argue again, but I shoulder-bump her and put a finger to my lips. We follow Brian down the metal stairs, doing our best to tiptoe. None of the bare lightbulbs are on in either of the hallways. Maybe @PRTruth isn't down here after all.

"Let's split up and check both hallways," I whisper. "Elijah, you come with me. You three check that hall." I point toward the shortest half of the L hallway that ends at the file storage room. "Nobody use your phones as flashlights. We want to catch him by surprise."

I take off before Brian can argue, Elijah breathing heavily behind me. A whispered argument rages behind us, then silence. I smile, confident Trish just triumphed again. My heart is pumping double time, but my earlier resolve fades as we stop outside the door to the creepy mannequin room. Maybe we should've stuck together after all. Or called security.

"You okay?" Elijah whispers, and I nod, even though I'm not. We eyeball each other like panicky droids who don't know what our next move should be.

"Finn and Rey would bust the door down," Elijah whispers.

"So would Han and Leia."

Elijah squares his shoulders like a true Resistance fighter.

"May the Force be with us," I whisper.

Together, we shove the door open and rush into the room…and crash into the evil mannequin, which topples onto a hulking figure crouched on the floor.

"Hey!" hollers the blob on the floor. "What the hell?" He pushes the mannequin aside and stands up.

Elijah and I jump back. I squint my eyes, scanning the

room for something we can use as a weapon, but no lightsabers leap to my hand.

The guy points his lit phone screen at us, and when he does, I can see just enough to make out Lewis's face.

"Of course it's the princess," he growls, "and her lackey."

Something inside of me snaps. All of my worries about Jason and my dad and his company explode inside of me. I dart forward and smack the phone out of his hand. He reaches out to grab me, but I'm smaller and faster. I grab the mannequin from the floor and ram it into Lewis's stomach like a knight with a lance.

"We have him!" I yell at the top of my lungs as Lewis doubles over, gasping for air.

"It's Lewis!" Elijah fist pumps the air. "We got him!"

I hold onto the mannequin, pointing it at Lewis like a weapon. Elijah blocks his exit as footsteps thunder down the hallway. Lewis knocks the mannequin out of my hands and shoves Elijah out of the way. He makes it through the door, but just barely.

A vigilante posse awaits, trapping him where he stands. We encircle him like vultures with roadkill. Trish yanks the string on the bare bulb in the hallway, revealing Lewis's sputtering, tomato-red face.

"You son of a bitch." Brian pokes him in the chest. "How could you do this?"

Lewis shoves Brian, but Brian stands his ground, and the rest of us move in close. He's a big dude, but we outnumber him, and I can feel our outrage powering us. Even Ashley looks like she could poke his eyes out.

"It was worth it," he snarls. "I don't need this crappy job anymore."

"It's not a crappy job!" Trish's vehemence startles me. "I can't wait 'til my dad cans you."

"I should've had Jiang's promotion." Lewis's voice vibrates with anger. "But she got it because she's a chick, and a minority."

Brian steps in close to Lewis, looking ready to punch him. "Shut the hell up. Jiang's a million times smarter than you."

"You're a bigot and a chauvinist," Trish snarls, fire shooting from her eyes. "And a perv, based on that mannequin."

"What do *you* know about working hard?" Lewis demands. "You and princess here get everything handed to you—college, an easy summer job." He scowls at the other interns. "And the rest of you, maybe you need scholarship money, but so did I. Nobody gave me a sweet summer internship where I got paid and a shot at a free ride."

"Gosh, I can't imagine why not." I finally find my voice. "Especially with your sparkling personality." My friends snort with laughter as Lewis puffs up like he wants to lash out. "You're pathetic. You sabotaged Jason. I know you Photoshopped that picture." I step toward him and poke him in the chest like Brian did. "And you cheated at foosball, too.'"

He rears his head like a trapped animal, but the sound of feet trampling down the metal stairs makes all of us turn. My dad and Mr. Mantoni charge toward us, followed by the security guard. Lewis surges forward, trying to bust through our human ring of justice, but we don't let him.

When they reach us, my dad glances at me, worry creasing his face. "I'm okay," I mouth, and he turns on Lewis.

"We know what you've done, Lewis," Dad says. "Stop fighting these kids." He unleashes the full-power Vader glare on Lewis. "It's over. Laurel figured out someone Photoshopped Jason's picture with the fake beer, and the tech gurus found the incriminating photo on your laptop today." Dad inhales, nostrils flaring. "They found the @PRTruth Twitter login and password, too."

"Go, nerds, go," Elijah whispers under his breath next to me.

"You've been sneaking down here setting up this mannequin so you could tweet it and embarrass Mr. K." Brian's eyes are steely with anger. "I saw that Insane Clown Posse T-shirt stuffed under your desk." He squints like he's Clint Eastwood, and I bet he's wishing for his Nerf gun. "You're a sick fu—"

"Whatever," Lewis spits out. "This place sucks anyway."

The Manicotti can't take it anymore. He points a vibrating finger at Lewis and utters the words we've all been waiting for.

"You're fired!"

My Scooby Gang regroups at a nearby coffee shop after the security guard hauls Lewis away. Jason joins us after Ashley texts him to tell him what happened, and he surprises me by hugging me.

"Thanks for proving that photo was fake." His green eyes shine with gratitude. "Your dad said he's happy to have me back. I don't know how to thank you."

"Maybe get my name right," I tease, playfully slugging him on the shoulder, and he laughs.

We all giddily replay the Twitter drama, our weird night trapped in the basement, and congratulate ourselves on tonight's bravery.

All that's missing is Carlos.

Elijah texts him as we huddle over mochas and pastries, flashing me his phone screen after he's been typing for a few minutes.

Elijah: *You missed out, dude. We busted Lewis red-handed. Laurel went all Han Solo on his ass.*

Carlos: *??*

Elijah: **She saved the day. Attacked him with the mannequin. He was @PRTruth. That photo of Jason was a fake. Mantoni fired Lewis. It was epic.**

Carlos: **Is she okay?**

Elijah: **The mannequin? She'll be fine.**

Carlos: **Don't screw with me. Is Laurel okay?**

"What should I tell him, Jedi?" Elijah asks, smirking.

My heart pitter-patters as I reread the text convo. Maybe Carlos hasn't turned off his feelings for me after all. Though just because he asked if I'm okay doesn't mean he's interested in kissing me anymore. And I'm still mad at him about Jason.

"Tell him we're all fine here."

"He won't get it," Elijah says with an eye roll. "Padawan, remember?"

"Tell him anyway." It was true—we all were fine. Jason was relieved and excited to be exonerated. The dads told us how proud they were of our teamwork. My dad lectured me on no violence in the workplace, while also hugging me and telling me he was proud of his warrior princess. Totally mixed message, Vader, but it still made me all warm and fuzzy.

Elijah types quickly, then shows me his phone again.

Elijah: **Come meet us.**

Carlos: **Can't. I'm working the restaurant 'til closing.**

Elijah: **Don't you want to see for yourself that Special K is OK?**

Carlos: **Gotta go.**

"Is that supposed to cheer me up?" I ask Elijah, disheartened by Carlos's response.

"He'd be here if he wasn't working. He asked about you, Jedi, no one else."

I meet Trish's gaze. Her lips slide up in their usual smirk, but her eyes are full of laughter, the friendly kind.

It's true—we're all fine here, even if one of us is missing.

Chapter Twenty-Three

*T*oday is my day. Saturday— Comic Con day, with over 100,000 people expected. My phone pings with a text as I put the finishing touches on my makeup. I've applied a small silver infinity tattoo next to my left eye. It looks cool—subtle but effective.

On your way?

Elijah. I grab my phone and type, careful not to get silver eye shadow on the screen.

Whoever gets there first gets in line.

The lines to get into the convention center usually wrap around the building before the doors open. I don't mind, though, because everyone's in a fantastic mood, excited for the day and checking out each other's costumes.

I can't wait for a full day of nerdvana. After the dramatic unveiling of Emergent's Twitter criminal, life at work has been sort of crazy.

Cruz quit after his buddy Lewis was canned, Dad managed to salvage the Stockwell Suds account, and things are looking good for the Rockies Roast account, too. Dad had a big staff meeting in which everyone processed their feelings and ate donuts and pledged their undying loyalty and corny stuff like that. Afterward, everyone adjourned to the roof to play foosball and bond.

Also, Trish and I have eaten lunch together every day since the troll takedown. She helps me scout photo locations and I give her…romance advice. Don't ask me how that happened, but apparently she has a crush on an uber-nerd at CU, so she wants tips on how to woo a geek.

My love life is still nonexistent. I told my heart to officially give up on Carlos. Not because I'm still mad at him—looking back on everything, I can see why he was unsure about Jason's innocence. He was worried about Jason ruining the internship for everyone. I think he was even worried about my dad's business, since he admires him so much.

I haven't seen Carlos for days, since he's been traveling around with his mentor checking out local restaurant chains. I'm glad for him because I know how much he wants his experience to pay off for his family. One day last week when he was gone, I finally snuck a peek at that book he's always reading. It wasn't a novel like I'd hoped; instead it was a fat, boring textbook about small business expansion.

Then after I left work yesterday, Trish texted me a blurry photo of Jason and Carlos up on the roof playing foosball together. *"**Look who's bonding.**"*

I wasn't surprised—Carlos was the kind of guy who admitted when he was wrong. I hoped he'd stay friends with Jason after this summer was over.

Pushing aside thoughts of Carlos, I remind myself it's my day to celebrate. I can't wait to spend it hanging with Colorado's nerd herd. My phone pings again.

I am Groot.

I smile as I reply to Elijah. ***I thought you were Star-Lord.***

You know what I mean, Jedi.

I laugh because *I am Groot* means whatever we need it to mean. That was the genius of his character. I practically skip down the stairs from my bedroom.

Dad looks up from his coffee and newspaper when I enter the kitchen. "Will we see you at all this weekend? Or is your cult holding you captive until Monday?"

I fake-scowl at him as Mom hands me a toasted bagel with cream cheese, wrapped in a napkin so I can eat it on the train.

"Thanks, Mom."

"Remember the first time we took you to Comic Con?" Mom sighs happily.

Like I could forget. I was twelve years old and dressed as Violet Parr from *The Incredibles.* Being around so many other nerds made me realize I wasn't alone in my love of sci-fi and fantasy, and I'd had the best weekend of my short life.

"That was when you wanted me to wear a red bodysuit, right?" asks Dad.

"Yep." I'd wanted our whole family to dress like The Incredibles, but they hadn't. Still, my parents had taken me to the event all three days and indulged me with awesome souvenirs from the trade booths. Kendra had only joined us for one day, but she'd been cool with my geek rapture.

"Don't be out too late," Mom warns. "I don't want you downtown by yourself at night."

"Panels go until eleven tonight." And I'm staying until the bitter end.

Mom and Dad exchange a glance that means trouble.

"I can pick you up," Dad says, but he doesn't look happy about it. "You're not riding the train home that late."

I huff out a frustrated sigh. I don't want to drive because parking will be impossible. Downtown Denver isn't exactly a hubbub of criminal activity, but I understand their worries.

Fortunately, I have a plan B.

"Lexi's coming to get me, then I'm spending the night at her house." I wish she was coming to the con, too, but she's stuck working at the water park all day.

Mom frowns. "When were you planning to let me know that?"

I shrug. It's a constant tug-of-war lately with Mom as I push for more independence and she holds on tight. I know it's because she realizes I just have one more year at home. Plus the Twitstorm sort of freaked her out, especially me confronting Lewis.

"Better Lexi than me." Dad snaps his newspaper closed. "And this way Mom and I can have a date night without having to pick you up in the *Millennium Falcon*." He's been a barrel of bad jokes ever since Lewis was caught.

"I appreciate your concern, Vader."

He grins, then turns his attention to Mom. "She'll be fine. She'll be in the company of harmless nerds." He stands up and swoops Mom into a hug. Next thing I know they're kissing, which is my cue to leave.

At the light rail station I join a crowd of costumed revelers lining the platform. I love how the con celebrating starts on the train. We all admire each other's costumes and answer questions from the regular passengers who are amused or confused by our appearance. At each train stop, we pick up more cosplayers and by the time we get downtown, it's a full-on train party, everyone bouncing and chattering with excitement.

I text Elijah as soon as I step off the train and he says to me to meet him at the bear. The Denver Convention Center has an enormous two-story statue of a blue bear peering into the building.

At the base of the statue I spot Star-Lord and Gamora waving at me. Giddy with anticipation, I run to meet them. They look as excited to be here as I am, which makes my stomach swirl with happiness.

"Laurel, this is Alisha, AKA Gamora. Alisha, this is…" Elijah scratches his head. "So who are you?"

"She's Qa'hr!" gushes Alisha, and I immediately love her. "I love those books," Alisha scans me up and down, her dark eyes dancing with excitement. "Great costume. You made it, right? I wish I could sew. I bought mine online and paid a small fortune."

Elijah grins at us. "You two were separated at birth."

Alisha and I smile at each other, then I realize we're going to have to go to the very back of the line since they didn't save us a spot.

"Dude, I thought you were going to wait in line."

Elijah looks smug. "Got it handled, Jedi. Somebody's saving our spot."

"Don't call her Jedi," Alisha admonishes. "It's Qa'hr. Show some respect."

We all laugh as we cruise the line, Elijah scanning the crowd for our space saver. The creativity of the costumes thrills me. I can't wait to start taking photos.

"There he is." Alisha points.

When I follow her finger, my heart stutters to a halt, because standing in the midst of superheroes, manga characters, videogame villains, and comic book characters is Carlos, wearing jeans and a faded *Avengers* T-shirt. Next to him is a boy about ten years old, I'd guess, based on his size. I can't see his face because he's wearing a giant cardboard Minecraft head.

I don't realize I'm frozen in place until Alisha gently squeezes my shoulder. "We should get in line." Her face softens with concern. "Laurel? What's wrong?" She glances toward Elijah's retreating back as he heads toward Carlos.

"Uh, I didn't expect..." I take a breath and swallow. Realization dawns in her beautifully made-up eyes as she follows my gaze. Her lips curve into a reassuring smile.

"I see." She nods. "Take a deep breath. It's going to be okay."

"Did you guys all come here together?" I ask, plotting to kill Elijah later for keeping this a secret.

Alisha shakes her head. "No. Carlos and his brother got here early to get a place in line." She takes a step toward the line. "Come on. It'll be fine." Her smile veers from reassuring to speculative. "You look fantastic, if that's what's worrying you."

Of course that's worrying me, along with a hundred other things, like untangling my feelings for Carlos. I'd planned on a fun day of geekiness with Elijah and Alisha, but now...

"Yo, Jedi! Gamora!" Elijah hollers, causing the people around him to stare. "Get over here!"

"He just can't get your name right today, can he?" Alisha loops her arm through mine. "Come on, Qa'hr. Since when are you scared off by a hot guy? You vanquished an entire alien platoon in your trilogy."

Maybe she's right. The whole point of Comic Con is to revel in fantasy worlds. Today I am Qa'hr, not Laurel.

"You're right." I square my shoulders as we walk toward the guys. I keep my eyes on Elijah until we're just a few feet away, then I let my eyes drift to Carlos. I catch him scanning me from head to toe, and when his gaze returns to my face, he swallows. We stare at each other for a long moment, until Elijah breaks the tension.

"Name that character, Rubio," Elijah challenges. "Do you know who Laurel is?"

Carlos shakes his head. Why isn't he saying anything? Maybe he thinks I look ridiculous. Maybe he thinks this whole con is ridiculous. Maybe he wishes he'd stayed home. I turn my attention to the boy with the cardboard head.

"Hi," I say. "Cool Minecraft head, bud. I'm Laurel; what's your name?"

"Christopher," says a muffled voice. "But today I'm Minecraft Steve."

"Yes you are." I glance at Carlos, whose dark eyes are fixed on me. "Today I'm Qa'hr. Nice to meet you, Minecraft Steve." I reach out to shake his hand and he obliges, his hand sticky with something. Food, probably. I take a breath and look at Carlos again.

"Too cool for a costume?" I tease, because that's what Qa'hr would say.

Carlos blinks, then shrugs. I'm still waiting for a smile but it's not happening.

"I…uh…yeah. I mean, no, not too cool. I'm not good at stuff like that." He points to his *Avengers* T-shirt and a hint of dimple flashes. "This is the best I can do."

"He helped me tape my head together," says the muffled voice.

"That's great." I grin at Minecraft Steve head, wishing I could see Christopher's face. At some point I'm sure I will, when he's hungry or thirsty and needs to access his mouth.

Elijah and Alisha wrap their arms around each other's waists and whisper together. Their cozy intimacy destroys some of my fake Qa'hr cool. Carlos must feel awkward, too, because he turns away from them and nods at me.

"So your costume is, uh…great. Really, um, nice." His gaze strays to my legs clad in thigh-high boots and my entire body flushes with prickling heat.

"Thanks." I face forward, staring at the backs of Elijah and Alisha so Carlos doesn't see me blush. I should've gone with green skin paint like Alisha. *Note to self: never show up at Comic Con without knowing the entire guest list.*

The line starts to move and the crowd's energy level amps up. Somewhere behind us a chant starts: "Comic Con! Let us in! Nerds Unite!" Pretty soon everyone's chanting and laughing as we surge toward the doors. A huge, gorgeous guy dressed like Thor stumbles into me with an apologetic laugh. Carlos reaches out to steady me, his hand lingering on my waist a beat longer than necessary. We glance at each other, then quickly avert our gazes.

Once inside the convention center, Elijah leads us to the prop check-in table.

"What's this?" Carlos asks, as we stand in line with a crowd of people carrying all sorts of props.

"Peace bonding," Elijah says. "They give you a wristband to show your prop is approved. They don't allow real weapons or anything that looks too realistic." He holds up his 3D molded blaster gun. "As epic as this is, it's obviously a prop, so it's allowed."

"Wow." Carlos glances down at his brother. "Good thing I didn't let you bring your metal sword."

Cardboard-head shrugs. "Maybe I'll buy a new one."

"Did you drive or take light rail?" I ask Carlos.

"We drove. I'm not sure how long Chris can hang in, so I figured I'd drive in case we leave before you—"

"I'm staying the whole time!" the muffled voice is loud and gets a laugh from the Deadpool standing in line behind us.

Carlos ducks his head, looking slightly embarrassed. "I guess he's stoked for this."

"As he should be."

We finally smile at each other for real. I tell myself to pretend we're at work, that this is just a normal day, but it doesn't help.

After Elijah gets his wristband, we huddle up. Carlos flips through the program while I retrieve my camera to get ready to take photos. Elijah and Alisha are my first official posers. Minecraft Steve photobombs the picture, making us all laugh.

"Dude," Carlos warns, "dial it down."

"Oh, cut him some slack," I tease. "He's in heaven."

Carlos sighs and runs a hand through his hair, which I know by now is one of his nervous tells. "Yeah, I guess you're right. I told him he can't mess up the day for you." His neck blotches. "And, um, Elijah." He glances at Gamora. "And Alisha. I know this is a big day for you guys."

I study him, trying to determine if he's sincere or condescending. Considering his spreading blush, I'm going with sincere. And that makes me even more nervous.

"Hey Qa'hr." Elijah brandishes his program like a weapon. "You gonna do sci-fi speed dating?"

Now it's my turn to blush. "I think you have to be eighteen." I cringe inwardly and try to restore my Qa'hr confidence. "Anyway, I'm not here to hook up." Oh, *much* better. Way to make it really awkward.

Everyone gapes at me, even Minecraft Steve, who tilts his cardboard head back to study me through his eyeholes. "I thought you were Carlos's girlfriend." And this time, his voice is barely muffled.

Argh. I grab my camera and hold it up to my face. I frantically snap photos while Carlos leans down and speaks to his brother in a harsh whisper.

"All right," Elijah announces, "time to indoctrinate the newbie. I say we go upstairs and check out the merch and displays. I'm not interested in any of the panels until after lunch."

We crowd onto the jam-packed escalator. A trio of girls dressed like Sailor Moon, in very short skirts and plunging sailor tops revealing a lot of cleavage, are on the step right above Carlos. I don't even want to know if he's checking them out.

We fan out at the top of the escalator. I move to the edge of the balcony looking down on the main level. I love taking photos from up here because it's a great vantage point. Part of me knows that if I don't stick with my friends, odds are good we'll get separated and lose sight of each other in the swarming crowds.

A finger taps my shoulder. It's Carlos, minus his cardboard shadow.

"Elijah said I should wait for you, that you won't be able to find the group once we go in there." He tilts his head toward the doors. Security guards man the doors, checking badges and herding people inside the exhibition hall.

"Yeah, he's probably right. Is your brother with Star-Lord and Gamora?"

Carlos nods. "Yeah. He can tell they're much cooler than me. In a nerd way." He bites his lower lip, which is not good for my equilibrium. "I mean that as a compliment."

I nod and turn back to the balcony railing, putting my camera up to my face. "I want to take more photos." I glance over my shoulder. "You don't have to wait for me. I'll find you guys." That sounds harsher than I intended, but I need a few minutes to myself, to breathe. To absorb the energy of the con. To get into my Qa'hr groove, which is proving much more difficult than anticipated.

Carlos takes a step away from me. "At least give me your cell number so we can find each other." He frowns, and I wonder if we're both remembering how I never texted him after our park kiss.

It's a reasonable request, so I search my contacts for "Poe" and text him. "That's me."

"You had my number in your phone but you never texted?" His dark gaze locks on mine and I shrug, embarrassed. He doesn't even glance at the sexy Harley Quinn who brushes past him.

"Okay, whatever. Text me or Elijah." A frown flits across his face. "If you want to connect. I mean, if you're doing your own thing with photos or whatever, maybe we'll see you later." He shrugs. "Or not."

Is he mad at me? I study his face. Unreadable emotions cloud his eyes.

"I won't be long. I'll find you guys soon."

"Up to you." He shrugs, then strides away.

Is it possible he came to the con to hang out with me? But that can't be it. He brought his little brother, who's clearly a legit nerd. And to hang out with Elijah. This isn't about me.

I return to what I do best—hiding behind a lens and experiencing life vicariously.

After I'm satisfied with the photos I've taken from the balcony, I enter the main exhibition hall. Once inside, I absorb the cacophony of noise and endless aisles of merch booths. Freestanding booths sell everything from manga to steampunk costumes to weapon replicas to every possible nerd T-shirt a geek like me could want.

The crowd jostles me as I slowly make my way down an aisle of comic book artists signing books and posters. Two girls about my age dressed like Poison Ivy in sexy green skintight dresses, long red wigs, and ivy leaves twined around their arms pause to check out my costume.

"Are you Qa'hr?" asks one.

I nod and her face breaks into a grin. "Awesome! Do a selfie with us!"

Flattered, I pose with them on either side of me as they snap selfies with their phones. A few people walking by take photos of us, and I feel my con energy returning.

I wander down another long aisle, checking out booths full of tempting merch. I've learned it's best to scope out all the booths before making any purchases, because you never know when you'll find something you love even more than the item you just bought.

A booth of custom chocolates catches my attention. I doubt I'll find another chocolate spaceship vendor, so I buy three ships—a *Millennium Falcon*, an *Enterprise*, and a *Serenity*, planning to share them later.

My phone buzzes in my hand.

Where are you, Jedi? Your boy is grumpy.

Elijah.

I step out of the crowded aisle, finding a quiet spot near an emergency exit door. My thumbs fly over the screen.

Sorry. Where are you?

I watch the dots, hoping my text gets through. It's time to buck up and stop hiding out. Carlos is a great guy, and I don't want us to end this summer on bad terms. I've forgiven him for the Jason stuff.

Today we're just…us. Friends having fun at my favorite event of the year. Or we will be, once I track everyone down.

Elijah's reply finally pings my phone: **Ghostbusters car**.

That'll be easy to find. Last year the *Knight Rider* car was a big hit, and the iconic *Ghostbusters* car is here every year. I make my way toward them, telling myself it's time to have fun and relax.

I spot Star-Lord and Gamora first, hamming it up and

posing for photos, and then I spot Carlos and his brother. Christopher poses in front of the iconic white station wagon while Carlos takes photos with his phone. My pace speeds up; I should take photos of them; I can offer that much, at least.

Carlos jumps when I tap his shoulder, spinning around to face me. His dark hair falls over his eyes, and his hesitant smile pinches my heart.

"Hey," he says. "We thought maybe you ditched us."

I guess I deserve that.

"I'm sorry. Got carried away with the photography." I point to his brother, who's attempting to crawl into the open car window, his cardboard head crashing against the window frame. "Want me to take a picture of you guys together?"

"Probably a good idea, before he destroys his fake head." He yanks his brother up and away from the car. Christopher's arms flail in the air, his muffled yelp making me laugh.

"Lean against the car. Cross your arms over your chests like you're tough Ghostbusters." They follow my orders and I take a burst of photos. I love how bursts capture fleeting expressions and movements. Also, I now have another legit reason to take Carlos's photo.

"Hey, what about us?" Elijah asks, sidling up next to me.

"You're next." I turn back to the Rubios because I might as well take some close-ups while I can, right?

"I know what you're doing, Special K," Elijah whispers in my ear. "You're gonna be drooling over those pictures later, aren't you?"

"Whatever he said, ignore him." Alisha whacks Elijah on the shoulder, but he laughs and hops out of her reach. I motion for them to join Carlos and his brother by the car. I take more photos, laughing at their silly poses.

"We need one with you," Alisha calls out. She waves over a mom who's been watching us, along with her two young boys who are also fascinated with the car. "Can you please take our picture?"

Alisha reaches out to pull me into the group, and I find myself sandwiched between her and Carlos. I'm 90 percent sure she did that on purpose. Carlos drapes his arm over my shoulder and Alisha's hand squeezes my waist, like she's sending me a secret message.

I'm unable to breathe, but it's not because of Alisha.

"Say cheesy!" Minecraft Steve hollers through the cardboard and we all laugh as the mom takes our picture. Carlos's arm is still around my shoulder. I don't know whether to extricate myself or stay frozen in place to soak in the feel of his warm hand on my bare shoulder.

"Let's see," Elijah demands. We crowd around as Alisha scrolls through the photos. We're all laughing in the first two, which is great, but in the last photo Elijah and Alisha are grinning at each other and Carlos is looking right at me, as I smile dorkily at the camera.

I shrug out of Carlos's grasp, nervous energy spiking through me. Photos can reveal a lot, and this one…this one definitely reveals something. Something that takes my breath away.

"I'll text these to you," Alisha gives me a sly smile, then glances at Carlos. "To you, too."

"Cool, thanks," Carlos says, distracted by his brother's antics.

Maybe he doesn't look at photos the same way I do—that wouldn't be a surprise. I'm used to deciphering emotions through the filter of a lens, but not everyone is. Alisha winks at me; she's clearly seen the same thing I have.

"I'm starving," Elijah announces. "Let's get some grub."

• • •

After we stand in long lines for food and eat together, we split up. Elijah and Alisha go downstairs to an author panel about villains and anti-heroes, while Carlos, Christopher, and I stay upstairs to cruise the display booths.

Carlos is exactly the big brother I knew he'd be: patient and indulgent, with a sliver of frustration showing through just when I start to think he's too perfect.

As his brother agonizes over how to allocate his twenty dollars of personal spending money, Carlos heaves a huge sigh and gives me an apologetic shrug.

"This probably isn't how you planned to spend your day, watching a kid have a brain freeze over which plastic sword to buy."

I laugh. "It's exactly how I planned to spend it; I just didn't realize I'd know the kid." I lift my camera and tell Christopher to pose. He does, striking threatening poses with each sword.

Another boy wanders over to give his opinion on the swords, and the two kids launch into a vigorous debate about the swords' various abilities.

Carlos steps closer to me. Part of me longs for his arm to wrap his arm around my shoulder again, while the rest of me panics as he leans in close. He speaks softly so that only I can hear him.

"How long are you staying down here? For the duration?" His breath tickles my ear and I inhale sharply.

"I, um, yeah. My friend Lexi is picking me up since my dad doesn't want me taking light rail late at night."

Carlos glances at his brother, who's still engaged in a heated debate with his new friend, then turns the full power of the Hershey's eyes on me. "I can give you a ride home. If you want."

My throat constricts as I try to form a reply. Unfortunately he mistakes my hesitation for a *no* and steps away, stiffening his shoulders. "Hey, Chris, hurry up and decide already."

His brother shoots him a glare, then returns to his debate.

"I, um, thank you for the offer," I squeak. "But I live pretty far, almost to Castle Rock, and I wouldn't want you to go out of your way."

He nods, his eyes still on his brother. I feel a wall of ice building between us. I briefly imagine the Wall from *Game of Thrones*, and me climbing it with ice picks, aiming straight for my own version of Jon Snow.

A barrier between Carlos and me is the last thing I want, but I'm not sure how to melt it. Maybe I should launch myself at him and plant a kiss on those lips I can't stop dreaming about, like that crazy redhead did to Jon Snow.

"No fraternizing." Carlos speaks so quietly I'm not sure if I heard him right.

"What?"

He turns to face me. "Rule number eight. Are you planning to stick to that rule and pretend that kiss in the park never happened?"

My heart stutters in my chest. I've got one shot at melting the ice between us. One shot at telling him how I really feel.

"Some rules are made to be broken. With the right person." I say this with my Qa'hr voice, strong and confident, and I can tell he's as surprised as I am.

Craacck. I feel the ice between us thaw. Even better, heat builds between us as his gaze locks on mine. A fire starts in my toes and works its way up to my chest. "So…do you—" he starts, but a voice interrupts him.

"Hey, Carlos!" Christopher calls out. "I need five more dollars."

Carlos squeezes his eyes shut, then opens them to shoot a glare at his brother. "No more cash, dude." He mutters something under his breath that almost sounds like "worst" and "date." Christopher reluctantly puts both of the swords back, then wanders to the next booth to check out the enormous Funko Pop selection.

"You're such a mean brother," I joke.

"I know, right?" Carlos grins, rolling his eyes.

We follow Christopher to keep him in our line of sight, but hang back so we can talk just the two of us. Even though we're surrounded by thousands of people, it's like we're a tiny island of two, occasionally crashed into by a wave of aliens. Like, literal aliens.

"My sister texted me. She's picking Chris up at six o'clock," Carlos says. "He's gonna pitch a fit, but he's got a sleepover at a friend's tonight that I didn't know about."

I nod, wondering where this is going, not daring to get my hopes up.

"So that's why I can give you a ride home if you want. I figured I'd hang out with you…um, and Elijah…until whenever." He reaches out to grab a small Rey figurine from a display. "You should get this. It goes with your collection."

"What collection?" I take the tiny plastic Resistance fighter and make eye contact with her instead of Carlos as my pulse thuds in my ears.

"The one on your desk."

"Oh, right." I hand the Rey figure back to Carlos, a flush heating my cheeks as our hands touch.

Christopher races over carrying a Minecraft Steve mini-figure. "I need this," he announces. "Like, badly."

"Like, no," Carlos retorts, but he ruffles Chris's hair. "Your twenty should cover it."

Christopher's dark eyes widen in mock horror, looking so much like his brother I want to laugh. "It's only five dollars."

"Great," Carlos says. "That leaves you enough to buy a present for Landon's sleepover."

Christopher blinks up at him. "What sleepover?"

"Tonight. Rose is picking you up later. Much later."

Christopher opens his mouth to protest, so I jump in.

"You won't miss anything," I say. "All the good stuff is done by dinner time." It's a white lie, but definitely allowed under the circumstances.

"Pick out a present for Landon," Carlos says. "He likes dorky stuff, too, right?" Carlos glances at me. "I didn't mean dorky like a bad thing…I, uh…"

"It's okay." I'd forgive just about anything right now.

Christopher's calculating gaze moves between Carlos and me. "Okay, but you have pay for Landon's present."

Carlos shakes his head. "Nice try, kid. Remember what Mom said. Presents mean more when you pay for them and pick them out."

"That's true." I jump in before Christopher can protest. "My favorite presents are surprises from my friends, ones they picked out just for me."

Christopher's shoulders slump, but he turns back to the overflowing display shelves with a new mission. Carlos and I smile at each other and he steps close, his gaze sweeping over me from head to toe. The energy between us shifts, and blood thunders through my veins.

"Not the best place to break the rules," he says, his voice low. "Unfortunately." He glances at his brother, then back at me.

"I'll take a raincheck."

That earns me both the dimples, and I take a mental picture because I don't want to ever forget the way he's looking at me right now.

• • •

As the con winds down for the night, Elijah, Alisha, Carlos, and I walk the downtown streets, surrounded by laughing and yelling cosplayers and other Saturday night partiers. I texted Lexi hours ago to tell her I had another ride home. She sent back an entire paragraph of emojis letting me know exactly how she hoped I'd spend my evening.

"We're parked down here," Carlos says as we stop at corner and wait for the walk light. "Catch you guys later." He and Elijah do the bro dude hug, while Alisha hugs me.

"Cold?" he asks.

I am sort of cold in my thin Qa'hr shirt. A cool breeze has moved in, making me shiver. His eyes are as melty as that day at his restaurant. He wraps an arm around my shoulder and pulls me in close.

Omigod. Is this really happening? I glance up at him and notice the chin stubble in the glow of the streetlight. Why am I so obsessed with this? Probably because I've never kissed someone with actual man stubble before. That afternoon in the park he was clean-shaven. Not that he's going to kiss me again. I mean, I hope like crazy he will, but—

"Laurel?" We've stopped walking and he's staring down at me.

I meet his intense gaze. "Yes?"

He pulls my body around so that I'm pressed against him, wrapping me in his arms. "I have a lot to say. But I don't want to mess it up." He glances up at the dark high-rise buildings surrounding us and his grip on me tightens.

"I've spent all summer trying not to break the rules. But then I did, because I wanted to. And then that crazy Twitter stuff happened, and I freaked out. I worried I'd get fired, that I'd lose my chance to help my family." He looks down, his eyelashes brushing his cheeks. "And I was confused…honestly, I was jealous. About Jason." He sighs. "I'm sorry. For pulling away from you, and for not trusting you about Jason." He tucks a stray curl behind my ear. "Jason's a good guy. His dad situation sucks. I can't even imagine it."

"I know." My voice is soft. "You and I have great dads." I reach up to touch his stubbled jaw, and his arms tighten around me. "I forgive you for your temporary jerkiness. 99 percent of the time you're pretty amazing."

"I am?"

"Like you don't know that." I run my finger along his jawline to his throat. I feel his Adam's apple as he swallows. "But I should remind you—I'm the boss's daughter and technically off-limits for three more weeks." He starts to speak but I keep going. "It's why I pulled away after that park kiss. You could be disqualified if anyone knew we—"

He touches a finger to my lips.

"I don't care whose daughter you are, or how many days I'm supposed to stay away from you." His hands slide up my back, over my shoulders, and when his fingers slide into my hair, my bones melt. "I practiced a whole speech for you, Qa'hr. Princess Leia. Whoever you are tonight." His eyes are as dark as the sky above us. "But I can't remember any of it right now."

"You know what's better than speeches?"

"What?"

"Kissing," I whisper recklessly, "and I already know you're good at that."

And then Qa'hr takes over—or maybe it's me. Somebody does. Someone pulls his head down and presses his lips to mine and feels the planet start to spin…and then I forget to think about who's doing what because all I can feel and taste is Carlos.

Yeah, he's definitely skilled at kissing. Expert level, in fact. And the stubble? It's kind of scratchy but I like it. After a long, long time, we pull apart.

"Wow," Carlos breathes.

"Yeah. Wow."

Carlos reaches around to his back pocket, then hands me something small and plastic. It's the Rey figurine from earlier. "Don't hide her in a drawer."

"I won't." I squeeze my fingers around the best present ever.

I wonder if my smile could light up all of downtown Denver, but I don't get the chance to find out because suddenly we're kissing again, and my mouth has much better things to do than smile.

Chapter Twenty-Four

It's here: the final day of the internship. The interns gave their individual presentations to the Emergent executives, their mentors, and Cal Stockwell, since he's funding a chunk of the scholarship. Trish and I sat together since she's not competing. Everyone did well, each presentation reflecting their individual personalities and goals. Now the executives are huddled in the conference room to vote.

The interns went to the corner bakery for a sugar hit, but Trish and I are in the sky box, going over our plan one last time.

"Ready?" Trish asks.

I glance over my shoulder. No more spying on Carlos from across the room, or laughing at silly faces from Elijah. No more shy smiles from Jason. No more eye rolls from Trish, or observing Ashley's lip gloss application.

"Showtime." I raise my palm and Trish high-fives me. We march down both flights of stairs, across the lobby, and to the conference room, united in our mission.

Ms. Romero doesn't even try to stop us as we burst into Dad's office. I think she secretly likes it. Dad, Ms. Simmons, the Manicotti, and Cal Stockwell gape at us. My dad, in particular, looks ready to blow.

"I hope you didn't start without us."

"What are you doing here? You said you weren't voting." Dad levels me with the Vader glare. "You told me you have a conflict of interest."

I did tell him that, but I'd refused to reveal the specifics of my "conflict."

"I'm not voting, but you wanted feedback on the interns. A peer review, right?" I glance at Trish, whose expression is fierce and determined. She stares down her own dad. "Trish and I spent a lot of time with the interns and we think you should hear what we have to say before you vote. Also, at the beginning of summer you said I had two votes. I'm giving them to Trish."

Dad scrubs a hand down his face, but Ms. Simmons's eyes flash with interest. Cal Stockwell's expression is inscrutable. To my surprise, Mr. Mantoni looks almost…pleased.

"Let's hear it." Mr. Mantoni's words startle me. Ms. Simmons nods, and my dad and Cal Stockwell shrug in defeat.

"Okay." I take two deep breaths, like Trish coached me. "They all deserve to win." I glance at Trish, who nods encouragingly. "Every one of them needs the money." I meet my dad's appraising gaze. "They all worked hard this summer. And put up with *a lot*." I side-eye Mr. Mantoni, who squints behind his glasses.

"You wanted us to become a team," Trish says. "And we did." She turns to Cal Stockwell. "Together we figured out who was sabotaging you, and Emergent."

"That's true, but—" my dad begins, but Trish puts up a hand to stop him.

"I couldn't stand any of the interns the first week," Trish continues. "Especially Laurel."

"The feeling was mutual." We grin at each other. The executives look stunned.

"But I changed my mind about Laurel. Not just her. I thought Jason was an idiot, but he's not. He's brave. Every single day, he's braver than I will ever be."

"And I thought Ashley was a ditzy blonde." I clear my throat, telling myself not to be intimated by Ms. Simmons's frown, or my dad's scary eyebrows. "But she's smart, and thoughtful. She doesn't have the support at home that Trish and I do, yet she holds on to her dreams."

"I disliked Elijah the least, at first." Trish grasps her spider pendant, so I know she's more nervous than she appears. "I wondered why he was even here in his designer duds." She swallows. "Now I know." Trish shoots her dad a look that would make me whimper. "He's brilliant, Dad. And funny. He's the heart of his family."

My turn. I take a deep breath. "I, um, wasn't sure about Carlos at first." I can't look at Trish. "I thought he was sort of arrogant. But then I got to know him…and his family." My dad's gaze sharpens, but I keep going. "He's a remarkable guy. His whole internship was focused on helping his family, not his own college plans."

I make eye contact with Cal Stockwell, whose facial muscles are on lockdown.

"You know how it is on a team, Mr. Stockwell." I wait for a reaction from him, but I get nothing. "Teammates don't always like each other, but the more they train and compete together, the tighter they get." I dart a quick smile at Trish. "Unexpected allies team up."

"Word." She reaches out to fist-bump me.

My dad sighs and runs a hand through his movie star hair. "All right, we get the message. You're all one big happy family now. And that's great—really, it is." He glances at Mr. Mantoni, whose attention is fixated on Trish. Something is brewing behind those beady eyes, but I can't tell if it's good or bad.

Dad clears his throat. "But we have to choose a winner." His gaze softens as he studies me. "You know that, honey. You've known all summer."

Trish turns to me, desperation in her eyes.

"You're offering a one-hundred-thousand-dollar scholarship." My fingernails dig into my palms. "That's a lot of money." My knees are trembling, but I keep going. "Why not give each of them twenty-five thousand?"

"I second that," Trish says. "With both my votes."

Dad blinks in surprise. Mr. Mantoni and Ms. Simmons exchange confused glances. Cal Stockwell is a frozen statue.

"We know that's not enough for a full ride for any of them," Trish says quickly before they can argue. "But 25K is a good start. And you can give all of them fantastic recommendation letters for other scholarships."

No one speaks.

"You've given us your opinions," Dad finally says, his brow creased with frustration or anger—maybe both. "Now please leave. We need to choose the winner."

Shoulders slumped in defeat, I turn away, anxious to escape. Trish shadows me, and somehow reading each other's minds, we head for the rooftop to commiserate.

"One thing our dads have in common," Trish says as we climb the stairs, "they're both too damn stubborn."

Two hours later, everyone gathers for the scholarship announcement. Employees line the stairs and fill the lobby. Laughter echoes off the brick walls and anticipatory energy bounces through the crowd—for the announcement, but also for the surprise party that will follow on the rooftop. Somehow everyone has managed to keep it a secret from my dad.

The interns stand on one side of Miss Emmaline's desk. Carlos wore a tie today, as did Jason and Elijah. Ashley, as always, looks lovely. I don't feel envy anymore when I look at her. I'm impressed at how determined she is, in spite of her mom's low expectations.

I can tell by their body language and anxious glances the interns are nervous. I desperately want to stand next to Carlos and hold his hand, but I stay where I am, next to Trish, my stomach roiling with worry. Lexi has texted me three times to ask who won, which only made me more anxious, so my phone is on Do Not Disturb.

Carlos's gaze scans the crowd and locks on me. My heart dances in my chest. He doesn't smile, but his eyes are full of warmth. I pray that no matter what happens with the scholarship, our new relationship isn't just a summer fling.

Miss Emmaline stands behind her desk, scrutinizing the crowd over the rim of her eyeglasses. When I catch her attention, she studies me with a long, appraising look, then reaches into the candy bowl, slowly unwraps a Crazy Cowboy, and pops it into her mouth. I guess I'll never understand her, and she'll never get me. But that's okay—she's devoted to my dad and Emergent, and that's what matters.

The crowd parts as my dad, Mr. Mantoni, Ms. Simmons, and Cal Stockwell make their way across the lobby. Vader doesn't even have to ask for everyone to be quiet. At the beginning of summer, I would've said his minions were scared of him. Now I know the reason for the silence is respect.

As sad as I am that Dad rejected our idea to split up the scholarship award, I can't deny how much my view of him and his company has changed.

Trish shoulder-bumps me. "Here we go," she whispers. I

nod, unable to speak. Carlos isn't looking at me anymore; he's focused on my dad.

"Thank you all for gathering to celebrate our first summer internship program." Dad flashes a quick smile. "You all know we experienced some unexpected drama this summer, and our interns suffered for it. Some more than others." He nods at Jason, who blushes. "All of them deserve a round of applause for sticking it out."

The crowd claps enthusiastically. Brian blows an air horn, probably from his desk toy collection. I'm trembling with nerves. Why didn't I argue my case better? Why didn't I wheedle my dad about the scholarship money on our drives to work this week?

"Deciding on a scholarship winner might be one of the toughest decisions I've made at Emergent." Dad gestures to the other bigwigs. "I think I speak for all of us." Each of them nods, including Cal Stockwell.

My heart is in my throat. The interns are frozen in place, eyes wide.

Please, Dad. Don't do this.

Dad nods at Mr. Mantoni, who takes a step forward. He gestures toward the interns, who eye him warily.

"This is a great group of kids," he says, surprising me, and probably them, too. "I might've been too hard on them, but as Mr. K said, they stuck around anyway." He runs a hand over his gleaming bald head.

Brian and Jiang have moved to the front of the crowd, phones and cameras ready to take pictures for social media and a press release, I assume. For once, I don't want my camera. The last thing I want is a picture of one happy intern and three crestfallen ones.

"You all know a college education is expensive these days," says Mr. Mantoni.

A rumble moves through the crowd. I wonder how many of them are still paying back student loans? The profound realization of how fortunate I am hits me square in the chest and to my dismay, tears fill my eyes.

Ms. Romero watches me from across the room, sympathy in her warm brown eyes. I chew the inside of my lip as my attention returns to the interns. I want the best for all of them, but I failed them. Only one person's life will be changed today.

"The four of us spent a long time debating," Mr. Mantoni continues. He pauses and all I can hear is the muffled sound of traffic outside, and the thudding of my heart.

"As you know, the intent of the scholarship is to provide one hundred thousand dollars to the winner. Depending on which college they attend, that could be a full ride, or a big chunk of the final tab." He glances at my dad, who steps forward as Mr. Mantoni steps back.

I wonder if that's what happens when you work so closely together for so long—reading each other's invisible signals. Dad and Mom do that at home, too. Maybe someday I'll be lucky enough to find that closeness with someone.

"Most of you know my story." Dad's voice is strong and clear, reaching the employees on the stairs. "I worked my way through college. It was hard, but I don't regret it." He faces the interns, who shift nervously. "But when I started this company, I vowed that someday I'd make earning a degree easier for others than it was for me."

Trish is vibrating next to me. Or maybe it's me that's shaking.

"I was hell-bent on making sure one of you got a full ride, at least to a state college."

Dad's never looked more intense than he does in this moment.

Jiang is discreetly taking photos with her camera, but my

dad doesn't notice. Brian's riveted by my dad, not taking any photos. I smile to myself. I see why Jiang got the promotion.

"However."

The word floats in the air, taunting me. Trish grasps my hand, squeezing it hard. Dad's penetrating stare searches out Trish and me and stays there.

"I've learned a few things over the years." Dad's lips twist in an ironic smile. "Such as wisdom sometimes comes from unexpected sources." For a long moment, he looks only at me. Trish's grip on my hand tightens.

"So." Dad tears his gaze from me and strides toward the interns, who look ready to keel over from stress. "We've made a change to the award."

Carlos tugs at his Windsor knot, Jason's blush returns, Elijah stands up straighter, and Ashley smooths her skirt. Trish and I dare to look at each other, but we don't speak. I think we're afraid to jinx whatever's coming next.

Dad talks directly to the interns, but we can all hear him. "From what we've observed, and based on what we've learned from those who worked with you closely, we've decided that all of you are winners."

A murmur begins in the crowd, but the Vader side-eye stops it.

"Now, splitting the pot four ways gives you each twenty-five thousand, but it's not what you signed up for."

The interns look shell-shocked. I can't tell if they're excited or disappointed. Trish is definitely vibrating. So am I.

Dad motions for Cal Stockwell to join him. Cal's almost seven feet tall; his height combined with his stern countenance are intimidating as he looms over the interns. Jason stares at the floor, and I know he feels guilty about the Twitstorm, even though he didn't do anything wrong.

"I got my degree by winning a basketball scholarship."

Cal's booming voice matches his size. "I know one of you sees that as your only option." He stares at Jason, waiting until he lifts his head. "But it's not."

Jiang's camera is getting a workout.

"Mr. Kristoff and I have spent the past couple of hours on the phone. A lot of the guys I played with went to school on scholarship, too." He cracks a small smile, the first one I've seen. "And Mr. K knows how to call in a favor."

My dad's words echo in my ears: *When you have friends in powerful positions, you don't ask for random favors. You choose wisely, holding onto the big-time favor until it's something important, for someone special.*

"Ms. Simmons, join us," my dad says. She beams as she hurries to his side. Now the four bigwigs face the four interns. The crowd whispers excitedly, but this time my dad ignores it.

"Due to the generosity of a whole lot of people who want to pay it forward," Dad announces, his voice booming almost as loud as Cal's, "we're able to award each of you eighty-thousand dollars."

Cheers and applause roar through the room, echoing off the brick walls, along with Brian's air horn, followed by the pounding beat of Van Halen. Someone just launched my dad's surprise party playlist.

My whole body goes numb, like I'm having an out-of-body experience, floating up and up, over the excited, chattering crowd below me. The interns hug and laugh and fist pump and mug for the camera. My dad and Cal laugh together, punching each other on the arms like dorks. Ms. Simmons makes each intern pose with her, holding their certificates. Mr. Mantoni watches it all like a benevolent dictator.

A swirl of warmth and happiness floods my body, bringing me back to the ground, to reality. A squeal builds in my throat but I tamp it down—until Trish grabs me and spins me around and around, crashing into the employees standing nearby.

"We did it, princess!"

I've never seen her so happy. I release my squeal and join her in a goofy celebration dance to the famous Van Halen "Jump" song. I spin around again, jumping in sync with the lyrics…and crash smack into Carlos, whose arms lock around me, pinning me close.

He smiles down at me with those stupid dimples, then slowly lowers his forehead to mine. "I think you have something to tell me," he murmurs.

I'm dimly aware of the flash of camera lights, and the other interns joining us for the expanding dance party, but I tune it all out.

"You're breaking rule number eight." Our lips are just millimeters apart, but the party is now dancing its way upstairs to the roof, so no one's paying attention to us.

"The internship's over, Special K. The only rules I'm following are my own." He kisses me softly, gently, and I sigh into his mouth.

To my horror, my phone buzzes in my bra. Carlos leans back, bestowing me with the teasing smirk he wore the first day I met him.

"Don't say a word," I warn him. "My dress doesn't have any pockets so—"

"I have sisters, you know. Rose's bra is always buzzing." His grin is distracting, so I turn away and reach into my bra.

My phone buzzes again. *Where are you, sweetie? We're all on the roof. Slideshow is about to start!*

Mom. I grab Carlos's hand and drag him toward the stairs and we race each other to the rooftop.

Chapter Twenty-Five

The anniversary video plays on a screen under a canopy. I drag Carlos up to the front so I can wave to my mom. From her spot by Ms. Romero, she waves back, glancing at Carlos curiously.

Jiang did an amazing job, weaving together photos and music that effortlessly portray the past fifteen years in reverse. Dad's eyes look shinier than usual when the final slide lingers on the screen—one of him and Miss Emmaline way back in the day when they shared an office. Mom, Kendra, and three-year-old me are in the background. Miss Emmaline looked crabby back then, too, but Dad is grinning in the photo. He doesn't have strands of gray hair in that picture, or any crinkle lines around his eyes. It's easy to picture him as the handsome college guy who won Mom's heart.

Carlos steps away to join the other interns as the slideshow ends. Mom tackles me with a big hug, wiping a few tears from her eyes as everyone toasts Dad with champagne, and sparkling cider for the interns, under Cal's watchful eyes.

"This was a fantastic idea," Mom tells Jiang, who's joined

us. "Thank you for coordinating it."

Jiang winks at me. "I had a lot of help pulling it all together. Your daughter was a terrific intern this summer."

"Assistant," I correct automatically, but Jiang shakes her head.

"You were much more than that." She grins. "If it weren't for you and that mannequin attack on Lewis, who knows what would have happened?"

Mom sighs and shakes her head.

"I had a lot of backup." I glance at Brian and the interns, who are taking selfies together.

"Yes, but now you're an Emergent legend."

Mr. Mantoni commandeers the microphone and treats us to a high-pitched feedback whistle. From across the roof, Trish catches my attention and rolls her eyes. I shrug and grin in solidarity.

"Today's a special day," the Manicotti begins. The crowd is chattering, but as his voice booms over the portable speakers, they have no choice but to listen. "We're thrilled with our scholarship awards and now we get to celebrate Emergent's fifteenth anniversary." He pauses to take a sip of champagne. "Twelve years ago, I applied for a job at this small start-up company called Emergent. I interviewed with Rhett at a bakery that's no longer in business, which is surprising, since I'd never seen a guy put away so many pastries at once."

The crowd laughs as Mom and I share knowing looks.

"I didn't know what to think about his company. It was young, and so was he."

More laughter. Who knew the Manicotti was a comedian?

"But I liked his energy and his ideas. And for some reason, he liked me."

He smiles at Dad, and Dad grins, a big sloppy one

like he's a human Golden Retriever. I wonder how much champagne he's had.

"I was at the end of my rope," Mr. Mantoni says, his voice now serious. "My wife had died of cancer and I was raising my young daughter on my own." He pauses and rubs his hand over his shiny bald head. "I didn't know what I was doing, as a dad or in any other area of my life, but I knew I needed to get it together, for Trish."

I glance at Trish, whose eyes are wide as she stares at her dad.

"Anyway." Mr. Mantoni clears his throat. His audience is completely quiet, respectfully waiting as he composes himself. "I'd had at least twenty interviews before I met Rhett. But no job offers. I was running out of money. Running out of hope." He pauses again, taking a deep breath. I glance at Mom, whose eyes are shiny with tears. My own eyes are blinking rapidly, too.

"So after he ate one of everything in the bakery, Rhett offered me a job. And I was able to pay my rent. And take care of Trish. And each year I worked here, my life, and my daughter's, got easier." He holds my dad's gaze, and all the pieces fall into place — why he's so loyal to my dad, and vice versa. Why he was so tough on Trish here at work. Why he almost lost his mind over the Twitstorm. Why Dad will never fire him, no matter how wacky he is.

Mr. Mantoni wipes a hand across his brow. "Okay, I wasn't supposed to kill the buzz. Somebody else come up here and talk before I make things worse." A few people laugh. He glances at my dad again and touches two fingers to his forehead. "Thanks for everything, Mr. K." He raises his glass in a toast and my dad does the same. Dad looks suspiciously near tears.

Ms. Simmons takes the mic from the Manicotti and starts

her own tribute to my dad. She's funny, too, but I tune her out because I'm watching Trish and her dad. He bends down, and she whispers in his ear. His frown disappears as he smiles down at her, and I turn away because they're having a private, special moment.

The party goes on for another two hours, and by the time three o'clock rolls around, Dad tells everyone to go home and take Monday off in celebration of the anniversary, and everyone cheers. Yeah, I think I get why his staff is so loyal. Lewis was an anomaly.

After everyone leaves, Mom and Miss Emmaline sit on couches in the lobby, deep in conversation. So basically Miss E likes everyone in my family but me.

Oh well, can't win 'em all.

I make my way to Dad's office to tell him how thrilled I am about the scholarship money. He's been surrounded by people ever since the announcement and I want one-on-one time with him before he and Mom disappear on another date night. Ms. Romero sweeps me into a hug.

"It's been quite the experience for you, young lady. I hope you don't regret a minute of it."

There are definitely parts I regret, but today was the big payoff—the culmination of a crazy roller coaster of a summer. I couldn't be happier about the scholarship money. And the rest of it? I wouldn't change a thing, because it's true what Dad says—Kristoffs never quit.

"No regrets," I tell her, and she smiles wide, eyes crinkling. I've entered her photo, along with a dozen others, in my Faces of Denver collage contest entry. I don't even care about winning; I just hope my photos move others to feel what I felt when I took them.

She pats my shoulder as she heads to the door, then stops and turns. "Your dad's in a meeting, so don't knock on his door."

"What? Now?" Why would he be in a meeting after a party, and after sending everyone home early?

Ms. Romero shrugs, an impish smile tugging at her lips. "It shouldn't last long." She gestures to a chair. "Why don't you wait? I know he wants to talk to you."

I take a seat.

Tonight Carlos and I get to officially be a couple. He told me we're having a date night, but he disappeared after the flurry of congratulations and goodbyes to the other interns.

Dad's office door swings open and I glance up, startled to see Carlos and my dad emerge together. Carlos winks at me, then turns to shake my dad's hand.

"Thanks for everything, Mr. K. I can't thank you enough."

My dad nods as he shakes Carlos's hand, but he looks almost shell-shocked. Carlos tilts his chin as he glides past me. "Meet you at the elevator."

I blink up at him. "Okay, but I need to talk to my dad first." I stand up, and my dad and I both watch him leave, though I doubt my dad is scoping out his backside like I am.

My dad coughs and I turn to face him. "What was that about?"

Dad scratches his head, looking puzzled. "I think I just gave him permission to date you."

"What?! What do you mean permission? Like it's the 1800s or something?" I can't believe this. Did my dad figure out our feelings and call Carlos into his office? I'm going to—

"It was his idea," Dad says, and now his confused look is replaced by something closer to amusement. "He asked for permission to break rule number eight, even though the internship is over." Dad grins. "He's something else, that guy. Smart, charming." His eyes narrow. "Good at winning over bosses and dads. I hope he's not all talk."

A blush heats my face as I think about the secret kissing

sessions we've engaged in on the rooftop when we could escape for a few minutes to ourselves.

"Definitely not all talk," I say, and Dad's eyes narrow even more. "And by that I mean he's the real deal. Not fake, if that's what you're worried about."

Dad sighs and shakes his head. "It was bound to happen sometime. You and some…some…*guy*."

I laugh at his morose expression. "Don't act like he just blew up your Death Star, Vader. He's on your side. And so am I."

Dad grins. "You're not part of the Rebellion anymore?"

"Something like that. I think this summer taught me a lot about enemies turning into allies." I keep my voice strong even though there's a lump in my throat. "I love you, Dad. And I love your weird company, too. I can't believe what you and Cal did." My eyes blur with tears. "You changed four lives, Dad. *Four*. They can all get degrees now. They might need small loans but—"

Dad puts a finger to my lips. "You're the one they should thank, not me. You and Trish." He shakes his head and blows out a breath. "Sometimes I get so stuck on doing things my way I don't see other options. You made me see there was another way, Laurel. A better way."

He wraps me in a hug and I squeeze him tight. "However," he says into my hair, "next time you have a 'conflict of interest' you'd better let your boss know what it is." He releases me from the hug and ruffles my hair. "You know I want to meet anyone you date, Laurel."

"I know. But I was afraid you'd disqualify him if you knew he had, um, feelings for me. And we haven't even had a real date yet."

Dad cocks an eyebrow. "He showed me the website you designed. Great work, kiddo. But you were obviously seeing each other then."

"We weren't." I shake my head, embarrassed. "I was just stalking him."

Both of Dad's eyebrows shoot up.

"Don't freak out, Vader. He was a gentleman, I promise. We hung out at Comic Con, but that wasn't a date, either, because he had his little brother with him, and Elijah was there and—"

Dad puts up a hand. "I'm getting the picture. You've been pining for each other all summer." He grumbles under his breath, but I can hear what he says, and I laugh.

"You're right—Jason was never the one to worry about."

Dad crosses his arms over his chest. "So how's the food at his restaurant?"

"Fantastic! You'd love it."

"Excellent. We'll go there soon. You can introduce me to his family. Since you already know them."

I blush under his scrutiny, but his eyes are twinkling with mischief.

"Don't you have your own date night?" I ask Dad.

"Indeed I do." He grabs his briefcase from a chair and flicks off the overhead lights.

"Good, because I have to go. My suitor awaits, and since you've given him permission…"

"Home by midnight." Dad points a warning finger.

I snap a crisp salute. "Whatever you say, Vader."

Dad and Mom wave goodbye to me as I cross the lobby to the elevator. Carlos waits, leaning against the wall.

"I can't believe you asked *permission*," I whisper as he presses the elevator button.

He shrugs and wraps his arm around me, pulling me in close. "I figured it was a good strategy." He slants me a sly grin. "I cleaned out my desk and found this."

He hands me a crumpled napkin. I open it to discover he

completed the list we started at lunch weeks ago, filling in numbers six through ten.

Degrees of Fraternization
1. Introductions
2. Shared Interests
3. Joint Projects. Teamwork.
4. Friendly banter.
5. Nicknames
6. Joke book present
7. Creating a website without being asked
8. Kissing at a park
9. Kissing in a hot sci-fi costume
10. ☺

My cheeks grow hotter as I read each item, but when I get to number ten, I glance up. "What's number ten?"

He grins down at me. "What it always was—being able to date you for real."

"Oh." I hope he can tell how much his answer means to me. We step into the elevator.

The doors are sliding shut when a wobbly voice calls out to hold the elevator. Carlos shoots his arm into the gap, forcing the doors to bounce open. Miss Emmaline totters into the elevator, narrowing her eyes at me, then beaming at Carlos.

"Thank you, *Carlos*," she says, like I wanted to slam the door in her face but he saved the day. I shoot him an exasperated look and I can tell he's trying not to laugh.

"Hey, Miss Emmaline," Carlos says as the elevator lurches downward. "What do you get when you cross a snowman with a vampire?" He winks at me, and I vow to make him pay later. Probably with more kissing.

Miss Emmaline looks from Carlos to me, then back to Carlos. "Frostbite."

My mouth drops open and Carlos blinks in surprise.

The elevator jerks to a stop and the doors slide open. Miss Emmaline steps out, then turns to face us, or, more specifically, me.

"I always liked the jokes, Laurel, but you need to work on your delivery." She glances at Carlos, and her eyes sparkle with humor behind her glasses. "I'm sure Carlos can help you, in between kissing sessions." She winks at us. "I'm glad you two don't have to sneak up to the roof anymore."

As Carlos and I gape at her, she lifts her hand in a wave and walks to her car.

"How did she—"

"She never goes up to the roof—"

We look into each other's eyes and realization hits us at the same time.

"She's a super spy," I whisper. I can't believe it.

We both come to a halt when we round the corner. The whole gang is waiting. Trish sits on the hood of Carlos's car, twisting Ashley's hair into something complicated and pretty. Elijah and Jason are playing hacky sack, laughing and smack-talking. Trish glances up, smirking when she sees us.

"Hit it, maestro," she calls over her shoulder. Elijah startles, fumbling the hacky sack as he lunges for his phone…which is apparently Bluetooth-connected to the Death Star speaker perched on the roof of Carlos's car.

"What the—" I begin, but the music blasting from the speaker drowns me out. As the lyrics wash over us, Carlos and I stare at each other, laughing when we recognize the song.

Trish slides off the hood of the car, twirling Ashley around. They dance horribly, awkwardly, like every bad 80s movie I've seen. Jason and Elijah join in, laughing.

"Don't you forget about me!" We all sing at the top of our lungs in synch with the iconic song, ignoring the weird looks from other people headed for their cars.

Jason dance-bounces over to me. "I don't know how to thank you, Laurel." His eyes are misty, which makes my throat swell. He side-eyes the anarchist doing the lawn mower dance with Barbie. "And Trish, too. You're both amazing."

I look around at my friends. We're *all* amazing.

Carlos pulls me into his arms, grinning down at me as the throbbing beat of the song echoes off the garage walls. "Bet you didn't think your summer would end like this."

"Never in my wildest—" but I don't get to finish because Carlos's lips are devouring mine. Honestly, if a person could earn kissing trophies, he'd have a million. *Show off.*

Behind us, our friends whistle and yell. Somebody cranks up the Death Star volume. And as Carlos ratchets up his kissing game, I smile against his lips.

This wacky summer has been best summer of my life.

And it's not over yet.

Acknowledgments

I began writing this book shortly after my father was diagnosed with Alzheimer's. Writing a romantic comedy during this time wasn't a smooth process, as my editor and agent will attest, and I want to thank Liz Pelletier (and everyone at Entangled) and Nicole Resciniti for their patience, encouragement, and compassion, especially as my father's condition worsened, leading to his passing.

As I read this book one last time before it went to print, I realized that as I was losing my own father, I channeled my love and memories to the creation of a father on the page. And not just a father, but a father-daughter relationship that I hope brings joy to readers.

Thank you to my critique partners Laura Anderson, Laura Deal, Pamela Mingle, and Lynn Rush. You read this when it wasn't ready for prime time, for which I'll always be grateful.

Thank you to Liz Pelletier for, as always, finding what was missing.

Thank you to Candace Havens for a fresh editorial perspective, and gently pointing out my obsession with Carlos's dimples.

Thank you to Nicole Resciniti for cheering me on and lifting me up when I wasn't sure I could keep going.

Thank you to my family and friends, who provided extraordinary love and support during an overwhelming time. My husband and son never cease to amaze me, rising to every occasion and doing what needs to be done. I couldn't do this without my guys.

Finally…in loving gratitude to my father. Unlike the father in this book, he didn't run an empire. He lived a simple life, but one of such profound 12-step service to others, I've no doubt his gentle guidance will echo through generations.

My dad always believed I'd be a writer someday. I'm so proud to have proved him right.

GRAB THE ENTANGLED TEEN RELEASES READERS ARE TALKING ABOUT!

BY A CHARM AND A CURSE
BY JAIME QUESTELL

Le Grand's Carnival Fantastic isn't like other traveling circuses. It's bound by a charm, held together by a centuries-old curse, that protects its members from ever growing older or getting hurt. Emmaline King is drawn to the circus like a moth to a flame… and unwittingly recruited into its folds by a mysterious teen boy whose kiss is as cold as ice.

Forced to travel through Texas as the new Girl in the Box, Emmaline is completely trapped. Breaking the curse seems like her only chance at freedom, but with no curse, there's no charm, either—dooming everyone who calls the Carnival Fantastic home. Including the boy she's afraid she's falling for.

Everything—including his life—could end with just one kiss.

NEVER APART
BY ROMILY BERNARD

What if you had to relive the same five days over and over?
And what if at the end of it, your boyfriend is killed…
And you have to watch. Every time.
You don't know why you're stuck in this nightmare.
But you do know that these are the rules you now live by:
Wake Up.
Run.
Die.
Repeat.
Now, the only way to escape this loop is to attempt something crazy. Something dangerous. Something completely unexpected. This time…you're not going to run.

Combining heart-pounding romance and a thrilling mystery *Never Apart* is a stunning story you won't soon forget.

LIES THAT BIND
BY DIANA RODRIGUEZ WALLACH

Reeling from the truths uncovered while searching for her sister, Anastasia Phoenix is ready to call it quits with spies. But before she can leave her parents' crimes behind her, tragedy strikes. No one is safe, not while Department D exists. Now, with help from her friends, Anastasia embarks on a dangerous plan to bring down the criminal empire. But soon she realizes the true danger might be coming from someone closer than she expects...

BRING ME THEIR HEARTS
BY SARA WOLF

Zera is a Heartless—the immortal, unaging soldier of a witch. Bound to the witch Nightsinger ever since she saved her from the bandits who murdered her family, Zera longs for freedom from the woods they hide in. With her heart in a jar under Nightsinger's control, she serves the witch unquestioningly

Until Nightsinger asks Zera for a prince's heart in exchange for her own, with one addendum: if she's discovered infiltrating the court, Nightsinger will destroy Zera's heart rather than see her tortured by the witch-hating nobles.

Crown Prince Lucien d'Malvane hates the royal court as much as it loves him—every tutor too afraid to correct him and every girl jockeying for a place at his darkly handsome side. No one can challenge him—until the arrival of Lady Zera. She's inelegant, smart-mouthed, carefree, and out for his blood. The prince's honor has him quickly aiming for her throat.

So begins a game of cat and mouse between a girl with nothing to lose and a boy who has it all.

Winner takes the loser's heart.

Literally.

entangled teen

an imprint of Entangled Publishing LLC